THE HARD EDGE OF MAGIC

THE RUPTURED KINGDOM
BOOK 1

ALLAN N. PACKER

LUMINANT PUBLICATIONS

THE RUPTURED KINGDOM SERIES

The Hard Edge of Magic (Book 1)
The Riven Land (Book 2)
The Weight of Interference (Book 3)
Waking the Dragon (Book 4)

Companion Novelette
The Renegade: A Prequel to The Hard Edge of Magic

Other epic fantasy by Allan N. Packer

THE STONE CYCLE SERIES

The Stone of Knowing (Book 1)
The Cost of Knowing (Book 2)
The Stone of Authority (Book 3)
The Struggle for Authority (Book 4)
The Stone of Vitality (Book 5)
The Hope of Vitality (Book 6)

Companion Novelettes
The Seer: A Prequel to The Stone of Knowing
The Rending: A Prequel to The Cost of Knowing

The Hard Edge of Magic
The Ruptured Kingdom Book 1

Copyright © 2024 by Allan N. Packer

First edition (v1.0.5) published in 2024
by Luminant Publications

ISBN 978-1-922636-84-3

Luminant Publications
PO Box 305
Greenacres, South Australia 5086

http://www.allanpacker.com

Cover Design by 100 Covers
Map illustration by Brian Plush

To Lawrence, newly established but already making a mark in your unruffled way.
May you experience great delight as you discover your niche in life and learn to influence the world around you for good.

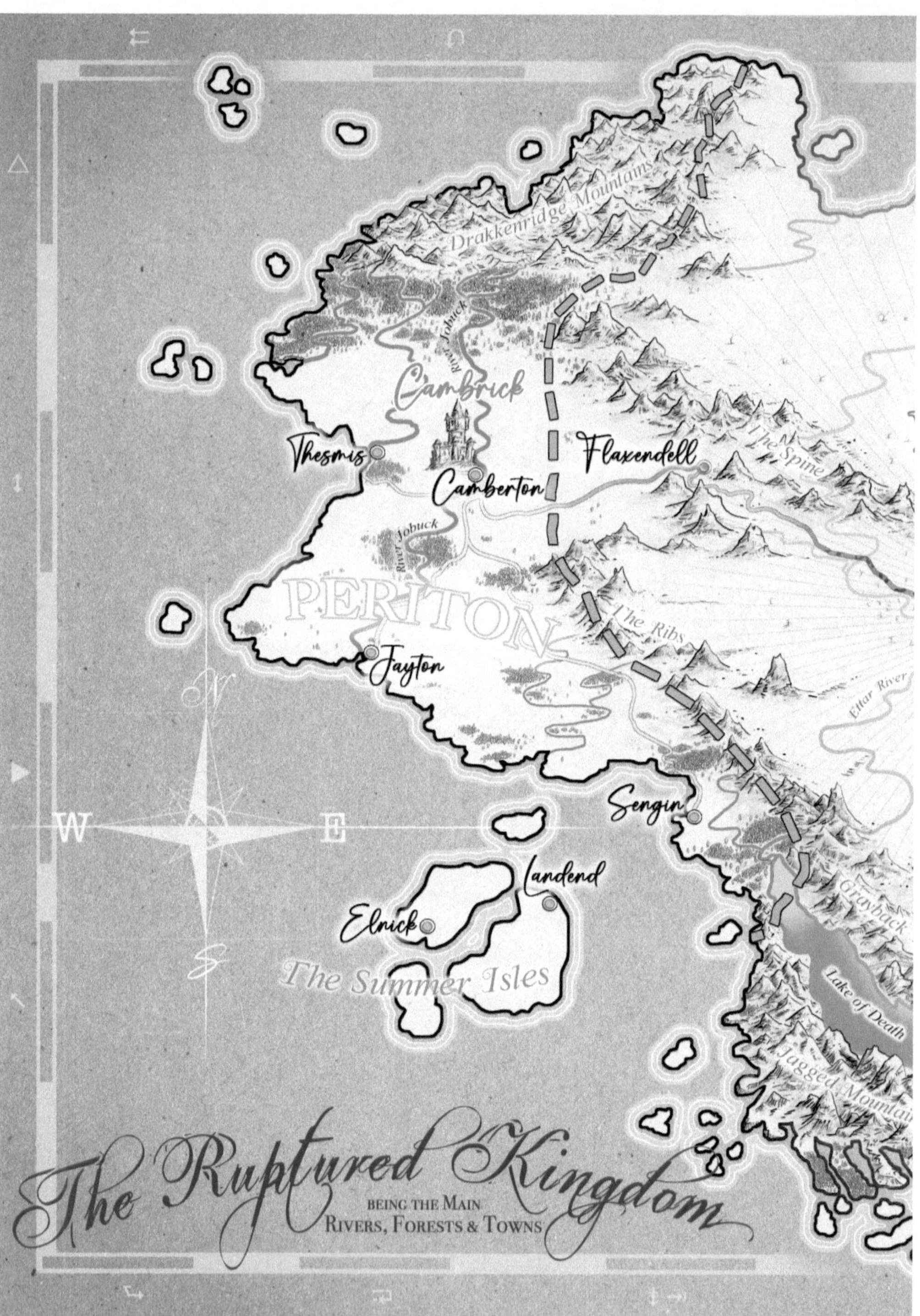

Drakkenridge Mountains
River Johnick
Cambrick
Thesmis
Camberton
Flaxendell
The Spine
River Jobuck
PERITON
Jayton
The Ribs
Ettar River
Sengin
Landend
Grayback
Elnick
The Summer Isles
Lake of Death
Jagged Mountains
N
W
E
S
The Ruptured Kingdom
BEING THE MAIN
RIVERS, FORESTS & TOWNS

Northport
Forshem
METHESIA
Ruined Kingdom
Ettaran
Ettar River
Souther
Bane Mountains
Mountains
Brynford
Brynburn River
Firetip Mountains
TANTEL
Artilin
River Antil
Shelmar
Dynsdale
Nairb H'Sulp • Royal Cartographer & Geographer • High Street • Cambrick

VOLUME 1—FOUNDLING

PROLOGUE

Tremors shook the mountain to its roots, splashing rivers of molten rock onto barren slopes.

In a vast cavern below the summit, an ancient creature slumbered fitfully, untroubled by the convulsions. Hidden from sight and long forgotten by all who scurried about on the surface of the earth, it brooded silently and it slept.

Joy no longer penetrated the darkness of its heart. Decades turned into unnumbered centuries, and one thing remained constant in the ebb and flow of its jaded desires—its craving for the annihilation of humankind.

Remarkably, its most effective allies were the humans themselves. They seemed eager to pave the way to self-destruction, their brightest and best pursuing it with no less energy than the most stupid among them. It was a marvelous mystery.

Of late the prospect of a new devastation had threatened its lethargy. There was no need for undue haste. When the moment was ripe the creature would bestir itself.

And this time, it would find a way to ensure that the little parasites eradicated themselves completely.

CHAPTER 1

Kylen peered attentively down at the ever-increasing mound of loaves below him. His rooftop perch offered him an uninterrupted view of the huge cooling tables that stretched across the rear of the bakery.

Steam rose lazily from the golden brown crusts, and the intruder pushed from his mind the insistent rumbling of his stomach. So much depended on him. He would not be the only one going hungry if he failed. Maintaining his silent vigil, he watched and waited, calling upon his almost boundless store of patience.

Remaining motionless was far from easy. Having settled into his current position well before dawn, he had every reason to feel uncomfortable. Nevertheless, he stubbornly refused to acknowledge the aching in his joints and the stiffness in his muscles. It would all be for nothing if he didn't choose the right moment.

At first the baker had peered around suspiciously while setting down the latest tray of crusty bread, fresh from the ovens. Now, a couple of hours later, he seemed relaxed and untroubled. Kylen reasoned that the man had little cause to concern himself—with so many loaves laid out, the baker could surely afford to lose a few.

Dawn was lightening the sky when Kylen finally decided to make his move. A steady stream of customers would be lining up to buy fresh bread, and the baker would be distracted. Swinging his legs silently over the edge of the roof, he eased himself down onto a strategically placed water barrel and from there to the ground. Nothing apart from a rickety wooden fence now lay between him and his goal. After pulling his hood low over his face, he stood perfectly still for a moment, listening intently for any sound from the rear of the bakery. He heard nothing.

In a single smooth motion he was over the fence and scooping loaves into a sack.

His sack was barely half full when he sensed movement. A hurried glance revealed two dark figures looming from the shadows at the back of the building. They sprang toward him, wooden clubs raised purposefully.

There wasn't time to think. Scaling the fence in a heartbeat, he scrambled onto the water barrel before clambering awkwardly onto the roof. The sack weighed him down, but he refused to relinquish it. Hoisting the spoils into his arms, he raced for freedom.

Even in the half light of dawn he knew his way around the rooftops. Let them catch him if they could. This was his domain.

Loud thumps sounded as his pursuers pulled themselves onto the roof. The men dwarfed him if Kylen's quick glimpse had offered any indication. It would have ended badly if they'd caught him in the bakery.

It was a different matter on the rooftops. Above the ground big meant clumsy, and clumsy people were a danger to themselves and anyone beneath them.

No one could accuse Kylen of being big. He was lean and trim, not just from constant exertion, but because he was forever hungry. His pursuers would never keep up with him.

With his thoughts wandering he failed to notice two new figures rising up directly ahead of him. There was nothing big or clumsy about them. Lithe and nimble, they sprang at him. One grabbed the sack with both hands. His companion grasped his arm tightly with one hand while pulling back his hood with the other.

With a violent twist to one side, he broke free of the hand on his arm, relinquishing the sack at the same moment. Slipping through their flailing arms, he flew away, not daring to look back.

The loaves were gone, but it was too late for regrets. All that mattered now was to avoid being caught. Racing from one roof to another, he jumped down and scrambled higher almost without conscious thought. At times he was forced to leap across yawning gaps, ignoring the serious injury or death awaiting him if he misjudged and fell.

His pursuers were proving difficult to shake off. While never managing to catch him, they weren't far behind. He soon realized something unexpected would be needed to shake free. Heading for a nearby section of the city where the buildings reached up three stories, he turned a corner where he would be hidden for a moment then boldly stepped off the roof. A crude scaffold had been erected beside the uppermost story of that particular building for renovations. It had been in place for several weeks. Landing on it lightly, he climbed in through the open window before him.

Anyone familiar with the area knew the building was unoccupied. Not waiting to see if he was followed, he hurried down the stairs and slipped through an open space into a narrow lane. Pausing long enough to ensure no one was in sight, he twisted and turned through a network of backstreets and alleyways until he was certain he had eluded any stalkers.

Finally, he climbed carefully up onto a roof and peered about him. Impossibly, he spotted his pursuers, silent and watchful, perched on the roof of an adjoining house. They had their backs to him, but the smallest sound would surely alert them to his presence. How had they managed to track him here?

He was in real trouble now. It was bad enough that he'd failed to lose them. Even worse, the light had been strengthening when they tried to grab him. He was confident he'd recognize their faces if he saw them again. That meant they had an equally good look at him, especially with his hood pulled back.

It was pointless to keep running. The time had come to retreat to a place where no one would find him. Easing himself to the ground, he set off for his refuge of last resort.

His path led him through busy streets as well as abandoned back alleys, but he was practiced at remaining inconspicuous.

Eventually he wound his way to the more affluent quarter of the city. He didn't belong there, and everything about his appearance demonstrated it clearly. But there was little he could do. Keeping his head down, he hurried toward his destination.

Fortunately, no one challenged him before he slipped at last into a dark lane behind a building formerly occupied by the Jewelers Guild. Scaling an external drainpipe, he made his way onto the roof.

At one point the roof dipped on four sides to direct rainwater into a channel leading to a drainpipe. The design had created a small sunken area hidden from view on all sides. Clambering into it, he settled down among the tiles. A glazed window overlooked the section of roof where he was hiding, but he was not concerned. Long disused, the building had always been dark and empty in recent times.

He released a deep sigh. He wouldn't be leaving anytime soon. A waterskin hung at his belt, but he had nothing to eat. Fresh bread from the bakery had been intended to deal with that. It didn't matter. He was no stranger to hunger.

His hiding place offered no shelter from the elements, and it would be cold on the rooftops. That was nothing new either. At least it wasn't raining. Besides, he wouldn't be stuck there for long. With winter almost upon them the days were getting shorter.

With time at last to reflect on his experience, he saw that he had visited that particular bakery once too often. The baker had clearly anticipated a visit from Kylen or someone like him. Along with the men at the rear of the building, he had apparently positioned a couple of street rats on the rooftops in case the first two weren't quick enough.

The baker had little to lose. All of his guards had appeared lean and poorly dressed themselves. They were probably paid nothing more than a few loaves, with a handful of coins as a bonus if they caught someone in the act.

The strategy had worked perfectly. The baker had done more than just protect his loaves—he had sent a clear message. Word would get around. No one, Kylen included, would be targeting his bakery anytime soon.

The outcome was partly Kylen's own fault. Busy congratulating himself as he raced away with his half-full sack, he had forgotten the most basic rule of foraging on the streets: never celebrate until both you and the spoils are safely hidden away.

His thoughts turned to Jonno and Bella. They wouldn't be worrying about him yet—he was often forced to stay away for long periods. They'd be disappointed when he returned empty-handed though.

Raff and his cronies wouldn't care what happened to him. They did nothing to help anyone who didn't bow and scrape to them, although it didn't stop them insisting on a share of whatever Kylen came back with. He didn't care about them or their hypocrisy. For the most part they left him alone, and if sharing the spoils was the price of independence, he was willing to pay it.

If something ever did happen to him, he comforted himself that Jonno and Bella would survive without him. Both of them had the mental and physical toughness to get by on the streets. They might grovel before Raff for as long as they thought it necessary, but sooner or later they would follow Kylen's example and strike out on their own.

Sadly, not everyone was so well equipped. An image of Elspeth came into his mind. Two years previously he had noticed her on the streets and taken her under his protection. It was only thanks to her he knew of the building where he was sheltering. She was familiar with it because her father had been a goldsmith—a respected master craftsman in the Jewelers Guild. When both of her parents died suddenly, leaving her as their sole heir, distant relatives had swooped in. Supposedly holding the family assets in trust for her, they were interested only in enriching themselves. The guild should have looked out for her, but too many craftsmen were distracted in the rush to secure her late father's customers.

Unfortunate enough to be both innocent and attractive, Elspeth had discovered by accident how her relatives planned to exploit her beauty. With no one to turn to, she fled her home in dismay. Kylen found her wandering alone and downcast on the streets.

He had done what he could, but she proved too delicate and other-worldly to survive for long in the harsh conditions of her new environment. Losing hope, and with it any enthusiasm for life, she slowly faded away. In the end, an ordinary cold had developed into a dangerous fever. In her weakened state she hadn't long resisted.

The tragic and bitter end to her life haunted Kylen still. He readily accepted his own situation, but someone like Elspeth didn't belong on the streets. In his anger he briefly considered finding a way to avenge her death on those responsible for it. But he couldn't bring himself to make the attempt. Survival was a daily battle, and others among the living needed him. Besides, his instinct had always been to avoid violence and conflict.

Her grasping relatives weren't unique. The city would never lack people deserving punishment. It didn't seem fair that they lived and died without any kind of reckoning.

Nevertheless, he had enough self-awareness to acknowledge it was easiest to see fault in others. He himself would be numbered among the evildoers. The baker would certainly see it that way.

Kylen sighed. He didn't like to think of himself as a thief. In his mind he was foraging.

It wasn't as if he had a choice. Most others his age were raised by family. Parents or other adult relatives took responsibility for providing shelter, food, and clothing for younger dependents. They were also expected to steer the young into apprenticeships or something similar.

Those with no one to provide for them had to fend for themselves.

It hadn't taken Kylen long to discover that Cambrick, the capital city of the kingdom of Periton, was a forbidding place for a foundling. City officials offered no support, and few others showed the slightest pity for the disadvantaged. You toughened up and looked after yourself. Either that, or you ended up like Elspeth.

Kylen shook his head. Where had the gloomy thoughts come from? It wasn't as if he had been entirely bereft of friends and support in his life on the streets. Most likely it was the loss of the loaves.

The hours dragged slowly on. Restless as he was, Kylen had decided to remain hidden until the light was gone completely, especially now his face had been seen by his pursuers. It seemed unlikely anyone would still be looking for him, but he wasn't willing to take any chances.

Once the sun set, it became dark remarkably quickly. Heavy cloud cover blotted out the stars, and the moon hadn't risen yet. As he was about to leave, a glimmer of light showed in the window overlooking his little section of roof. Why would anyone be roaming around in an abandoned building? Surprised and intrigued, he climbed to his feet and tiptoed cautiously toward the window.

Peering in, he saw the light grow in intensity as others brought candles into the room. The dimly lit figures gathered around a table. Then a candle floated toward the window. Startled, he pulled himself to one side and froze. A face appeared at the window and peered out. He held his breath anxiously, but after a few moments the face disappeared. Apparently the candlelight had not penetrated far enough to illuminate the eavesdropper outside.

Moving carefully back to the window, he stared in once more. Six people sat around the table. One attendee was a man clad in a simple black robe. He could have been a merchant or someone wishing to hide his identity. Three of them, a woman and two men, wore brightly colored robes—one blue, one yellow, and the other green. There wasn't sufficient light to reveal details, but Kylen was certain that each robe would feature some kind of fur around the neck. If so, these three were nobles.

The other two—a man and a woman—wore black robes edged with a distinctive broad crimson strip. His heart skipped a beat when he realized that their garments identified them as mages. A wave of fear washed over him. Anyone living on the streets instinctively avoided people who wielded power, and mage power was the most frightening of all. It was unnatural.

With the first moments of surprise behind him, Kylen became curious. He was well accustomed to observing without being seen.

Pressing his ear as close to the glass as he dared, he tried to listen in on their conversation. Voices were occasionally raised, but even then he couldn't make out what they were saying. Nevertheless, the longer the meeting progressed, the more apprehensive Kylen began to feel. Occasional furtive glances toward the window suggested the meeting was clandestine.

A new wave of fear rose up within him. Even seeing these people together might be enough to put him at risk. Remaining on the rooftop would be madness. Stepping carefully away from the window, he headed across the roof toward the drainpipe at the back of the building.

He had barely taken a step when he felt lightheaded. His head began to spin, and the night sky disappeared entirely from view. He felt as if something was pressing down on him. The sensation of being smothered increased until he was gasping for breath.

Then suddenly, although his feet never left the tiles beneath him, it felt like he was soaring among the stars. The experience was unnerving. He couldn't comprehend what was happening.

The dizziness became overwhelming. Falling abruptly backward, he hit his head hard. Everything went black.

When Kylen regained his senses, he opened his eyes to the terrifying awareness that he couldn't see. Glancing desperately around he discovered to his relief he wasn't blind. It was nighttime, and it was very dark.

Everything came rushing back. He was still on the roof, and his head hurt. No trace of light flickered from the window. Climbing unsteadily to his feet, he heard people shouting from the streets below him.

His presence must have been discovered. He would have made plenty of noise when he fell and hit his head. If the meeting had been secret, the attendees would have wasted no time getting out of the building. Once they were clear, one of them would have undoubtedly 'spotted' the intruder on the roof and raised the alarm.

How long had he been unconscious? Had his face been visible from the window once they knew he was there? Would any of the six recognize him if they saw him again? Almost without thinking he pulled his hood forward to hide his face.

Leaving the area had become pressing. He was still a little shaky on his feet, but he was able to make his way safely across the roof. Hurrying to the drainpipe as quickly as he dared, he looked down to find the back alley deserted. That suggested he hadn't been unconscious for long. All too soon the building would be surrounded with people trying to find a way onto the roof.

Shinnying down the drainpipe, he ran along the alley a short distance to another building. Having scaled this building on a previous occasion, he knew what to do. Within a couple of minutes, he was on the roof and heading away from the commotion below him.

As he hurried away he was surprised to catch a glimpse of someone he recognized. Rowan—a street dweller a couple of years older than him—was perched on the roof of an adjoining building, in a perfect position to observe Kylen's hasty departure.

Had Rowan recognized him? The possibility of being identified was alarming. His hood had been in place, and although Rowan wasn't exactly a friend, he had no reason to want Kylen harmed. In any event, he wouldn't be aware of the clandestine meeting or who had witnessed it.

Pushing the chance encounter firmly from his mind, Kylen focused his attention on getting away.

Another two hours passed before he allowed himself to return to familiar territory. After escaping pursuers twice in one day, he would need to lie low for a very long time.

The derelict building he called home lay before him at last. Relieved and sobered, he hurried toward it. Jonno and Bella at least would be pleased to see him. Raff might give him a hard time, but he didn't care.

A figure stood outside in the darkness. As he approached, the light of the newly risen moon dimly revealed a face. It was Raff.

"He's here!" Raff shouted smugly.

Before Kylen could react, he was pounced on from both sides. Leering faces appeared before him—the faces of his rooftop pursuers from that morning. After tying his hands tightly behind his back, one of his captors tossed something in Raff's direction. No doubt the price of his betrayal.

His captors mocked him as they hauled him into the night.

"The little thief thought he got away, did he? Not so clever now, are you? You'll cop it this time!"

CHAPTER 2

After a miserable night in a cold cell, Kylen woke to the dubious prospects of an imprisoned thief.

His captors had hustled him to the city lockup, where he was handed over to a grim faced constable. After pushing him into an empty cell, the constable locked the door and ignored him. Water was available in the cell; no food was offered, then or later.

Others had been imprisoned around him, and when the sun rose the prisoners were led out one at a time. Noon must have come and gone before Kylen's turn came at last. By then his courage had long deserted him. His legs were so shaky he could barely walk.

Escorted into a richly furnished room in an adjoining building, he was shoved forward to face the city sheriff. Flanked by armed guards, the official was adorned in a lavish black robe, capped by a broad-brimmed hat fringed with purple ruffles. He was seated in an ornate wooden chair at one end of the room. The wall behind him featured a broad panel decorated with carved images of a crown, a royal standard, and a huge set of scales.

Stern of face, the sheriff frowned down at the newest miscreant. Kylen had never imagined someone so intimidating.

"Who is this, and why is he here?" growled the sheriff.

An aide was shuffling pieces of paper, a harried expression on his face. "Err, he was…Err…He was caught stealing from a baker, m'lord." He triumphantly flourished the document containing the information.

The sheriff addressed himself to the prisoner. "What is your name, boy?"

"K…Kylen," he stammered in response.

"Where is the complainant?" the judge demanded.

After a hasty look around, the aide hurried to a side door and bustled in the baker, a rotund man with a red face. "The victim is a worthy citizen by the name of Jonas Spelling, Your Worship," he announced.

The baker bowed low in the direction of the sheriff.

"What was stolen?"

"Bread, Your Worship. A sack full. Freshly baked loaves!" sputtered the baker. "And not for the first time, either!"

The judge pointed to the accused. "How do you know it was him?"

The baker appeared bemused by the question. "He's the one my guards caught."

The sheriff glowered at him. "I meant how do you know he's stolen from you before?"

"My guards asked around. It turns out he has quite a reputation!" the baker assured him. He nodded repeatedly as he said it, as if he thought the gesture somehow added weight to his assertion.

The officer raised his eyes heavenward. Turning his attention to Kylen, he asked, "Why did you steal his bread?"

"I…I was hungry, m'lord." Overawed and completely unnerved, it never occurred to Kylen to lie.

The sheriff frowned at him.

"Surely your parents feed you?"

"I don't have parents."

"Well your relatives, then."

Kylen shook his head helplessly. "I don't have relatives."

The officer frowned again. "Why steal a whole sack full of loaves?"

"The others are hungry too. The bread would have fed us for a week."

"What others?"

"My friends." He shrugged helplessly. "Others like me."

The sheriff scowled. "Being hungry doesn't give you the right to steal. You *buy* what you can afford. With money. We'd have anarchy if everyone simply took whatever they wanted."

Kylen wasn't entirely sure what anarchy was, but he understood money well enough. Thus far in his life he'd seen precious little of it.

It was becoming apparent to Kylen that the sheriff was totally ignorant of the daily realities of his life. It was hardly surprising. Kylen couldn't begin to imagine the sheriff's world either.

The officer seemed to have lost interest in him.

"Have we seen him before?" he asked the aide, jerking his head in the direction of Kylen.

"Err...I...I believe so, m'lord," the aide replied.

"More than once?"

The aide appeared flustered.

"Well?" demanded the sheriff.

Squeezing his eyes shut, the aide bobbed his head repeatedly. "Yes, yes, we have!"

"It isn't true!" sputtered Kylen.

The sheriff ignored him. "Clearly this is not an isolated incident. In view of your repeated misdemeanors it is incumbent upon me to send a message—to you and to others like you. Stealing is never the way to solve your problems. You need to find honest ways to feed yourself. I hope your punishment will remind you and your friends of that." He turned to a stony-faced guard waiting off to one side. "Carry out the usual penalty, then release him. See that it's done at once." He turned brusquely away. "Next case!" he bellowed.

Grabbing his arm roughly, a constable dragged the condemned thief from the room. The baker left ahead of them, a gloating look on his face.

Kylen had begun trembling with fear. He knew exactly what to expect from the sheriff's verdict. He'd seen others on the streets with only one hand. It left them useless for any practical task. The toughest among them found a way to survive, but for some the punishment amounted to a death sentence.

As he was led into position, he dimly noticed a crowd had gathered. A few onlookers heckled, but most remained silent. The constable stretched out his left hand, and he spread his fingers wide involuntarily. A brute of a man approached, grasping a medium-sized ax.

Squeezing his eyes closed, Kylen sucked in a deep breath. He grimaced as a strange sensation washed over him.

The crowd went quiet. Then the ominous silence was broken by a loud thud, accompanied by sudden pain.

Too frightened to look, he kept his eyes clamped shut tight.

The constable beside him broke the silence. "You bungled it!" he said in disgust. "You'll have to do it again!"

Daring to open his eyes, he almost swooned when he saw his little finger detached from his left hand.

As the ax man began to raise his weapon a second time, a voice called commandingly, "You get one attempt, and one attempt only. That's the law!"

Kylen stared wide-eyed into the crowd. He couldn't spot the speaker.

The constable opened his mouth to argue, but a woman with a cultured voice got in first. "He's right! Let the boy go." He heard her adding in a lower voice, "The very idea of it is barbaric!"

He saw that the speaker was a noblewoman, surrounded by a sizable group of servants. She was glaring at the constable. From the look in her eye, she was on the brink of commanding her servants to intervene.

The first voice spoke again, more authoritatively. "Release him, and do it now!" Kylen finally identified the speaker—a tall man in a gray robe, his face hidden in a large hood.

The noblewoman was growing impatient. "Do I need to call for Lord Mardell?" she demanded. Her tone left no doubt that she knew Lord Mardell personally. Kylen had no idea who the nobleman was, but the constable did—he'd gone pale.

Other voices joined in.

"Let 'im go!"

"You 'ad y'r chance!"

Abruptly recognizing that this battle was lost, the constable yielded. Grasping a cloth soaked in some kind of liquid, he thrust it at Kylen. Then he pointed away with a scowl. "Go before I change my mind." Bending closer, he added in a harsh whisper, "Next time we'll take a lot more than your hand!"

Kylen wasted no time pushing forward into the crowd, positioning the cloth gingerly over the stump of his finger as he went. He felt so lightheaded he could barely stay on his feet.

The hooded stranger who first spoke out on his behalf appeared beside him. "You'd better come with me," he murmured.

After a moment's hesitation, Kylen swung in behind the man. As he did so, he caught a glimpse of several figures in black robes, their garments fringed with a distinctive broad crimson strip.

Mages had arrived! One of them called out loudly, pointing in his direction.

"Quickly!" urged his rescuer.

Not waiting for a response, the stranger pressed deeper into the crowd. Kylen set off after him, his heart pounding and his hand throbbing painfully. His panic grew as the clamor of pursuit swelled behind him.

The secret meeting he'd disturbed had slipped entirely from his mind, pushed aside by his captivity and subsequent trial. Now it all came rushing back. One of the mages must have recognized him as he lay exposed and vulnerable on the roof after fainting. He didn't want to think about what might happen if they caught him. Fear propelled him forward, his injury forgotten. Nothing mattered except to escape.

Weaving their way frantically through the crowd, the two fugitives ducked between alleys and busy streets, until the noise of pursuit slowly died away. By that time Kylen was flagging badly. He vaguely recognized that they had reached a seamy quarter of the city. It didn't bother him—he felt at home in this environment. Apparently his rescuer did too.

Coming to a halt before a nondescript dwelling, the tall guide pushed through the door. Once inside, he stepped behind a rough wooden cupboard and moved aside a hidden panel. Stepping through it, he paused long enough to wave Kylen in after him. After a moment's hesitation, the weary youth followed him in.

He didn't follow heedlessly, even in his reduced state. But something told him that the stranger did not intend to harm him. He knew how to recognize the signs.

In his experience, most people were like Raff—they acted solely from self-interest. There had been exceptions over the course of his short life, but precious few in number. The exceptions had become the only people he counted as friends.

They slowly ascended a narrow staircase, emerging into a large upper room. Shutters covered a window, and the stranger pulled them open to admit rays of afternoon sunlight. The window offered a view across the rooftops of the city and up to the large stone castle perched above it. The view might have been striking, but Kylen couldn't take it in. His hand was throbbing, and the tension of all that lay behind had left him weary beyond words.

"Please, sit," ordered the stranger gently, pointing to a low bed.

Kylen obeyed.

"My name is Dalthinir," the man announced, watching him closely. When Kylen gave no reaction, a fleeting look crossed his face. Was it relief? "Who are you?" he asked.

"I'm Kylen."

"May I see your hand, Kylen?"

Kylen slowly removed the cloth, wincing at the sight that greeted him. Then, after hesitating for a long moment, he held out his hand for inspection.

After examining it gravely, Dalthinir disappeared into a corner of the room. Loud mumbles sounded as he rummaged about energetically. "Why do those herbs keep disappearing whenever I need them? Where might they be?"

Eventually he seemed to find whatever he was looking for. Seating himself at a small wooden table, he worked away quietly for a few minutes before turning to Kylen once more.

"Apply this to the wound," he said, handing over a small quantity of paste on a square tile. "It will keep it clean and encourage healing."

He held out an unsoiled rag. "Wrap this tightly around your hand when you're finished."

"Thank you," Kylen managed. He was blinking with weariness by the time he was done.

"How long since you've eaten?" asked Dalthinir.

Kylen responded with a shrug.

His rescuer retrieved bread, some cheese, and a skin of water. "Once you've had this you'd better lie down for a while." He waved a hand at the bed Kylen was sitting on.

Kylen drank deeply from the water, then he took the food and chewed it absentmindedly. He peered at his benefactor. "I'm a thief. Aren't you afraid I'll steal from you?"

A wry grin came to Dalthinir's face. It was the first hint Kylen had seen of a smile. The older man waved a hand around the room. "I have very little worth stealing."

"Why are you helping me?" Kylen persisted.

The man shrugged. "Someone helped me once," he said simply. "I wouldn't be here today otherwise. I had no opportunity to repay him. This is a way I can express my appreciation."

His face became thoughtful. "Beyond that, I try to remind myself that life is short. Too short to miss an opportunity for unselfish conduct."

Making sense of such statements was beyond Kylen at that moment. By the time he had swallowed the last mouthful, he could barely keep his eyes open. Even the throbbing in his hand couldn't keep him awake. Stretching out on the bed, he drifted off the moment he closed his eyes.

The room was dark when he awoke. The shutters had been left open, and moonlight shone dimly about him. There was no sign of Dalthinir.

Ignoring the pain in his hand, he moved to the window and gazed out across the city. Tiny lights twinkled here and there, especially from the castle, but very little sound reached his ears. He couldn't be certain of the time, although he must have slept well into the night.

His mind returned to his rescuer. Who was Dalthinir? How did he earn a living? Why had he been present at Kylen's punishment? Was it only by accident?

He sighed. Many questions and no answers.

With his rescuer gone, it seemed like an ideal opportunity to explore his room. Every corner and every available surface was filled with books, papers, and all manner of strange things. It was no surprise that Dalthinir had struggled to find the herbs.

The man had spoken the truth—Kylen saw nothing worth stealing. He did wonder what was written on the books and papers, and for the first time he wished he knew how to read.

A few minutes later his host returned. He appeared restless and distracted.

"We need to go," he said as he hastily lit a candle. "We'll leave the moment I've packed a few things."

With that he grabbed a sack and hurriedly began throwing items into it.

"What's happened?" asked Kylen nervously.

Dalthinir's reply set his heart pounding. "Mages are looking for us. They have ways of searching. They're already close. They'll be here in a few minutes at most."

Despair washed over Kylen. He had no idea what powers a mage might call upon to aid their search, but they could do just about anything—everyone knew that. How could he possibly hide from them? He broke out into a cold sweat.

Strangely, Dalthinir didn't seem intent on casting him aside. Nevertheless, vulnerable and hopeless as Kylen felt, he couldn't allow himself to be the cause of trouble coming upon his rescuer.

"I'll go," he said, his heart as heavy as a millstone. "You've already done enough for me."

He got up and headed for the stairs.

Dalthinir got there first, the sack over his shoulder. "That's very brave of you, Kylen. But I'm not going to abandon you to your fate. We'll go together." Clapping the youth cheerfully on the shoulder, he set off down the stairs.

After a moment's hesitation, Kylen followed him.

They emerged onto the street in almost total darkness. Dalthinir led the way.

Nothing unusual was evident as they hurried along the street. "Around there. Quickly!" His guide pointed to an alleyway just ahead of them.

They were entering it when a group of people appeared from a different direction bearing blazing torches.

"Grab him!" shouted a voice imperiously.

Before Kylen could react, a dark figure leaped toward him. To his complete astonishment, the lunging figure pushed past him, snatching at his rescuer instead. Spinning away out of range, Dalthinir grabbed Kylen's arm and pulled him into the alley.

All they could do was run. Sprinting back and forth through dark streets and darker alleys, they didn't stop until a huge double gate loomed before them. A glimmer had appeared in the sky, a sign of the approaching dawn. In response, guards emerged and swung wide the gates. Resisting the urge to dash forward heedlessly, the two fugitives ambled through the gates to freedom.

They didn't pause until the city lay far behind them. Then Dalthinir rummaged in his sack until he located bread and waterskins. Sharing them with his younger companion, he sat down on a fallen log to break his fast.

"What just happened?" asked Kylen. "I don't understand."

"You were under the impression they were chasing you," observed Dalthinir calmly. "Surely that's not just because you're a thief who escaped the full intended punishment." He raised an eyebrow knowingly. "There's a reason why you believe a group of mages is anxious to capture you. I'm curious to know what that reason is."

Kylen stared back at him uncertainly. Then he shrugged. What was the point in holding back? The older man had so far given him no reason to mistrust him.

Speaking slowly, he outlined everything that had happened on the roof. It felt like an incredible relief to get it out.

Dalthinir listened intently. "So you saw six people. Two mages—a man and a woman—as well as a noblewoman with a blue robe, a nobleman with a yellow robe and another nobleman with a green robe, plus another man with a simple black robe?"

Kylen nodded.

"That's interesting. Very interesting indeed!" Dalthinir was gazing at him thoughtfully. "And while you were still on the roof you suddenly became dizzy and collapsed. It felt like you were being held down, while at the same time floating above the ground?"

Once more Kylen nodded.

"Your magic has only just been awakened, then," Dalthinir mused. "And you don't know what any of it means." He nodded firmly. "It's time you knew the truth. First of all, those mages weren't chasing you —they were chasing me."

Kylen stared at him wide-eyed.

"You apparently haven't heard of me. I'm not sure whether to be pleased or disappointed." He smiled wryly. "I'm a mage, Kylen. A mage who isn't a member of the Compact—the council of mages. That makes me a renegade."

Before Kylen could recover from his shock, the older man added, "And that's not all. Thankfully, they don't seem to have realized what's happened yet, although I suppose it's only a matter of time. But thanks to your adventure on the roof, you're a mage as well. And just as much a renegade as I am."

CHAPTER 3

Two weeks earlier

The day was drawing to a close when Master Petria stepped through an ornate archway and briskly descended a short flight of stairs. The imposing building she was exiting housed an extensive library for the exclusive use of mages. The library included books and documents covering a wide range of topics, most especially magic in all its forms. A wealth of useful material awaited anyone persistent or fortunate enough to locate it.

The collection was maintained by the council of mages, commonly known as the Compact. As a member of the Compact, Petria was entitled to unrestricted access to the library during daylight hours. She also enjoyed many other privileges, including the right to be addressed by the honorific 'Master'.

As she crossed the road, a formally dressed man in his middle years intercepted her. His light cloak marked him as a representative of the Notaries Guild, a body that handled legal matters on behalf of individuals as well as institutions of every kind.

"Are you Master Petria?" he asked.

She nodded curtly.

He bowed stiffly, handing her a small piece of parchment. "Please accept this invitation to a meeting tomorrow evening at sundown. The meeting will be hosted in a private room in the headquarters of the Notaries Guild. The gathering is being convened in accordance with instructions contained in an addendum to the will of the late Master Banadin."

Her eyebrows went up at once.

He ignored her surprise. "Please treat the meeting as highly confidential. Master Banadin's instructions were very explicit on that point."

"Of course," she replied crisply.

With that he departed.

She was left bemused and extremely curious. Master Banadin had been one of the most powerful and influential mages in Periton. She had come to know him well.

Her mind drifted, recalling the time when first she had met him. In the months prior to his violent and unexpected death ten years previously, he had invited her to join him at a secluded location. At first suspicious of his intentions, she quickly realized he was interested only in becoming a guide and mentor. Inexperienced as she was, he seemed to appreciate someone unspoiled by the intrigues and infighting that came with life as a mage.

"I wish to lay before you an unusual proposition," he had said. "I hope you will find it intriguing. But let me begin with a demonstration."

Showing her a small, golden talisman shaped like a clenched fist, he asked, "Could you please invoke a fireball? Send it wherever you like. Note its dimensions and intensity, but keep the information to yourself."

After a moment's hesitation she agreed and did as he requested. To her astonishment, her fireball failed to appear.

"I will now send your fireball into that body of water," he told her.

Holding aloft the talisman, he sent a fireball into the lake.

"Can you confirm that the fireball matched the characteristics of the one you invoked?" he asked.

"It did," she confirmed in astonishment.

"This talisman is able to capture and store magical power for later use. I made it myself, and it responds only to me," he told her. "I trust that I have captured your interest."

She nodded, her eyes wide.

"Are you willing to swear that you will keep our conversation private?" he asked.

When she agreed, he made her take an oath. "I swear that I will speak of this conversation to no one. If I break my word, may my magic follow crooked paths and rebound on me."

Once the oath lay behind them, he dipped his head in satisfaction.

"A vast treasure of knowledge was lost in the destruction of Methesia," he began. "Yet the full power wielded by mages in its best years can be recovered! Why should mages be limited to one or two magical abilities?"

He shook his head sadly. "The Compact has long banned a range of magical pursuits out of fear of another Great Desolation. I have come to see this approach as unnecessary and unhelpful. However, any suggestion of change is fiercely opposed. The inevitable conclusion is that only a massive upheaval in the social order will bring about the kind of environment needed to promote a restoration of the lost skills and abilities."

He had been studying her reaction closely. "Are you willing to explore these matters further?"

She swallowed. Then she nodded.

"You may be wondering how I came to these conclusions. And how I created the talisman. The inspiration for all of it came only after an ancient being of immense intelligence and power contacted me, offering both insights and practical knowledge. This being, whom I shall refer to as my magical patron, used unusual means to make contact. I can say no more at this time, beyond assuring you that my patron has pledged to furnish whatever magical assistance might be needed to achieve these goals."

He eyed her keenly. "You are young, and new opportunities do not seem to frighten you. Your ability with fire is impressive, but perhaps you would welcome additional abilities. And perhaps you could expand your responsibilities in other ways. Would you be willing to participate in an effort to bring about the changes I have described? I can see you taking a leading role in a new order—if you are interested."

Petria's eyes had almost popped out of her head. From her earliest years, opportunities to improve her lot had been denied her. Her upbringing had been harsh and restrictive, with no one to protect her from the relentless bullying and belittling of her siblings and other children in her circle. She had been treated as troublesome and worthless.

Becoming a mage had been a heady experience. But her ability with fire had quickly paled beside the greater power and broader range of abilities wielded by others. Her deep-rooted desire for recognition had yet to be satisfied.

Now she had been singled out by a mature and experienced mage and invited to play a key role in an endeavor of immense consequence. Petria fully understood she was wading into forbidden waters, but she hadn't hesitated. "I am keenly interested."

"I will be in touch in the future," Banadin promised her. "Do not forget your oath!"

In the months that followed, he had been as good as his word. While he never revealed names, she was given to understand that other key individuals had also committed themselves to work beside him.

Busy as he was, he took time to share his experience and knowledge with her. He pushed her too hard—even to the point of cruelty on occasion—but she was used to it, and he was at least unstinting in his praise as she developed in her skills and ability.

Hints about his activities had surfaced when Master Dalthinir approached the Compact leadership, claiming he had witnessed Banadin dabbling with forbidden magic. Banadin escaped sanctions only because Dalthinir was not able to offer proof of any kind. It also emerged that Dalthinir had been monitoring meetings between Banadin and his supporters.

Banadin made no secret of his bitter hatred of his accuser. From that moment, Petria worked tirelessly to undermine Dalthinir at every opportunity, as did a number of others. The likely identities of her fellow secret conspirators became apparent as she took note of the mages who rallied to Banadin's support.

Petria had been shocked when Banadin's body was discovered soon after. He had suffered a violent and messy death.

Masters Clarree, Roza, and Garmer, all of them senior and influential mages, immediately accused Dalthinir of murder. Petria, along with Master Lars, another junior mage, joined them in a demand for charges to be laid. Pressuring the chief master relentlessly, the mages successfully badgered him into acceding to their demands. The chief master at the time was old and well past his prime, and Banadin's supporters had celebrated when he yielded to the pressure. He died before the inquiry took place, and it was presided over by the newly appointed Chief Master Adrastas.

Dalthinir was not found guilty—hardly surprising given his solid alibi and the absence of evidence against him. Nevertheless, during the trial Banadin's allies asserted that Dalthinir had tarnished the good name of Banadin without proof. They also howled that he had been snooping on them, and in doing so had engaged in conduct unbecoming a member of the Compact. They called for Dalthinir to be sanctioned, their demands loud and strident.

In an attempt to appease the vocal minority, a number of limitations were imposed on Dalthinir's freedom and the exercise of his abilities. He responded by protesting that Master Clarree and others had tarnished his good name in accusing him of murder without evidence. To the satisfaction of Banadin's supporters, Adrastas disregarded his objections.

Masters Clarree and Garmer in particular had pursued Dalthinir with unusual energy and vindictiveness, and they showed no signs of relenting. Apparently recognizing there was little future for him in the Compact, Dalthinir severed all connection with it and fled Cambrick. In doing so he declared himself renegade.

The inquiry had polarized the mage community, and the Compact leadership had demonstrated its weakness and ineptitude. Nevertheless, with their leader gone, there was little Banadin's supporters could do to take advantage of the situation.

With this history churning through her mind, Petria arrived at the headquarters of the Notaries Guild at the nominated time. She was ushered into a small room where she found a number of others already assembled. Prince Evran, the brother of the king, was among them. The only other mage was her contemporary, Master Lars.

After a few minutes, the member of the Notaries Guild who had delivered her invitation approached Prince Evran and handed him a sealed document. "Please open this and read it when I have left. The building has been emptied to ensure your privacy. Feel free to take whatever time you need to conclude your business."

Having fulfilled his duty, he left the room, securing the heavy wooden door behind him.

Prince Evran examined the seal carefully before breaking it. "This document is from Master Banadin," he announced. Then, pushing back his chair, he stood up and read the letter.

You have been assembled according to my directions by my legal representative. He has been instructed to ensure your privacy. He has no knowledge of the purpose of this meeting, nor of the contents of the documents you will receive from him.

He will have handed the prince the sealed document that is now being read to you.

The fact that you are receiving this letter demonstrates that I have failed the test of time. It therefore falls to others to complete what I have begun. I must emphasize that there is no reason why my absence should negatively affect the outcome of the endeavor that lies before you.

I have engaged individually with every person in the room, giving and receiving oaths from each of you. However, until now you have never met as a group. In view of my demise, any of you who wishes to withdraw from the commitments you made may do so now, without hindrance or penalty. If you remain in the room, you will be bound forever by unbreakable oaths. Only death can free you.

The reading of this document must be paused at this point to allow each attendee to make their binding decision...

EVERY PERSON in the room began glancing around, assessing the other attendees.

Of the mages who directed their fury upon Dalthinir after the death of Banadin, Masters Garmer, Roza, and Clarree had been the most powerful and experienced. Petria had concluded at the time that each of them must have been recruited by Banadin.

All three were absent from the room. While none of them had been young, Banadin must have expected them to enjoy typical lifespans. Nevertheless, each of them had died of natural causes in the decade since his passing.

In any event, she could not fail to notice that, apart from herself and Lars, every person in the room was a prominent and distinguished figure in the life of the kingdom.

Mages must surely have featured strongly in Banadin's designs. Her stomach began to twist as she considered the possibility that the others might get up and leave now they could see who their hopes rested on.

Nobody moved.

Realizing she had been holding her breath, Petria exhaled quietly through her teeth. She was committed now. And so was every other person in the room.

CHAPTER 4

Holding up Banadin's document, Prince Evran continued to read.

> *I have important instructions to those of you who remain. I have included with this document a packet that is of value only to the mages in the group. It should now be handed to Master Roza for her to deal with at a later time. If she is not present, her place should be taken by one of Masters Clarree, Garmer, Petria, and Lars, in that order.*

So she had guessed correctly about Banadin recruiting the three mages.

The prince handed the packet to Petria before continuing.

> *The timing of this meeting has been carefully chosen. A unique opportunity is about to present itself, due to the rare total solar*

eclipse that will occur in the near future. If each of you does what you need to do, this occurrence will set in motion a series of events that will decisively lead to a new order, with control in the hands of the people in this room. The mages, led by Master Roza or her replacement, will find their powers vastly increased by what is about to occur. They will be chiefly responsible for bringing about the changes.

Assuming all of the following have remained in the room, Prince Evran is to become king, and Lady Mardell will become the kingdom's most senior official with Lords Marklo and Rostem her deputies. None of this should come as a surprise to any of the people named.

The Compact will undergo many important changes. I expect one of the mages present to be appointed chief master. Each of the mages present in this room will enjoy new prominence and prestige due to their greatly enhanced power and abilities. They will have the opportunity to lift all restrictions on magic, allowing mages to rediscover the lost powers of their forebears.

Beware the mage Dalthinir! He will oppose you with all his might! Dispose of him swiftly.

Do not waste the opportunity before you! Nothing like it will arise in your lifetime.

Master Banadin

A LONG SILENCE FOLLOWED. It was broken by the prince. "We should not ignore Master Banadin's warning about Dalthinir. As a renegade, he is no longer in a position to oppose us openly, but he remains at large. If he learns anything of what we are planning, he will do whatever he can to block us. None of us should underestimate him."

He then addressed the two mages. "All of us are placing a great deal of faith in you. Do not disappoint us!"

With that he nodded gravely and left the room. The others filed out after him, closing the door behind them.

Lars didn't try to hide his excitement. "Let's find out what the packet contains!"

She frowned at him. "The packet was placed in my keeping, not in yours."

He wasn't deterred. "There are only two of us now. We need to work together!"

Ignoring him, she opened the packet and examined its contents. Two objects fell onto the table before her. Made of gold and shaped like a clenched fist, both resembled Banadin's talisman that captured and stored power. She pictured once more his demonstration of the talisman's power, remembering her astonishment.

Seeing the hunger in Lars's eyes, she grasped both of them firmly in her left hand before placing the hand on her lap beneath the table.

The packet included a covering letter, which she read silently.

By the time she finished Lars could barely contain himself. "What does it say?" he demanded.

Seeing no good reason not to share it with him, she read it aloud.

Master Roza,

The key to acquiring the power needed to bring about change is a book, Ode to the Fallen One. *The book had long been lost, with almost no one believing it could ever be found.*

I long suspected that crucial information about the book was held by Olatiren, keeper of the Compact library and a man well acquainted with the library's contents. Having learned of a past dalliance between Olatiren and the wife of a key mage, I threatened to expose them both if Olatiren refused to hand over to me every piece of information he had on the book.

After bowing to my demand, Olatiren resigned his position and disappeared.

I have included in the packet the document he gave me. It will lead you to the book. You will learn from the document that the power you need will be released when you open the book. Along with unlimited power, you will acquire the full capability of every magical sense.

I will not deny the evil reputation of this book. However my patron has convinced me that opening the book will not destroy the world as claimed by the ignorant, provided you have in your possession one of the talismans included with this packet.

You witnessed for yourself the talisman's effectiveness. It is able to trap and store power for later use, thereby nullifying any immediate impact of the power.

I have included two identical talismans with this packet. Keep them safe! Take one of them as your own. After you have used it for the first time, it will respond only to you. If used correctly, there is no limit to the power it can trap and store. You may use the second talisman in whatever way you choose.

One word of warning. I learned from my patron that although the talisman may be used many times, the amount of power it is capable of storing will be determined by its first use. The talisman I demonstrated to you was first used to capture and store a relatively minor expression of power. I later found it incapable of storing greater amounts of power. For that reason I always planned to use one of the two remaining talismans when opening the book.

I trust that my meaning is clear. DO NOT use the talisman for any other purpose. If you do, the capacity of the talisman will be compromised, making it unable to store the vast amount of power unleashed when you open the book. My source left no doubt that under such circumstances the excess power will be released upon the world, resulting in terrible destruction.

It will already be obvious that my knowledge of these subjects owes a great debt to the ancient being I have spoken to you about previously. The practical steps I have taken to ensure a successful outcome would not have been possible without assistance from that same source.

My patron revealed to me that in times past it had become trapped. It required only two things in return for its assistance —first, in view of the fragility of humankind, that I prepare a contingency plan to take effect in the event of my demise, and second that I release it from the place where it is trapped as soon as I have the power to do so. I solemnly agreed to both undertakings. The first I have done, as you can bear witness. The second pledge now passes to you. I expect the creature will find a way to make contact at an appropriate time.

I will not be there to witness the new order you will usher in. I do at least have the satisfaction of knowing I laid the foundations.

I wish you good success.
Master Banadin

BOTH OF THEM sat silently for many minutes.

Lars spoke first. "Read the other document!" he urged.

Picking it up, she saw that it was an old parchment, still in good condition. She focused her attention on the spindly script that covered its surface. Unfamiliar at first, the words began to make sense once she recognized familiar characters in the flowery handwriting. In a halting voice, she began to read.

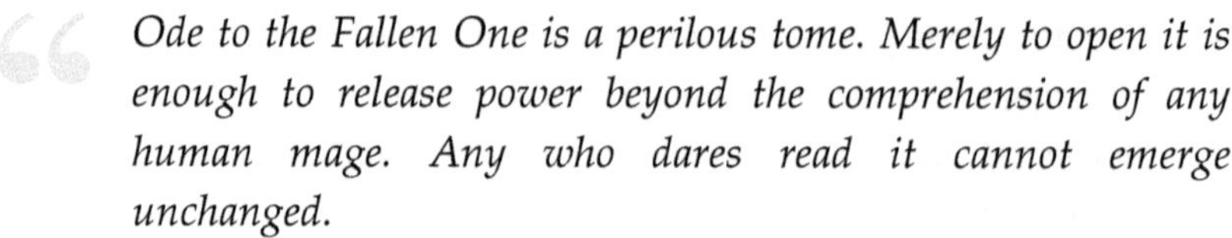

Ode to the Fallen One is a perilous tome. Merely to open it is enough to release power beyond the comprehension of any human mage. Any who dares read it cannot emerge unchanged.

PAUSING, she glanced at Lars. He sat transfixed, his usual brashness replaced by an almost primal hunger. She could hardly criticize him when his reaction so closely mirrored her own.

She bent to the parchment once more.

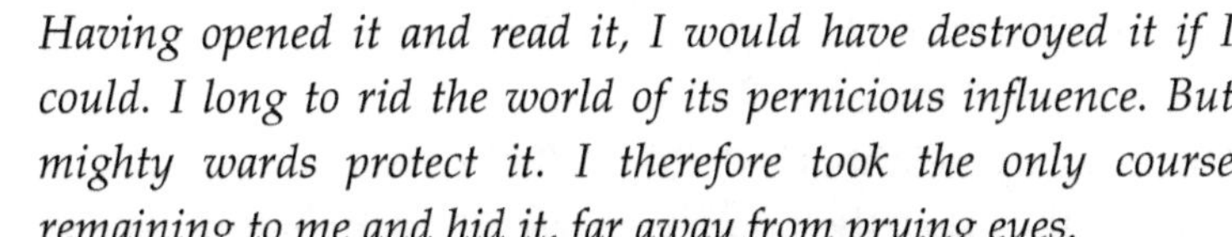

Having opened it and read it, I would have destroyed it if I could. I long to rid the world of its pernicious influence. But mighty wards protect it. I therefore took the only course remaining to me and hid it, far away from prying eyes.

And yet having done so, I find myself strangely compelled to describe its whereabouts. Here are the clues, unwillingly though I write them. Any mage determined to seek the book must brave the deadly hazards of the Drakkenridge Mountains. Once within reach, the book will draw you to itself. You must pass a door, taller than me and outlined faintly in the rock. Press twice at the top, twice at the bottom, and thrice on each side, then hard in the middle. The book rests within a boulder, positioned on a rock stand inside the chamber. Only great heat can release it from the enfolding rock. Human hands cannot grasp it—mage power alone will draw it forth. The book will be accessible only during a total solar eclipse, in the moment between times.

So I have yielded up its secret. I have fallen low, low indeed. Surely the ode must have been written with me in mind.

To whomever finds and reads this, I leave a final warning. If you lust after power, beware!

May you be blessed with the wisdom I lacked.

Once more they sat without speaking for a considerable period.

Eventually Lars looked pointedly at the document in her hand. "We need to take this parchment with us!"

She shook her head. "It would be much too risky. But we cannot afford to forget the smallest detail. It isn't long. I will read it one more time so we can commit it to memory. Pay close attention!"

She began again, her voice trembling.

Ode to the Fallen One is a perilous tome. Merely to open it is enough to release power beyond the comprehension of any human mage...

They sat silently once more after she had finished.

"*Ode to the Fallen One*," breathed Petria at last. "As Master Banadin acknowledged, it has an evil reputation."

"So does my neighbor's dog," scoffed Lars.

"The author sees the book as extremely dangerous," she persisted. "Doesn't that bother you at all?"

Lars waved a hand dismissively. "Power has always been dangerous to the weak-minded. The author's misgivings reveal little more than his timidity. He has nothing to say about actual risks from opening the book."

She shrugged. "Now that we have committed ourselves, I suppose it is no longer relevant. It seems heat is needed to release the book from the rock, and it needs to be picked up magically. Banadin's magical abilities allowed him to do both."

"The same was true of Master Roza," replied Lars. "That's undoubtedly why he put her at the top of his list."

"It had nothing to do with her experience and power?" asked Petria ironically.

He didn't respond.

She shrugged. "I can arrange for the heat. And your mage touch ability will allow you to pick the book up magically."

"You need to be aware that I will do nothing to help unless you give me one of the talismans," he told her flatly.

She raised her eyes heavenward. "There will be plenty of time to consider such details. The talismans are of no value until we gain access to the book. In the meantime far too many questions remain. How can we find out when the next total solar eclipse is due? And how will we get to the Drakkenridge Mountains?"

With no answers forthcoming from Lars, she added, "There must be some benefit from having a member of the royal family involved. I will ask Prince Evran to find the date of the next total solar eclipse and also to provide a guide who can lead us into the mountains."

"If that's all he's good for, I don't see why Banadin bothered to involve the prince in the first place," grumbled Lars. "Or the nobles for that matter."

Petria stared at him in disbelief. "Have you never grasped that society cannot be stable unless power is shared? The most important institutions in Periton are the Crown, the Compact, and the Conclave of Nobles. No king long survives without the support of the kingdom's key institutions, and the most powerful mage in the world can't do it either. The prince belongs to the Crown, we are both members of the Compact, and Banadin involved several key members of the Conclave. It is in all of our interests to work together."

He fell silent.

Lars apparently had little interest in sharing power with anyone, her included. It was fortunate indeed that Master Banadin had entrusted the talismans to her and not to him.

CHAPTER 5

Kylen stared at Dalthinir, his mouth hanging open in astonishment. It had been shocking enough to hear his rescuer claim to be a mage, but a renegade mage? Even he knew that renegade mages were dangerous and unpredictable. It was well known that they bore the blame for most of the trouble in the world.

So far he hadn't seen the slightest hint that Dalthinir was dangerous, but he knew very little about him. The man might be lying when he claimed to be a mage.

As for the suggestion that Kylen was one himself, it was ridiculous.

The older man was watching him silently. He seemed content to wait for Kylen to speak.

Eventually he found his voice. "I'm no mage!" he protested. "I know nothing about magic!"

"None of this must be easy for you," Dalthinir replied patiently. "And I'd be lying if I told you your life is about to get any easier. Would you like me to try to explain what I know?"

Kylen's first instinct was to escape into denial, to shut it out and refuse to hear any more about it. But he quickly saw that withdrawal would get him nowhere. He nodded reluctantly.

Waving him to another log nearby, Dalthinir began, "Do you know what pushing magic is?"

He sat down, shaking his head.

"It's one expression of a magical sense we call mage touch—but it basically involves moving objects by magical means. Not all mages can do it, and of those who can, some are more capable than others."

Careful as Kylen was to appear attentive, he was struggling to take any of it seriously.

"I happen to be among those able to do it," the self-professed mage continued. Then he paused, eyeing Kylen knowingly. "I can see you don't believe me."

Not knowing what to say, Kylen was wise enough to say nothing. But Dalthinir was right—he didn't believe a word of it. He could barely make sense of anything that had happened in the last couple of days. Now he was being asked to accept all this talk about magic, and from a man who claimed to be a mage without offering the slightest evidence of it. It was all too much.

He remembered a donkey cart he had seen in the city once. The cart had been so overloaded the donkey couldn't move. His mind felt like that—weighed down to the point of absurdity.

A slight sound caused him to glance to his left. A pine cone was rolling slowly but steadily in his direction. A thump sounded on the other side of him, and he swung his head in time to see a small rock quivering on the ground. As he stared wide-eyed, it headed toward him in a series of small hops.

Thoroughly alarmed, he leaped to his feet, peering wildly around him.

"You needn't worry," Dalthinir assured him. "The demonstration's over."

Too shaken to sit, Kylen stood staring at him in dread.

"You truly have nothing to fear," Dalthinir insisted. "The more so since you're capable of doing the same yourself."

Kylen frowned, not certain if the mage was mocking him.

The older man was looking at him mildly. "You must have wondered why the axman missed your wrist." When Kylen offered no response, he added, "Hitting the right spot is his job. He's had plenty of practice, and he's very good at it."

It had surprised Kylen that the axman botched it so badly. He shook his head in confusion.

"I'm guessing you felt strange just before he swung the ax."

Kylen's brows drew together. "Yes. I did," he acknowledged reluctantly. "I felt...I can't quite describe the sensation."

Dalthinir nodded. "The ax missing your wrist was no accident. You saved your own hand. You instinctively called upon magic to push the ax aside as it came down. You're not experienced, of course, and your push was poorly directed. That cost you a finger. But you didn't do badly considering it was a first attempt, and an unconscious one at that."

"So you're saying I could move rocks and pine cones like you just did?"

"Based on what happened with the ax, most certainly. Don't expect too much without training though."

Kylen wasn't buying it, although he tried not to make his skepticism too obvious. He no longer doubted the mage's powers—not after the earlier demonstration. But the notion that he had power as well? That was another matter entirely.

Abruptly Dalthinir held up a hand for silence. He stood rigid for a few moments, his head cocked to one side. "We need to move! We're not safe yet."

Picking up his sack, he set off at a steady jog, heading away from the road and into the trees. Kylen kept pace with him easily.

"I don't hear anything," offered Kylen.

"Neither do I. I'm using farsense," Dalthinir told him. "A group of mages is heading this way. And at the rate they're moving, they must be on horseback."

A wave of panic washed over Kylen. "We can't outrun horses."

The older man was beginning to breathe heavily, and talking had become more difficult for him. "Outrunning them isn't my intention," he managed.

A noise ahead of them had been growing in volume as they ran, and as they burst out of a stand of trees Kylen was presented with a sight that astonished him. Water was rushing loudly and chaotically along a broad channel. Having spent his entire life in the city he'd never seen anything like it. He knew enough to give it a name though. It was a river.

Dalthinir began hunting along the water's edge. "There's supposed to be a coracle on the riverbank somewhere," he said, his voice strained. After glancing back the way they had come, he moved to the water's edge. "We're out of time. I hope you can swim, Kylen!"

"No, I can't!" Kylen called back anxiously.

The mage paused on the brink of throwing himself into the water. Casting rapidly about, he located and retrieved a large branch. "Grab this! It will keep you afloat." Then he urged Kylen into the river.

Approaching the water's edge uncertainly, Kylen hesitated. Apparently deciding the time for gentle persuasion had passed, Dalthinir gave him a healthy shove, then jumped in after him.

Kylen cried out in surprise, clinging desperately to the branch as water splashed over and around him. He sucked in air frantically, terrified of going under. The water picked up speed as it rounded a bend in the river, and he caught a glimpse of white foam around a series of large rocks ahead.

Swept forward relentlessly, he came to a jarring halt as his branch wedged momentarily between two boulders. Water rushed heedlessly around him. Then the branch came free, and he raced forward once more.

Dalthinir had now been carried beyond him. Seeing the mage's head bobbing in and out of the water, Kylen wondered how he could possibly survive. Then the river bent in the other direction. On the inside of the bend, the branch slowed, drifting closer to the bank. Kylen's feet touched the bottom, and he struggled toward the dry land, dragging the branch with him.

Soon he was only waist deep. Discarding his support, he surged out of the water, trembling with nervous energy. Only when he was safely ashore did it occur to him to wonder what had become of the mage. To his relief, he spotted Dalthinir struggling ashore a little further downstream. Remarkably, he still had his sack, although by then the contents must have been thoroughly soaked. Kylen moved quickly to join him.

Throwing himself onto the sand, the older man heaved in the life-giving air. Eventually he was able to speak again.

"Well, that was exciting," he said.

Kylen stared at him incredulously.

His attention elsewhere, Dalthinir didn't appear to notice. "We seem to have lost our pursuers," he finally announced.

Renegade mages, determined pursuers, raging rivers. The future suddenly seemed impossibly bleak to Kylen. "What are we going to do?"

"Find somewhere dry," the mage replied cheerfully. "Then have something to eat."

THE TWO FUGITIVES sat beneath the dense canopy of an ancient oak, drying themselves before a small fire while they munched on soggy bread and cheese.

"Will they find us?" asked Kylen.

"They'll try. But we'll be long gone by the time they get here."

"You're not going back to the city?"

The question clearly surprised Dalthinir. "We have no choice. The city isn't safe anymore—not for either of us. And I can't teach you what you need to learn unless we're in a safe place."

The mage must have noticed his quizzical expression. "You need to learn to swim, of course. Perhaps when the weather is more mild. But the crucial thing is to learn how to control and use your power."

Far from convinced he had any power to control, Kylen returned a frown of puzzlement.

Dalthinir sighed. "You have no way of knowing it, but mages are always aware when magical power is used. The ability to identify magical power is what makes a mage a mage. When the ax came down, you sent out a surge of power. A strong surge. But one that was unrecognizable to anyone from the Compact."

Seeing Kylen still frowning, he continued. "Perhaps an illustration might help. When people speak, they don't all sound the same. If you know someone, you recognize their voice when you hear them speak. Using power is similar. When a mage uses power, it's expressed in a unique way. A tiny amount of power won't be noticeable. Like when I moved the pine cone and the rock. Another mage would have needed to be nearby to notice it. And even if they were close at hand, a tiny amount of power wouldn't give away the mage who caused it, any more than a voice is recognizable when someone whispers.

"A substantial burst of power is different. Other mages can readily tell if it came from anyone they know. Mages belonging to the Compact—the council of mages—recognize each other's magic."

Kylen was still skeptical. "So you found me because I sent out a burst of power?"

"Not exactly. I was there already. But it was very clear to me when you did it. And it drew other mages as well."

"So that's why they're hunting me?"

Dalthinir shook his head. "They know nothing about you. They thought the power came from me."

Kylen stared at him wide-eyed.

"I've been living in the city under their noses for the last two years. They had no idea I was there. Then this happened. I doubt they believe another renegade mage exists, much less one capable of a surge like that. Their leaders will be desperate to know what I've been up to, and they'll spare no effort to find me."

"If they didn't recognize the burst of power, what made them think it was you? Don't they recognize your power?"

"That's a bit complicated," Dalthinir replied evasively.

Kylen had plenty more questions. "What's a renegade mage?" It wasn't a comfortable subject, but he needed to know, and sooner was surely better than later.

"It means one of two things. If you exercise magical power and you're not a member of the Compact, you're a renegade. You also become a renegade if you're a member who leaves the Compact, as I did."

"So I'm a renegade because I'm not a member?"

The mage nodded.

"How do mages join the Compact?"

"The Compact assigns some of their number to search tirelessly for people with the potential to become mages. Having a parent or grandparent who is a mage is a possible starting point, but there are indicators, such as the way someone instinctively reacts to a demonstration of power. As soon as they find a person with clear potential, they make them an apprentice. They have their own rituals for awakening magical power in an initiate, and they don't allow that to happen until the apprentice has been thoroughly trained in their ways and sees things the way they do."

"What if someone doesn't see things their way?"

"They're killed. Immediately—before they can become a problem."

Kylen was horrified. "Even if they've done nothing wrong?"

"Even then. I know it must seem like a huge overreaction. It applies equally to me. I've done nothing terrible, and I never will. But they'll kill me if they catch me." He sighed. "Terrible as it is, I do understand their reasoning. The truth is I'm capable of doing a lot of damage should I ever choose to. And I became answerable to no one apart from myself when I left the Compact." He gave a wry smile.

"Their policy was put in place for a reason. Many years ago, before I was born, there was a powerful mage who caused major problems. He had strong opinions, and he became increasingly angry with anyone who disagreed with him. He eventually decided to go off on his own. At first he stayed out of sight, so he was ignored. It later emerged he'd spent his time preparing an attack on the royal family. He intended to kill them all. When he launched his assault, no one knew it was coming. A lot of soldiers died. The royal family was saved only because a group of mages arrived. They were barely in time. Some of them were also killed before the rogue mage was finally stopped. After that, the king demanded that the mages take steps to prevent any of their number doing something like that again. He reminded them that any position of power and privilege came with responsibilities.

"The mages wanted to rule themselves, so they agreed to come under the authority of the Compact leadership. Anyone who refused to do so would either have to accept exile or die."

"So you could leave Periton! If you weren't in the kingdom, they'd stop chasing you."

Dalthinir shook his head. "After a while the leaders of the Compact realized that exiled mages were still dangerous. So they removed exile as an option. Now, it's very simple—if you leave, you die." He smiled grimly. "Provided they can catch you."

"Why don't you leave Periton anyway? Surely it would be harder for them to find you if you weren't in the kingdom."

"Unfortunately, that isn't practical. To begin with, no other kingdom is readily accessible. The nearest is Tantel, but the region between Periton and Tantel is uninhabitable. It's unsafe even for travel by land. The only way to reach it is by sea. And there's an agreement between the kingdoms to restrict the movement of mages. Mages must get permission from the council of mages in both kingdoms before any visit. In practice, it almost never happens. Even though the two kingdoms are at peace, there's a long history of suspicion between them. Especially where magic is concerned."

Kylen covered his face with his hands. He wasn't convinced he was a mage, but it made no difference what he thought. If the Compact decided he was a mage, they'd kill him as a renegade. And fleeing wasn't even an option.

"If I'm a mage, why can't I just join the Compact?"

Dalthinir had no comfort to offer. "I'm afraid it's too late for that. I'm sorry, Kylen, but you can never be a member of the Compact. Your magic has been awakened without their involvement. Worse, it happened without you having been immersed in their way of thinking. They'll always see you as a threat."

"So they'll want to kill me, even though I've done nothing to oppose them?"

Dalthinir nodded.

It was grossly unreasonable. They'd kill him to prevent him from putting them in danger. But how could he be a danger to anyone? If he truly did have powers, he had no idea how to use them.

If all of this was true, Dalthinir might offer his only hope of survival.

"Why are you a renegade?" he asked.

The mage's face was unreadable. "That's a story for another day."

There was so much he didn't understand. But there was one thing he did know. "If we're leaving Cambrick forever, I need to go back first."

"Why?"

"Two of my friends, Jonno and Bella, are still there. I won't leave them to get by on their own."

The look on Dalthinir's face made it clear he had no interest in taking on responsibility for anyone else.

"Don't worry, once they join us they'll look after themselves," Kylen assured him.

The mage shook his head. "I can guess what looking after themselves will mean," he stated flatly. "If you're joining me you'll have to give up your thieving ways. Getting that to happen will be enough of a challenge for both of us. What will they be doing in the meantime? Being bored and light-fingered is a bad combination—they'll draw attention to themselves, which also means drawing attention to us."

Kylen was unmoved. "If they don't come, I'm not going." The mage couldn't possibly know about his stubborn streak, but he was going to find out sooner or later. It might as well be now. "Don't worry. You won't need to do anything. I'll go back for them, and all of us will meet you here."

The mage was incredulous. "Do you *want* the Compact to find you and kill you?"

"Of course not. But you said they're looking for you, not for me."

"It isn't that simple." Dalthinir shook his head in exasperation. "You leak power like a skunk leaks bad smells. I first sensed it when I was passing by—that's why I was there when they carried out your punishment. It took me a while to figure out who it was coming from. I wasn't certain until the ax came down."

His face showed his concern. "The Compact are on the lookout for me. They'll have mages on high alert at every entrance to the city, and they'll sense your magic if you go anywhere near them. They'll be all over you the minute you step through the gates."

"Can't you teach me not to leak power?"

"I intend to try, but it will take time. And it isn't safe to do it here."

"Then I'll just have to find a way into the city that doesn't involve going through the gates."

The mage threw up his hands in helpless appeal. "If you go back there I can't protect you! I've explained why the city isn't safe for me."

"I understand that. But it won't matter. I've made it this far through life without anyone protecting me."

"You seem to have forgotten that you were just caught and punished!"

"Once! That was the only time it's happened. From now on I'll be a lot more careful."

"How do you propose to get into the city without going through the gates?"

"I'll think of something."

Such assurances clearly didn't satisfy the mage. He was shaking his head in disbelief.

What could Kylen say though? He wasn't willing even to consider leaving Jonno and Bella behind to fend for themselves.

He was confident he'd find a way to get them out. If he was caught in the attempt, then so be it.

CHAPTER 6

Entirely unaware of Dalthinir's silent scrutiny, the distant form climbed slowly upward, searching for a new handhold before hauling himself a little higher.

The rear of the city of Cambrick was protected by an almost sheer cliff. To secure the city's defenses, a massive semicircular wall had been constructed, anchored at each end by solid rock. The city was built within it. Expansive as the available area was, it had gradually been consumed over the years. The inevitable result was that dwellings had spread out beyond the confines of the walls. The sprawling township of Camberton now lay a short distance away on both sides of the main road.

Attacking the city from behind was unrealistic for an enemy army, but a determined climber could still find a way up the cliff and over the wall, provided they possessed the necessary skill. And provided they were willing to thumb their nose at death. From Kylen's own account, he was entirely at home on the rooftops of the city. That suggested he had a head for heights.

But attempting a climb like the one before him? And after losing a finger?

At times of war, guards would be posted to prevent such incursions. But the kingdom of Periton had enjoyed an extended time of peace, and no guards could be seen anywhere near the cliff.

The mage shuddered as his eyes scanned the rock face still towering above the youth. He had been fool enough to think Kylen would give up once he realized he couldn't enter the city by the gates. In his wildest imaginings he could never have dreamed he would attempt something like this.

Kylen had at least shown enough sense to heed his warning about entering the city by the gates. But the alternative he had chosen was beyond foolhardy. And how was he planning to escape? Surely his new apprentice wasn't expecting to climb back down the cliff with his two friends.

Dalthinir's eyebrows furrowed. He might think of Kylen as his new apprentice, but no actual agreement had been reached. The matter hadn't yet been discussed.

He sighed. Could he be bothered with an apprentice? His sense of responsibility became remarkably inconvenient at times. It would have been far less trouble to leave the boy to fend for himself from the beginning. But he knew Kylen wouldn't have remained undetected for long. Worse, he wouldn't even have been aware he was at risk. He would have been hunted down and executed without ever knowing why.

The mage's life would only become more complicated if these friends of Kylen's joined them. He couldn't begin to imagine what he would do with them, even if they somehow managed to escape the city.

He shook his head, dispirited by his own reluctance to do his duty. He had long believed that, while breath remained in his body, turning aside from duty was shameful and dishonorable. So much of humankind's effort and energy would come to nothing in the end. Why neglect any opportunity to cooperate in the work of Providence?

His eyes returned to the climber, inching closer to the top of the wall. Unable to bear the tension any longer, the mage headed for the city gates. Having failed to anticipate Kylen's solution to the problem of getting in, he could at least try to help him find a safer way out. Assuming the youth made it into the city without killing himself.

Dalthinir had asserted that he couldn't reenter the city, but he was more capable than he'd been willing to admit. Kylen wasn't the only one who knew how to make it through life without anyone to protect him. And Dalthinir had never been caught, not even once.

That was fortunate indeed, he acknowledged wryly. Because in his case it wouldn't end with the loss of a finger.

No one challenged the renegade mage as he hurried through the gates, swept along with a steady stream of farmers bringing their wares to market. Ever helpful, he was leading a horse and cart while the grateful farmer dealt with an overflowing pile of pumpkins threatening to bounce their way to freedom.

No trace of a magical aura leaked from him. He appeared no more magical than the horse.

Once clear of the gates, he returned control of the cart to the farmer and headed toward the poorest quarter of the city. Kylen had told him where he eked out a living. Having arrived in the right vicinity, he located a suitable place to monitor the area unseen and settled down to wait.

There was no way of knowing if Kylen had scaled the cliff safely, and as the hours dragged by, doubts began to cloud his mind. Nevertheless, he thrust his uncertainties aside and continued to wait.

A small band of louts had been strutting around prominently, led by a bully who evidently liked to throw his weight around. The light was fading when two others emerged from a tumbledown building across from the mage's position. One was a boy aged around fifteen, the other a girl who appeared a little younger.

"Where do you two think you're going?" demanded the bully.

"Foraging, Raff," the girl replied calmly.

"You haven't asked for permission," Raff sneered.

"If you please, Raff," offered the boy, executing a low bow that smacked of mockery.

The bully took the full meaning, and he stepped forward threateningly.

"Leave them alone, Raff."

The new voice drew the leader's attention immediately.

"Or what?" he sneered. "I'm so terrified of one-handed thieves."

Kylen had arrived at last. Raff's young thugs chortled as they surrounded him.

Dalthinir was stunned. He'd been alert for any sign of power, yet he was unable to sense anything from Kylen, even with him so close at hand. The leakage of power had somehow dried up.

He watched with growing concern to see what would happen next.

There was no denying Kylen's boldness. The youth surely couldn't have been more than sixteen or seventeen himself, yet he seemed unconcerned by the older boy's intimidation.

The two who'd emerged initially must surely have been Jonno and Bella. No longer the objects of attention, they had quietly slipped away to climb a nearby roof. Retrieving a sack from somewhere, they pulled several large objects from it and began pelting Raff and his followers.

The first missile struck Raff squarely on the back of the head. Clearly dazed, he staggered unsteadily, the remains of a rotten orange dripping down his body. The other members of the gang spun around to locate the fools stupid enough to attack their leader. Sprinting toward the two assailants, they became targets themselves. Few of them remained unstained by the time they reached the building where the two were perched.

Raff and Kylen hadn't moved. Having recovered himself, the bully puffed himself up and stepped forward menacingly. Dalthinir couldn't see Raff's face, but from his posture he had lost interest in threats. He wanted to inflict pain.

Kylen retreated, coming to a halt with his back to a building.

Raff aimed two rapid punches—a left fist jab at his belly, followed immediately by a right to his head.

The left fist struck Kylen squarely in his torso. Unaffected by the blow, he twisted aside, allowing Raff's right fist to smack into the building.

Raff cried out, holding up both fists in pain. Then as Dalthinir sensed a short burst of power, Raff was thrust backward, landing prostrate on the ground with a look of terrified astonishment on his face.

No longer needing protection for his torso, Kylen reached beneath his clothing and removed a large metal plate. After tossing it carelessly aside, he stepped forward and leaned down to whisper briefly in Raff's ear. Then he was gone.

Returning his attention to the drama on the roof, Dalthinir was in time to see Bella sprinkle a large jar of thick liquid over the boys climbing at that moment toward the roof. The liquid must have been some kind of oil, because the climbers immediately slipped and slithered helplessly, eventually landing in a pile on the ground.

Having disabled their pursuers, the two paused long enough to laugh at them. Then they raced away over the rooftops.

The mage had no idea where they were heading, but it was obvious he had underestimated all three of them. They didn't need his help.

One pressing issue did need his attention. Had other mages been close enough to sense Kylen's tiny burst of power? He had no desire to draw further attention either to Kylen or to himself.

Reaching out with his farsense he was relieved to confirm that no one else was nearby.

It was past time for him to be gone. Hurrying back to the gates, he managed to exit with a crowd of others just before the gates were closed for the night.

THE SUN WAS SETTING on the following day when Kylen and his two friends appeared at Dalthinir's small fire in a clearing deep within the forest. Their arrival almost startled the mage out of his wits. Certain they wouldn't be able to find him, he'd been planning to search them out in the morning.

"This is Dalthinir, the mage I told you about," Kylen told them. "And this is Jonno and Bella. They're twins, although everyone says they don't look like twins. They're fifteen."

After greeting them politely, the mage offered them all food. He studied the twins carefully as they devoured everything he gave them. Jonno had long dark brown hair and hazel eyes. Bella's hair was darker, cut severely short, and her eyes were green. Their clothing appeared serviceable—barely—although their overall appearance was quite unkempt. Both of them were much skinnier than any child ought to be.

"Tell me what happened," said Dalthinir, working hard to contain his curiosity. "How did you get into and out of the city? Did you have any trouble? Were you followed?"

"You needn't worry—no one followed us," Kylen assured him. "I got into the city by climbing the cliff until I reached the wall."

"How could you do that? You're missing a finger!"

Kylen glanced at the stump on his left hand. "It felt weird, and it throbbed," he acknowledged. "But it made me even more careful than usual."

He resumed his story. "The three of us left through the gates. As for what happened when I collected Jonno and Bella, you already know that, because you were there."

Dalthinir stared wide-eyed at him. "How did you know I was there? Did you see me?"

"No. I just knew. I'm not sure how. It's the same way I knew how to find you here."

The mage was astonished, although he was careful not to show it. For years he had successfully hidden his magic from the Compact's most powerful mages, yet Kylen, untrained and not yet in full command of his power, had no difficulty finding him.

The youth had also ignored his warnings. "Why did you leave through the gates? You were taking a fearful risk!"

"Well you told me it wasn't safe for you to go back into the city, and yet there you were. I decided you must have exaggerated the risk."

"I wasn't exaggerating! It's less of a risk for me because I'm able to hide my magical aura. I can also hide any use of my power, provided the burst of power is modest. That means I can be around other mages without them being able to detect me. What I didn't expect was for you to figure out how to do it. Not to mention discovering how to put your power to use."

Kylen shrugged. "I don't understand any of it. But I can see you were right. About me having power, I mean." He gazed quizzically at the mage. "Did you see me knock Raff down?"

"Yes. It was a minor burst of controlled power. Very impressive."

"I'm not even sure how I did it. I just imagined it, and somehow it happened."

It all sounded so matter-of-fact. Yet Kylen's demonstration of power was extraordinary. The mage could only guess at the raw power he might command once he knew how to do it.

Both Jonno and Bella had listened to the conversation without comment. Dalthinir soon discovered that such restraint was uncharacteristic.

"Kylen said you're a renegade mage!" If Jonno found such a notion at all frightening, there was no sign of it. He was bursting with eagerness. "Can you fly?" With no immediate response, he added, "Through the air?"

Bella was not to be outdone. "Can you turn people into toads? You could start with Raff!"

"You seem to have some strange ideas about mages," he observed calmly. "You might be in for some disappointments. To begin with, I'm a hunted man, and Kylen is too. If you're traveling with us, you'll be at risk yourselves."

"Nothing unusual about that," Bella stated flatly.

He frowned back at her. "You shouldn't dismiss it so lightly. They'll kill Kylen and me if they capture us. They'll most likely do the same to you if they catch us together."

Jonno shrugged. "Facing death is nothing new for us. One slip and it's all over when you leap across a roof."

They clearly weren't going to be put off. "If you stay with us, there'll be no more stealing," he told them firmly. "We can't afford to draw attention to ourselves."

They looked crestfallen. "How do you expect us to get food?" asked Jonno.

Dalthinir gazed calmly at him. "I'll pay for it."

"You have money?" They looked at him with sudden interest.

"I do. And don't even think about stealing it, or I *will* turn you into a toad."

The newcomers stared at him wide-eyed. Then both of them burst out laughing.

"What am I going to do with you?" he asked, throwing up his hands in helpless dismay.

"You'll be amazed how useful we are," said Bella seriously.

Jonno nodded energetically. "You'll never manage without us."

The mage grunted, unconvinced.

"Where are we going?" asked Kylen.

"Away from the city. Far away." The mage waved a hand vaguely toward the north. "We'll find a quiet place and settle there for a while. Then we'll move on. We won't stay anywhere for long. It won't be safe."

"What will we do while we're there?" asked Jonno.

"I'll be teaching Kylen to control his power. And to read and write, among other things. That's assuming he wants to become my apprentice."

Kylen responded with a stiff nod. His attempt at indifference couldn't conceal his eagerness.

Dalthinir was willing to tolerate a little excitement. There'd be ample opportunity for his apprentice to discover the deadly peril that shadowed any renegade mage.

Bella didn't look satisfied. "What about us?"

The mage didn't blink. "You'll be demonstrating how amazingly useful you are."

Bella and Jonno groaned in unison.

AFTER THE LITTLE group had shared food around a fire, Jonno and Bella wasted no time in settling down to sleep. Kylen's face suggested he was no less weary, which was hardly surprising after the eventful day that lay behind him.

Nevertheless, Dalthinir wasn't quite ready to release him.

"You've somehow managed to gain access to your powers. That's impressive."

Kylen yawned. "All I did was push Raff over. I have no idea how."

"You did a lot more than that. You masked both your power leakage and your magical aura. You weren't leaking at all when I saw you in the city, and you're not leaking now either. How have you managed to do that?"

The youth shrugged. "I thought about rich people with cloaks that keep water out when it's raining. I imagined I had an invisible sack around me that hugs my body and doesn't let power out. It must have worked."

The mage's eyebrows went up. "It more than just worked—it's still effective! That's remarkable."

Another huge yawn covered Kylen's face.

Dalthinir ignored it. "And you could tell I was nearby in the city?"

"Yes. I knew you were there, although I can't explain how. It's hard to describe. I sensed it somehow. It wasn't like smell or touch or sight or anything I'm used to—it felt like something different."

The mage nodded slowly. "What did you whisper in Raff's ear?" he asked curiously.

A wry grin twisted Kylen's face. "I told him that if he keeps pushing people around, he'd better expect them to push back."

Dalthinir grinned back, nodding in satisfaction.

The mage had one final question. "Can you still use your pushing power?"

"Right now? You mean move a branch or something?"

The mage nodded.

Glancing around, Kylen fixed his attention on a piece of wood lying near the fire. He stared at it with narrowed eyes. Then a frown of concentration came to his face. Finally he tried waving at it with his hand. The wood didn't budge.

"It isn't working," he said. He sounded disappointed.

"Don't let it bother you, Kylen. It will come with practice." Dalthinir rose to his feet. "It's time for both of us to get some sleep. We'll be making an early start in the morning."

CHAPTER 7

Master Inga worked hard at ignoring the self-important noblewoman who was at that moment pacing restlessly about the room. Lady Mardell had apparently found it necessary to invade the mages' sanctuary, violating the tranquility of their one haven from their many responsibilities. The invader exhibited no consideration at all for the busy lives of mages.

Lady Mardell rounded on her. "Where *is* Adrastas?" she demanded.

"I imagine Chief Master Adrastas will arrive when he is able, my lady," she replied evenly.

The noblewoman aimed a disdainful glance in Inga's direction before resuming her pacing.

Irritating as it was to be detained at the whim of such a person, there was little Inga could do about it. Even Adrastas could not afford to simply ignore her. Arguably the most powerful woman in the kingdom of Periton, she was a force to be reckoned with in her own right, and not merely because her husband had long held the office of Royal Chancellor.

Inga stared out across the rooftops of Cambrick, willing to embrace any kind of distraction. The late afternoon sun had bathed the sprawling city in a golden light, weaving its magic on mansions and hovels alike. The streets below might be thronged by hovel dwellers, but from this window everything about the vista appeared beguiling.

The two women were waiting in the reception room of the chief master's chambers. As head of the Compact, Adrastas enjoyed spacious and well-appointed quarters, and the outlook from the main window of his reception room was unquestionably the finest available in any of the buildings occupied by the mages.

According to tradition, during the reign of the present king's grandfather a wealthy merchant had dared commission a tower opposite this particular window. The chief master informed him indignantly that the structure would blight his favorite outlook, but the builder remained unmoved. A week before its opening ceremony, the tower collapsed. After reinforcing the foundations, the builder erected the tower again, only to see it suffer a similar fate. The merchant accepted defeat only after the structure degenerated into a pile of rubble for a third time.

The chief master at the time had been a mage with powerful elemental magic, giving him mastery over earth and water. If the merchant had ever dared accuse him of interference, there was no record of it.

Master Inga turned away from the view just as the door swung wide to admit the head mage at last. Despite Lady Mardell's snort of irritation, Inga didn't doubt there was a good reason for the delay. The demands on his time were extraordinary.

She was beyond busy herself. No mage in the Compact had farsensing ability to equal hers, and the ability kept her in high demand.

Adrastas waved them both to chairs.

Lady Mardell ignored his invitation, facing them with hands on her hips. "I have caught wind of an alarming development!" She stared pointedly at Master Inga. "Is it true that Dalthinir has been detected in this city?"

Inga nodded. "Your sources are accurate, Lady Mardell."

The noble rounded on the chief master with a frown of anger. "Then why has no one notified the civil authorities?"

The head mage's eyes narrowed.

It wasn't hard for Inga to guess what he would be thinking. Lady Mardell's questions were no less insulting than her disrespect in omitting his title. And influential as she was, she had no particular right to be informed of such matters. Her husband represented the civil authorities, but she did not.

Chief Master Adrastas decided to be diplomatic. "As you are no doubt aware, my lady, a long-standing royal statute requires mages, not civil authorities, to take responsibility for dealing with renegades among their number. The Compact is doing just that."

"Exactly what is the Compact doing? Since Dalthinir has clearly eluded you, the only reasonable conclusion is that your full resources have not been applied to the task."

"The Compact is capable of conducting its business without advice from the public," Adrastas replied coolly.

She glared at him. "I wonder if the king will treat the matter as flippantly as you seem to be."

Inga frowned in displeasure. Lady Mardell's manner was bordering on insolence.

"That is a matter for the king," Adrastas said stiffly, dropping his own use of her title. "Now, if you will excuse us, Master Inga and I have matters to discuss." He waved a hand toward the door.

Lady Mardell glared at him for a moment, then she spun on her heel and departed.

"The woman is insufferable," he growled. "Apparently it's beneath her dignity to show even the barest minimum of respect."

Not only was she insufferable, she wasn't as well informed as she thought. Inga knew that Adrastas had promptly informed the king as soon as Dalthinir's presence had been exposed. Lady Mardell clearly wasn't aware of that, in spite of her much-vaunted closeness to the monarch.

"I wonder why she's so interested in Dalthinir," mused Inga.

The head mage looked at her sharply. "An excellent question, Inga. You have a way of seeing to the heart of the matter." His lips quirked momentarily in a wry smile. "But I've often acknowledged that your powers of observation aren't limited to farsense."

Inga ignored his flattery. "Lady Mardell's bluster seemed out of proportion. How could Dalthinir's presence threaten her interests?"

She glanced out the window thoughtfully. "I wonder what Dalthinir would make of it."

"It makes no difference what he might think," Adrastas growled. "He forfeited his right to an opinion when he chose to become a renegade."

She made no reply, and his brows furrowed in irritation. "Don't expect me to indulge your fondness for digging up the past in connection with this matter, Inga. He knew what he was doing, and he fully understood the consequences."

She flicked him a glance before resuming her stare out of the window, making no attempt to hide the sadness in her eyes.

He sighed, but offered no further comment.

Inga had been far from satisfied with the process that led to Dalthinir abandoning the Compact. It had been obvious to her that the campaign against him was vicious and personal, not driven by any question of principle. She hadn't been alone in that view either.

She knew that the chief master had made a personal appeal to Dalthinir before he left. Perhaps he felt that absolved him of responsibility for the final outcome. If so, he had let himself off the hook far too easily. She believed his decision to sanction Dalthinir for his actions related to Banadin had contributed to Dalthinir's final decision to leave.

To be entirely fair to Adrastas, he had been new to the role of chief master at the time. He came with neither the experience nor the clout he'd developed in the decade that followed.

In any event, it was too late for regrets. Dalthinir had forfeited the rights and privileges of a Compact mage when he fled. Worse, he had forfeited his right to life. He was an outcast, and he would be hunted relentlessly until the day he died. That could well mean until the day he was found and executed.

"What will we do?" asked Inga.

He frowned at her, bemused by the question. "We'll continue to hunt him, of course. There is no other option available to us."

"I was referring to Lady Mardell and her unknown agendas."

He raised his hands helplessly. "I can put out some feelers for whatever that's worth. She's very proficient at keeping her agendas to herself. But I'll do what I can."

Inga was less than satisfied, and he must have recognized it, because he quickly redirected the conversation. "In the meantime, we have a responsibility to discharge. The crown demands that we track renegades down. It's beyond embarrassing that we failed to detect him when he was right here in Cambrick! He'll be long gone and far away by now. We have people out searching for him, but farsense offers the best hope of finding out where he's hiding." He fixed her in a glare. "What are you doing about that?"

She aimed an ironic glance in his direction. "He's very proficient at keeping his location to himself. But I'll do what I can."

"I want you to lead the search," he told her.

"Leading suggests that others are involved."

"Lars can join you. He doesn't seem to be doing anything more useful than complaining about the lack of progress in finding Dalthinir."

She screwed up her face. "Lars?"

"You'll be in charge. He can do the routine work. Give him the time wasters, like following up on reported sightings."

Before she could respond, he added, "I have another meeting to attend. It was good to see you as always, Inga."

He sent her a parting wave as he disappeared through the door.

She shook her head in dismay. Spending time in the company of Lars wasn't going to improve her quality of life.

MASTER PETRIA APPROACHED the ragged-looking youth and eyed him disdainfully. Would this latest lead prove to be another dead end? She could not afford to rest before identifying the person who fled the rooftop of the abandoned building. So much depended on swiftly finding and eliminating the spy who had dared to eavesdrop on the clandestine meeting. But she was already wearying of the search.

"Are you Rowan?" she demanded.

He nodded once without speaking.

Petria was treading a fine line. Of necessity, her inquiries had bypassed official channels. It was crucial that the search remained covert, like the interrupted meeting. For the same reason, she could not afford to be seen wearing her mage's robe with its distinctive crimson edging.

Robed or not, though, her full powers remained at her command. She would use them without hesitation if the need arose.

"I am told you were nearby when there was a disturbance outside the old headquarters of the Jewelers Guild a few nights ago."

He nodded again.

"Did you see anyone leaving the area?"

He stared back at her calmly, still choosing to say nothing.

Her immediate instinct was to terrify him into compliance, but something told her he needed to be handled differently.

Her face creased in concern. "Please! It's important. I believe he might be in trouble. I want to help him." The intruder might not have been male, but she decided it was worth taking a chance.

He appeared to be wavering. Holding up a silver coin, she added, "If you see him, can you please give him this?" Then, after feigning a moment's consideration, she produced a second coin. "This is for you. For helping him."

Even then Rowan hesitated. After a long moment he took the coins and held one of them up. "As far as I know he's gone away. But I'll give him this when I see him." He shrugged. "His name is Kylen."

"Can you tell me where he lives?"

To her satisfaction he told her what she wanted to know. After letting down his guard sufficiently to reveal a name, he apparently wasn't going to quibble about providing directions.

"One last question. Do you know anything of Dalthinir?"

He looked at her blankly before shaking his head. He was clearly telling the truth.

"Everyone should have a friend like you, Rowan," she said, turning away.

It didn't take long to find the location Rowan had given her. The first person she encountered was a swaggering youth surrounded by a small group of flunkies.

She stared at them coolly. "I'm looking for Kylen."

"Who wants to find him?" the leader asked haughtily.

She held up a silver coin. "I'm paying for answers. That means I get to ask the questions."

He eyed the coin hungrily. "What questions?"

"Let's start with your name."

He held out his hand imperiously. "It will cost you."

She tossed the coin onto the ground. His face darkened, but he didn't hesitate to bend down and pick it up.

"My name is Raff."

"Well then, Raff, if you want to earn more, you can begin by telling me where to find Kylen."

He shrugged moodily. "I don't know. He's disappeared with Jonno and Bella, a couple of his little stooges." He scowled. "I have a score to settle with all three of them if they ever dare show their faces here again."

Petria barely managed to suppress a sneer of contempt. She knew Raff's type only too well. He wouldn't be difficult to bend to her purposes.

"I can see you're an important person, Raff. Tell me more about Kylen." She threw another coin onto the ground, hiding her scorn as he scrambled to retrieve it.

"He was caught stealing," Raff said importantly.

"Who caught him?"

Raff waited pointedly for another coin to be thrown before answering. "A couple of locals employed by the baker on the main street. He can tell you who they are—I don't know them."

"And what about Kylen's friends? The two you mentioned."

"Jonno and Bella? They're nobodies," sniffed Raff, "just like Kylen. The three of them deserve each other."

She threw down one more coin. "This is to keep your eyes and ears open. I'll send someone by from time to time. If you hear anything more of Kylen or his friends, then make sure you let them know."

He nodded eagerly, pocketing the final coin.

"Oh. One other thing. What do you know of Dalthinir?"

He shrugged. "Never heard of him."

Raff was so transparent that it was obvious he wasn't lying. Turning her back on him, she headed for the bakery on the main street.

Several hours passed before she tracked Kylen's captors to a seedy part of the city. Most people in their right minds would never be seen alone in such a place, but she wasn't like most people.

She found the men she sought squatting beside a small fire. Both of them got up, stepping into her path menacingly. "You're the woman who's been asking questions about us," one of them snarled.

It was immediately obvious she wasn't facing another Raff. Young as they might be, these two were cruel and dangerous. They had yet to discover it, but so was she.

"What do you know of Dalthinir?" she asked.

Knives appeared in their hands. "We'll ask the questions," sneered the first one, stepping closer.

She waved a hand idly, and the fire behind them erupted, knocking them to the ground and singeing their hair.

"I know how to deal with parasites like you!" she snapped. "Drop your knives and stay on the ground, or I'll burn the flesh from your faces."

They complied at once, shrinking away in terror.

"Answer my question!" she shouted.

"We haven't heard of him!" they protested, both of them speaking at once.

"What about Kylen?" she demanded.

"He stole a bag of loaves. The baker hired us as guards—he promised us coins in return for a capture. We chased him. He went missing for a while, but we found out where he lived and waited for him. He eventually showed up. All we did was take him to the lockup."

"Where is he now?"

"We don't know! The baker told us he was going to lose his hand. He's probably off somewhere licking his wounds."

"If I discover you've been lying to me, or if you tell anyone about our meeting here today, I'll come back for you. Next time I'll fry you from the inside out! Now shut your eyes!"

They obeyed, whimpering in fear.

By the time they dared open them again, she would be long gone.

It was looking increasingly likely that Kylen was no longer in the city. Petria had found no evidence linking him with Dalthinir, but she was becoming convinced he'd fled with the renegade. That made it doubly important that Dalthinir was found, and soon.

It wasn't all bad news. She had no idea what induced Kylen to take a couple of his young friends with him, but a party of four would be hard to conceal, especially when only one of them was a mage. And Jonno and Bella—she even knew their names—would only slow Dalthinir down.

Petria had taken a big risk in revealing herself to the last two thugs. She might not be dressed as a mage, but she'd demonstrated her power. And her ability to control fire would make it easy to identify her.

Nevertheless, risks had to be taken at times. And she had the feeling they wouldn't forget her warning in a hurry.

As soon as it was fully dark, Lady Mardell wound her way through the streets and alleys to the agreed rendezvous location.

Most highborn women were too frightened to walk the streets of Cambrick at night; she had no such hesitation. Her indifference was not born of overconfidence; it had more to do with the dagger that accompanied her wherever she went. Slender and extremely sharp, the blade was a lethal weapon in the hands of anyone who knew how to use it. More than one attacker had learned the hard way she was a target to avoid.

Pushing through the heavy wooden door at the rear of an abandoned building, she made her way toward a pinprick of light visible through a broken window.

A silky voice greeted her. "Malia. I see you found us."

"Lady Mardell to you, Lars," she snapped.

The voice took on a sharp edge. "And that would be Master Lars to you, my lady. I presume you've met with our head mage. I trust you are bringing us good news."

She scanned the faces around the table. Both of the mages, Master Lars and Master Petria, appeared calm. The two nobles, Lord Marklo and Lord Rostem, showed every sign of nervousness. The other member of their company was absent.

"Where is he?" she demanded, pointing to the empty chair.

Marklo responded. "There's no point in asking us. He answers only to himself."

Lars broke in. "We were talking about good news."

"How can I possibly be bringing good news?" spat Lady Mardell. "You know as well as I do that Dalthinir has managed to slip through your fingers."

Petria waved a hand dismissively. "Some of our number are tracking him, accompanied by a large contingent of soldiers. He made a big mistake allowing himself to be discovered here in the city. Too many in the Compact have found it convenient to simply forget about him. They can't ignore him any longer. He will be flushed out before long."

So the mages hunting the renegade were accompanied by soldiers. That meant the king had been informed of Dalthinir's presence in the city. She suppressed a wave of irritation at not having been made privy to the news.

"The real question is what he was doing." Marklo sounded anxious. "Given the risk, he wouldn't have come here without a reason. How long was he here, and what was his purpose?"

Lars was unperturbed. "Whatever his purpose, Dalthinir is no threat. The best resources of the kingdom are bent on tracking him down and destroying him. He'll come to the same swift end as any rabid animal."

Rostem wasn't satisfied. "What about that boy? The one who eavesdropped on our meeting from the rooftop. He must surely have been working with Dalthinir. There's no telling how much he heard!"

"We're on the trail of the boy as well," Petria assured him. "We already know who he is—he's nothing more than a street rat. He won't be able to elude us for long. Even if Dalthinir and the boy are working together and have somehow become aware of our plans, there's nothing either of them can do to hinder us."

"But what if they talk? There's no telling how much they know!"

Lars snorted. "Let them squeal as loudly as they want. No one will believe them." He raised his hands in appeal. "None of us can afford to panic every time we're faced with a challenge!"

Lady Mardell had heard enough. "I have no interest in bickering. Contact me when you have some news worth talking about."

Ignoring them completely, she headed for the exit.

CHAPTER 8

King Durvaryn frowned at the three mages standing before him. He had asked to see the chief master and the mages actively involved in the search for Dalthinir. It was no surprise to see Master Inga accompanying Chief Master Adrastas. He hadn't expected Master Lars.

"Have you discovered where your renegade is hiding?"

Chief Master Adrastas bowed. "Not as yet, Your Majesty. But we are vigorously pursuing a number of very promising leads."

The head mage's demeanor radiated calm confidence, but Durvaryn was not convinced. The more basic question was why Dalthinir's reappearance warranted such a frenzied reaction.

"Just how dangerous is he? There's been no hint of him for years. If he intends harm to anyone, he's shown no sign of it."

Master Lars bowed in his turn. "It would be most unwise to underestimate him, Your Majesty," he assured the king smoothly.

Durvaryn stared back at him noncommittally. From the little he knew of Lars, he wasn't inclined to rely too heavily on his perspective.

"He is answerable to no one," the mage continued. "If he is planning to turn his particular powers against the kingdom, as many of us believe, he could do considerable damage."

When it came to the potential of Dalthinir's magical powers, Lars should know what he was talking about. Of all the mages, his abilities were reputedly most similar to those of the renegade, although with one important difference—by all accounts the power wielded by Lars was considerably weaker.

The inner workings of the Compact were carefully concealed from outsiders, even the king. Durvaryn had never been privy to the details behind the renegade's departure, but he strongly suspected that envy had much more to do with it than any misdemeanor on Dalthinir's part. And in the ten years since the renegade fled, renouncing his seat on the mage council, there had been more than one hint that Lars played a role in undermining his position and driving him away.

The king suppressed a sigh. The uncomfortable truth was that he had always liked and respected Dalthinir. It wasn't something he could say for Lars, or for some of the other mages.

Inga was one he did respect. "Do you have any insights to offer, Master Inga?" he asked.

She bowed. "None at this point, Your Majesty. It isn't clear why Dalthinir briefly allowed his presence to be exposed while he was in Cambrick, but he appears to have returned to his previous practice of carefully concealing his whereabouts."

"The reason for him being exposed seems simple enough," said Lars. "He needed to call on magical power for some reason."

Inga offered no comment, but Durvaryn had the impression she wasn't convinced. Did she doubt that Dalthinir needed to use power? Or did she believe that Dalthinir could have prevented it being detected if he chose to do so?

"We could speed up our search if Your Majesty was willing to provide more soldiers," noted Lars.

The king's brows drew together. Lars had couched his comment as an observation, but it nevertheless bordered on a request. Was he ignorant of royal protocol? A request of any kind would be inappropriate from anyone except the chief master, and the king had no intention of dignifying the remark by responding directly to Lars.

He clearly was not alone in his reaction. He couldn't help but notice the shocked look that flashed across Master Inga's face. The chief master said nothing, but the narrowing of his eyes was telling.

The king addressed himself to the head mage, ignoring Lars entirely. "Your request astonishes me, Chief Master. May I remind you that responsibility for dealing with renegade mages rests solely with the Compact? I have already assigned a large company of guards to the search. Do not expect more."

"Your Majesty," Adrastas replied with a stiff bow. "Thank you for making yourself available to meet with us."

The three mages filed quickly from the room.

The queen entered almost as soon as they had left.

"What was that about?" she asked. "I couldn't catch what he was saying, but the chief master was clearly furious with that other mage. The one who somehow seems slippery."

The king smiled grimly. "It's about Dalthinir, Karolin. They're trying to track him down. Lars effectively asked for more soldiers, and he did so with the head mage right there in front of him! The man has no right to make requests on behalf of the Compact! His behavior was inappropriate and disrespectful, and I'm not surprised that Adrastas was giving him a dressing down."

"I wish someone like him had run away instead of Dalthinir!"

The king's eyebrows rose in alarm. "Be careful what you say, Karolin!" he said, speaking in a low voice. "You never know who might be listening. The law is clear on the matter. The queen can't be seen to be sympathizing with a renegade."

Drawing him to her with a conciliatory embrace, she pressed her lips close to his ear. "Whatever you might say in public, my dearest, I know you sympathize with the renegade just as much as I do," she whispered.

Master Inga felt increasingly restless as the bickering continued. Full gatherings of the Compact had never inspired her, not since the vitriolic sessions that culminated in the departure of Dalthinir ten years previously. Things had settled down since, but the reappearance of the renegade had reopened old wounds.

Leaning over to Master Emmela, who was seated at her left, she whispered in frustration, "Could you find a way to make this look pretty?"

Her friend rolled her eyes, not bothering to reply.

Inga didn't blame her. It made no difference how strong Emmela's illusionary magic might be. There was no way that raw antagonism could be made to look good.

"This body has a legal responsibility to deal with renegade mages," Petria exclaimed. "It is shameful that after *ten years* the Compact has failed to fulfill that responsibility. We might have forgotten Dalthinir, but he has not forgotten us! Why else has he reappeared on our doorstep? We cannot ignore the possibility that a catastrophe is about to befall this kingdom at his hands, with us having done nothing to prevent it! The Compact will rightly be held responsible for his actions."

She glared at her fellow mages. "We cannot ignore our responsibilities any longer! Our current half-hearted approach to this crisis does us no credit."

"Master Petria is right!" Lars exclaimed. "There are no excuses for further idleness! It's time for us to put aside whatever else we're doing. Dealing with Dalthinir should become the primary focus of us all."

Other voices rose in agreement, and Inga noted that those voicing support for Petria and Lars were mostly younger mages. It wasn't surprising—most of them knew Dalthinir only as a renegade. Nevertheless, it irked her that the pair enjoyed so much influence over the less experienced members of the Compact.

There were reasons for their influence. The Compact provided accommodation and other essential services, but moving to the capital was still a major adjustment for anyone who grew up away from the city. With their own roots far from Cambrick, neither Petria nor Lars had found it easy to settle when they arrived in the capital. That had spurred Lars to offer assistance to newly awakened mages who lacked family support in Cambrick. Seeing the impact, Petria had soon done something similar, although the two of them had never worked together.

Admirable as the efforts of Petria and Lars undeniably were, Inga wasn't alone in questioning their motives. Lars in particular had reveled a little too blatantly in the resulting recognition.

When Master Kothlar rose to his feet, Inga quietly heaved a sigh of relief. After the tub-thumping of Petria and Lars, she was more than ready to listen to someone she regarded as moderate. Kothlar was well liked among the mages, respected as much for his common sense as for his unusually powerful mage touch ability in moving objects.

"I've heard enough of this nonsense," he growled. "Dalthinir has been gone for ten years, and in that time he has done nothing to justify any kind of hysteria. Nor have we been presented with a single shred of evidence to back the suggestion that he is planning to unleash a catastrophe upon the kingdom."

"Sit down, Kothlar!" called Lars. "Clearly you're either unwilling or unable to see the big picture. No one with any sense could possibly suggest we sit idly by at such a time."

"I will not sit down," Kothlar snapped back. "The law is clear about renegades—there is no disagreement about that. But I'm not the only one sick of your posturing, Lars. Your vendetta against Dalthinir is no more justified now than it was when you helped drive him out. As for your absurd suggestion that we drop everything else we're working on, you seem to have forgotten that the kingdom is heavily dependent on our magical abilities to support everything from manufacturing to agriculture. Our chief master has a plan, and he's following it. He deserves the full support of us all."

Cheering broke out across the chamber, with both Inga and Emmela joining in enthusiastically.

Growls of protest could be heard as well, but Kothlar remained unmoved. He stood there, hands on his hips, glaring at Lars and Petria. Inga reminded herself that in addition to his more admirable qualities, he had a reputation for being hard-nosed and uncompromising. On that particular occasion she couldn't have been more satisfied with his stubbornness.

Chief Master Adrastas got to his feet at last. "As I made clear in my report earlier, the Compact is far from sitting idly by as has been claimed." He directed a dark look at Lars. "We have been vigorously seeking out the renegade, supported by a squadron of the king's soldiers, and we will continue to do so until he is found and dealt with. In the meantime, it is abundantly clear that any proposal to change our current approach will not be supported by the majority of this council. I therefore call this meeting closed. I will convene another full gathering of the Compact when there is something of substance for us to consider."

Not all of the mages were pleased with the outcome, but none showed any interest in lingering. By the time Inga and Emmela reached the door, the Compact's Auditorium was almost empty.

Master Petria sat in a secluded room, huddled with Master Lars and the sixth member of their covert group.

Prince Evran, the younger brother of King Durvaryn, eyed the others darkly. "It's now apparent that Dalthinir has spent a considerable period of time in the capital, yet we have no idea what he was doing. We cannot rule out the possibility that he might have been observing us. What is he likely to do if he does become aware of our plans?"

Lars shrugged. "None of us can say with any certainty. Chances are he'll do nothing worse than run away and hide, since that seems to be his preferred way of dealing with problems." He leaned back in his chair. "It won't come to that though. Given that he's determined to remain hidden at all costs, how can he possibly find out what we're planning?"

The prince didn't seem entirely satisfied. Nevertheless, he moved on. "What of the youth who was spying on us in the abandoned Jewelers Guild building?"

"We can safely forget about him," said Petria calmly. "He was a petty thief, hiding on the rooftop to avoid getting caught. He didn't get away with it. They caught him anyway and took off his hand. He's since disappeared, but there's no evidence to suggest he's in any way connected with Dalthinir."

"How serious is the Compact leadership about catching the renegade? Banadin specifically warned us about him. He's capable of doing incredible damage to us."

"They're not serious enough," growled Lars. "A hunt is underway, but a lot of them are less than enthusiastic about it. Since he's kept out of sight and done nothing threatening for ten years, too many of them are convinced it isn't worth the effort."

"Can't you help make up their minds?"

"What are you suggesting?"

"Use your power to do some damage. Something serious. Perhaps an act that threatens our precious sovereign and his family. Then blame it on Dalthinir." The prince appeared to be licking his lips involuntarily.

Lars raised his eyes heavenward. "You apparently are not well acquainted with magical power, Your Highness. Whenever a mage uses power, it leaves behind a unique scent—a marker that identifies the person who did it. There's no way we could blame it on someone else."

The two mages exchanged a glance. "That's how it works for us now, anyway," Petria murmured.

Lars allowed Evran no opportunity to ask what she had meant. He glowered at the prince. "You speak of threatening your brother. We are poised on the brink of a very deep and very dark chasm. I trust none of us needs to be reminded of the importance of timing."

"You've read far too much into my wording," the prince replied airily. "I was merely offering an example of something that might catch the attention of other mages. I am not proposing an imminent attack on the king."

"If you're not proposing it, you would do well not to talk about it," said Lars pointedly.

"And you would do well to remember who you're talking to," the prince countered.

Petria threw up her hands. "Please! None of us can afford to lose focus!"

Both men glared at her, but they calmed down.

"So where does all this leave us?" asked Evran.

"Nothing has changed, Your Highness," Petria assured him. "We will proceed with our plans as before. We'll continue to apply pressure on the leadership of the Compact to do more about Dalthinir. Please do whatever you can to work on it through the king."

The prince waved a hand idly. "Don't expect him to pay any attention to me. If you're unable to do anything to escalate the situation, we'll be reduced to hoping for the best."

Having apparently lost interest in further conversation, the prince rose to his feet. He left after delivering a polite nod to Petria and the most cursory of farewells to Lars.

With their meeting concluded, both of them got up to go. They left with Petria acknowledging to herself that the prince might have been right. Unless they could force the hand of the Compact leadership, running Dalthinir to ground would involve little more than hoping for the best.

There had to be a way, and she was determined to find it.

THE OPPORTUNITY CAME the following day.

Petria had spoken the truth when she told Prince Evran there was no evidence to link the eavesdropping thief with Dalthinir. Nevertheless, she remained convinced that Kylen and his two friends had joined the renegade. For that reason she had promised Raff that her contacts would seek him out from time to time in case he had new information on the missing youths.

Through her contacts she discovered that a farmer on his way to the capital had caught a glimpse of a pair who reminded him of Bella and her brother. Having known them from their childhood years, he found time to seek them out while in Cambrick. By a roundabout route the farmer found his way to Raff and before long to Petria's contact as well.

Petria was able to meet with the farmer in person. Finding him alarmed to learn they had been living on the streets, she was able to convince him she was also concerned for their welfare. He innocently provided considerable background on the twins and their past. He also told her exactly where he had spotted the youths who prompted him to think of them.

The moment she left the farmer, Petria hurried to the quarters of Adrastas. Only he could arrange for a squad of soldiers to join the search.

She knew enough of Dalthinir's magical prowess to realize it would take a lot more than a squad of soldiers to overcome him. She would also need mages with combined power and abilities that exceeded his own.

As chance would have it, she met the head mage on his way out.

"At the full gathering of the Compact, you assured us you are serious about the search for the renegade, Chief Master."

He nodded tightly.

"I have just received credible information about a possible sighting, not far from the capital. Would you be willing to lend me a squad of the guards assigned to the search by the king?"

He eyed her cautiously for a long moment. "I am willing to send a squad," he finally replied, "provided the party is led by Master Kothlar."

The idea of the pig-headed mage leading the search was almost unthinkable. Nevertheless, there wasn't time to argue. "As long as we leave immediately," she conceded reluctantly.

Three painful hours passed before Adrastas was able to locate Kothlar. She put the delay to good use, arranging for Lars to join them along with two other mages suggested by Adrastas.

The small party had rejoined Adrastas when Kothlar finally appeared.

Adrastas came immediately to the point. "Master Petria believes she might know where to find our renegade, not far from the city. I intend to send a group of mages and soldiers to investigate. Would you be willing to lead the party?"

"I would," he replied loftily.

"Then we have no time to waste," Petria told him. "The trail is already going cold."

Kothlar was unmoved. "You've insisted that Dalthinir is extremely dangerous. That means we can't afford to set out until we're thoroughly prepared. The composition of the party will be crucial. We will need soldiers who aren't intimidated by magical power. And the whole party will need horses and other equipment."

The man's stubbornness was legendary, but Petria dared not offer him an excuse to dig in his heels. Gritting her teeth, she said nothing.

In the end, the party didn't set out until a couple of hours before dawn the following day. Petria was almost beside herself by the time the five mages rode through the gates of Cambrick accompanied by a strong contingent of soldiers.

Using the directions provided by the farmer, Petria led them at a rapid pace to the region. One of the mages in the party had farsense ability of moderate strength, and as they drew nearer she guided her horse alongside the leader.

"I'm sensing power, Master Kothlar. It's operating at a low level, but it's steady!"

A frown of concentration covered the face of Lars. "Now that you've alerted me, I can sense it as well."

"A hunted animal is never more dangerous than when it's cornered," Kothlar reminded them. "Dalthinir is stronger than any of us alone. We will need to work together. Each of you was chosen because of your magical abilities. Follow my lead, and we will remain safe."

He turned to the mage who had alerted him. "Lead on."

She set off, leading them toward their quarry.

They were now facing the imminent prospect of a confrontation. For all Petria's protestations about the danger posed by Dalthinir, she acknowledged that until that moment she hadn't taken the risks seriously. Kothlar's reminder had been sobering. Much as she had resented the delay in setting out, she now recognized the value of the preparation done by both Adrastas and Kothlar.

They were well prepared, and the renegade was almost within their grasp.

As they drew ever closer, she couldn't resist some silent self-congratulation. She had guessed correctly about a connection between the renegade and the three street rats. The twins had led them to a mage who was using power. It could only be Dalthinir.

He had not slipped away from the capital alone. The fool had burdened himself with three useless companions. It had been his first major mistake in the ten years since he abandoned the Compact.

It seemed appropriate that common street rats would bring about his downfall.

CHAPTER 9

Dalthinir soon discovered that Jonno and Bella were early risers. It proved fortunate that they were.

The sun had not yet risen when Bella came rushing into the clearing where the small group had spent the night.

"We have company," she called. "There are riders not far away!"

Dalthinir leaped to his feet. "Heading in this direction?"

"Yes. Some of them are mages."

Startled, he reached out with his farsense. She was right. No fewer than five mages. And they were close—alarmingly so.

At that crucial moment he sensed a steady flow of power around him. Hurrying to Kylen's side, he shook him urgently. "You're leaking power again! Can you re-establish your sack?"

Instantly awake but bleary-eyed, Kylen took a deep breath and screwed up his face. "Did that work?" he asked hopefully.

Frowning, Dalthinir shook his head. His apprentice had picked a bad time to lose his ability.

Masking them both needed to be done immediately. Without conscious thought, the mage grasped hold of Kylen's idea of power-resistant sacks. In little more than a heartbeat imaginary sacks were in place and protecting them. No more than a vague notion had been needed.

The simplicity and effectiveness of the strategy astonished him. The traditional approach was to place a bubble around whatever was being protected. It invariably needed to be reshaped, both to ensure it was big enough without being too big and to ensure that unnecessary objects weren't inadvertently included within it. When protecting anything that wasn't stationary, the bubble also needed to move with whatever it was protecting.

Although there were complexities involved, Dalthinir had learned from the beginning to do it that way, and he was able to achieve it almost without thought. Nevertheless, he found it easier to envisage a shield that hugged the protected object in the same way that a close-fitting garment enwrapped a person. It was also much simpler to bind to the object so they moved together, and simpler to exclude other unwanted items.

With the immediate issue resolved, the reality of their situation hit him full force. The Compact had sent *five* mages. And almost exactly to the right location. He broke into a cold sweat when he realized how close they were to disaster. Kylen had probably been leaking power all night.

It was his own fault. He had put wards in place and masked his own magical aura as always. But Kylen had still been providing his own masking, and Dalthinir had wrongly assumed he could continue to do so. It was completely unrealistic. Kylen was a novice in the ways of magic.

A confrontation was looming, and what could he do? Harming others had never been an option for him, even though he knew no mercy would be granted him if he was caught.

His own situation was not entirely hopeless. He knew how to defend himself. And they had to catch him first. But Kylen was another matter. He was defenseless, and they would kill him without hesitation as soon as they learned the truth about him.

An impossible choice lay before him. Was he willing to harm others to prevent harm being done to his apprentice?

And what about the twins? In his distraction he had failed to notice that Bella had disappeared again.

"Where have those two gone?" he asked in exasperation.

Kylen simply shrugged. He didn't look surprised.

As if in answer, faint cries and the high-pitched screaming of horses reached him. Then all went quiet.

Reaching out with his farsense, he discerned to his surprise that the mages were further away.

"Kylen, remove all traces of our campsite! I need to see what's become of your friends."

He had barely taken a step when Jonno and Bella reappeared.

"Anyone hungry?" called Jonno, grinning as he held up a large hare by its ears.

"Where did that come from?" sputtered the mage.

"I trapped it," said Bella matter-of-factly. "We were out setting the traps when we first spotted the mages."

Dalthinir tried to remain calm. "Where are they now?"

"We sent them packing," Bella replied, waving her hand toward the city.

"How?!"

Each of the twins held up a slingshot.

The mage's head was spinning. "Where did they come from?"

"We borrowed them when we were leaving," said Jonno innocently. "From Raff. Do you think he'd mind?"

Dalthinir stared at them in bemusement. "How did you send the mages packing?" He was almost too frightened to ask.

Bella grinned. "We let fly with the slingshots and hit a few of the soldiers' horses on the rump. We used to do it when we were younger. There's no better way to get horses moving."

Jonno took up the tale enthusiastically. "They blamed it on horse-flies. None of the mages cared until they got bitten as well. That decided them in a hurry. Once they were underway, we let fly at every horse in sight until we ran out of stones."

"They took off as if dragons were hunting them," Bella continued. "By the time the riders get their horses under control, they won't be anywhere near here."

Both of them burst out laughing.

"Now, about the hare," said Jonno, settling down after a final chuckle. "If someone has a sharp knife, I'll get it ready for cooking. You can build the fire, Bella."

"We're not cooking anything," Dalthinir told them emphatically. "We're getting away from here, and we're doing it now!"

"It'll be slow going if we're walking. Would you like us to borrow some horses?" asked Jonno.

"Aargh! No, I would not! I told you—no stealing. *Especially* from mages!"

Horses were not an option anyway, because Dalthinir's farsense told him the mages were no longer within reach. He had dealt with Kylen's power leakage, and the intervention of the twins had bought some crucial time for the little party. Combining woodcraft with a little magic, he now made sure that even the best tracker would never find their path.

That didn't mean his trials were over. As the morning progressed, the offer of horses started to seem more and more appealing. It might at least have prevented the continual grumbling of the twins about long walks before breakfast when they could have been riding on full stomachs.

After a couple of hours of their complaints, he could bear it no longer. Putting Kylen's innovation to use once more, he quickly established an invisible sound-proof sack around them both.

The noise stopped immediately. At first completely bemused, they quickly guessed what had happened. They might have been silenced, but the dark looks on their faces spoke eloquently.

He'd never resorted to such measures before, and by the time he finally allowed the party to come to a halt, he was thoroughly ashamed of himself. Releasing them from the invisible gag, he made an immediate attempt to make it right.

"I apologize sincerely, Jonno and Bella. Silencing you in that way was heavy handed, and it wasn't fair." He couldn't resist adding, "Even if it meant I did enjoy a bit of peace and quiet for a while."

To his amazement, both of them accepted the apology with good grace.

"We did do quite a bit of grumbling," Bella acknowledged.

Jonno winked. "Can we cook the hare now? I'm hungry!"

Amazed at their buoyancy, Dalthinir readily agreed. As Jonno skinned the hare and Bella built a fire, he made an effort to be a bit more friendly. He hoped it might go some way toward making up for his earlier behavior.

"How do you both know so much about trapping and cooking? And using slingshots?"

"We lived in the country," Bella told him. "Country children grow up needing a lot of practical skills."

"Then both of our parents died unexpectedly," Jonno continued. "It was only a couple of years ago. We wanted to carry on looking after ourselves, and we could have done it too. But the village elders decided we were too young. A wealthy merchant was passing through, and he convinced them there would be better opportunities for us in the capital. He talked up how good the food was, how comfortably people lived, and how every child learned to read and write. The elders agreed to let him take us with him."

"When we arrived in the city," Bella continued, "we soon found out what his real intentions were. He turned us into servants. He had more than enough of them already, none of them better than slaves. No pay, never enough food, no freedom at all. We lasted six months."

"What happened?" asked the mage.

Jonno shrugged. "We decided it was time to fend for ourselves." He grinned. "We left him something to remember us by."

One of Dalthinir's eyebrows went up. "Dare I ask what it was?"

Bella laughed. "We didn't want to do anything that would create more work for his other slaves. He had a huge property in the city, with four milking cows. So we led them to the market, and whacked them hard on the rump to get them going. They knocked over quite a few stalls before they settled down. A city official came up, red in the face, and one of the cows dumped a load of manure onto his feet. He was not happy!"

Jonno was grinning broadly. "We told him the name of the merchant who owned the cows. And we said that the manure seemed like an appropriate gift, because the merchant was always telling people that city officials are about as useful as cow dung. The official got quite excited. He was running around yelling at the top of his voice, demanding that the merchant be arrested."

"We ran for it," Bella told him. "Kylen eventually found us wandering the streets and took us in. Raff and his gang found us too, of course." She winked. "We did level the score a bit when we left."

The mage was impressed, although he was careful not to show it. He wasn't sure he wanted to be seen as condoning some of their more erratic behavior.

The twins were clearly forces of nature. They were also resourceful and unusually capable, especially considering their age. And having heard what they'd been forced to endure, he felt a great deal of sympathy for them.

"You're welcome to stay with me for as long as you want, and I'll never treat you like slaves," he promised. "But it's important for you to understand that I can't guarantee your safety."

They both nodded cheerfully. "We'll manage," Jonno replied simply.

AFTER EATING, they set off again. The mage set a brisk pace, but his younger companions had no difficulty keeping up. Walking made for slow progress, so he was determined to keep them at it until just before sundown.

Kylen had nothing to say while they were walking, and occasional glances in his direction suggested the apprentice was dispirited.

"What's on your mind?" asked the mage.

There was no answer at first. Then Kylen told him, "I've been trying to use my magic, and it won't work anymore. Maybe I've lost it completely."

Dalthinir grinned. "I wouldn't worry. Your power hasn't gone anywhere. You're leaking enough of it to cause a problem if I stop masking it."

"Why does it work sometimes and not at others?"

The same question had been exercising Dalthinir. "I'm not sure. It wasn't the same for me. It took me a while to get access to my power, but once I did, it was always available, even though it was quite weak at first. Your power seems to work—and work incredibly well—when you're not consciously trying to access it. The problem arises when you are trying."

"What use is that?" asked Kylen miserably.

"We need to figure out what's causing the blockage." He glanced thoughtfully at his apprentice. "There are plenty of other unanswered questions. Like how your power was awakened in the first place."

"Why does that matter?"

"Perhaps it doesn't. But I'm not aware of any mage whose power was awakened in the same way. It's a mystery."

"How does it normally happen?"

The mage drew closer and lowered his voice. "Normally apprentices are led by a small group of mages to a secluded place on a night with a new moon. Then they're given a drug to put them into a trance. The other mages chant an incantation, then they leave the candidate alone in the darkness. The apprentice emerges from the trance to find their magic awakened. This method has been used for generations. The Compact has lots of fancy explanations for the mechanism, but the truth is that no one knows why it works. No one has any idea what actually happens."

"Where does magic come from, and why doesn't everyone have magical power?"

"I can't tell you why some have magical power and some don't. But the same is true of any ability. Some people are better than others at solving tricky problems, and not everyone has enough physical strength to make them a good blacksmith.

"As to where magic comes from, no one knows for certain. But mages who have studied magical history agree that the most powerful magic came from dragons."

A shocked look came to Kylen's face. "But dragons aren't real, are they?"

"They were real enough once. In fact I've seen some ancient documents that suggest it was dragons who originally awakened magical power in mages. Whatever the truth, when mages became powerful enough and numerous enough, they drove dragons from human lands. They're generally regarded as extinct now."

"Why did the mages drive them away?"

"Because the dragons turned on us. I've read the accounts. It was terrible. Ferocious firedrakes roamed the land, viciously killing people and destroying everything they built. They came to be known as the Winged Death."

Kylen looked baffled. "Why did they hate humans so much?"

"No one knows. It wasn't like that at first, but at some point they apparently took it upon themselves to annihilate humankind."

Kylen was looking pensive. "Have mages ever gone crazy like dragons did?"

Dalthinir looked at him knowingly. "Are you worried about magic corrupting you? All good mages ask themselves that question, especially when they discover what their power is capable of. Power changes people. It's an important reason why mages need to be apprenticed, like any craftsperson. Learning to recognize and restrain your own worst impulses is a key part of an apprenticeship."

"What about pushing Raff with magic? I wasn't trying to—I didn't know I could. It just happened. Was that wrong?"

"He clearly deserved it. But it's an important question. The law strictly prohibits mages using magical power against other people."

"Do mages always obey that law?"

"Unfortunately not. You asked about mages going crazy. There have been mage revolts in the past. They were dark times. There haven't been any revolts in recent times, but some mages don't hesitate to act in unscrupulous ways."

"Do mages have to answer to the Compact?"

"Supposedly. In my opinion the Compact is a big part of the problem."

"Is that why you left?"

"It was one reason. I didn't like what the Compact has become. In the old days, experienced mages took on apprentices. That's how magical abilities were developed and encouraged. An apprentice learned on the job, working alongside an older mage. That's what I'm planning to do with you. That approach was abandoned a few generations ago, replaced by training at the Conservatory for Magical Arts. The goal was to make learning more consistent and more efficient, and to make sure young mages were taught commonly accepted values and conventions. But the conservatory became hidebound and hopelessly compromised. It turned into a forum for the most powerful mages to promote their own ideologies and agendas. Training apprentices in the use of magic almost seems like an afterthought these days."

A glazed look had come into his apprentice's eyes. "A lot of that didn't make any sense to me."

The mage winced. "I've dumped a bit much onto you, Kylen. Ignore my ramblings. There's no reason for you to worry about mage politics right now."

A large village had appeared in the distance as the light began to fade in the sky. Dalthinir had no intention of going anywhere near it. They were still much too close to Cambrick for his liking.

"Once we've skirted around this village we'll find somewhere to camp," he announced.

No one voiced a complaint, and he was grateful to be traveling with companions accustomed to sleeping rough.

The moment they found a suitable location, the twins disappeared, returning before long with a pair of partridges. Kylen had already built a fire, and the twins began dressing the birds. Dalthinir leaned back against an obliging tree trunk with a sigh of satisfaction, his stomach already beginning to rumble.

Having almost been caught out the previous night, the mage put protections into place as they were settling down to sleep. After ensuring that Kylen's power was fully masked, he invoked a simple ward to alert him if anyone approached their campsite.

His circumstances had changed completely in the previous few days. He had an apprentice. That was momentous enough. It would be a long and arduous process to guide and protect him to full maturity as a mage, but Dalthinir didn't doubt that both of them would find it fulfilling, in spite of the twists and turns.

It was true that he'd acquired significant new responsibilities, but there were benefits. Bella had spoken truly. The twins were already proving themselves to be incredibly useful.

More significantly, he was no longer alone. After fleeing the Compact, he had been forced to carefully limit his contact with other people. He was beginning to discover how much he had missed normal human companionship.

He settled down to sleep more contented than he had felt for a long time.

CHAPTER 10

Several days had passed since the mage and his companions set out from Cambrick. From Kylen's point of view, the time had been uneventful. Provided he didn't count the almost daily escapades of the twins. The previous day they had almost started a major forest fire. A disaster was averted only thanks to the mage's timely intervention.

That morning Dalthinir had been discoursing on the history of the kingdom of Periton. Bored and restless, the twins moved ahead, soon disappearing from sight. Half an hour later, the lesson was interrupted by the bellowing of cows.

"What are those two up to now?" grumbled Dalthinir.

They hurried forward to find Jonno and Bella frantically pulling at a wooden sluice gate on the downstream side of a small dam. They had already opened it enough to allow a steady trickle of water. Then, thanks to a coordinated tug from both of them, it came fully open. The trickle become a torrent, almost carrying the twins away with it. A small wall of water was soon racing down the stream below the dam.

The reason for the twins' intervention was not hard to determine. Two cows had somehow become trapped in the dam. Unable to escape, and out of their depth, they were clearly tiring in their efforts to keep their heads clear of the water. Fortunately, the dam was emptying rapidly due to the outflow of water.

With the level dropping rapidly, the twins hurried into the dam, yelling and clapping their hands. Taking the hint, the cows desperately tried to escape. Their progress was hindered by the slope of the dam wall and the cloying mud that dragged at their legs.

As he looked on, Kylen willed them to do it. To his surprise, his magic flared, giving a sudden boost to their desperate attempts to break free. Lowing loudly, they clambered over the top and stumbled away to safety.

The twins tried without success to close the sluice gate. It was jammed open and refused to budge.

Dalthinir stared at them. "What have you done?" he asked despairingly, waving a hand to encompass the fleeing cows and the empty dam.

"Cows in these parts seem to startle easily," said Jonno innocently. "For some reason they decided to go for a swim."

"But we couldn't let them drown," added Bella.

The mage threw his hands in the air. "You've drained the farmer's dam!"

Neither of them were at all perturbed. "A dam like that serves no useful purpose in a region like this," asserted Jonno. "There's plenty of rain and more streams than anyone could possibly need!"

Dalthinir glared at them. "Leave! Now! All of you," he commanded.

Turning their backs on the scene, the three of them headed off obediently into the trees.

Barely ten minutes had passed before the curiosity of the twins became more than they could bear.

"Let's go see what he's up to," exclaimed Bella excitedly.

They ran off without waiting for a response from Kylen. No less curious, he hurried after them.

They arrived to find the sluice gate closed and the dam refilled with water. How the mage had done it remained a mystery, because he refused to enlighten them.

The twins greeted Dalthinir's efforts with euphoric delight. Kylen wondered wryly if his effectiveness in undoing the damage might now encourage them to do whatever took their fancy.

The same possibility must have occurred to his mentor.

He glared at them furiously. "Next time you try a stunt like that there will be dire consequences!" he told them. "You grew up on a farm—you should know better! And I don't want to hear another word about the rainfall of the region!"

They tried their best to look dismayed. Kylen didn't find their efforts even slightly convincing.

Before long they came upon a farmer. After friendly greetings had been exchanged, the travelers paused for a conversation. The twins joined in politely.

After a while, Jonno addressed the farmer. "You seem to have quite a few dams around here." He spoke earnestly, without the slightest trace of irony in his tone.

"Yes, we do," the man confirmed. "And we're grateful for them! In a dry year the ponds and streams around here dry up almost completely. Thankfully, we have one spring that reliably delivers fresh water in every season. Between that and the dams, we find we can manage."

Jonno nodded wisely, congratulating him on his foresight in building dams to supplement the reliable spring.

Dalthinir had gone red in the face. He remained silent, but it clearly cost him an effort.

To anyone who didn't know the twins, they must have seemed totally chaotic, but Kylen knew better. Their exuberance, erratic as it was at times, disguised skills and resourcefulness remarkable for anyone their age.

Watching Jonno and Bella in action in the countryside had been a revelation for Kylen. In spite of his best efforts to help them in the capital, they had never entirely settled there. He was beginning to understand why—they simply didn't belong in a city.

In this environment the roles had been reversed. They were knowledgeable and proficient. He was very much the learner. He knew he wouldn't have lasted long if left to his own devices. Even Dalthinir was increasingly relying on their practical skills.

In leaving Cambrick, Kylen had been wrenched away from everything familiar. He had nothing useful to contribute, and consistent access to his magical power was proving frustratingly elusive. It would have been easy for him to feel entirely worthless. Instead he was more determined than ever to develop the skills needed to adapt to his new circumstances.

He was soon trailing after his younger companions to learn how to set traps and snares. He surprised himself with how much he enjoyed it. After a few days they were congratulating him on his progress with a slingshot. If he was less than enthusiastic about skinning rabbits and dressing game birds, he reminded himself that his main goal was to become proficient. He didn't have to enjoy every aspect of what he was learning.

Ten days out from the capital, Kylen was becoming more settled in his new environment. Everything around him was different, with each new sight, sound, and smell providing a fresh source of wonder. On one occasion as they were wandering across open fields, Kylen spotted a bird of prey hovering nearby. Gazing upward at the predator, he tried to imagine what it must be like to stare down upon the earth from such a vantage point. There'd never been anything wrong with his imagination, and it didn't let him down. He could readily picture the countryside below and the creatures great and small moving upon its surface. Shifting his attention he could see a wood to one side. Beyond it he saw tilled earth, with smoke rising lazily from a farmhouse nestled beside a stream.

Lost among the clouds, his mind was far away, soaring with his imagination. Unfortunately for him, his feet were still moving forward across uneven ground. Reality intruded unexpectedly when he stumbled into a rut and came crashing down.

Picking himself up unsteadily, he dusted off his clothes, grateful he hadn't broken anything. He shook his head at his own stupidity, deciding ruefully that in future he would keep his mind on what he was doing.

The open ground led to a wood, and they spent an hour picking their way through the trees before crossing a stream and emerging into the open again. Splashing their way across another small stream, they came suddenly upon a man sitting against a tree with his head down. The man looked up in alarm at the four strangers.

A dog appeared, barking ferociously and coming at Dalthinir with bared teeth. "Keep away, strangers!" it seemed to be calling. The mage said a few quiet words, and the dog calmed down immediately, wagging its tail in welcome.

The man had risen to his feet, but his alarm quickly abated. The change might have been due in part to the non-threatening appearance of the new arrivals. Equally likely it was in response to the dog's acceptance of them.

"Are you well?" called Dalthinir.

The man looked anything but well.

"It's my milk cow," he replied grimly. "My only one. She's trying to deliver a calf, but something isn't right. She can't get the calf out."

The mage didn't hesitate. "Can I help? I have some experience with animals."

After a moment's consideration the farmer nodded, waving for Dalthinir to join him. They set off toward a small barn. As Kylen followed them in, he noticed that the twins had disappeared.

The cow was lying on its side inside the barn, a small hoof poking out of her birth canal. Kneeling beside the animal, the mage reached inside and felt around carefully.

"The calf is twisted inside the womb," he said. "I'm going to try to turn it."

Sensing a brief burst of magic, the apprentice stole a wide-eyed glance at the farmer. The man showed no awareness that anything unusual had happened.

The cow lowed noisily, and Kylen looked on in awe as a calf slowly emerged. A tear rolled down the farmer's cheek. Dalthinir was grinning broadly.

As the exhausted cow nosed the newborn, the farmer ran excitedly to call his wife. When she arrived, the relief on her face said more plainly than words how important the cow was to them. Losing it would have been a heavy blow.

"I told you our luck would turn today," she told her husband, giving him a knowing nod. "I saw a toad on the path," she explained to her visitors.

"Aye," the farmer replied soberly.

Kylen was baffled, but there was no opportunity to ask the mage what she had meant.

Both of them were soon bustled into the small farmhouse to enjoy freshly baked cakes and hot tea.

"What happened to your other two young 'uns?" asked the farmer.

A fleeting look of alarm flashed across the mage's face before he managed to school it into a blank expression. Kylen grinned to himself. It wasn't hard to guess what his new mentor might be thinking.

The farmer's wife disappeared outside to find them. She reappeared a few minutes later, her face shining.

"What a pair!" she enthused. "You know what I found them doing?"

Both Dalthinir and Kylen shook their heads dumbly.

"The lass had a bucket. The water barrel was nearly empty, and she's just finished refilling it from the stream. The young lad's been hard at work repairing the holes in our hen house fence. What a sweet pair!"

She disappeared again, returning a few minutes later with the twins in tow.

"These two grew up on a farm," she announced proudly. "I said as much, and they didn't deny it!"

The farmer and his wife insisted they stay for the night. Sent off to the barn with clean blankets, the three youngsters made themselves comfortable on beds of hay. Dalthinir settled beside the fireplace in the house.

Even before the sun rose the twins were hard at work around the farm. At the end of a busy day, the travelers stayed a second night. By then the farmer's wife had extracted the twins' sad history.

"You poor, poor dears!" she crooned. She eyed the farmer sternly. "It's clear what we need to do. We need to adopt them, here and now!"

"We'd like nothing better," Bella assured her with a sad smile. "If only we hadn't promised our aunt!"

Jonno nodded glumly. "Yes, our dear, doting aunt. Alone with our uncle on their huge farm, with only the hired hands to keep them company."

"She made us promise to come to her if ever we found ourselves in need," Bella told them mournfully.

The farmer's wife was crestfallen. "Oh well. A promise is a promise, I suppose. But I won't let you all leave without some necessaries for the journey."

After loading them down with a range of supplies for their journey, she waved them off tearfully.

As soon as they were well clear of the farmhouse, Bella heaved a huge sigh of relief. "That was a close call! We barely escaped with our lives."

Jonno raised his eyes heavenward, and both of them laughed.

"We escaped with a lot more than that," Dalthinir told them, patting the sack full of provisions.

He seemed to suddenly notice a pack Jonno had acquired. "What's in there?" he asked suspiciously.

Reaching in, Jonno extracted a large metal pot. He held it up, his face a picture of innocence.

"I warned you about stealing," exclaimed the mage in dismay. "We'll have to take it back."

"There isn't any need," said Bella hastily. "We found it on the scrap heap. Due to the broken handle and the dents." She pointed them out. "The farmer said we were welcome to it, if it was any use to us."

Dalthinir appeared to be considering their story when a loud squawk emerged from the sack. "What's that?" he demanded in alarm.

Reaching in, Jonno removed a scrawny chicken.

"You stole a chicken?!"

Seeing the scandalized look on his mentor's face, Kylen struggled to stifle a laugh.

"They won't miss Henrietta," Jonno insisted. "Besides, the poor little thing was being treated abominably by the other hens."

It was true. Kylen had been shocked at what he witnessed until Bella explained the pecking order in a hen house. In his innocence he'd thought that mean spirited behavior was limited to humans.

"We told the farmer's wife that Henrietta had escaped," Bella said. "She told us not to worry, because the foxes would have taken a lot more than Henrietta if we hadn't repaired the hen house wall."

"We can't carry a chicken around with us!" protested Dalthinir.

"Why not?" asked Jonno reasonably. "What's wrong with fresh eggs every day? Besides, if Henrietta doesn't deliver, we can always cook her in our nice new pot."

The mage covered his face with his hands, provoking a new burst of laughter from the twins.

In the end, they kept the hen. But only after Dalthinir had made the twins renew their promise not to steal. "If you break your promise again, I'll be searching out a nice little pond for a couple of new toads," he growled.

They did their best to appear suitably chastened.

CHAPTER 11

After traveling for several hours, they stopped for a break in a small clearing among the trees. Dalthinir had been unusually pensive, and when they were ready to settle he called them over.

"Before we left, the farmer warned me about a small group of brigands operating in the region."

Kylen had witnessed the interaction. "There are three of them," the farmer had said grimly. "They've done their share of looting, and even killed a few people." He pointed to a pitchfork positioned near the door. "They haven't bothered us yet. But I'll give them something to think about if they do come here. Jess always gives us fair warning if strangers approach, don't you girl?"

Lying contentedly before the fire, the dog had thumped her tail a few times when she heard her name.

"Is there anyone you can turn to when the law needs enforcing?" Dalthinir had asked.

The farmer shook his head. "There are no large towns nearby. People have to look after themselves. Some of us band together when we need to, but most of the time we're isolated on our farms."

His mentor hadn't made any promises to the farmer, but Kylen had the feeling he might try to do something about the brigands. He quickly discovered that he had guessed correctly.

"If mages are on hand when people break the law," Dalthinir was saying, "they're expected to act on the king's behalf. That doesn't exactly apply to me any longer, but the people in these parts still need protection."

He eyed each of them thoughtfully, and Kylen couldn't shake off the impression that he was being measured and found wanting.

"I'm going after them. Things are likely to get very dangerous when I find them."

"Sounds exciting!" exclaimed Bella.

Jonno was no less enthusiastic. "Count us in!"

The mage shook his head emphatically. "You won't be coming. I've dealt with brigands before. This is not Raff and his little group of bullies. These people will kill you without a second thought."

"We're not afraid," Bella assured him.

"That's what worries me," he replied. "You'll be staying here, and that's the end of it."

Kylen couldn't quite match the twins' appetite for excitement, but he was eager to take every opportunity to learn from his master. "What about me?" he asked.

The response was a firm shake of Dalthinir's head. "It's much too risky."

"But I need to see how you handle difficult situations."

"I'm sorry, Kylen. You can join me once you're able to use your power, but not before. I'd have to protect you, and that might be a distraction I can't afford."

He included them all in his glance. "I need to know you'll be safe while I'm gone." He waved a hand around him. "This clearing looks like a suitable location. There's shelter beneath the trees if you need it, there's a stream nearby, and you know how to find food."

"How long will you be gone?" asked Bella.

"I can't be certain. As long as it takes to find them."

The mage had nothing further to say. With his mind made up, he was gone in a moment.

"Your friend's a cheery one," said Jonno, aiming a wink at Kylen.

"He's good-hearted for a renegade," Bella conceded.

Kylen sighed. "I'm sorry I've landed you in trouble."

Both of them laughed immediately. "We never had half as much fun in Cambrick," Bella assured him. "Not even with Raff and his merry clowns to entertain us." They laughed again.

Never idle for long, the twins began preparing the campsite. Jonno released Henrietta. Having helpfully clipped the wings of all the chickens before they left the farm, he wasn't worried about her wandering far. Then he built a fire while Bella headed off to set some traps.

After collecting firewood, Kylen filled the old pot with water from the stream and brought it to the fire. A part of him was happy to be far away from deadly trouble, but it also rankled that he had no way of controlling his power. He knew the power was there, but it might as well not be. What use was it if he couldn't access it?

Would he ever become a true mage, or would he forever be nothing more than an apprentice?

Needing a distraction, he raised a question that had been on his mind. "The woman at the farm said she knew they'd have good luck today because she'd seen a toad on the path." He shook his head in bemusement. "What's that supposed to mean?"

"Country people have a lot of superstitions," Jonno told him.

"A lot of city people do as well," Bella reminded him.

Her brother nodded. "That's true. Raff is incredibly superstitious."

Kylen chuckled. He'd seen the twins use Raff's superstitious nature against him on occasion. Like the time they'd seen him heading for the market. It was a Tuesday, and they turned him back by reminding him that a task started on a Tuesday would bring bad luck and mishap. Then they heard that a baker had brought more pastries than he was able to sell. Knowing he freely handed out what was left when the market closed, they decided to take a risk for once and went themselves. They made certain that Raff witnessed them eating the final mouthful.

"Country or city, people are careful not to do things if the omens aren't favorable," Jonno continued. "Everyone likes to see a good omen."

"Did you notice the horseshoe hanging above the main door into their house?" asked Bella.

"There was one over the barn as well," added Jonno. "Both of them were pointing down."

"What's that supposed to mean?"

"Horseshoes attract good luck. But only if the shoe comes off the horse on its own. It doesn't work if it's a new shoe, or one that's been taken off a horse. Pointing it up means the good luck collects in the horseshoe. Pointing it down means the good luck pours down onto whoever enters the house."

"Surely you don't believe things like that?" asked Kylen.

"I do," said Bella without hesitation.

Jonno didn't reply, but his manner made it clear he saw it the same way.

What would the mage have to say about it all? Kylen decided he would ask him as soon as he had an opportunity.

That night as they were preparing to sleep, he felt suddenly aware of their vulnerability without the mage nearby. He wasn't willing to leave it to luck.

"Dalthinir sets wards around our campsite each night to alert him if anyone comes near." He shrugged helplessly. "I can't do it. Do you think we should take it in turns to keep watch tonight?"

Jonno didn't seem too concerned. Nevertheless, he nodded in agreement. "If you want to. You go first. Wake me after a few hours."

The twins settled themselves near the fire, and Kylen positioned himself some distance away with his back against a tree. He felt uncomfortable and tired in equal measure.

His thoughts turned to Dalthinir. It was one thing to move pine cones and small rocks and to turn a calf in its mother's womb. But did he have the power to deal with armed bandits? So far he'd gone to great lengths to avoid trouble—he clearly preferred to run rather than to stand and fight. How would he handle a group of brigands? Violence was a way of life for men like them.

The mage didn't seem to question his own ability to deal with the situation, and Kylen could only hope his confidence was not misplaced.

Already feeling cold, Kylen glanced regretfully at the fire. Wriggling his toes in an attempt to keep them warm, he settled in for a long night.

KYLEN NEVER INTENDED to go to sleep. Nevertheless, he discovered he'd done just that when something woke him with a start just before sunrise.

A pre-dawn glow was beginning to lighten the sky. Cold and uncomfortable, he peered about with bleary eyes, trying to discover what had startled him awake. Nothing remained of the fire except a few glowing coals. It was too dark for him to make out the outline of either of the twins.

"What do we 'ave 'ere?" asked a cold voice from just beyond the fire.

A bulky form grasped hold of a writhing figure he guessed was Jonno. A second figure leaped up and dashed away, pursued by two others.

Taking advantage of the distraction, Kylen quietly moved further into the trees.

As the light strengthened, he could make out Jonno sitting trussed on the ground, angrily watching a bearded man with a prominent scar help himself to any food he could lay his hands on.

Two other men appeared, one skinny and the other unusually tall. "The other one got away," spat Skinny. Hearing his tone, Kylen shrank further into the shadows.

Scarface grabbed Jonno and hoisted him up. Pulling a knife, he held it to his throat. Then he bellowed into the half-light, "Whoever you are, come into the open. Do it now, or I'll slit your friend's throat! You have until I count five! One...two...three...four..."

"All right. I'm here," called Bella.

The skinny man marched over and struck her hard across the face, felling her to the ground. Then he leaned down and spat, "That's for making me trip in the dark when I was chasing you, wench."

After trussing her, he dragged her over to her brother, who'd been thrown back onto the ground.

"What are you two doing here?" Scarface demanded.

"We're just travelers passing through," Bella said, her voice quavering. Her fearfulness seemed only partly an act.

At that moment Henrietta appeared, clucking quietly. Lunging toward her, the tall man grabbed her and wrung her neck in a practiced motion. "Here's dinner," he said with a repulsive leer.

Jonno couldn't contain his fury. "We're under the protection of a powerful mage," he spat. "When he gets back, he's going to wring *your* necks!"

Scarface laughed. "A powerful mage, eh? Sounds like we better have our fun before he arrives then."

He hauled Jonno to his feet. "I wonder if I can get you to squawk like a chicken," he taunted, before punching him in the midriff. Jonno bent double, groaning in pain.

The skinny one lifted Bella and slapped her back down to the ground.

Unable to bear it, Kylen tried to imagine a protective sack around his friends. Scarface punched Jonno again, and this time his victim didn't wince. Heartened, he dared to hope his protection was working.

Concentrating on his friends, he didn't notice he was moving about restlessly until he stepped on a fallen branch. A loud crack sounded.

Everything went quiet as every eye turned in his direction. In the growing light the tall man spotted him through the trees.

"Ha! That's no powerful mage. It's another chicken to pluck!" he called. He raced toward Kylen, a nasty smile on his face.

As the brigand reached out to grab him, something erupted in Kylen's head. The attacker came to a jarring halt, as if he'd hit an invisible wall.

A number of things were happening at once. Scarface resumed his assault, prompting a cry of pain from Jonno. Kylen's heart sank. His protection of his friend must have failed, no doubt because he was distracted protecting himself. His own attacker chose that moment to go after him again. This time he was able to move forward unimpeded. His own protection had failed as well.

Kylen's mind was spinning. His successes had been short-lived, with every one of his shields failing. Hopelessly overburdened, he saw he lacked the skill to protect himself and the twins at the same time. Worse, he wasn't confident he could repeat anything he'd done for any one of them.

The tall man came at him again with his knife raised high. He was enraged now. Kylen's hasty attempt to push him back with magic proved futile, his panic and dismay blocking any access to his power.

As the knife plunged downward in a killing stroke, a roar of fury sounded from across the clearing.

Dalthinir had returned.

RAISING HIS HANDS HIGH, the mage clapped them together. Attackers and victims were knocked from their feet as a shock wave shook the ground and bent the trees.

After lying dazed for a moment, all three of the brigands sprang up and charged the mage with knives raised.

He didn't move. When they reached him, they stabbed viciously at him to find their weapons deflected by an unseen shield surrounding his body. Immediately they began pounding on him with their fists. He remained unaffected.

"Grab some hostages!" roared Scarface. Turning away from Dalthinir, the bandits raced toward their former victims. The twins and Kylen had been lying on the ground, watching open-mouthed as the mage calmly withstood the assault. Now they scrambled to their feet in alarm.

They had no cause for concern. Careering forward heedlessly, the three men came to a dead stop. Falling stunned to the ground, they lay sprawled awkwardly. With an effort they staggered to their feet, only to find themselves barely able to move. No barrier of any kind was visible, but somehow they'd been hemmed in on every side. Then they screamed in terror as the ground beneath them began to boil.

Ignoring them, Dalthinir moved purposefully to the twins. After kneeling beside each of them in turn and examining them carefully, he rose to his feet, a look of relief evident in his eyes. "Your injuries aren't significant. You'll recover with some rest." He had to yell to be heard over the howls of the brigands.

The mage returned his attention to the beleaguered men, watching in satisfaction as the earth slowly swallowed them up. By the time the ground finally ceased its rumbling, only their heads remained visible. They were whimpering rather than bellowing now. Barely able to breathe, they were panting shallowly. They seemed unable to fill their lungs sufficiently to shout.

Calling his little group together, Dalthinir spoke to them quietly. "I am sorry you had to endure that. I should never have left you alone, not with men like these in the area."

He pointed away through the trees. "I discovered another farmhouse only a short distance from here. I wanted to hear what they knew about the brigands, so I accepted their hospitality for the night. Fortunately, that meant I was never far away. When I sensed your burst of power, Kylen, I wasted no time getting back here."

He smiled at his apprentice. "When we get a chance, I want to hear what you did with your magic. First, though, I'm going to return to the farmhouse. They have a couple of adult sons on the property, and I'll ask them to take these bandits to the authorities. It's time they were held accountable for their crimes."

He threw a glance in the direction of the three men. "They can stay here, with you keeping an eye on them, Kylen. They won't be going anywhere, so I don't expect you'll be in any danger. The twins need to come with me so I can monitor their condition. It isn't a long walk—they should be able to manage it."

Kylen nodded mutely, still trying to recover from his shock. He had been rescued by the narrowest of margins. In the process he had seen the full power of the mage revealed at last. It had been awe-inspiring.

It was still difficult to comprehend everything that had happened. The shock wave, the mage's protective shield, and the invisible wall around the brigands were incredible enough. But then Dalthinir had caused the earth to swallow them up—while attending to the twins at the same time. It was beyond astonishing.

The mage helped Bella and Jonno to their feet. "We won't be gone long," he promised Kylen. "If anyone comes along, make sure they don't take pity on these men and dig them up!"

A couple of minutes later they were gone.

The brigands began whining the minute the mage was out of sight. If their protestations could have been taken seriously, they were nothing more than victims. Kylen could only shake his head in disgust.

Heading away from them, he emerged into open ground almost immediately. After locating a suitable rock, he sat down. He could still see their heads, but mercifully he was no longer within earshot.

Absently glancing upward he noticed a hawk hovering high above. Once more he was quickly able to picture the view from the hawk's perspective. He imagined a tiny figure on a rock below—himself—and, further afield, three figures heading for a nearby farmhouse. Then his attention was diverted by a small movement below. A mouse had emerged briefly into the open before drawing back again. Still and silent, the tiny creature was almost invisible. But its location had been compromised.

The mouse and its surroundings suddenly loomed ever larger, and Kylen, startled out of his absorption, looked up to see the hawk diving swiftly toward the ground.

Only then did it occur to him to wonder if what he'd seen was more than just imagination. Could he truly have seen the world through the eyes of a hawk? Was such a thing possible? Did mages possess such abilities?

The hawk had soared aloft once more. To his disappointment, every attempt to see through its eyes was in vain. Perhaps his imagination had deserted him. Perhaps his power was once again resistant to his conscious effort to control it. Either way, he could see nothing beyond the reach of his own eyes.

Time dragged painfully by as he waited for Dalthinir's return. A scream from one of the brigands briefly drew him back to the clearing to investigate. He found a couple of large ants crawling over a brigand's head, leaving the man terrified that insects would make a meal of him. Rolling his eyes, Kylen left them to their imaginings.

The mage and the twins eventually returned, accompanied by a heavyset farmer and his two sons. An elderly woman trailed behind them. Seeing the men buried in the ground, with no sign of digging anywhere, the new arrivals aimed awed glances in the direction of the mage.

The elderly woman immediately shuffled up to the imprisoned brigands and studied them carefully.

"That's the one who killed my husband," she exclaimed, pointing angrily at Scarface.

The brigand spat at her. Indignant and furious, the woman kicked dirt in his face.

Bella appeared at the side of the bereaved woman. Speaking quietly, the twin took her arm and led her gently away.

The farmer had brought ropes and shovels, and his sons dug up the men one at a time and bound them securely. The brigands had plenty to say to their captors, and the farmer must have anticipated it. Retrieving cloth gags, he stuffed one into each of their mouths, securing them with long strips of material.

"Where are you planning to take them?" asked the mage.

"To Cambrick," the farmer replied.

"How will you travel?"

"By horse. No point in prolonging the journey. We'll tie each of them over a horse. Will you come with us?"

Dalthinir shook his head. "We have business away to the west," he said. "When will you leave?"

"We'll leave today. I saw three ducks flying in that direction earlier."

One of the sons approached him and handed over a bundle. "My mother guessed you'd be leaving. She packed some supplies."

Dalthinir accepted the gift gratefully, asking him to pass on sincere thanks.

After farewells were exchanged, the farmer and his sons led the captives away. The elderly lady followed after planting an affectionate kiss on Bella's cheek.

When they were gone, Kylen turned to the mage. "What was that about three ducks flying in the right direction?"

"It's a superstition."

"Like having horseshoes over the entrances to houses or barns, or seeing toads in the path."

Dalthinir nodded. "No mage pays regard to such things. But superstition dominates the lives of a lot of people, even intelligent and educated people."

"I don't believe in it either," he said impassively.

It brought to mind the occasion when one of Raff's toadies had found an iron needle. A find like that was supposed to be especially lucky, and the boy had celebrated wildly until he somehow managed to sit on the needle. The wound in his leg eventually became infected, leaving him dangerously ill for a long time. When a raven appeared inside the building—an omen considered especially unlucky—he thought he was done for. Instead he began to recover that very day.

Kylen had never been able to take superstitions seriously after that.

"You said we're heading west?" he said.

The mage shook his head. "No, that's just what I want people to think." He sighed. "As soon as the farmer reaches Cambrick and reports what just happened, I might as well have shouted to the world, 'Dalthinir is here'. The Compact will be crawling all over this place before you can blink. And few of them will thank me for ridding the world of murderers and thieves." He shrugged. "It's the price we pay for doing our duty. Who would have stopped the brigands if we only cared about avoiding exposure?"

Like it or not, once more they would be fleeing for their lives, hunted relentlessly. The local people might be grateful for the mage's intervention, but to the Compact he was nothing more than a renegade.

Eager as Kylen was to gain access to his powers, he was beginning to see that it would never be safe to use magical power anywhere other people could witness its effects. Not if they wanted to stop running.

It was obvious that his mentor placed a lower priority on staying safe than on doing what he believed was right. Kylen recognized that if he was to learn everything Dalthinir had to teach him, he would need to embrace the same priorities.

"Where will we go?" the apprentice asked.

"Somewhere they'll never find us," Dalthinir replied calmly. "It's time we disappeared for a while."

VOLUME 2—APPRENTICE

CHAPTER 12

Plodding along behind the mage, Kylen struggled to come to terms with the massive upheavals in his life. He had become a fugitive—facing death if he was caught, and for no reason other than his newfound status as a mage. But he wasn't a mage. He was merely an apprentice. He was classed as dangerous because of powers he could neither master nor understand.

Dalthinir swung in beside him. "It's time I started teaching you about magic, Kylen," he said, a purposeful look on his face. "The place to start is magical senses. But it might be helpful to talk about our physical senses first."

He paused, looking expectantly at his apprentice. Kylen nodded readily, so he continued.

"Everyone has physical senses. Do you know what they are?"

"You mean seeing and hearing?"

"That's two of them. The others are touch, smell, and taste." The mage gazed expectantly at him. "What do you need to do to get these senses working?"

After a moment's thought, Kylen replied, "Nothing. If I'm awake, I can see."

"Does it work that way for the other senses?"

Kylen nodded.

Dalthinir's raised eyebrow told him a cursory response wasn't good enough.

"Er, hearing is the same," he added hastily. "I can hear whenever I'm awake. I can even hear if I'm asleep, because noises wake me up sometimes."

"All of that is true," the mage acknowledged. "While we're awake we see and hear constantly, unless we close our eyes or block our ears. But the other senses aren't quite like that."

Kylen frowned. "Why not? If there's smoke in the air I smell it. I don't have to try. And I don't need to do anything special to feel the cold."

"I'm delighted to know you're thinking," the mage told him. "And what you say is correct. But there are times we need to do something particular to take advantage of touch, smell, or taste. For example, to smell a flower I might have to bend low to bring my nose close enough to it. And I can't appreciate the taste of freshly cooked venison until I put it in my mouth. The same applies to touch. If you're sleeping and I want you to wake up, I have to go to you and shake you. Sometimes senses just happen, and sometimes we need to do something specific before we can put them to work."

Kylen nodded. None of it was hard to follow so far.

"For most of us, senses are part of our earliest experiences. We use them without thinking. But magical senses aren't like that. To begin with, we don't have them when we're children. And we only begin to experience them after our magical awakening. Even then it takes time and practice before we can get them working fully. They do become more like second nature over time, and on occasion we use them without conscious effort. Like when you diverted the ax to save your hand."

He paused. "How is your hand?"

Kylen held it up and peered at it. It both looked and felt strange to have a finger missing. "It still throbs occasionally. But the wound has healed."

The mage examined it briefly before nodding with satisfaction.

"Where was I? Ah, yes, differences between magical senses and physical senses. Another important difference is that mages usually only have two or three magical senses. It's extremely rare to have four, and I don't know of anyone with five."

"What do you mean by magical senses?"

"I mean mage smell, mage touch, mage taste, mage hearing, and mage sight."

Kylen frowned. "I've seen your magic, and it's nothing like seeing or hearing, or any of the other senses."

"You're right. It's going to seem confusing at first. Magical senses aren't like physical senses. Nevertheless, mages find it useful to think of them in that way. It offers a simple way to group together the kinds of things you can do with magic."

Seeing that Kylen was confused, he added, "An example might help. Can you guess which magical sense is shared by all mages?"

"Mage sight? Is that what farsense is?"

"Farsense is the correct answer. But farsense is mage smell rather than mage sight."

Kylen screwed up his face in surprise. "Smell? Why smell?"

"You've spent your life in the city, so you're probably not aware of it, but animals in the wild like to mark their territory to warn off other animals. They do it by urinating in different locations around their domain. The particular smell identifies the animal. When a mage uses magical power, it leaves behind a unique scent, one that identifies the mage. It isn't something we smell with our physical noses. We use a magical ability, one that we refer to as a mage sense of smell."

An earlier conversation came to Kylen's mind. "I remember you said that every mage can tell when magical power is used."

"Yes, provided they're reasonably close at hand. You wouldn't be a mage otherwise."

"How close is reasonably close?"

"That depends on the mage. Weaker mages can only sense power when it's used near them. More powerful mages can detect power from a considerable distance away."

"And every mage can also tell who did it? Because every mage's magic has a different smell?"

"That's right."

He shook his head. He understood what Dalthinir was saying, but it felt strange.

Dalthinir must have sensed his mood, because he said, "That's probably enough for now. We can come back to it another time."

Seeing that the conversation was coming to an end, the twins joined them. "We're heading in the direction of Cambrick," said Bella.

"I thought we wanted to get away from the capital," Jonno added.

Dalthinir nodded. "It's about time we discussed plans. Find yourself somewhere to sit."

After they were settled, he dug out a few of the supplies sent by the farmer's wife and handed them around. "I said earlier that we need to go somewhere no one will find us. That's why we're heading back toward the capital."

"Cambrick? Surely not!" Kylen exclaimed. "That's where all the mages are!"

The twins looked equally surprised.

The mage was unmoved. "We'll be safe as long as we're careful. It will never occur to anyone to look for us there."

"But there are people in the city who will recognize us!"

"They'll never see us, because we won't go to Cambrick. We'll stay outside the walls. There'll be somewhere for us to stay in Camberton. The town's more than big enough to lose ourselves in it."

Kylen wasn't entirely convinced, but he was willing to follow Dalthinir's lead. And the twins seemed willing to accept the plan.

The mage wasn't quite finished. "There is one small complication."

All eyes flicked to him.

"I'm going to need to keep an eye on the comings and goings of a couple of the mages. I was hoping Bella and Jonno might be willing to help."

The twins brightened immediately. "We said you'd never manage without us!" Jonno said with a grin.

Dalthinir rolled his eyes. "It might be dangerous."

"It wouldn't be interesting if it wasn't," said Bella with a wink.

Kylen eyed the mage uncertainly. His entire reason for extracting the twins from Cambrick was to ensure they wouldn't be left there on their own. "Who do you want to keep an eye on?"

After a brief hesitation, his mentor appeared to reach a decision. "That meeting you saw from the rooftop. You said it involved two mages, three nobles, and another person. I think I can guess who one of the mages might be and the other person as well. But I need to be certain. Something tells me it might be very important."

"Important to us?" asked Jonno.

Dalthinir shook his head. "Important to the whole of Periton. And to other kingdoms as well."

"Why do you care about Periton?" Jonno asked curiously. "The king and the mages want to kill you, don't they?"

He waited in vain for an answer.

The mage's frankness had come to an end. "Time to go," he announced, climbing to his feet and striding away without a backward glance.

All three of them leaped up at once and followed him.

"You've only just discovered the country, and you're leaving already," Jonno told Kylen with an exaggerated sigh.

Receiving nothing more than a grunt in return, he redirected his attention to Bella. The two of them were soon chattering away as if nothing unusual was going on.

FOUR DAYS PASSED before they spotted the walls of Cambrick in the distance. Camberton lay before them, a few bowshots from the city walls. It was a substantial town, having spread outward over the decades until its population almost rivaled that of the city.

"I've lived in Cambrick all my life, and I've never been to Camberton," mused Kylen.

"Then it's time you did!" Dalthinir replied. "I love the place, rough edges and all. It might be helpful to give you a brief description of the town. Some will tell you Camberton is for poor people. That might be true, but the quarter closest to the city has its share of mansions, mostly occupied by merchants. Traders from the Kingdom of Tantel are not permitted to own property in Cambrick, so they have a presence in Camberton along with the local merchants. Another substantial quarter primarily hosts guild members."

"There are guilds in the city too," said Kylen.

The mage nodded. "There are. But dwellings and workshops in Camberton are cheaper than in the city. That means members of lesser guilds are well represented. Such as cobblers, weavers, dyers, saddle makers, and masons. It's also easier to find blacksmiths and armorers in Camberton than in Cambrick."

He waved at the buildings ahead. "There are shops, inns, and respectable workshops on both sides of the main road. The poorer you are, the further you live from the road. A lot of the dwellings aren't much better than hovels. I should warn you that cutpurses and criminals of a more dangerous variety live among the shanty dwellers."

Pulling his hood low over his face, Dalthinir led them away from the main road. It soon became clear that he intended to lead the little party into the poorest quarter of the town. Given their pressing need to stay out of sight, Kylen saw the sense of it. That didn't make the place any more attractive.

The moment they set foot in the quarter, a rank stench assaulted Kylen. It felt oppressive after the clean country air they had left behind. As they pressed on, unsmiling eyes peered at them out of grubby faces. Most of the stares were unwelcoming; a few radiated hostility.

He had more reason than most to feel at home in a place like this. Nevertheless his former refuge in the city almost seemed like a haven in comparison, even with Raff and his cronies constantly finding ways to make life difficult.

The mage showed no signs of uneasiness, and Kylen took heart from that. He reminded himself that nowhere would ever be entirely safe now that he was a renegade. Besides, he wasn't entirely helpless. He was a mage too, even if his powers still remained largely untapped.

Dalthinir stopped outside a ramshackle building and banged on the door. It wasn't difficult to understand why this place might be appealing. The dwelling stood apart from other buildings, so no one was on hand to witness their arrival.

After a long delay a sour-faced man appeared. His expression changed the moment he saw who was at his door.

"Dalthinir! Come in!" he said enthusiastically. "Your friends too!"

Standing back, he waved them in and shut the door behind them.

He embraced the mage, clapping him on the back. "My friend! You honor us."

A woman and a young boy appeared, both of them beaming with delight. Kylen couldn't guess what had prompted such an enthusiastic welcome, but it must have been significant. Witnessing their genuine pleasure at Dalthinir's arrival, he found it hard to imagine them quickly betraying the mage or his friends.

The mage seemed equally pleased to see them. "I don't know if it's possible for you to accommodate us, Grudem, but all of us need somewhere quiet to stay for a while." He nodded toward his companions, briefly introducing each of them.

Pulling his other hand from within his robe, he held it out. A handful of coins shone dully in the candlelight, and Jonno and Bella gasped in surprise. Kylen understood their reaction perfectly—all of them were looking at a small fortune in gold.

"No, no! It ain't necessary, my friend." The man was wincing, trying not to look.

"Necessary or not, you will take it, Grudem. I insist! Besides, you need it more than I do. That's the truth, plain and simple."

As Grudem continued to hesitate, the woman stepped forward to resolve the impasse. Accepting the coins with a respectful bow, she turned a shining face toward her benefactor. "Once more y're savin' us from disaster, Dalthinir. Right on time, as always! It's our honor to have ya—and y'r friends—for as long as ya might need shelter."

She handed the coins to Grudem. "Buy a few supplies, me love. I'll make sure our friends are comfy an' all. Then I'm gonna prepare us a feast. We'll celebrate their arrival!"

Accepting the inevitable, Grudem mumbled thanks of his own to Dalthinir before pushing through the door and disappearing.

As soon as he was gone, the woman turned toward Kylen and the twins. "Y're all welcome! I'm Marta, and this is Keemun, our boy. Wait here!"

After a few minutes she returned. "C'mon up! I'll show ya all to y'r rooms."

Leading them up a flight of stairs, she ushered Bella into a small room, then led Kylen and Jonno into another. Dalthinir followed her further down the passageway.

Kylen and Jonno's room was simple. A small pile of blankets lay in the corner beside a bowl with a pitcher of water. The room boasted no other adornments. Kylen was more than satisfied. Sleeping on the floor under a roof had to be better than sleeping on the ground in the open.

With nothing to do in their room, Kylen and Jonno headed downstairs, joined by Bella. Grudem had not yet returned, and Marta was boiling water. Her son, Keemun, who might have been seven or eight years old, was hovering nearby.

The mage had been nowhere to be seen, but at that moment he appeared. He ruffled Keemun's hair affectionately. "The people of Camberton have always been very good to me," he told them. "Even so," he said, a tone of pleading entering his voice, "it would be good if no one knows I'm here."

"So the mages ain't stopped hunting ya?" asked Marta.

He confirmed it with a shake of his head.

She sighed sadly. "Nothin' ever changes, does it? Y'r right to worry too. There's plenty o' tattle tales 'round here. But we'll keep our lips sewn shut, won't we Keemun?"

The boy agreed without hesitation.

"Bella and Jonno will need to come and go a bit. Could you put it about that they're relatives of yours?"

"Consider it done!" she replied. "From now on, the pair o' ya can be me sister's kids. She even has a couple y'r age." She favored them with a beaming smile.

The door opened to admit Grudem. He held up a sack bulging with supplies, a big grin on his face.

"Now," said Marta, "it must be time for a party!"

CHAPTER 13

K ylen sat in the corner of Dalthinir's room as the mage finished preparing the twins for their first foray into the city.

"Do you understand what you need to do?" asked Dalthinir.

The twins nodded in unison.

"Promise me you'll get out the minute you see any risk of danger!"

Neither of them spoke a word, but their unapologetic smirks said plenty.

The mage grimaced. "The pair of you will be the death of me."

For that he was rewarded with a laugh. "You needn't worry, Dalthinir," said Jonno. "To anyone glancing in our direction, there'll be nothing to see. We'll be invisible."

"Except for our gigantic ears," added Bella.

The mage could only shake his head in despair, which set them off laughing again.

After they finally left, Dalthinir strode around restlessly until Kylen began to wonder if he was going crazy.

"Who are the twins trying to find?" he asked.

"A mage I was watching when I was in Cambrick," the mage told him. "It's nothing for you to be concerned about."

The answer only left Kylen more curious than ever. But he could see he wasn't going to get any more at that moment. "Were you planning some magic lessons?" he asked hopefully.

The mage stopped pacing and released a deep sigh. "That's a good idea, Kylen. I need something to get my mind off those twins of yours."

Kylen grinned at him. "They seem to be more your twins than mine these days."

The mage ignored the comment. "I've been wondering about your parents. Do you know who they were?"

He shook his head. "I have no idea."

"Do you remember them at all?"

He shook his head again.

"What do you remember of your early years?"

"Almost nothing. One of my earliest memories was on the streets when I was almost beaten up by a couple of thugs. I was terrified. They left me alone in the end. I think I must have looked so pathetic they decided that pummeling me wasn't worth the effort. I don't remember much at all about how I survived those years."

"You're a mystery. Your power is remarkable, and I'd love to know who your parents were."

"Do mages inherit magic from their parents?"

"Yes, although it's unpredictable. Powerful mages might produce offspring who turn out to be weak in magic, or even have no magic at all. And it's possible for weak mages to have a child who turns out to be powerful. There are cases of mages coming from bloodlines with no obvious sign of magic, but they're very rare."

"So the chances are that at least one of my parents was a mage?"

Dalthinir nodded. "I wish I had access to the Compact's records. It would be interesting to see if any mages died around the time you were born. It's surprising that no one cared for you. Usually a relative steps in, or someone close to the family."

Kylen shrugged.

"There's another thing I'm finding curious," the mage told him. "The twins were clearly brought up by parents who were intelligent and articulate. They don't speak or think like street rats. And neither do you. Why is that, especially since you remember nothing before your life on the streets?"

"That's easier to answer," Kylen replied. "An old man befriended me in my early years. He ended his life on the streets, but he was well educated and intelligent. Most of his life he was keeper of the royal archives or something like that. He couldn't help with finding food or dealing with people like Raff. But he took an interest in me and spent a lot of time teaching me things. He kept telling me a lot of wealthy children had tutors who weren't half as good as he was. We must have had eight years together, and I miss him a lot. He only died two or three years ago—just before I met Jonno and Bella. I still think of him most days."

"But he didn't teach you to read and write?"

"No. He didn't have anything to write with. And there was nothing for me to read, so I wouldn't have been able to practice. He told me that oral traditions used to be the main way of passing on knowledge. He said that once people started writing things down, oral teaching faded into the background, and a lot of knowledge was lost as a result. His view was that oral learning is the best way to start an education, because it teaches you to listen. You shouldn't learn to read until you can do that well."

"He sounds like an intelligent man," said Dalthinir. "What was his name?"

"He was called Olatiren."

"Olatiren?" The mage's jaw opened with surprise. "So he ended his life on the streets. He was a lot more than keeper of the royal archives! If he was your teacher, I'm no longer surprised at your speech and your comprehension. And I can well understand why you're not taken in by superstition."

Kylen's curiosity was thoroughly aroused. "He was a true friend to me. What do you know of him?"

To his surprise and frustration, Dalthinir refused to be drawn, quickly changing the subject.

"I think it's time we did something about the obvious gap in your education."

So saying, he retrieved from his sack a piece of parchment, a quill, and a small vial of what was apparently ink.

"Today is an important day," he announced. "It's the day you begin learning to read and write."

THE REALM of books and letters had always been a strange and foreign land to Kylen. Access to it was denied to all but a select few, and he had never dared imagine he would one day be included in that number.

Yet there he was, learning to read and write.

So far it was proving less difficult than he'd feared. Although he clearly had a great deal to learn, after a solid day of hard work he began to see glimmers of hope.

Positive as Kylen's day might have been, it was a different story for the mage. Long before the day ended, he was becoming restless again, and he showed no sign of settling before the twins appeared.

They arrived not long after sunset and came up to Dalthinir's room. By then he could barely contain himself.

"Well?" he exclaimed. "Did you get into any trouble? Did you find him?"

"Not exactly," Bella replied.

"It took us a while to find the place where the mages hang around," Jonno told them. "Eventually we spotted a mage who seemed to fit the description perfectly. We followed him around for most of the day."

"He's an incredibly boring person!" Bella told them. "He spent the whole afternoon in a library. Can you imagine it?"

Jonno snorted. "We'd just figured out a way to get in there when someone called him to the door. They called him by name, which finally showed us he wasn't Lars."

"You can't go into the Compact library!" protested Dalthinir in horror.

Bella ignored him. "We thought about starting again, but the day was almost over by then," she concluded. "So we headed back here instead."

"You did the right thing coming back. But we need to stop this right now. It's a bad idea," Dalthinir told them frankly. "I don't know what I was thinking."

Both of the twins looked baffled. "What's the problem?"

When the mage didn't immediately answer, Kylen decided to help him out. "Dalthinir was a bit restless." Then he shook his head. Why soften it? "If you want to know the truth, he was edgier than a cornered rat. He was worried about you." Whoever Lars might be, tracking him was apparently a high risk undertaking.

"I can't let you do this!" The words burst out of Dalthinir. "It's much too dangerous. I won't let you do something I'm not prepared to do myself."

Bella waved a hand dismissively. "We were fine," she said. "I even earned this, running an errand for one of the mages." She held out a small copper coin.

"Which mage?" asked Dalthinir anxiously.

"Her name was Inga."

"Inga?" Dalthinir turned away as he said it, but not quickly enough to hide the bright red blush that covered his face.

Jonno was ecstatic. "Oh ho! Dalthinir has a sweetheart!"

A serious look came to Bella's face. "I can see why you like her. She was very nice, and she did strike me as unusually attractive for a woman her age."

Both of them burst out laughing, which further deepened the mage's embarrassment.

"Is she someone important?" asked Kylen gravely.

His attempt to change the tone must have worked, because Dalthinir finally managed to master himself. The flush of embarrassment had been replaced by a scowl directed at the twins. "She's a senior mage," he grumbled.

"In that case the connection might be useful," Bella said thoughtfully. "I'm glad I decided to run the errand instead of just walking away with the coin."

Another burst of laughter followed her comment.

Kylen rolled his eyes. The twins were enjoying themselves far too much. It was only too apparent that the mage brought out their mischievous streak.

Dalthinir frowned at them. "This isn't a joke," he snapped. "It's deadly serious. For me and for Kylen especially, but for you as well if they find out who you're helping."

Their faces instantly became sober. "We do understand," Jonno assured him. "Truly. We would never treat the mission as a joke. But if you could see your reaction!"

They managed to keep straight faces, although clearly it was a struggle.

"I'm sure we'll have better success tomorrow," Bella assured him. Then she added casually, "If you would like me to pass on your love to Master Inga, just let me know."

Jonno snorted loudly, subsiding only when Bella nudged him hard in the ribs.

"I'm going downstairs to see if there's any food," she announced. Grabbing her brother's arm, she dragged him out with her.

"They'll be the death of me. Of us all!" said Dalthinir gloomily the moment they had gone.

"Of course they won't," Kylen assured him. "We just need to give them a bit more time. And you need to stop provoking them!"

"Provoking them? What on earth are you talking about?"

"Oh, never mind," he replied helplessly.

"It's time for another lesson," the mage asserted grimly.

THE FOLLOWING days gradually settled into a consistent pattern. The twins disappeared as soon as the sun rose. The mage and his apprentice stayed indoors during daylight hours to avoid being seen. Several hours each day were set aside to work on Kylen's literacy.

After dark the four of them conferred as soon as the twins returned. Then Dalthinir and Kylen left the dwelling to stretch their legs. They were usually gone for two or three hours, and the mage almost always used the opportunity to continue teaching Kylen about magic. He focused on the magical senses they had already covered, both describing how he routinely applied them in everyday situations and demonstrating them in small ways. He also gave Kylen many opportunities to do a bit of practice of his own, always masking the use of power to ensure they were not exposed.

On one occasion the twins decided not to go to the city. They said it was because they were tired. It was only later that Kylen realized it had been a Tuesday. When the following Tuesday came around, they again took the day off. Raff had been superstitious about setting out to do something on a Tuesday, and they hadn't missed the opportunity to poke fun at him. He could have done the same to them, but he let it go. It would have seemed churlish.

The twins eventually identified Master Lars. The man was suspicious by nature, and it took time before they were able to tail him without him realizing it.

By then it was obvious they were neither reckless nor impatient, and Dalthinir finally allowed himself to relax. The twins remained as buoyant as ever. None of the Camberton locals ever bothered them, apparently accepting them as Marta's niece and nephew.

Thus far there was no hint that Dalthinir's presence in Camberton had been exposed. Nor was there any evidence that Master Lars was up to no good. Nevertheless, the mage remained convinced it was just a matter of time.

Whatever Dalthinir feared must have been significant, and more was at stake than his own well-being. Otherwise he would never have let the twins put themselves so much at risk.

On one occasion Kylen asked directly, "Why are the twins trailing this mage? What do you think he might be up to?"

The mage remained tight-lipped. "Don't think about it, Kylen. There's enough else for you to worry about."

Kylen's dissatisfaction with the answer must have been obvious to the mage, because he added, "If my worst fears are realized, you'll be one of the first to know."

And that was that. It was undeniably true that their situation was dire already. He could only wait, hoping that the mage was concerned for no reason. However he couldn't shake the feeling that the outcome wouldn't be encouraging.

ONE EVENING KYLEN and the twins were enjoying the meal prepared by Marta. After bolting down some food, Dalthinir had left with Grudem on some kind of errand.

The twins had returned from Cambrick earlier than usual that day, and they were clearly feeling relaxed.

"How is it you know Dalthinir?" Bella asked Marta.

"Well, young Bella, there's quite a tale b'hind it! It were a few years ago. There was this huge storm. Terrible winds, with hail big as a baby's fist. All of a sudden, boom! We lose the roof! Our Keemun—just two at the time—is sleepin' upstairs. And we can't get to him! Not with all the wreckage in the way."

She lowered her voice conspiratorially. "Now our Dalthinir, they might call him a renegade, but he's a mage. A real one." She winked. "I'm sure ya all know that. Well, at the time he's staying right here in Camberton, not far away. Someone tells him we need help, and he rushes in and uses his powers to hold up the roof, so Grudem can race upstairs to grab the young 'un. Just as they're comin' down the stairs, the staircase collapses! Course, none of that's a problem for Dalthinir! He gives 'em a soft landing." She was grinning ear to ear.

"While this's goin' down, the other mages—the high and mighty ones up in Cambrick—they find out he's here. All 'cause he's using his magic. Next thing we hear, soldiers are comin', and mages with 'em. We tell Dalthinir, but he don't care! No stoppin' for him, not 'til both of me men are safe!" She shook her head in wonder.

"People here don't hold with fancy mages and soldiers. It gets 'round pretty quick that they're comin'. Rain's hammerin' down, and the wind's howlin', but quick as ya like everyone's out on the streets, milling around 'til the outsiders couldn't barely move." She brushed a tear from her eye at the memory. "Dalthinir escapes afore they get here, but only just!"

All of them had been listening wide-eyed.

"Fixing your house must have been a big job," offered Bella.

"Big? I'll say! But, just before our Dalthinir slips away, he goes and plops a little bag into Grudem's hand. Enough gold coins to fix our house and then some! We ain't the only ones he's helped either—not by a long shot." Her face was shining.

She winked at them. "People from the city like to say this part of Camberton ain't safe for decent folks. Not if ya ain't a local. But no one here would ever lay a finger on Dalthinir! Nor on his friends!"

CHAPTER 14

The twins might have been accepted as the niece and nephew of Marta, but Kylen had acquired no such status. As far as he knew, none of the locals were aware he existed. Given the importance of remaining unnoticed, he avoided going outside in daylight hours.

That didn't mean he was satisfied with the arrangement. He longed to be able to wander about freely like the twins, whatever the risk.

During this period he came to appreciate darkness as never before. He walked regularly with Dalthinir, but he also ventured out on his own whenever the mood took him. The mage didn't mind as long as he stayed reasonably close to the house.

On one occasion while meandering a little further from the house, he was alerted by the terrified yelping of a puppy. Hurrying in the direction of the sound, he heard harsh shouts drowning out the animal's squeals. Then everything went abruptly quiet.

Fearful for the puppy's safety, he hesitated to leave, even though he guessed he wasn't safe there himself. But with no further sound to follow, he headed reluctantly for home.

Unable to put the puppy's distress from his mind, he returned to the area more than once in the days that followed. His persistence was finally rewarded four nights after his initial contact. The sound of whimpering drew him to a small puppy hiding among some rubbish. Trembling violently, the animal watched in fear as he approached. When he knelt down and spoke soothingly to it, its little tail began to wag tentatively and a tiny tongue emerged to lick his offered hand.

Abruptly his viewpoint switched, the world taking on an unfamiliar appearance. As if seeing through the puppy's eyes, he saw an ill-favored man approaching from behind. Standing hastily and spinning around, he saw that the vision had been accurate.

The puppy began to whimper fearfully.

"That's my animal! Git away from it!" demanded a coarse voice.

Setting his jaw defiantly, Kylen stood his ground.

Wading immediately to the attack, the man swung a heavy fist toward Kylen's head.

The youth dodged it easily.

He had encountered bullies in his years on the streets. Where possible he avoided them. He had also developed a happy knack of calming hotheads before confrontations turned physical. Usually. Experience had taught him that some brutes could neither be talked down nor avoided.

Very occasionally he had been forced to choose between fighting or fleeing. On occasion he had decided to stand and fight, usually in defense of the helpless. More often than not, he'd received a fearful beating as a result.

This particular man wasn't interested in being placated, and Kylen had no intention of leaving the puppy to his dubious mercy. That meant it was going to come to blows.

He wasn't overly troubled though. His attacker's movements suggested the man had been drinking heavily. While he was undoubtedly dangerous, he was unlikely to be well coordinated.

Rushing forward, the man tried to wrap thick arms around him. Moving rapidly, Kylen dropped to his knees.

Unable to slow himself in time, the man stumbled heavily into the kneeling youth and crashed to the ground.

He didn't get up.

Thoroughly alarmed, Kylen picked himself up and hurried over to examine him. He could see no sign of injury, and as if to confirm his observations, the man began snoring loudly. Satisfied that he was seeing nothing worse than a drunken stupor, the youth ignored the man and hurried to the puppy. Scooping the little creature into his arms, he hurried back to Marta's house.

Everyone looked up in curiosity when he arrived.

"Where did he come from?" asked Marta in surprise.

"It's a she," he replied. "And I rescued her."

Marta peered at the puppy. "Looks like some brute has been beatin' her."

Stepping closer, Dalthinir examined the dog. "I think you're right, Marta. Her cuts and bruises suggest she's been beaten severely. I think her leg might be broken as well."

"Can you mend it?" asked Kylen anxiously.

"I've never been much of a healer. But I'll try."

Everything went quiet, then the puppy gave a little yelp.

"That seems to have done it," the mage said. He was looking especially pleased with himself.

Keemun ran over and began stroking the little creature behind its ears while Marta searched out something for it to eat and drink. When the food and drink arrived, Kylen put the puppy down. After sniffing cautiously, she ate frantically. She was clearly famished.

With everyone distracted, Dalthinir drew Kylen aside, "Did you use power to get her away from her master?"

He shook his head. "I didn't need to," he replied. "I haven't done anything that might give us away."

Then he frowned in puzzlement. "It's strange, but using power never even occurred to me!"

The mage didn't seem surprised. "In a situation like that you probably reacted instinctively, like you would have back on the streets. Old habits die hard."

Then he leaned forward to whisper in Kylen's ear. "I hope you realize you won't be able to keep the animal. We won't be able to take a dog with us when we go."

A stubborn frown came to Kylen's face.

"It wouldn't be fair to the puppy," insisted the mage. "Marta and Keemun will look after it."

The twins were taking their turn fussing over the newcomer.

"Kylen has always been drawn to the helpless," said Bella with a smile. "When it comes to strays, he can't stop himself. One time he rescued a bird with an injured wing."

"It's the only time I've seen him really angry," said Jonno.

"What happened?" asked Marta.

"We were living in an abandoned building," Jonno told them, "along with a bully called Raff and his lackeys. The bird was getting better—it could fly for very short distances. The three of us had been out foraging, and when we came back the bird was lying still in its little box. It was dead."

Bella took up the tale. "Raff was smirking. He said there was a little accident when he was playing a game with the bird."

"What did Kylen do?" asked Keemun eagerly.

"His face went red!" said Bella. "Raff had a decorated wooden chair he loved to sit on. He'd found it somehow."

"Stole it more likely!" interjected Jonno.

"Everyone called it Raff's throne. Kylen grabbed it and smashed it into the ground until it broke. Raff went pale. Kylen stood there calm as you like. He said there'd been a little accident when he was playing a game with the chair."

Jonno chortled. "Raff was furious. He headed straight for Kylen, but Kylen didn't back off at all. He picked up one of the broken legs and waited for him."

"Did they fight?" asked Keemun eagerly.

Jonno shook his head. "For once Raff showed a bit of common sense and left."

"Kylen picked up the bird very gently," said Bella. "He went outside and dug a hole, and then he buried it."

Feeling very awkward, Kylen dropped his gaze.

The incident had happened at least a year ago, but it was still fresh in his mind. He'd been filled with rage. After one glance at his expression, Raff decided not to take his chances. He'd been smart. Kylen was angry enough to have beaten the bully senseless if given the opportunity.

When he had finally calmed down, Kylen emerged from his

anger shocked to discover what he was capable of. He promised himself that day he would never again allow himself to be ruled by rage.

But he'd also learned an important lesson. Bullies enjoyed preying on people who lived in fear of them. If you weren't willing to live in fear, sooner or later you needed to stand up to them.

Raff's bullying hadn't stopped, but it had never seriously troubled him after that.

"The bird wasn't the only thing he rescued," Bella was saying.

"Not even close!" said Jonno with a grin. "Bella and I are two of his strays ourselves. We were doing it tough on the streets of Cambrick when he found us and took us in."

Embarrassed by the attention, Kylen quickly changed the subject.

"Whatever you did must have worked, Dalthinir," he said, picking up the dog. "She seems much more comfortable."

"Can she stay, Ma?" pleaded Keemun.

"Course she can!" Marta replied. "We'll need to give her a name. 'Queenie', I reckon! Ya don't have to be born in a palace t' be important."

Grudem didn't seem convinced. Approaching the puppy for a closer look, he was taken by surprise when the little creature shrank back fearfully.

"She seems to think she'll get a beating when a grown man approaches her," suggested Dalthinir.

"Poor li'l thing," muttered Grudem, holding out a finger for the puppy to lick.

The puppy appeared to have made another conquest. Kylen reluctantly acknowledged that Dalthinir was right. The dog would be better off with the family.

Heading outside, he wandered alone into the night, keeping near the house.

He thought about what the twins had said. He hadn't set out to rescue strays. It had just happened.

He'd never been one to make plans for his life—surviving from one day to the next had always provided enough of a challenge. He'd received help along the way, most notably from Olatiren, and doing what he could to help others gave him a practical way of expressing his gratitude.

Becoming a mage would surely expand his opportunities. It had certainly worked that way for Dalthinir. Kylen himself had benefited directly from his unselfishness, and it had been inspiring to hear Marta describe some of his acts of compassion.

It wasn't going to be easy though. It hadn't taken long to discover the hard edge of magic. For Kylen, acquiring magical power amounted to a death sentence. No matter how much he might do to improve the lot of the vulnerable, the Compact and the Crown would always want him dead.

It would be easy to be bitter, but he was determined not to allow their malevolence to change him. He would continue to rescue strays whenever he could. Thankfully, it was worth the trouble, because the strays he rescued had mostly thrived. That was another thing to be grateful for.

Then, with a pang of grief, he remembered Elspeth. She hadn't thrived, for all his efforts.

KYLEN TRIED TAKING Queenie on his next nighttime walk with Dalthinir. It was a disaster. They had barely left the house when a dog apparently smelled the pup. It immediately started barking frantically, soon joined by every dog in the neighborhood.

When they next went walking, Kylen asked Keemun to look after her. Having taken an eager interest in the pup, the boy agreed readily.

Free from distractions once more, Kylen raised a question that had been playing on his mind.

"You told me about farsense. Is that all there is to mage smell?"

"Mage smell has a number of different expressions. The most basic form is the ability to sense the use of magic. As you already know, every mage can do that, at least when it happens nearby. Detecting the use of magic at a distance depends on the power of a mage's farsense. The stronger the power, the further away they can sense it."

Kylen nodded. It made sense.

"Another expression of mage smell is sensing a magical aura," continued Dalthinir. "Magical aura is also known as magical glimmer. It's often shortened to just glimmer."

"Does that involve sensing the magical presence of a mage, even if they're not using power?"

"It does, and you've described it well. When someone with that ability is nearby, It's almost impossible for a mage to hide."

"You're able to detect magical auras, aren't you?"

"Yes, I am. Very few mages are capable of it. Of those who are, the strength of their magical power decides how far away they can do it. In that way it's similar to the most basic type of farsense."

"Does farsense allow you to detect anything other than magical power or magical glimmer?"

"Yes. Some mages have been able to sense the presence of non-magical creatures as well, especially humans. The most adept practitioners could also sense the mood and intent of a creature they detect. Whether the creature is hostile, for example. I don't know of anyone alive today who can do that though."

"As well as sensing magical auras, you're able to hide your own aura, aren't you? And you do it for me as well."

"Yes, that's true. It's the only reason I've been able to survive as a renegade. It isn't anything new though. Supposedly dragons were able to mask their glimmer."

"Can other mages do it?"

"I'm not aware of other mages who can. Apart from you, that is! You somehow managed it when you first collected the twins—before you even knew about such things. You were also able to recognize my aura when I had it shielded." He shook his head in bewilderment. "I didn't think that was possible."

"Doesn't it require power to mask power? Isn't the act of masking detectable?"

"That's a good question, Kylen. No. When I mask power I'm able to remove every trace of it."

Kylen's curiosity was by no means exhausted. "If you weren't hiding our magical auras, would the mages in Cambrick be able to sense our presence?"

"Most of them aren't strong enough to do it from that far away. Master Inga would go the closest, but even she probably can't detect glimmer from that distance."

"But you can detect them all, can't you? From here, I mean."

Dalthinir shook his head. "I'd need to get quite a lot closer to be able to do that."

Seeing the look on Kylen's face, his mentor asked sharply, "Are you telling me that you can?"

Kylen blushed sheepishly. "I'm sorry—I didn't realize it was unusual! I'm not practiced at any of this. I recognize your aura—I guess I should say I know what it smells like. And I'm aware of a large number of auras in the direction of Cambrick. I presume they're from other mages."

The mage seemed astonished and excited in equal measure.

"Can you tell them apart?"

He nodded. "I do recognize them as different 'smells'. But I don't know who any of the smells belong to, so it isn't very useful."

"Can you detect anyone who isn't in the city?"

Kylen paused for some magical sniffing. "Someone's been riding along the main road. They've stopped not far from here." He pointed.

Dalthinir had been doing some sniffing of his own. "I sense them as well," he reported. "But I don't recognize their smell, so it's someone I don't know." He paused. "I wonder why a mage might want to visit Camberton at night. Let's go and take a look."

"Isn't that dangerous?"

"Not if we stay out of sight. Especially since it's nighttime."

Pulling their hoods low over their faces, they hurried toward the main road. Neither of them had any way of knowing how long the mage intended to remain in Camberton, so they couldn't afford to delay.

Only a few minutes had passed when Dalthinir grabbed his arm.

"I'll go first," he whispered. "See if you can get a good look at them —so you can put a face to the smell."

With that he crept closer.

They found themselves approaching a blacksmith's smithy from the rear. Red light from the forge provided dim illumination. A man in a plain cloak was standing with his back to them. The blacksmith stood to one side.

Dalthinir turned briefly toward him, one eyebrow arched. Kylen guessed at his meaning. The man's cloak had no crimson edging. It had to mean he didn't want to be recognized as a mage.

The two men appeared to be arguing, although they were too far away to hear what was being said. Open ground lay ahead of them. If they moved any closer, they risked being seen.

Before either of them could do something foolish, the mage left the smithy. He didn't seem happy. Going to his horse, he mounted and rode back in the direction of the city.

Dalthinir jerked his head back the way they had come, and they set off in the direction of Grudem's dwelling.

"What do you think that was about?" Kylen asked as soon as they could speak freely again.

"I don't know. If I knew who he was I might be able to guess, but I didn't see his face. One thing I can be confident about, though. When a mage conceals his identity and travels under cover of darkness, he's up to no good."

CHAPTER 15

After a frustrating morning with the group tasked with tracking down the renegade, Master Inga escaped the bickering and emerged gratefully into the sunshine.

Her eye fell at once on the slight figure of her errand girl. Of late she seemed to hover nearby most mornings, and Inga had the feeling the coins she earned weren't her real reason for being there.

"Good morning, Jen," she called.

Inga had guessed from the beginning that Jen was not her real name, and the momentary hesitation before the girl responded further reinforced that view.

She brightened visibly when she saw the mage. "Good morning, Master Inga! What do you have for me to do today?"

She sighed. "What I need more than anything else is some sensible company for a while. Would you describe yourself as sensible, Jen?" She allowed a note of pleading to enter her voice.

"I'm renowned for being sensible! Most of the time, anyway." Her words were accompanied by the infectious grin that had so captivated Inga from the moment they met.

In addition to her exuberance, Jen was unusually buoyant by nature. Nevertheless, Inga, widely recognized as an astute judge of character, had also noted a sadness and vulnerability lurking beneath her carefree abandon.

"I'm sure the local baker has some fresh pastries. I was hoping you might sample them with me."

Jen swung in beside her enthusiastically. The two of them were soon engaged in an animated conversation that ranged from favorite foods to most embarrassing childhood memories.

Once they had acquired a small stack of pastries, they set off wandering in the sunshine.

"Do your parents live in Cambrick, Jen?"

"No. They died a couple of years ago. My brother and I came here hoping for a better life."

"Where do you live now?"

"With our aunt in Camberton."

The brightness in Jen's tone didn't fool Inga. "It's a big thing to lose your parents, whenever it happens. But especially so at your age." Their eyes met. "You miss your mother, don't you?" she asked gently.

The girl turned away, but not quickly enough to hide the tear welling in her eye.

"What was she like?"

"She was wonderful. Always cheerful, even when everything started going wrong."

Inga listened quietly, offering the girl her full attention.

"She used to say that her life had been a grand adventure, and that the biggest adventure of all was having my brother and me. I miss her so much."

This time the tears could not be held back, and she began to sob, her body heaving uncontrollably in her distress.

Putting her arms around her, Inga held her close.

Eventually the sobs came to an end, and she mastered herself.

She drew back from the older woman, glancing up at her in great embarrassment. "I'm sorry. I'm not usually like this. I've made a fool of myself."

"Grieving is never foolish," Inga assured her. "Those unwilling to grieve are the real fools."

She squeezed the girl's hand. "Your mother was clearly a remarkable woman, Jen. She must have been to produce someone like you."

Jen took in a shuddering breath. "I have to go. I've taken so much of your time. Thank you for the pastries!"

She turned away before impulsively running back and throwing her arms around Inga.

"Goodbye!" she called as she hurried away.

A wave of compassion washed over Inga. Resilient as Jen might be, beneath the surface she was a vulnerable girl who needed to be loved. She acknowledged the truth—the waif had wormed her way into her heart. Compelled by a motherly protectiveness she didn't fully understand, she quietly set off after her.

Someone had been waiting for Jen. Inga readily recognized him as Jen's brother, having briefly glimpsed him on an earlier occasion. She'd said his name was Rob.

He didn't look happy. Although she wasn't close enough to hear what they were saying, it was clear that they were arguing. It took her by surprise. Jen had said she was close to her brother, and Inga had the impression they almost never disagreed.

She kept her distance. Whatever the squabble was about, they needed to resolve it themselves. She had no business interfering.

In the end, Jen wandered slowly away, her head down, while Rob stormed off in a different direction.

On impulse, Inga followed Rob.

He knew his way around, and she was hard-pressed to keep him in sight. She was barely in time to catch a glimpse of him disappearing into the back of an abandoned building. Foreign as it felt to be sneaking around spying on someone, she crept in after him.

To her immense surprise, she found a meeting in progress. Several figures were huddled around a table. Her farsense told her that two of them were mages. She had no difficulty recognizing the magical auras of Lars and Petria. The dim candlelight showed her that three others were nobles. It took a moment, but she eventually recognized Lady Mardell among them. The sixth member of the circle was immediately recognizable. It was Prince Evran.

The meeting could only be described as furtive. What was its purpose?

Peering around in the darkness of the building, she spotted Rob's hiding place directly ahead of her. She was too far away to pick up the conversation, but he was close enough to hear what they were saying. Why would Jen's brother be spying on a group like this?

What were they saying? She began to edge closer, her heart pounding uncomfortably. At that crucial moment, her inexperience as a spy betrayed her. Stumbling on something underfoot, she blundered into a loose pile of building material, sending it crashing loudly to the ground.

The people around the table immediately leaped to their feet in alarm. Inga saw at once that anyone coming to investigate would quickly discover Rob. Feeling a strange need to protect him, she called out, "Is anyone in there?" Then she stepped forward into the open.

"Who is it?" demanded the harsh voice of Lars.

"Master Inga," she replied without hesitation.

As Lars stepped forward, candle in hand, Inga was relieved to catch a glimpse of Rob silently slipping deeper into the darkness.

"What are you doing here, Inga?" Lars asked, his challenge anything but welcoming.

"I thought I saw a light and came to investigate," she replied boldly. "What are all of you doing hiding away in here?"

Petria answered, her casual tone suggesting that nothing extraordinary was taking place. "There have been suggestions that a few youths have become entangled with Dalthinir. I have an informal network keeping an eye out for them, just in case. We meet occasionally to share information. I trust it's obvious why conversations of this nature need to be kept confidential."

"What youths?"

"Street rats. One is called Kylen, and also twins known as Jonno and Bella."

The fog suddenly cleared for Inga. "Well I'm sorry to have interrupted your meeting," she said.

"Think nothing of it," said Petria smoothly. "We were just about to leave anyway."

So saying, she headed out of the building, the others close behind her.

"Your Highness," said Inga with a bow as the prince reached her. She nodded to the others as they passed.

After following them out, she stood silently until all of them had gone. Then she reentered the building. "It's safe to come out now, Jonno," she called.

For some time there was no response, then he emerged.

"How long have you known who I am?" he asked, an irritated look on his face.

"It was Master Petria who gave it away," she replied. "The woman I was talking to. I guessed some time ago that Jen wasn't the real name of your sister. But I had no idea who the two of you might be."

She looked at him seriously. "I hope you know what you're doing spying on these people, Jonno. Master Lars, the one who first challenged me, and Master Petria are not people you want to cross. Prince Evran was here too. It should be obvious that he carries a great deal of authority. The other three were nobles. I know only one of them—Lady Mardell—but her husband is the most powerful official in the kingdom, and she isn't a person to trifle with."

He said nothing in response.

"Why were you spying on them?"

Still he remained silent.

She frowned. "Is it true you have a connection with Dalthinir? If so, you need to understand that it's a very dangerous association. Is that what you want for Bella?"

"What's Bella got to do with it?"

"I've come to care for her a lot. I hope you realize that she's hurting and vulnerable and needs support."

Jonno wasn't impressed. "If you care about her, then stop upsetting her!"

Inga frowned. "How am I upsetting her?"

"She doesn't need you reminding her to miss her mother," Jonno said resentfully. "Our mother's gone, and no one can bring her back. Bella was managing perfectly well until you came along!"

Inga sighed. "I'm sorry you feel that way." She paused. "I hope you'll heed my warning about getting involved with Dalthinir."

And with that she turned on her heel and left.

She headed back to her quarters with a great deal to think about. She couldn't regret her interactions with Bella, and Jonno's irritation with her approach had only reinforced her concerns.

But bigger questions had been raised. What was the purpose of the clandestine meeting? Petria's explanation did not satisfy her at all. The group included mages, nobles, and even royalty. Prince Evran had no real power, but he had symbolic authority at least. His involvement was surely important.

And why was Jonno spying on them? Were he and Bella truly involved with Dalthinir? And if so, what was Dalthinir's agenda?

Her questions were significant. And they needed to be answered.

THE SUN SET OVER CAMBERTON, bringing another day of toil to an end. For the first time, neither Jonno nor Bella had returned.

Kylen was concerned, but he had confidence in the ability of the twins to navigate their way out of trouble.

Dalthinir was a different matter. As the night wore on, his restlessness became unbearable—for Kylen as well as for him.

"They might need my help. I have to go to the city."

Kylen shook his head firmly. "I'm sure there's no real reason for concern. They were probably delayed. If you try to go there, the only thing you'll do is get caught! And how will you even get into the city? The gates are closed at sundown."

"That didn't stop you."

Seeing Kylen's blank look, he added, "You climbed over the wall."

"In daylight! No one could do it in the dark! It would be suicide!"

The mage began pacing again. "There has to be something that can be done!"

Kylen stood up purposefully. "Then I'll go." Having watched the twins disappear off to the city every day, he was more than ready to take his share of the risks.

"What, and climb the wall?" asked Dalthinir incredulously. "There isn't another way into the city at night!"

He promptly sat down again. "If that's the case, there's nothing any of us can do. We can only keep waiting and hoping."

It felt incongruous that Dalthinir was the one who needed a calming word and wise counsel. But no one could reasonably fault him. His mentor wasn't distressed on his own account. He was anxious solely about the safety of the twins, and Kylen could readily share in that concern.

In the end, Dalthinir accepted the inevitable and resigned himself to waiting until the morning. Kylen reconciled himself to a sleepless night in the room next to a caged bear.

Sleep proved elusive for Inga. The events of the afternoon swirled endlessly through her head.

What was going on? And how had Jen—Bella, she corrected herself—and her brother Jonno become involved? What had they entangled themselves in?

The more she pondered it, the more convinced she became that the meeting she surprised could only be viewed as highly suspicious. The three people most insistent about action against Dalthinir—Lars and Petria at the full gathering of the Compact, and Lady Mardell in her meeting with Adrastas and Inga—had all been present at the meeting.

Why was it so important to them to have Dalthinir permanently out of the way? And why now, after all this time?

She had asked a similar question of the chief master the day Lady Mardell marched away from their meeting after arrogantly parading her insulting demands. She was beginning to wonder if it had been a major miscalculation to allow the question to lapse.

To whom should she turn? The logical person was Adrastas, although she was certain he wouldn't take any of it seriously. Not without hard evidence to support her suspicions.

The night was well advanced by the time she finally reached a decision. She would seek out Adrastas in the morning. It would need to be handled delicately. No accusations. She would simply tell him what she had observed. At the very least it might help him make sense of whatever was going to happen in the future.

CHAPTER 16

To her surprise, when Inga approached Adrastas a couple of hours before noon the next morning, he agreed to meet her immediately.

"Master Inga." His greeting was surprisingly formal.

"Chief Master Adrastas. Thank you for agreeing to see me."

The look on his face made it clear he had something on his mind. He didn't keep her waiting to find out.

"Early this morning I found myself confronted with a number of serious accusations. Against you."

She stared at him, too astonished to speak.

"From no less a person than Prince Evran."

Her forehead twisted in a frown of bemusement. She couldn't begin to guess what might be coming next.

"His Highness expressed grave concern at your dereliction of duty. He made it clear that the most dangerous fugitive in the kingdom is currently at large, and that, as the mage with the most powerful farsense capability, you bear an unusual responsibility. He claims you've made no attempt to take that responsibility seriously. While Dalthinir roams freely somewhere in the kingdom, just yesterday you were observed wandering the streets of Cambrick, enjoying pastries with a street urchin!"

He glared at her. "We can't afford to antagonize the royal family. What progress *have* you made in your search? Is it accurate to say it isn't a priority to you?"

Her mouth opened, but nothing came out. The plain truth was she hadn't made it a priority. She'd put in no more than a token effort. What was the point? To begin with, she'd never been convinced Dalthinir meant any harm. Beyond that, he was incredibly skilled at hiding his glimmer. He simply didn't leave a trail to follow.

"There's worse!" he told her. "It's well known you were sympathetic to him in the past. Prince Evran accused you of collaborating with him. These are serious charges, Inga!"

She found her voice at last. "It's all complete nonsense! What evidence did he present?"

"The girl you were sharing pastries with is strongly suspected of being an associate of Dalthinir."

"They've been snooping on me?!"

"According to him, a small group has been meeting to share information, and you've been snooping on them! What possible motive could you have for doing that?"

"I haven't been snooping on them! Last night I stumbled by accident upon a small group meeting in an abandoned building. I came here to make you aware of it. The meeting consisted of Lars, Petria, Lady Mardell, the prince, and a couple of other nobles I don't know. It's the only time I've seen them together. As for his 'evidence', I was seen with a girl 'suspected' of being an associate of Dalthinir? Is that the best they can do?"

She had indeed been spending time with the very girl they were looking for. But she had no intention of confirming it.

It seemed unlikely they knew Bella and Jen were the same person. Or that the girl they sought had been wandering freely about Cambrick running errands for a senior mage. The twins would have been pounced on long ago if their true identity had been known. She shuddered to think what might have happened if they'd discovered Jonno listening to the conversation during their secret meeting.

All that aside, these people themselves had questions to answer.

"If they have suspicions about possible associates, why haven't they passed those suspicions on to the authorities so others can confirm and take advantage of them? And if they know so much about who Dalthinir associates with, why haven't they found him themselves? You know as well as I do that he's a master at hiding himself. I've searched day and night and still come up with nothing. He doesn't leave a trail to follow!"

Planting her hands on her hips, she glared at him. "Do *you* believe these accusations he's spouting about me, Adrastas?"

He shuffled uncomfortably but didn't reply.

"DO you? I demand to know!"

Finally he sighed. "Of course not. But the prince has placed me in a difficult position. I can't be seen to be ignoring the crown."

"Then speak to King Durvaryn. Find out if the prince *is* acting on behalf of the crown, or only on behalf of himself."

When Adrastas hesitated, she added, "If you don't do it, I will!"

He waved his arms placatingly. "Calm down, Inga!"

"I will not calm down! I've been accused first of negligence, then of treason! You said it yourself—these are serious charges! I won't rest until my name has been cleared!"

"Leave it with me." Adrastas was visibly wincing. "Your suggestion about speaking to the king is a good one. I'll apply for an audience at once."

Inga's eyes narrowed. "This isn't just about me. I want to know what this little group is up to, holding secret meetings in an abandoned building, passing around 'evidence' they've failed to share with anyone else, and making wild accusations about the first person to uncover their little secret. It sounds a lot like they correctly guessed I would report what I saw, so they got in first. Throw enough mud around and you can divert attention away from yourself."

She glared at him. "What is the agenda of these people? Have you asked yourself that?"

She left without waiting for an answer.

It was Adrastas's turn to be surprised when his request for an audience with the king was granted immediately.

"Chief Master Adrastas, you are welcome."

"Thank you, Your Majesty."

"What's this I hear about Master Inga? My brother met with me earlier this morning to voice some serious concerns about her recent behavior."

Adrastas was stunned. The prince had been very busy that morning.

"He met with me as well, Your Majesty. In fact my reason for meeting with you was to find out if you shared his concerns."

"I do. It isn't acceptable for mages to spy on members of the royal family."

"I'm not convinced that Master Inga was doing that, Your Majesty."

"Neither am I, Chief Master. I'm sure your inquiry will confirm that, and life will be able to continue as normal."

"Inquiry? What are you suggesting?"

The king sighed. "Justice must be seen to be done, Adrastas. It's a price all of us must pay for the effective rule of law."

No doubt seeing the alarm on Adrastas's face, the king added, "I'd be happy to arrest her if that would make it easier for you."

The head mage bristled. "I'm sure you are well aware, Your Majesty, that mages have always been tried and sentenced by the Compact. That agreement might long pre-date both of us, but it is a key pillar in the institutions of Periton."

"Of course! I did not intend to suggest that a body other than the Compact would try or sentence her. I was merely offering to have her brought in. I thought to spare you the need for direct involvement in that part of the process."

Adrastas bowed stiffly. "I thank you for your consideration, Your Majesty. I can assure you that the Compact is well able to handle such matters where the need arises." He frowned. "I hope you will pardon my confusion, but if I were to have Master Inga arrested, what would be the charges?"

"I am happy to leave that to you, Chief Master. If my brother has met with you, I'm sure you are well aware of his views."

"I am. If I may speak plainly, he made a number of accusations without presenting substantial evidence of any kind. He made no mention of an arrest, and even if he had it would never have occurred to me to arrest a mage of the standing of Master Inga on such flimsy grounds. With respect, Your Majesty, it is you alone who is calling for an arrest."

The king winced. "Both of us find ourselves in a difficult position, Adrastas. My brother was not sparing with his accusations. He accused me of going soft on Dalthinir, among other things." He raised his arms helplessly. "The Crown is a core institution of Periton. We present a united front, fragile though it might be on occasion. It would not benefit the kingdom for cracks to emerge at a time like this."

It would have been inappropriate to scowl, but Adrastas desperately wanted to do it. The king was essentially saying he was unwilling to deal with his brother, and that he expected the chief master to arrest one of his mages on trumped-up charges to keep the man satisfied.

He bowed. "Your Majesty. I will endeavor to find an appropriate way forward."

As he returned to his private rooms, he pondered the situation carefully. He couldn't see a way to ignore the king's request, unpalatable as it might be. But clearly he was free to choose the charges.

He arrived to find Masters Lars and Petria waiting for him.

"Well?" he asked curtly. "What do you two want?"

"We were wondering if Prince Evran has met with you," Petria began.

Adrastas crossed his arms and glared at them. "Is it true that Master Inga was snooping on the two of you and your meeting?"

"Yes, she was," Lars confirmed brusquely. "And she deserves to be reprimanded for doing so."

"Well in that case you'll be pleased to know that His Majesty has called for her arrest."

Both of them looked shocked. They apparently hadn't expected such a strong response.

"Who will try the case?" asked Lars.

Adrastas eyed him disdainfully. "The Compact, of course. A group of mages is the only body that can pass judgment on one of our own."

Petria was horrified. She obviously understood the implications of the matter becoming public. "I am distressed that it has come to that. I cannot see that Master Inga's actions warrant her arrest. I would like to volunteer to serve on the investigative panel. It's true that the prince was angry, but I am eager to ensure that her case is judged fairly."

"Neither one of you is eligible."

Petria's brows drew together. "Why not?"

"Lars made it clear that her actions negatively affected those attending the meeting. As aggrieved parties, it would be a conflict of interest for either you to take any part in the inquiry, except as witnesses."

It took considerable effort for Adrastas to contain the smug smile that threatened to cover his face. His question about Inga snooping on them had been a carefully laid trap, however casual it might have seemed. Lars had jumped in, feet and all.

From the look on Petria's face, Lars would soon be benefiting from a few of her insights. But it was too late for recriminations now.

He adopted a bored expression. "Now if you two will excuse me, I have an arrest to make."

"Can I ask what the charges are?" asked Petria.

"You can. But you needn't expect an answer." They could find out about the charges at the same time as everyone else.

Their little group had pulled some fast maneuvers since being exposed by Inga the previous evening. It was now abundantly clear to him that they were up to no good and needed to be monitored covertly. He would get onto it as soon as Inga was dealt with.

Calling for an aide, he told him to locate Master Inga and return with her immediately.

The two of them returned within the hour.

After dismissing the aide, he addressed Inga. "I met with the king, but the prince got there first. This situation has now become highly political. I regret to say I have no choice but to arrest you."

Ignoring her wide-eyed disbelief, he pressed on. "I don't doubt that the goal of Prince Evran and his little band was to send a clear message that anyone who dares to interfere with them will pay a heavy price.

Even if the interference was trivial and unintended. They want to keep themselves and their dealings out of the light."

"What are the charges?" she managed.

"Failing to promptly report an unauthorized meeting involving representatives of the Compact, the nobility, and the Crown."

A moment of stunned silence was quickly followed by a peal of delighted laughter. "Adrastas, you are a genius! Every mage is taught about the laws prohibiting unsanctioned consultations between institutions, but I have to confess I'd completely forgotten about them."

He permitted himself a grin—he'd earned it. "We'll see how well that satisfies their desire to avoid exposure."

CHAPTER 17

The daylight was almost spent by the time Bella and Jonno returned to Grudem's residence. They had been gone for almost thirty-six hours.

Kylen was downstairs with Marta and Keemun when they arrived, Queenie resting contentedly in his lap. He had long since left Dalthinir to his relentless pacing, unable to bear his agitation any longer.

By then the mage had convinced himself the twins had been discovered, taken into custody, and almost certainly tortured. He had wasted several hours hatching and discarding a range of schemes to locate and release them.

None of the schemes impressed Kylen at all. At one point he had asked, "If these are examples of the ideas you dream up, how have you managed to stay out of trouble for so long?"

The mage had looked at him seriously before replying. "Before now it's only been my life at risk. I can't bear the thought that I sent the twins to their deaths. The very idea confounds me. I feel like my brain isn't working properly anymore."

Everything changed the instant the twins returned. If his relief seemed somewhat pathetic, he did at least quickly return to normal. That was worth celebrating.

After making sure nothing dire had happened to the twins, the mage called the four of them together in his room.

"You have news," he said. "I can tell! I want to know everything that happened. Especially why it took this long to get back to Camberton."

"That last one's easy," Jonno told them. "It was dark by the time I finished what I was doing yesterday. The city gates were already closed by then. So I found somewhere to sleep."

All eyes turned to Bella. "I waited for him," she said simply. She seemed more muted than usual, although Kylen couldn't quite put his finger on what had changed.

"You're right about there being news," Jonno said. "I found out that Lars and the others had been meeting in an abandoned building, so I went there last night. All of them showed up. I even know the names of most of them now."

"How?" asked the mage.

"Thanks to Master Inga."

Seeing the shocked look on Dalthinir's face, he pressed on. "She followed me in there."

"She followed you?!"

Jonno shrugged. "I have no idea why. But she isn't good at this kind of thing. She tripped on something, and it gave her away. She almost got me caught! She distracted them by talking her way out of it. After they left, she told me their names. They were Master Lars, Master Petria, Lady Mardell, Prince Evran, and two other noblemen she didn't know."

Dalthinir punched his hand in excitement. "I knew it! The prince is in on this. And Lady Mardell too. You've done excellent work! What else did Master Inga say?"

He waved an arm vaguely. "She mostly warned me about the risks of what I was doing."

Kylen knew him well enough to realize he was holding something back, but he decided to bide his time rather than pursue it.

"Were you seen talking with her?"

He shook his head emphatically.

"Why didn't you come back as soon as the gates opened?"

"I was curious. I wanted to see what would happen once the secret meeting wasn't quite so secret anymore."

"What did happen?"

"It all got very interesting, as you would say. People were talking about nothing else. Palace gossip says that the prince pressured the king to move against Inga."

"That's no great surprise," said the mage bitterly. "He would have wanted to warn off anyone stupid enough to inquire into his doings. What happened?"

"The head mage visited the king. The king wanted him to arrest Inga. The mage wasn't happy about it, but he wasn't given a choice."

"*Arrest* her? Why!"

"To keep the prince happy, apparently."

"And he actually did that?"

"He did. But it didn't quite work out like the prince and Lars and the others expected."

"Why not? What were the charges?"

"It was something like she didn't report a meeting that involved more than just mages. I have no idea why that should be a problem."

The mage laughed heartily. "That's brilliant!" he chortled. "I take back everything I've ever said about Adrastas!" He shook his head in amazement. "I can explain. There's an old ordinance that prevents representatives of different institutions from meeting without getting approval first. It was intended to stop secret deals between nobles and mages, or mages and the crown."

"And this meeting involved mages, nobles, and a member of the royal family," said Kylen.

"Exactly!" the mage replied. "The beauty of Adrastas's charges is that the inquiry will bring this secretive group right into the open. In the name of prosecuting Inga, he'll shine a light on what they've been doing. They'll lie, of course, but they won't find it quite so easy to meet secretly in the future."

He looked at Jonno, trying not to be too eager. "Did you hear anything at all of what they were talking about during the meeting?"

Jonno nodded. "It didn't make much sense to me. But there was talk of a book. It had something to do with dragons. They're pretty desperate to find it."

Dalthinir sucked in a sharp breath. "What book?"

"They only mentioned it once. I don't remember the name."

"*Ode to the Fallen One*?"

"That was it!"

The mage had gone pale. "So it's true. They really are fool enough to do it."

"Apparently if a mage opens it, they get a whole lot of new powers."

"And the kingdom is destroyed in the process!" said Dalthinir fiercely. Kylen had never seen him so grim.

"Lars brushed it off when one of them brought that up. He claimed no such thing would happen."

"And he would know, of course," said Dalthinir sarcastically.

Everything went quiet for a time.

The mage broke the silence. "What did the prince have to say?"

"Not a lot. He was mostly demanding they hurry up the process."

"And the nobles?"

"Lady Mardell did the most talking. She said she's done everything asked of her, and she wanted to know when she'd get what was promised. She didn't say what it was."

The mage covered his face with his hands. "It's every bit as bad as I feared," he said despairingly. "These fools aren't just playing with fire. They're playing with active volcanoes! I can't believe they're actually planning to do it. Unless someone stops them, they'll destroy us all."

"Why do they need you out of the way?" asked Kylen.

Dalthinir shrugged. "Because I'll do everything in my power to stop them, and they know it."

Kylen looked at him expectantly. "What are we going to do?"

"I need to think about that. In the meantime, everyone should get some food. Jonno and Bella, there's no reason for you to go to the city now, so there's no need for you to get up early tomorrow."

Neither of the twins argued. Jonno got up immediately and went downstairs.

Something about the interaction troubled Kylen. Jonno had done almost all of the talking. Normally the twins interspersed conversation almost as if they were a single person. Getting up quickly, he sidled alongside Bella as she was heading for the stairs.

"Are you all right?" he asked.

She didn't reply. But the glance she shot in his direction left him in shock. He hadn't seen such desolation in her face, not even in their darkest times on the streets of Cambrick. Something had happened. Something significant. Jonno appeared barely affected, but Bella was devastated.

Dalthinir didn't know the twins well enough. He would have no idea there was any kind of problem.

Kylen knew he wasn't good at raising this kind of issue. But nothing would happen if he didn't at least try.

He waited until he found himself alone with Jonno in the little kitchen. "What happened?" he asked.

"What I said," Jonno replied through a mouthful.

He shook his head stubbornly. "That isn't what I meant. What happened between the two of you?"

A brief shadow passed over Jonno's face, but he said nothing.

"You've always supported each other, no matter what you've had to face. Whatever happened in there, you can't let it come between you!"

With no response forthcoming, Kylen threw up his hands helplessly and headed upstairs.

Jonno had nothing to say when he settled for the night beside Kylen. Bella had already disappeared into her own room. He was sure neither of them had spoken since he last saw them.

It wasn't encouraging, but tomorrow would be a new day.

JONNO WAS STILL SLEEPING when Kylen got up. Heading downstairs, he found Dalthinir biting into some freshly baked bread.

"Have you seen Bella?" he asked.

The mage shook his head distractedly. He appeared absorbed in his own thoughts.

A full hour passed before Jonno emerged, yawning. When Bella still didn't appear, it occurred to Kylen to check her room. He found the door slightly ajar and the room empty. There was no sign of her.

Beginning to feel alarmed, he hurried downstairs. "Has anyone seen Bella?"

Both Jonno and Dalthinir looked at him blankly for a moment. Then they got up to look for themselves.

A brief search quickly reinforced the uncomfortable truth. Bella was gone.

ALTHOUGH SHE WAS TECHNICALLY under arrest, Inga had not been required to spend the night in a secure facility. Given the nature of the charges and her impeccable reputation, she was allowed to return to her quarters until the commencement of the trial. The guard posted outside her door provided the sole reminder of her current status.

The trial got underway early the following morning. The chief master had appointed Master Kothlar as head of a panel of five mages who would conduct the inquiry. Compact members filed in until the meeting place was almost bursting, and a keen sense of anticipation filled the room.

Master Inga sat at the front, facing the panel presiding over the trial. Glancing around, she spotted Masters Lars and Petria sitting among the observers. Both of them were looking relaxed. Inga could only conclude they were not yet aware of the charges.

Master Kothlar climbed imposingly to his feet. "Order!" he called. As soon as the low hum of voices died away, he referred to a document before him.

"Master Inga, you are charged with failing to promptly report an unauthorized meeting involving representatives of the Compact, the nobility, and the Crown."

A loud murmur broke out across the room, quickly silenced by another call to order from Master Kothlar.

"Do you accept or deny the charge?" he asked.

She got to her feet. "I deny the charge," she called firmly.

This time Kothlar waited for the murmuring to die down.

Chief Master Adrastas was called as the first witness.

"I first became aware of this meeting the following morning when Prince Evran called on me. Among other things he complained about Master Inga snooping on the meeting, as he put it."

"Did he say who was present at this meeting?"

"He did. He named Masters Lars and Petria, Lady Mardell, and Lords Marklo and Rostem as well as himself."

This time Master Kothlar was forced to call twice for order before the hubbub in the room died down.

He turned to Petria.

"Do you deny this, Master Petria?" he asked.

Petria shook her head numbly.

"Master Lars?"

He shook his head as well.

Inga smiled to herself. The look on their faces went a long way toward compensating her for the indignity of her arrest.

Master Kothlar addressed the chief master once more. "Did the prince explain the purpose of the meeting?"

"He *claimed* it was intended to share information relevant to the search for the renegade mage."

Loud exclamations greeted this statement, along with a couple of mocking guffaws. Master Kothlar wisely decided to wait it out, contenting himself with pointed glares in the direction of the worst offenders. Eventually the din subsided.

The none-too-subtle emphasis Adrastas had placed on the word 'claimed' made it abundantly clear what he thought of the prince's explanation. A small grin had twisted Inga's lip, and she made no attempt to hide it.

"Did Master Inga report this meeting to you at any point, Chief Master?"

"She did. She reported it later the following morning, although not until after Prince Evran had left."

Master Kothlar was frowning in bafflement. "If she reported the meeting to you, why has she been charged?"

"The charge states that the matter was not reported promptly."

"Promptly?!"

"The meeting was a serious breach of a long-standing statute of the law of the kingdom. I believe I have the right to expect an immediate report in a matter of this nature."

Kothlar then called Inga to answer questions.

"Has Chief Master Adrastas accurately described the sequence of events?"

"He has."

"Yet you denied the charge. Why?"

"While I acknowledge I did not report the meeting immediately, I believe I did report it promptly."

"Do you have anything further you wish to say in your own defense?"

"No."

Kothlar addressed the other members of the panel. "Do any of you wish to call other witnesses, or further question the chief master or Master Inga?"

All of them shook their heads.

"In that case, the panel will retire to make a deliberation."

Loud conversation broke out across the room as the five members departed. They were gone for no more than ten minutes, and the din did not abate until they returned.

"Master Inga will rise," ordered Master Kothlar.

As soon as she had done so, he continued. "The panel has determined that the charge against you centers entirely around an interpretation of the word 'promptly'. Panel members hold a view not dissimilar to your own. While you failed to report the unsanctioned meeting immediately, your action could nevertheless reasonably be described as prompt. The panel therefore finds in your favor. You are free to go."

A cacophony threatened, and he raised a hand imperiously. "Silence!" he demanded loudly.

With order again restored, he added, "I have two statements to make on behalf of the panel of inquiry. First, notwithstanding the verdict, we trust that this incident will serve to remind us all of our shared responsibility to rigorously observe the law in all its detail. Second, while this body bears no responsibility for the conduct of representatives of the nobility or the Crown, the unauthorized meeting did involve two members of the Compact. We accordingly recommend that charges be laid against Masters Lars and Petria. Thank you for your attention. I hereby pronounce these proceedings closed."

With the final removal of official restraint, a deafening roar engulfed the room. Taking her chance, Inga hurried from the building. A sea of smiling faces greeted her, calling out congratulations as she passed. Responding with a cheery smile and a wave, she slipped away in search of somewhere quiet.

Her feet led her toward a small park not far from the building where the trial had been held. Finding a peaceful corner, she sat down, finally allowing herself to heave a sigh of relief.

Inga could only be in awe of the brilliant strategy employed by the chief master. The proceedings had borne all the hallmarks of a serious legal inquiry. Yet although she was the one called to account, in practice her involvement had been little more than incidental. The wording of the charges, the appointment of the no-nonsense Master Kothlar to preside over the inquiry, the chief master's own testimony—all of it had ensured that the focus was unerringly directed where it had always belonged.

The trial itself might reasonably be described as a farce. It had nevertheless achieved its intended purpose magnificently.

The crunch of leaves interrupted her thoughts. Someone was approaching. Company was the last thing she needed at that moment. Turning to firmly but politely rebuff the intruder, her eyes went wide with surprise.

"Bella!" she exclaimed in astonishment, climbing immediately to her feet.

She pulled the girl into a worried embrace. "What are you doing here? Cambrick isn't safe for you!"

CHAPTER 18

"Where has she gone?" Kylen asked Jonno. Having witnessed the uncharacteristic distance between the twins the previous evening, he felt sure Jonno could make a reasonable guess at what she was doing.

"She's gone to see that interfering mage," he replied bitterly.

"Who are you talking about?" asked Dalthinir.

"Your dearest friend," he snapped. "Master Inga."

"I think it's time you told us what's going on," said the mage calmly.

For a moment Kylen wondered if Jonno was going to respond at all, but then it all burst out.

"It started when Bella ran an errand for her. Next thing they're going on walks and talking about girl things. Two days ago she had Bella crying about losing our mother."

Dalthinir nodded. "I'm not surprised. Inga has that effect on people. If it helps, I don't doubt that she truly cares about Bella."

"I don't care why she's doing it! That isn't the issue. We promised we'd talk only to each other about what happened to our parents. No one else has a right to know! It isn't the business of some mage she's only known for a few days."

He shifted restlessly. "We had a big argument about it. Then I went off on my own to eavesdrop on the prince and his little group. After the others left, I had it out with Inga. I told her to stop upsetting Bella."

"What did she say?"

"She just warned me about the risks of associating with you."

The mage looked puzzled. "Why would she think you have anything to do with me?"

"The prince's group somehow figured out that Kylen, Bella, and I are connected with you. They told her they're trying to find us in the hope it will lead them to you. We've been calling ourselves Rob and Jen instead of our real names. But after Inga heard what they said she figured out who we really are. She doesn't know for certain that we're connected with you, but she suspects it."

This latest information filled Dalthinir with alarm. "So you're saying that these people are actually looking for all three of you? And that Inga at least knows your real identity?"

Kylen braced himself for a new bout of agonizing from the mage, but it didn't happen.

"I've been sending the two of you off to do my job instead of doing it myself. Now Bella's in serious trouble because of it. I'm going to Cambrick."

"You can't do that," protested Kylen.

"I can and I will. I won't allow anyone else to put themselves in danger for my sake. I'm finished. You need to wait here until I get back."

Something settled firmly in Kylen. It had never sat comfortably with him to play it safe while the twins took the risks. He was done with it. "I'm coming too."

"No, you're not."

"You've forgotten I was the one who went in and got the twins out in the first place. Bury me in the earth if you think it will stop me. I'll find a way out."

The mage laughed. "Very well. In that case I'll put you to good use while we're there."

He turned to Jonno. "You can wait for us here."

"Forget it," said Jonno simply.

Dalthinir shrugged. "It seems that all of us will be going. Jonno, why do you think Bella wants to see Inga?"

"Maybe she thinks she's found someone to replace our mother," Jonno said coldly.

The mage chose to ignore his tone. "Whatever the reason, we clearly need to look for Inga. If we find her, sooner or later we'll find Bella."

GETTING into Cambrick proved less difficult than they might have expected. Neither Kylen nor Dalthinir detected mages anywhere near the gates.

Once inside, they soon found out the reason. All gossip centered on the mage trial taking place that very morning. All of the mages had undoubtedly gathered for the spectacle.

If Dalthinir had concerns for his friend Master Inga, he showed no sign of it. Guessing exactly where the trial would be held, he led Kylen and Jonno there directly. He stopped as soon as they were in sight of the Auditorium used by the Compact.

"We need to find somewhere we can observe people coming and going without being seen ourselves," he said.

Both Kylen and Jonno immediately looked up and began scanning the surrounding buildings.

"There," said Kylen, pointing.

The two of them scrambled up onto a nearby roof, waving the mage up behind them. Following them proved less than straightforward for him. In the end, Kylen was forced to climb down and help him up.

Once they were on the roof, Kylen led them to first one then another adjoining roof. Before long they were positioned inconspicuously in a location that gave them a perfect view of the access points to the building.

The mage turned to Jonno. "Your task is to closely watch Inga. When Bella appears, you'll be responsible for finding a way to get her safely out of Cambrick."

With that settled, he whispered to Kylen, "This is an unusual opportunity. You can identify magical auras at a greater distance than anyone else, but you don't know who they belong to. Every mage in Cambrick will be here for the trial. I'll point out key individuals so you can associate them with the scent of their glimmer."

Kylen nodded.

"Something just occurred to me," the mage added. "When you try to use power, where do you picture it coming from?"

After a puzzled silence, Kylen said, "From my head I suppose—I am thinking about it."

Dalthinir punched his palm. "That's why your access to power is unreliable when you're consciously trying to use it! Power comes from your gut! You instinctively draw it from there when you're not trying. You need to consciously draw it from there as well."

Kylen nodded slowly.

There wasn't opportunity to explore it further. People began pouring out of the auditorium building almost immediately.

Dalthinir pointed as a woman emerged. "Inga!" he said. "The trial must be over. And she's been freed!" He sounded relieved.

Jonno didn't need to be prompted. He was already hurrying across the rooftops to keep her in sight.

Many of the mages who emerged were ignored by Dalthinir. "I don't know all of them," he explained quietly. "Some of them only joined the Compact after I left." But he soon pointed urgently to a pair of mages hurrying away from the building. "Lars and Petria! Make sure you take special note of the auras of those two."

"Adrastas, Kothlar, Emmela," he said, along with a handful of others he thought worth noting.

The flow of people soon diminished.

"We need to find Jonno and Bella and go," Dalthinir whispered. "Sooner or later there'll be mages on the gates again. We'll be taking a big risk if we're still in Cambrick when that happens."

Jonno lost sight of Master Inga when she retreated to the little park set back from the restless bustle of the streets of Cambrick. Creeping around in search of a different vantage point, he eventually spotted her. Sitting peacefully on her own, she didn't appear to be waiting for anyone. Being absorbed in her own thoughts was hardly surprising if she'd just been on trial.

Then Bella appeared.

He was close enough to hear Inga's immediate response. "What are you doing here? Cambrick isn't safe for you!"

Dalthinir had convinced himself that Inga truly cared about Bella. Maybe he was right. But it made no difference to Jonno. Whatever the mage's attitude, she was putting all of them in danger, Bella especially.

Now it came to the point, Jonno began to doubt himself. What if Bella refused to go with him? He had very little experience of navigating major disagreements with her. He knew she was upset with him and feeling hurt. What would he do if she insisted on staying with Inga, risk or no risk?

He decided to wait a few more minutes before making a move.

"I was worried about you!" Bella was saying. "When I found out they were putting you on trial, I felt like I was to blame."

"You mustn't blame yourself! There is a lot more going on here than either of us know. It goes well beyond the hunt for Dalthinir. But even so, you're still in danger. You won't be safe until you get far away from Cambrick! That's true for Jonno as well."

"But I won't see you again!" Tears had come to Bella's eyes.

Inga embraced her again. "I won't see you either. And I'm going to miss you! I mean it."

She pulled back from Bella and took her by the shoulders. "I want you to go because I care about you. I don't want them to get hold of you."

Jonno decided his moment had arrived. Moving out of his hiding place, he hurried over to them.

"She's right, Bella! We need to go. Now!"

He looked at Inga, although he couldn't meet her eye. "I'm sorry you got into trouble. It was more my fault than Bella's."

"It doesn't matter," she replied. "They've cleared me of the charges. The two mages at that meeting are the ones in trouble now." She eyed him intently. "Did you hear what they were talking about?"

He hesitated for a moment. Then he remembered she'd protected him from being exposed. He couldn't think of a good reason to hide what he'd discovered.

"They're looking for a book that somehow involves dragons. It's called *Ode to the Fallen One*."

She sucked in a sharp breath. "Are you certain?"

He nodded.

"This is worse than I could have believed possible! They must be stopped! But how?"

"Someone *is* going to stop them," he assured her. "But every one of us is at risk until we get Bella safely away from here."

The hint was not lost on Inga. She gazed at Bella with shining eyes. "Tell him...I've never doubted him," she breathed. "I don't doubt him now either."

"Tell who?" called a loud voice.

Two figures swung into view and strode quickly toward them. Jonno recognized them at once.

"Ah, you must be Jonno," said Lars. "It's nice to meet you at last. I didn't quite catch everything you were saying, but I'll look forward to hearing every detail once we have you in custody."

Lunging forward, he grabbed Jonno by the arm. Jonno twisted and turned, but the mage was too strong.

"Leave him alone!" protested Bella.

"Or what?" retorted Petria, grasping her arm firmly.

Inga grabbed Bella's other arm, and the two of them wrestled back and forth with her between them.

"You might as well let her go, Inga. You can't win," sneered Lars. "You'll never talk your way out of this."

KYLEN AND DALTHINIR located Jonno and Bella at the same moment Lars and Petria arrived. They hung back out of sight as the two mages moved to take control of the situation. It was immediately obvious that Inga would not be able to protect the twins on her own.

"I can't rescue them," whispered the mage. "My magic will be limited if I have to mask it as well as using it. It's up to you. Do whatever you need to, but be sparing with power. As long as you keep the power down, I'll be able to mask it. There'll be no sign that magic has been used."

"But what should I do?!"

"Start by keeping them quiet! There'll be a crowd here in an instant if they start yelling."

Recalling what Dalthinir had done with the brigands, Kylen imagined an invisible sack around each of them. For the first time, he consciously drew his magical power from his gut. It was almost effortless and it used very little power.

Astonishment showed on the faces of both mages as they discovered they'd been silenced.

Encouraged by his success, Kylen built a solid barrier around each sack. In spite of increasingly frantic struggles, neither of them were able to do more than twitch.

Jonno and Bella quickly pulled free.

Inga looked on in astonishment. "How?" she asked quietly. "No one is using any power."

"We need to go!" said Jonno.

"Yes, go! Both of you!" Inga replied. After a last hug, she pushed Bella after her brother.

"Once everyone is well clear, you need to release those idiots," Dalthinir whispered to Kylen. "After that, don't waste a minute catching up with us."

Kylen nodded his understanding, and Dalthinir set off to join the twins.

Reaching out with his farsense, Kylen saw that Dalthinir was heading for the gates as expected. To his surprise he also detected the presence of another mage nearby. The scent of the other mage was known to him now—it was Chief Master Adrastas. And he was heading directly for the park.

The moment he appeared, Kylen released Petria and Lars.

Adrastas arrived to see the two newly freed mages writhing about and shouting incoherently.

Seeing the chief master, Lars seemed to come to his senses.

"We just caught her with two known associates of Dalthinir," he sputtered, jabbing a finger at Inga. "They were discussing the renegade! She can't be allowed to get away with it this time!"

"Where are these people?" asked Adrastas reasonably. "I don't see anyone. Are they invisible?"

"They got away," howled Lars. "But only because she silenced and incapacitated us! That's illegal! Arrest her!"

"She silenced and incapacitated you? Magically?"

"Yes!" they both insisted.

"Congratulations!" Adrastas said dryly, addressing himself to Inga. "You must show me how you managed it. I've wanted to do it on more than one occasion."

He turned back to Lars and Petria. They looked entirely wild.

A scowl came to his face. "You claim to have been magically silenced and incapacitated. Then why can't anyone smell it? Every mage in Cambrick will confirm that no magic has been used. How do you explain that? You also claim that Inga was consorting with two associates of the renegade mage, yet they're nowhere to be seen."

He glared at them disdainfully. "I've had more than enough of your ranting and raving! Both of you are now facing charges as a result of your little secret meeting. I'm beginning to think I was overly generous, letting you roam freely while the inquiry is being set up. If I hear another word of accusation against Inga—from either of you—you'll be facing a new round of charges. And they'll be charges you won't wriggle out of! You can expect to be out of circulation for a very long time."

They looked at him sullenly.

"DO YOU UNDERSTAND?" he bellowed.

After poisonous glances at Inga, they nodded. Then they slunk away.

Adrastas rolled his eyes.

He turned to Inga. "I came looking for you, Inga. I wanted to apologize for what I just put you through. I don't believe your reputation has been damaged, but I'm only too aware of my own need to convince myself of that."

She laughed heartily. "There is no need for apologies, Adrastas.

That trial was the best entertainment I've witnessed in a very long time. Before those two arrived, I was sitting here reflecting on the brilliance of your strategy." Her face turned serious. "They need to be watched."

He nodded. "I've already arranged it. Keep that to yourself, of course. As of this afternoon, they will be followed day and night. Among other things, that means they won't get away with another intrusion like the one you were just forced to endure."

"Thank you!" she said with feeling. She looked like she wanted to say something more, but to Kylen's relief she remained silent. What could she say anyway? The slightest word about Jonno and Bella would only lend credibility to the claims of Lars and Petria.

He'd seen enough. Setting off after the others, he barely caught up with them before they reached the gates of Cambrick.

Passing through without incident, the four of them set off for Camberton.

For Kylen, the day had been incredibly satisfying. They had achieved everything they set out to do in the city without being caught, thanks to Dalthinir's tip he had been able to call upon his magic reliably, and all four of them were heading home safely together.

They had even taken Lars and Petria down a notch or two. It had been a day worth celebrating.

CHAPTER 19

Two days had passed since Master Inga's trial in Cambrick. Dalthinir had seen no sign that they were being actively hunted, and Kylen had been able to confirm that both Lars and Petria were still in the city. They were probably safe enough in Camberton for the moment.

Yet he felt restless for reasons he couldn't articulate.

That night he tossed and turned for several hours after lying down. It must have been the early hours of the morning before sleep finally took him. When he slept, he dreamed.

The experience was so vivid it could have been real, yet his profound sense of calm detachment told him it was a dream.

Soaring high above Cambrick, he caught sight of the sleeping city below. Then the capital slid away as he sailed over the cliffs beside it. He was heading north, gliding silently beneath a night sky breathtaking in its brilliance.

There was no need to look down for him to know he was riding on the back of a golden dragon. Its wings beat steadily around him, driving them forward.

When the sun rose to drive away the darkness, he was not surprised to see mountains taking shape ahead of him, with the glitter of open seas beyond them. Nor was he surprised to sense the anger welling up about him—fierce anger prompted by the threatened violation below. A hidden chamber in the mountains had been exposed, and human mages were poised, ready to unleash desolation on an unimaginable scale.

A blinding flash momentarily blotted out the sun, and clouds of darkness welled up to obscure the light. In the dimness he saw that every living thing below him had been destroyed. The desolation stretched to the far horizon.

The dragon flew ponderously back the way it had come, exposing him to the full impact of the magic released on the kingdom and its inhabitants. When he reached the cliffs overlooking the capital, he saw nothing but ruin. The city and its inhabitants had been obliterated.

DALTHINIR WOKE WITH A START, sweating freely. Nothing in the dream was new to him. Ten years earlier, the same dream had finally sealed his decision to leave the Compact. At the time he had understood the dragon to be symbolic, but the menace to be real. The dream had been a warning.

Only one conclusion made any sense. The warning had been repeated because the danger was now imminent.

WITH THE DRAMA BEHIND THEM, the days were beginning to feel unbearably routine to Kylen. He was now able to track the location of mages known to him from Camberton, but even the excitement of that had quickly worn off.

One morning he was relaxing downstairs at the table, enjoying a hot cup of tea. The mage was brooding in a corner on his own. He had apparently slept poorly the previous night.

Bella had been almost completely silent when she first came back, but she gradually seemed to be returning to normal. If the twins' relationship wasn't quite what it had been, they were at least talking to each other again. Importantly, Bella no longer showed any desire to run off.

Almost as if prompted by his thoughts, she appeared in the room, heading straight for Dalthinir.

"I need to give you a message," she said. "From Inga."

The mage's eyebrows went up in surprise. "She knows we're connected?"

Bella nodded. "She guessed. But not because of anything I said."

"When did this happen?"

"After the trial. Jonno told her about the book Lars and Petria are looking for."

Dalthinir looked horrified. "Jonno told her about that?!"

He quickly recovered his poise after a moment's reflection. "He did the right thing," he said with a nod. "It's important that others are aware of what the prince and his lackeys are up to."

"She said that someone needs to stop them. Jonno told her someone would. That's when she passed on the message."

"And what was the message?"

"She wanted me to tell you she's never doubted you, and she doesn't doubt you now."

He sat quietly for a long moment.

"She's figured out what we've been doing," he observed. "She always was more intuitive and insightful than the rest of us."

Inga's message moved the mage, although he tried not to show it. "It would be good to see her one last time," he murmured, shaking his head sadly.

Nothing further was said until Jonno returned a few minutes later. He seemed restless.

"How much longer will we be staying here?" he asked.

Dalthinir glanced toward him. "We won't be staying—it's time we were gone. We'll head out as soon as it's dark."

The decision pleased Jonno. Pouring himself a cup of tea, he settled onto a chair with a loud grunt of satisfaction. Bella gave nothing away, but she soon disappeared upstairs into her room.

"I suppose I'll have to say goodbye to Queenie," said Kylen sadly.

"It isn't practical for us to take her," the mage confirmed. "We can't afford the distraction. I'm sure Keemun will be happy to have her."

Kylen nodded. He wasn't surprised. "Where will we go?" he asked.

"North," was the only reply.

He shrugged. The direction meant nothing to him. A bit of distance from the mages couldn't be a bad thing, though—for any of them. Even the twins were being hunted now.

He would be content if it meant more freedom to learn about magic. Thanks to Dalthinir's advice about using his gut rather than his head, he'd been able to call upon his power the last time he needed it. But he still had so much to learn, and Camberton wasn't a safe place to practice. There were too many mages nearby who might notice uncontrolled bursts of power.

"How far away will we go?"

"That will depend on you."

Seeing Kylen's quizzical look, he added, "I need you to keep track of our friends in Cambrick. You won't be able to do it if we're too far away."

He nodded slowly. "Why are we heading north?"

"Lars and Petria will find a way to go after the book. I don't know where it is exactly, and maybe they don't either. But the direction they'll take is north."

"But the chief master wasn't happy with Lars and Petria. He won't let them go anywhere, will he?"

"Never underestimate a person who lusts after power. If they're determined enough, they'll find a way."

AFTER LEAVING a final payment with the grateful Grudem and Marta, Dalthinir and his companions thanked the family for their friendship and hospitality. Kylen was sorry to say farewell to little Queenie, but it needed to be done. Keemun's delight went a long way toward reconciling him to it—the boy looked as if he were king of the world.

Eager to be gone, the mage led his companions into the night. Reaching the main road, they traveled along it briefly before turning off onto a lightly used track. Within a few minutes they found that the track ended at a farmhouse. When a dog began barking, they quickly headed into the surrounding fields. Keeping well clear of the farm buildings, they crossed tilled earth until they reached a stand of trees. Pasture land lay beyond the trees, and they set off across it, ignoring the sheep that scurried out of their way. Passing two more farms, they pressed on until they finally reached land that wasn't cultivated.

By then Kylen felt more than ready for a break. Dalthinir had apparently reached a similar conclusion.

"We'll pause here for a few minutes," he said softly. "I'm not planning to walk much further tonight anyway. We'll stop as soon as we find somewhere suitable to camp."

His face turned toward Kylen, illuminated dimly in the pale moonlight. "Can you still sense their magical auras?"

"Yes," he replied.

"Let me know if they start fading out."

He nodded.

They soon resumed their journey, continuing until they found themselves in a lightly forested area. When they came upon a small clearing near a stream, Dalthinir called them to a halt.

"We'll spend the night here. Jonno and Bella, please gather some wood for a fire. Kylen, you need to make sure our friends in Cambrick are still within reach. I'll set some wards."

After the mage completed his tasks, he approached Kylen.

"Are the auras of the mages still within range?"

Kylen nodded.

"Can you distinguish individuals?"

He nodded again. "At this distance they're all clustered together. But I can still tell who they are." He hesitated before asking, "Is that surprising?"

"Very surprising. But it makes our task easier. And it's less dangerous for all of us if we can monitor them without needing to be nearby."

"What about the prince? I can't tell where he is."

"I don't care about the prince. It's Lars and Petria we need to be concerned about. The prince probably thinks he'll be able to snatch the crown if they find the lost book. The poor fool doesn't realize there'll be nothing left for him to rule."

Every new mention of the lost book intrigued Kylen more. The part of him that welcomed peace and quiet was glad he knew nothing about it. Another part of him was inquisitive and hungry to learn— eager to find out exactly what the book was and why these people wanted it so badly.

If Dalthinir was right, a similar fascination was driving the two mages, and the kingdom with them, ever closer to disaster.

He pushed the book from his mind.

"What if they don't go north? They might set off while I'm asleep and be out of range before I even know they've gone."

"They'll go north. If the book's anywhere it'll be in the Drakken-ridge Mountains."

THE NEXT MORNING they continued walking for several hours, heading in the same general direction. Each time Dalthinir checked, Kylen was able to confirm he had no difficulty identifying individual mages in Cambrick.

Having reached a region that seemed barely populated, they set up camp in a forest, sleeping in the open and living off the land for several days. Kylen was now capable of setting traps, and the mage taught him to identify plants, mushrooms, and nuts that were safe to eat.

One morning they sat together around a fire, breaking their fast.

"It was chilly last night," offered Kylen, shivering a little in spite of the fire.

"The nights are becoming cooler," the mage observed. "Sleeping under the stars won't be quite so appealing soon." He stood up and stretched. "It's a couple of weeks since we left Camberton, and we've benefited from a break from other people and their challenges. It's time we reconnected with humankind."

His announcement was well received. They set off the moment their campsite had been cleared, passing through an extensive forest before eventually emerging into grazing land.

A herd of cows stood in the distance, the sound of their lowing growing louder as they drew closer. A farmer was moving among them, stroking their backs with a tree branch.

"What is he doing?" asked Kylen.

"Being superstitious," replied the mage gruffly.

"He's relieving the aches and pains of the animals," explained Bella.

"With a branch from a shrew ash," added Jonno.

"What's a shrew ash?"

Dalthinir rolled his eyes. "These people believe their animals are in pain because shrews have been running over them. Their solution is to bore a hole in an ash tree, put in a live shrew, then seal the hole. Supposedly that gives the branches of the tree magical healing properties."

"Farmers have always done it," said Bella simply.

"Because it works," Jonno asserted.

The mage shook his head helplessly.

It sounded bizarre to Kylen, but he decided not to comment.

Crossing a stream, they came upon several farm buildings.

"I think we need to stop soon," Kylen told the mage.

"The auras?"

He nodded. "I can still detect them all, but they're starting to feel a bit thin."

"Your range is remarkable," Dalthinir told him. "And this is as good a place to stop as any."

He glanced at the twins. "Why don't you see if any of the farming folk could benefit from our help? They might even give us a barn to sleep in."

His suggestion was greeted with enthusiasm by the twins. They had soon disappeared in the direction of the nearest farm.

Returning to the country was clearly good for them. Jonno had been visibly more relaxed since leaving Camberton, and Bella seemed happier than she had been for a long time. They'd even resumed their old habit of finishing sentences for each other.

Kylen could only conclude that they had agreed to some kind of truce. He sat down with his mentor, content to enjoy the afternoon sunshine while the twins established new connections.

Dalthinir was the first to break the silence. "So Lars and Petria are still in Cambrick?"

He nodded. "You seem to be expecting them to make a move sometime soon."

The mage shrugged. "It's impossible to guess what they'll do. You overheard Adrastas saying they were going to be tried. That will have happened by now, and even if they weren't locked up, a city full of sneering mages will feel like a prison. After everything that's happened, I imagine they'll see it as a high priority to get away from Cambrick."

"To look for the lost book?"

He nodded. "I imagine so, if they believe they have information about its location. They should be well aware of the dire warnings about using the book. But they might have convinced themselves they can somehow avoid being affected. If so, they're fooling themselves."

"Will you be able to stop them?"

"They seem to think so." He gazed off into the distance. "I honestly don't know. But I mean to try."

Kylen's curiosity could be contained no longer. "What's in the book? Why is it so dangerous?"

The mage's brows furrowed deeply. "It's a pleasant afternoon, Kylen," he growled. "Let's not change that."

An answer like that was guaranteed to further increase both his curiosity and his frustration. But what could he say?

THE TWINS DIDN'T REAPPEAR until the light was fading from the sky.

"If you hurry, there might still be some hot food left at the farmhouse," said Jonno cheerfully.

"What have you been doing?" asked the mage.

"A bit of this, a bit of that," said Bella vaguely. "But we've found a barn where we can stay for the night."

Not waiting around for further questions, they headed back toward the farmhouse. Kylen hurried after them, his belly rumbling loudly.

He noticed that this dwelling also featured a horseshoe over the door, in this case pointing up. Presumably that meant the occupants were more interested in collecting good luck than in pouring it out. Inside they found a gruff-looking man sitting at a large wooden table with three children. A woman stood behind them, bouncing up and down with a screaming baby in her arms. She managed a thin smile, but she looked harried.

"Your young 'uns have earned you a feed," said the man, nodding gratefully to the twins. He pointed to a couple of empty places at the table.

"Thank you," said the mage, settling himself at the table and pointing Kylen to the other seat. "I have a little skill as a healer. Would you like me to examine the baby?"

"We'll see," said the man guardedly. "If he's no better by dawn, we might let you take a look."

An inscrutable look came over the mage's face, although by now Kylen knew him well enough to know he was consciously restraining himself from responding. He was left wondering what might happen before dawn.

After they had eaten, the four travelers made their way to the barn. Mounds of hay lay about, and they had soon prepared resting places that felt much softer than usual.

Dalthinir nodded to the twins appreciatively. "The two of you clearly know how to make yourselves indispensable," he said.

Bella didn't respond. "I'm going to help settle the children," she said, slipping out of the barn.

Jonno shrugged. "On a farm there's always more to do than hands to do it. Especially with a sick baby."

"I did offer," grumbled the mage.

"People have their own ways of dealing with trouble," Jonno murmured.

No more was said. Too weary to ask what they meant, Kylen drifted off to sleep almost immediately.

He woke with a start just before dawn. Had something wakened him?

His thoughts flew at once to the mages in Cambrick. Climbing quietly to his feet, he stole away from the barn, focusing his attention on the distant glimmer that had become so familiar. None of the mages he was monitoring had left the capital, and he allowed himself to relax.

Then he heard the muffled cry of a baby. Straining his eyes in the darkness, he sensed rather than saw dim figures moving away from the farmhouse. His curiosity aroused, he silently set off after them.

The flicker of candlelight warned him they had come to a halt. Slipping behind a tree, he watched with fascination the scene unfolding before him. The farmer stood on a hillside before a large tree with his wife at his side. Cradled by the woman, the baby had begun to whimper unhappily.

Something about the tree didn't look right—there appeared to be a dark gap in the middle of it. Straining his eyes to see clearly in the dim light, Kylen watched in bewilderment as the farmer took the baby and passed it through the gap in the tree. Someone on the other side of the tree took the baby, passing him back around the tree to the father. The action was repeated twice more.

Then the third person began chanting softly. Kylen could tell from the voice that it was an old woman. While she chanted, the father handed the baby to his wife and began removing blocks of wood from the gap in the tree. Then he wrapped something around the trunk of the tree, bandaging it tightly.

A hand settled suddenly on Kylen's shoulder, almost startling him out of his wits.

"Shh," warned the voice of the mage.

It took a long minute before his heart stopped pounding wildly.

Then abruptly the old woman turned in their direction.

"Destiny draws near!" she called in a quavering voice. "The child of prophecy has awakened! He will rise up in power, and the mountains will shake. Our doom rests upon his shoulders—deliverance if he stands; destruction and ruin if he falls!"

Her voice fell silent, and she turned away.

"Superstitious nonsense," mumbled Dalthinir.

Kylen stood transfixed. A shiver had run up his spine as she spoke. Somehow she was aware of him. The child of prophecy she spoke of was him. He couldn't explain how he knew, but he did.

"We'd better go before they notice us," whispered the mage.

With an effort Kylen turned away and plodded back toward the barn.

As soon as they arrived he turned to his mentor. "What just happened?" he asked, trembling for reasons he couldn't explain.

"It's a ritual as old as superstition," came the terse reply.

So the mage thought he was asking about the baby.

"People make a cleft in an ash tree, then pass the baby through it while chanting some suitably poetic—and entirely nonsensical— gibberish. Then they mend the rupture in the tree. Supposedly, the baby will heal along with the tree."

He couldn't make sense of any of it. "Is that why they didn't want you to look at the baby? They wanted to try this first?"

"That's the idea. I didn't argue with them. I'd have been wasting my breath."

Dalthinir turned toward the barn. Kylen opened his mouth to ask about the woman's pronouncement, but he couldn't find anything to say. He crept into the barn troubled and confused.

The twins appeared to still be sleeping, and both he and the mage lay down quietly.

Further sleep eluded Kylen. He kept churning over all he'd seen and heard. The woman's words had shaken him, but he eventually decided the mage must have been right. It was superstitious nonsense.

If that was the case, there was no substance to the ritual either.

He couldn't bring himself to ridicule the parents though. Elspeth came to mind. It had been too long since he thought of her. So much had been happening. But the tragic end to her short life had shown him that without hope people couldn't thrive. Sometimes they couldn't even manage to cling to life.

CHAPTER 20

When Kylen and Dalthinir emerged in the morning, they found the farmer and his wife glowing. The baby, no longer unsettled, was gurgling contentedly.

"Thank you for your offer," said the woman, "but the baby seems to be feeling much better this morning."

The mage nodded politely, ignoring the smugness in her tone. "Are there other things we can help with?"

"Your Jonno is off chopping wood," the farmer said.

"And young Bella is seeing to the older children," added his wife.

They weren't saying it directly, but they seemed to be suggesting that if he couldn't see for himself what needed to be done, he had nothing useful to offer.

"We'll have a look around the farm," Dalthinir said mildly.

As soon as they were clear of the house, Kylen said, "The baby seems to be feeling better."

The mage nodded firmly. "There's a useful learning experience here. How would you describe the facts of what happened?"

"The baby was sick. They passed the baby through a gap they'd made in the middle of an ash tree. They closed the gap in the tree. The baby got well."

"Are all of these facts connected?"

"What do you mean?"

"Did the baby get well because of what they did? Or would the baby have improved if they'd done nothing at all?"

"I don't know."

"No. None of us do. They're convinced the baby got well because of their trick with the ash tree. I'm convinced the baby's improvement has nothing whatever to do with that. Each of us believes that the facts support our own view. So what is the truth?"

"No one can say."

"That's the correct answer. We can't both be right, of course. The tree either healed the baby or it didn't. I'm confident I know what the truth is! But I can't prove it, and neither can they. You'll often hear people asserting that the facts prove their point of view. Never be frightened to dig deeper."

He sighed. "There are mages in Cambrick convinced I'm working hard to destroy the last trace of good in the world. As they see it, the facts demonstrate how dangerous I am. They're wrong, but there's no way I could convince them of that."

Kylen understood perfectly. "And you've told me they'll decide I'm dangerous if they ever find out about me. Too dangerous to be allowed to live. Just because my powers weren't awakened the way they think it should happen."

The mage hadn't mentioned the old woman's words, and Kylen saw no reason to raise the matter.

They had been walking toward a stream that ran past the farm-house. A track ran on either side of the stream, with a ford in the middle. The stream was knee-deep at the ford, and it undoubtedly ran deeper in some seasons.

Piles of logs lay on both sides of the stream. A covered wagon also stood nearby, which Dalthinir briefly examined. It was apparent that the farmer had been planning to build a bridge across the stream.

"How would you like to build a bridge this morning, Kylen?" asked the mage with a wink. He jerked his head toward the logs and the wagon. "The farmer has already collected a pile of suitable logs, and there's lime and straw in that wagon. But he has a big job ahead of him."

"I'm willing to do whatever I can to help!"

"Good. Before we get started, let me make it clear that for a mage with any sense, a task like this isn't just about raw power. Careful planning is needed before we build anything. It would be easy to throw up something that looks like a bridge, but it wouldn't be of any use if it collapses the first time a herd of cows goes across it."

Kylen had nothing to say. It was a good thing Dalthinir knew what he was doing.

"First, we'll find some large rocks to place in the four corners. We'll place two rocks on each side of the bridge and run a wooden beam between them, parallel to the stream. Each end of the beam will rest on one of these bearing rocks. Then we'll run logs across the stream. They'll sit on top of the wooden beams on each side of the stream. Once that's done, we'll place smaller pieces of wood on top of the logs, perpendicular to them. The final step will be to put a firm surface on top of it all."

He looked at Kylen. "Do you get all that?"

He laughed when he saw the bewilderment on Kylen's face. "Don't worry, it will make more sense when we do it."

It took a while to find four large rocks with flat tops. Dalthinir used magic to remove the top layer of soil where they were to be positioned. The ground beneath was firm, but he added a layer of gravel from the bed of the stream to ensure the rocks would sit on a firm and level base. The rocks were heavy, but Dalthinir soon placed three of them with pushing magic. Kylen was delighted when he managed to get the fourth into position.

Beginning on one side of the stream, the mage positioned two poles beside each rock and used magic to drive them into the ground. The result was a pair of poles on the outside of each rock.

The farmer had already split several logs. Choosing a piece as their wooden beam, they rested it on the rocks between the two pairs of poles. The rocks now supported the beam, and the pairs of poles at each end prevented it from moving.

A similar piece was placed on the two rocks on the other side of the stream, held in position in the same way by a pair of poles. Both sides of the stream now had a simple base for the logs that would run across the stream.

Choosing suitable logs was difficult, because each of them needed to be large in diameter and reasonably straight, as well as long enough to span the stream. They found several acceptable logs among those the farmer had prepared, and selected a few suitable trees to provide the others.

Kylen was bemused when the mage used an ax to fell the trees. "Why didn't you use magic to bring down the trees?" he asked.

"Some mages think magic is the right tool for every job," the mage told him. "It isn't true. Every mage has muscles, and most mages have brains as well," he added with a wry smile. "There's no reason to be shy about using them."

In the end, they placed twelve logs across the stream, resting side by side on the piece of wood they had placed between the rocks. The pairs of poles securing the original beam of wood also served to prevent the logs from sliding off the beam.

The logs were heavy, and getting them into position would have been difficult without magical assistance. Kylen tried to magically place a couple of the logs, but although he had more than enough power, he didn't have the necessary finesse to do it precisely. In the end, Dalthinir did what was needed.

The final step was to place branches and smaller pieces of wood across the twelve logs—enough to provide a surface without gaps. The mage used magic to speed up the process of collecting the raw material.

When they were finished, a sturdy bridge spanned the stream.

Kylen walked across it, testing it for strength. "The surface is very uneven," he reported. "I wouldn't want to walk across it in the dark."

"There's plenty of clay soil and sand near the stream," the mage replied, "and we can use the farmer's lime and straw. After we've mixed it all up, we'll use a layer to smooth out the surface."

Having witnessed Dalthinir burying the brigands up to their necks in earth, it didn't seem surprising when he prepared a pit, moved clay, sand, lime, and straw into it, and mixed them thoroughly, all without either of them lifting a finger. However, the final step astonished him a lot. With the weather mild and sunny with no clouds anywhere in sight, Kylen was startled to see a light shower of rain gently soaking the mixture. The rain was falling only over the pit.

He stared at it wide-eyed.

"That should be enough," said the mage casually.

The shower came to an abrupt end.

"How...did you do that?"

"Magic, of course. I find it a bit more difficult to move water than to move soil, but the basic idea is the same."

He eyed his handiwork with satisfaction. "I'll use magic to smear a thick layer of it over the top of the bridge, and then we can just let it dry in the sun. It will set hard given the right amount of time."

Glancing up, Kylen saw the sun heading for the western horizon. Building the bridge had taken several hours. It would surely have taken much longer if the farmer had done it.

The two of them paused for a well-earned break.

"Is it possible that any of the mages in Cambrick might have detected our use of magical power?" asked Kylen.

He felt a little foolish asking, because he couldn't imagine Dalthinir taking the smallest risk. The answer came as a surprise.

"A mage with powerful farsense might have detected it. If their timing was perfect and they were looking in precisely the right direction."

"Are there any mages powerful enough?"

"There is one," he replied with a sheepish smile.

"Ah. Master Inga. And you don't think she would give us away, even if she did detect us using magic?"

He shrugged. "I can't say for certain. But the chances of anyone detecting what we did are tiny. And there isn't likely to be a repeat performance anytime soon."

"You're able to mask uses of power. Why didn't you mask it this time?"

"Because it takes power to mask power. If I want to mask whatever I'm doing, the amount available for me to use is more limited. Sometimes it's simpler to use power openly, in spite of the risk."

A no-nonsense look came over his face. "It's time we continued with your training. Do you know which magical sense we've just been using?"

Kylen shook his head. "Mage touch?"

"An intelligent guess. It's good to see you using your head! Mage touch is a practical and extremely useful expression of magical power. It takes a number of forms, and you've now witnessed all of them. Can you try naming some of them?"

"Pushing magic?"

"Yes. Thrusting power, which encompasses pulling as well as pushing, is a description of the ability to control, manipulate, or move objects magically instead of manually. We used it to move the logs. I also used it to put the clay mortar on top of the bridge at the end. What's another example?"

"What you did with the calf? Moving it inside the cow so it could be born?"

"Yes, good. Healing ability is another form of mage touch. External parts of the body can be manipulated without needing to directly touch them. And more usefully, internal parts can be manipulated without needing an incision to expose them. It might look like a mage is doing nothing while they're actually hard at work inside a living body. I'm sure you won't be surprised to learn that if you want to use healing ability effectively, you need a detailed understanding of the bones, muscles, and organs inside a body and how they work. You can't just go poking around inside someone. I don't have that degree of skill. What I did with the calf was relatively straightforward."

"How can a mage change things safely if they can't see what they're doing?"

"I've seen mages who are incredibly adept. They can use their magical ability to somehow sense what's gone wrong inside a person."

A chilling thought had taken hold of Kylen. "Does that mean a mage can intentionally damage a person by doing things inside their body?"

"I'm sorry to say it, but you're right. Anyone with the right kind of mage touch ability doesn't need a spear or a club to kill another person. It's one of the reasons shielding ability is so important. It can be used to protect the body from arrows, spears, or any other kind of physical attack. It can also protect against magical attack. I use a different form of shielding ability to block farsense of my magical aura."

A somber look came over his face. "It's a good reminder for both of us, Kylen. We can't assume I'll always be around to protect you. You've already demonstrated some degree of ability with shielding. We need to make sure you are capable of shielding yourself without conscious thought."

"I would value that a lot!" said Kylen with feeling.

"The other main expression of mage touch is elemental magic. It involves harnessing the elements—earth, air, fire, and water—to produce magical results."

"Like you did to make it rain on the clay on top of the bridge?"

"That was more to do with pushing ability than elemental magic. All I did was move the water from the stream. An example of elemental magic involving water might be to make it rain when there's no water anywhere nearby. An example involving fire might be to heat a mass of air without using a fire."

Kylen couldn't help feeling a bit dispirited. "There's so much to learn! And you've only covered two of the mage senses."

Dalthinir slapped him cheerfully on the back. "Be grateful you're not learning it in a stuffy classroom in the mage headquarters in Cambrick."

A grunt was the best he could manage in reply.

THE FARMER CAME upon them late in the afternoon. Coming to an abrupt halt, he stared at the bridge in astonishment. "How did you do that?!"

The mage's expression was unreadable. "We went looking for something useful to do."

"Thank you," the farmer managed. He appeared almost as fearful as he was grateful. It probably wasn't surprising given how superstitious he was. "Are you a mage?" he asked nervously.

"You have no cause for concern," Dalthinir replied. "We just wanted to thank you for your hospitality."

The man bowed low. "There'll be hot food very soon. I hope you will accept our hospitality again tonight."

"Thank you. A bit of hard work always makes us hungry."

They followed him back toward the farmhouse, although he scurried along so rapidly they couldn't keep up with him.

KYLEN WOKE ABRUPTLY from an unsettling dream. Dawn must have been close, although it was too dark to see anything.

He lay still, listening quietly. No unusual noises were reaching his ear, yet something had startled him.

Then all at once he knew.

Getting up, he hurried to the mage and shook him firmly. He was forced to shake him twice before the snoring stopped.

"What is it?" Dalthinir asked sleepily.

"It's Lars and Petria. They've left Cambrick."

CHAPTER 21

Master Inga sat in Adrastas's reception room, watching the head mage pace restlessly back and forth.

"They're impossible—the pair of them!" he said.

This wasn't the first time Inga had listened to him venting about Lars and Petria. It surely wouldn't be the last.

"I was fool enough to think their trial would bring them to heel. But even two weeks of house arrest taught them nothing." He threw his hands up in frustration.

"What have they been doing?"

"They've been demanding permission to leave Cambrick! Lars claims that Petria is under doctor's orders to retire to the country due to ill health. Because of the trauma they've been forced to endure. The trauma, of course, has been caused by the brutal and unjust campaign of persecution waged against them! Can you credit it?"

His face twisted into a grimace. "The two of them are relentless! I seem to trip over them every time I turn around. I've instructed my aides never to allow them access to my quarters under any circumstances. Somehow they still find ways of getting in!"

"You aren't going to let them go, are you?"

"Never! I wouldn't give them the satisfaction."

"Are they still being tailed?"

"Constantly."

"Have you learned anything new?"

He shook his head. "They've been careful. Their little group appears to have stopped meeting entirely."

"I've been doing a bit of surveillance of my own," she told him. "I discovered that messages are being passed back and forth regularly between Lars and the prince."

Adrastas's eyes had gone wide. "How did you find that out?"

"Entirely by accident. I noticed Lars slipping a document to a servant. Later I happened to see the prince handing a document to the same person. After that I kept my eye out. I paid a street urchin a few coins to follow the servant. It was quite instructive. The servant never goes directly between Lars and the prince. He uses a roundabout route that takes him through a succession of back alleys as well as the busiest section of the market. Only the most determined tracker—or someone who lives on the streets and knows every inch of the city—would be capable of keeping up with him."

"Has your street rat managed to intercept any of the notes?"

"No. I would never ask it of him—it'd be far too risky. He might be tenacious, but he looks like the slightest puff of wind would blow him away."

He scowled. "They're up to no good. I feel it in my bones. But I have no idea what to do with them."

She nodded. "They're clearly eager to make a move. Otherwise they wouldn't be applying all this pressure. Have you thought more about what I told you?"

"About them wanting to find *Ode to the Fallen One*? I'm sorry, Inga, but I simply can't take it seriously." Seeing the look on her face, he added, "It isn't just because you refused to reveal your sources. Maybe they did talk about it at one of their meetings. If so, they're doing us all a favor. I'd rather have them wasting their time on fairy tales than doing any real damage."

"But what if it isn't just a fairy tale? Lady Mardell isn't a person to be easily taken in."

"Even sensible people can be taken in by smooth talkers. Look, I don't doubt the book existed once, but there's no reason to believe it survived, much less that it's sitting out there waiting for a couple of geniuses like Lars and Petria to find it! You're worrying for no reason, Inga."

She wasn't convinced, but there was no point in pushing it further. "If they're determined enough, they'll find an excuse to leave. We'd better make sure we're ready when it happens."

SCARCELY TWENTY-FOUR HOURS had elapsed before Inga was back in the chief master's reception room.

"I've decided to let them go," Adrastas told her. "I suppose that means they won." He shook his head dispiritedly. "They wore me down. It didn't help when my dog died. In the end, it was all too much. You said yesterday they'd find an excuse to leave anyway, and I decided I would at least control the timing."

"I'm sorry to hear about your dog. What happened?"

He shook his head miserably. "It's quite distressing—she was almost a member of the family. She became sick quite suddenly this morning. I had her examined, but by then it was too late. Twisted bowel, apparently. One minute she was fine, the next she was gone. I can't account for it at all."

Inga frowned. "Has it occurred to you that your dog might have been tampered with?"

"What are you saying?" The head mage's expression changed from puzzlement to indignation in a moment. "Are you suggesting that Lars killed my dog?! He wouldn't dare! He took the same vow as the rest of us!"

She rolled her eyes. Every mage vowed not to use magic to harm another living being except in self-defense, and even then only when no other options were available. Somehow she didn't think a vow like that would trouble Lars. Not if it didn't suit him.

Without waiting for a response, he hurried to the door and bellowed for his senior aide. Seeing the man approaching, he called, "Find out if anyone was anywhere near my dog this morning."

The aide bowed. "I did see someone petting the poor creature early this morning, Chief Master. When I let her out for her morning squat."

The head mage had gone pale. "Who was it?" he demanded.

"It was Master Lars. He's been around such a lot of late. I thought nothing of it."

Sucking in a sharp breath, he dismissed the aide and closed the door.

He swung around to face Inga. "I'll have his hide!" he breathed, trembling with fury.

She observed him calmly. "You do realize you'll never be able to prove anything."

For a long moment he stared at her with bulging eyes. Then with an effort he mastered himself, the unnatural color draining slowly from his face.

His eyes narrowed. "It seems he decided I needed a bit of a nudge. And I was too stupid to see it."

"He probably sees it as fair payback for you belittling him in public."

"I belittled you, and you've forgiven me." He shot her a glance. "Haven't you?"

"Of course!" she said, waving a hand dismissively. "You were only doing what you needed to do."

She paused for a moment. "When are they leaving?"

He hung his head. "They've gone already."

"You let them go?!"

He winced. "I couldn't wait to see the back of them. I'm not entirely stupid though—I've been planning all along to send a team to keep an eye on them. That's now become urgent!"

She nodded emphatically. Something had changed. Something that had driven the two mages to take action. Perhaps the house arrest had interfered with the timing of their plans.

"I need you to lead the team, Inga. It has to be someone I can rely on completely, someone who understands what they're capable of."

A long, slow sigh escaped her lips. It was the last thing she wanted to do. The awkward truth was she'd allowed herself to become soft. She found herself thinking of Dalthinir as she often had of late.

Growing soft had never been an option for him. Forced from his home, he'd been reduced to a life of wandering. For ten long years.

There was also the matter of the book. Adrastas might not take it seriously. But if he was wrong—she didn't like to think about the magnitude of the disaster they would face.

She would go, of course. What else could she do? It wasn't as if she had a choice. No one else took their plans seriously.

"I'll go," she said.

"Good!" he said, his face brightening. "Take a couple of others for support. I'd suggest Kothlar, but I'm not sure he'd have the patience."

"I'll take more than a couple of others. I'll need people who can match the combined power of Lars and Petria."

He frowned. "Do you think it might come to that?"

She shrugged. "I don't know. But I suspect Lars didn't kill your dog on impulse. I have no way of telling how far any of them might go."

"This isn't about the book, is it?"

"It's about them. They seem to have become desperate. Desperate enough for him to break a vow. I don't know why, and the reason doesn't matter. What matters is that I'm taking it seriously. I don't want to take any chances."

Adrastas nodded slowly. "I'll tell people you're tracking Dalthinir. That will undermine the prince's accusations about your supposed negligence, and it will also explain why you need a substantial team. Would you like a few guards as well?"

She shook her head. "It will be simpler if we travel light. But I might need your support in other ways. I'll be asking people to drop everything else without notice."

"I'm willing to provide whatever support is necessary." His face set hard. "I've asked myself at times if I was making too much of the danger Lars and Petria pose. What Lars just did to my dog has finally opened my eyes. It isn't just about killing an animal. He crossed a line when he broke the vow, and doing it once will make it easier to cross another one. Pretty soon there'll be no telling where it will end."

"I agree completely. The two of them have the potential to be extremely dangerous."

He grunted an acknowledgment. "How much will you tell your team members?"

She paused before answering. "I'm not sure. I think I'll wait a while before telling them everything. It might be wisest to see how the situation develops."

He nodded. "I'd better let you go. You have a lot of preparation to do in a short time."

"I KNOW it's a lot to ask, Emmela, but it would make a huge difference to me if you were willing to come!"

Inga was willing to beg and plead if that was what it took.

"All I can offer is illusion. That isn't going to be of much use to you."

"It's impossible to predict what magical powers we might need. What I do know is that I need someone I can trust implicitly. That's why I want you to join the team."

"And exactly what is this team supposed to be doing?"

Inga winced. "I can't go into detail yet. Not until we've set out."

"When are you planning to leave?"

"Tomorrow."

"Tomorrow?!"

"I know it isn't a lot of notice. I wasn't able to choose the timing."

Emmela sighed. "I want to support you in any way I can. You know that! But the timing is difficult for me. Especially with no warning."

"Is there anything I can do to help?"

"I have commitments at the Conservatory. I'm supposed to be teaching apprentices all next week."

"Adrastas will arrange for your sessions to be covered by another mage. What else?"

"It's my mother. She has become quite frail and needs active support. I have a sister who's willing to help, but she has other responsibilities that limit her availability."

"Would your sister be able to supervise a paid helper if you had one?"

"Yes, she would. But neither of us can afford to pay someone."

"Would it solve your problem if Adrastas came up with the funding?"

Emmela's eyebrows went up. "The mission is that important?"

"It is."

Her friend sighed in resignation. "Very well. I'll make the arrangements."

As relieved as she was delighted, Inga let out a joyful cry. "Thank you so much, Emmela! I'll speak with Adrastas the moment he's available."

It proved impossible for Inga's group to leave the day after Lars and Petria. In the end, two additional days passed before preparations had been finalized.

Inga began tracking their auras the moment she became aware they'd left, although they were quickly out of range. Nevertheless she at least had a rough indication of the direction they had taken. If they'd been heading for Lars's family estate as they claimed, they would have headed west. Instead, they immediately headed north, not even bothering to lay a false trail.

Inga wasn't at all surprised. They seemed increasingly willing to cast aside caution to achieve their goals.

Four others had joined Inga's team. In addition to Emmela and herself, the team consisted of two men and a woman, all of them relatively young. Ellis and Kaspra each had moderately strong mage touch ability. Arguably neither of them were as powerful as Lars, but together they should be more than a match for him. Alexis had the ability to manipulate all the elements—earth, air, fire, and water. Although his elements ability was both stronger and more complete than that of Lars, he would also need to match Petria's ability to control fire.

Adrastas sought Inga out on the morning of their departure.

"As you know, I've arranged a horse for each of you. You'll also have a sixth animal as a packhorse."

"Thank you. The packhorse might prove useful as a spare mount."

"I've also made the arrangements you requested on behalf of Emmela. And I've done everything necessary to smooth the way for the other members of the party."

"All of us appreciate it."

He waved it away. "It's the least I can do. I've had a rude awakening, Inga. It might have taken me a while to fully grasp the true character of these people, but now that I have, things are going to change."

His face became grim. "I've been making some discreet inquiries, and I've learned Prince Evran has gone missing. He disappeared the day after Lars and Petria, accompanied by half a dozen of his own royal guards."

"Does the king know what the prince is up to?"

Adrastas shook his head. "I had already sought an audience to brief him on your expedition. While I was there, I asked him if the prince was acting on the crown's behalf or his own behalf."

"And what did he say?"

"He was even more vague and evasive than usual. His Majesty seems more intent on preserving the appearance of royal unity than on calling his brother to account. So I told him about Lars and Petria and what they're up to—including what Lars did to my dog."

Noticing her mouth beginning to open, he hastily forestalled her. "Before you ask, I made no mention of your precious book! I told him it's likely the prince will join our two fugitives. Before any confrontation arises, it's crucial that we know if the prince is acting on royal orders. At that point he changed course and gave me an honest answer. The prince hadn't sought his approval—he didn't even have the courtesy to inform him he was leaving. For once the king actually showed some spine. He told me our mission has royal approval, and there will be consequences for the prince or anyone else who interferes with it. He even took the trouble to confirm it an official document, stamped with his seal! I have it in my quarters."

Inga was surprised and impressed. "Does he know that I'm leading the team?"

"He does, and he expressed great confidence in you."

That made no sense at all. "It's only a few weeks since he asked you to arrest me!"

"He did have the grace to apologize to me after that incident. I thought he'd be unhappy that I brought unfavorable attention to the prince. But he actually complimented me on the way I'd handled it. He told me he'd had stern words with the prince."

"That must have been a first," she muttered.

"I think we can both guess where the prince and his men are going. Your assignment has just become significantly more dangerous, Inga. I've therefore hired some men to ride with you."

She frowned. "Mercenaries? They'll just make our task more complicated!"

"Don't be so quick to dismiss them. They're not the cutthroats you probably imagine. I've known their leader since we were children, and I've called on his services before. His name is Ramond, and he's a good man. He's also the best swordsman in the kingdom, although I hope it never reaches that point. He's chosen six men he trusts, all of them capable fighters. Ramond will guard your team well. He also fully understands he'll be answering to you."

Reluctant as she was to include mercenaries, Inga could see that the involvement of the prince and his guards altered the balance. She reluctantly accepted the head mage's initiative. What else could she do? He hadn't actually offered her a choice.

Within the hour, Ramond and his men had joined her.

With preparations finally complete, the party set off without fanfare, riding through the gates of Cambrick at around noon.

They swung north at their earliest opportunity. They hadn't been riding for long when Ramond drew his horse alongside Inga's. "Where are we headed?" he asked.

She noticed others openly craning their necks in an effort to hear the conversation.

"North," she replied. "At least for the moment. I'll brief you all when we camp for the night."

CHAPTER 22

Petria sat opposite Lars, warming herself before a small fire. After many hours in the saddle since leaving Cambrick, she felt exhausted.

"How long do you think it will be before we're followed?" she asked.

"What makes you think anyone will follow us?" he retorted.

"Are you serious? It won't take Adrastas long to realize you killed his dog."

Lars snorted. "If he had half a brain he would have seen it coming when we first told him we wanted to leave."

"Before you congratulate yourself," she said scathingly. "you might want to remind yourself that his aide saw you working on the dog."

He grunted dismissively.

She got to her feet. "Mages are expected to take their vows seriously. It was never necessary to kill the dog! We were wearing him down very effectively. He would have let us go before long anyway."

"We couldn't afford to wait," he growled. "Not after being forced to sit on our hands for two weeks! Time is against us, as you well know. We get one chance at this. We'll be senile—or in our graves—when another total solar eclipse occurs."

"There's no point in arguing," she told him. "We both know what we need to do. Let's focus our attention on that."

PETRIA AND LARS had been waiting for hours when Prince Evran and his guards reached the agreed meeting location. The two of them had found very little to say while they were waiting, and that suited Petria perfectly.

As far as she was concerned, the prince hadn't arrived a moment too soon. He might be proud and arrogant, but at least his presence would take some of the focus away from the two mages.

Lars had been moody and silent since his interaction with Petria the previous night. She wondered how he would have reacted if she'd told him what she really thought. He could be infuriating at times. Not for the first time, she wondered what Banadin had seen in him.

"Are we being followed, Your Highness?" Lars asked the prince.

"At the time I left, Adrastas was putting together a small group to follow you."

"Who was leading it?"

"I don't know for certain, but according to rumor it was Inga."

"Inga?" Lars screwed up his face. "She's the best they could come up with?"

"Forget them," growled the prince. "They couldn't possibly know where we're going, and they're a long way behind us anyway."

The prince and his band had been riding hard. Nevertheless, the group set off again after a short break. They had long planned against this day, and having made a beginning they intended to press on until the end.

AFTER TWO DAYS of hard riding, Petria and her companions made their way to an abandoned barn. Lady Mardell had delivered on her promises. Plentiful provisions had been laid out inside, and they shared a nourishing meal before retiring to a double line of comfortable palliasses covered with warm blankets.

In the morning they rose early after a solid night's sleep and broke their fast. Then they exchanged their horses for fresh mounts waiting for them in an adjoining stable. Two long days of riding lay ahead of them before they expected to reach the next of her way houses.

The path to their intended destination carefully avoided centers of population, passing through uncultivated terrain wherever possible. It was impossible to bypass inhabited regions entirely. Two sections of their journey in particular would take them across expansive estates owned by Lords Marklo and Rostem, who had been part of their conspiracy from the beginning. The nobles had instructed their retainers to provision the travelers freely while treating every detail of their transit with the utmost confidentiality.

Two weeks of steady but uneventful progress saw them almost to the foothills of the Drakkenridge Mountains. Arriving at the last of Lady Mardell's safe havens, they were planning a full day to rest and recuperate before beginning the final stage of their journey.

"Just as I expected, there's been no sign of pursuit," said Lars.

Petria decided to ignore his tone. "It's hardly surprising. This location is remote by any standards. We could use magic freely, and even Inga would have no chance of spotting us. Tracking our auras is out of the question for any mage."

Lars smirked. "Inga won't be searching for us if she's distracted leading an expedition."

The prince glowered at them. "If you've finished congratulating yourselves, you might remember that the real danger lies in the mountains ahead of us. We're going to have a lot more to worry about than pursuers."

Petria got in before Lars had a chance to snap back at the prince. "Everything so far has gone entirely to plan, Your Highness. That's something worth celebrating."

Offering no more than a grunt in return, the prince turned and strode away.

"That man is full of himself," growled Lars.

"So are you most of the time," Petria retorted coolly before heading away herself.

WHEN INGA'S team first stopped for the night, all of them gathered around expectantly, eager for the promised briefing.

"You've been told we're pursuing the renegade, Dalthinir," she began. "That is the story being circulated, but it isn't why we're here."

Murmuring broke out at once, but no one interrupted her. "Our real purpose is to follow two mages, Master Lars and Master Petria, at the request of the chief master. Let me emphasize that our mission is sensitive. I expect all of you to treat it as highly confidential, both now and when we eventually return."

"Why are we following them?" asked Ramond.

"At this point I can't tell you any more," she replied. "I know you won't find that satisfying, but it's all I can offer for now. Many of us are saddlesore, and we can expect another long day of riding tomorrow. Once you've eaten, please take the opportunity to sleep. All of us could do with some rest."

They moved away, talking quietly among themselves.

Inga sought out Emmela and drew her aside.

"That's all very mysterious," Emmela ventured.

"Details won't matter until we come within range of Lars and Petria. There might be times when I need support though, which means someone else needs to understand the full picture. I'm sorry to say it will have to be you, Emmela."

Her friend raised her eyebrows hesitantly.

Inga pressed on. "You know from the two trials that the two of them were meeting with Prince Evran and three nobles, one of whom was Lady Mardell."

Emmela nodded.

"Adrastas wasn't at all satisfied with their explanation about the meeting, so he's kept them under constant observation. They've been more careful since then. But in recent days they've been pressing him to let them leave Cambrick, supposedly to visit Lars's estates to recover from the 'persecution' they've suffered."

Emmela's eyebrows rose higher.

"They'd been pestering him so much that he was sick of the sight of them. Then a couple of days before we left, they caught him at a weak moment, and he agreed to let them go."

"A weak moment?"

"He was mourning the sudden death of his dog."

Her eyes went wide. "You're not suggesting...?"

Inga nodded. "It was Lars who killed his dog. It was only later that he made the connection."

"Is he certain it was them?"

"As certain as he can be. His aide had seen Lars with the dog immediately before it got sick."

"That's contemptible by any standard! He broke a vow! It leaves me wondering what they're capable of."

"Adrastas was furious. Even without this interference, he would have had them followed when they left Cambrick. After this..." She sighed. "There's more, unfortunately. The day after they set out, Prince Evran left the city with a few of his most loyal guards. I think we can reasonably assume he's planning to join them."

"So that's why a group of guards have joined us." Emmela's brows had drawn together. "What kind of game are these people playing? Is the king aware of all this?"

"The king is aware of our expedition, and we have his official approval, even to act against his brother if he tries to hinder us," she replied. "The prince left without revealing his plans to the king. But sedition might be the least of our problems. The king isn't aware of it, but someone listened in on one of their secret meetings. They seem desperate to find *Ode to the Fallen One*."

Emmela's face paled with shock. "They couldn't be *that* foolish, could they?"

"It's only fair to tell you that Adrastas doesn't take that part of it seriously. He isn't convinced the book still exists, and he thinks any talk of it was nothing more than hot air."

"But you're inclined to take it seriously?"

"I can't shrug it off so easily." She shifted her feet restlessly. "I'll admit it's been weighing heavily on me."

"That's hardly surprising," Emmela told her emphatically. Holding up a hand, she began counting off fingers. "Secret meetings with the prince and three senior nobles. Getting you arrested when you exposed them. Killing Adrastas's dog to force his hand. Racing off to who knows where with the prince and a group of his guards. It's no wonder you're concerned. They're definitely up to something."

"Thanks for taking me seriously."

Emmela gave her arm a sympathetic squeeze. "Where do you think they are now?"

It was a troubling question. "They're far enough away that I can't track their glimmer. As long as they avoid using magic, they can essentially remain invisible. And without definite knowledge of their destination, trying to find them is like searching for a grain of sand on the riverbank."

"Why are we heading north?"

"If they're searching for the book, I'm very sure they'll make for the Drakkenridge Mountains."

"So you're betting on the book."

"I don't know of anywhere else to start looking."

Inga's team had been making steady progress in their journey northward. With no reason for secrecy, they were using major roads whenever possible. Established roads didn't always follow the precise direction Inga wanted to take, but the going was easier, and the party was making good time.

Whenever towns lay in their path, they paused only to restock their provisions. All of them would gladly have welcomed the comfort of an inn, but Inga knew only too well that tongues loved to wag. They instead slept in the open around a large fire. Ramond set a watch whenever they stopped, and Inga did nothing to discourage him. Unlikely as it seemed that they were in any danger, she saw no benefit in taking unnecessary chances.

The day came when Inga could see a dark smudge on the horizon.

The mountains were still too far away for her to detect auras, but she began to spend long periods scanning with her farsense.

The mountains were taking shape when they made camp the following night.

Ramond approached her as soon as they halted. "These mountains have a disturbing reputation," he said. "I know a man who ventured no further than the foothills, and if his report is to be believed, large and extremely dangerous predators are the least we can expect. I'll be doubling the guard each night from now on, and whatever protection your people can provide would also be welcome."

She nodded. "I will see to it."

Drawing the mages aside, she passed on what Ramond had said. "Ellis and Kaspra, I need you to set wards around our camp, and whatever protective barriers you can manage. The horses need protection as much as we do—we'll be extremely vulnerable out here without them."

"We can set wards, but we'll need to be awake to provide full protection," Kaspra told her.

"We can take shifts," added Ellis, "although it means neither of us will get a good sleep."

"Speak to Ramond. Perhaps his men can manage on their own for part of the night. They can still call on you if you're needed."

They both nodded their agreement.

"Alexis and Emmela, be ready to help if the need arises."

"Any sign of Lars and Petria yet?" asked Emmela.

"Not so far," she replied. "But I'm spending a lot of my time searching now."

By agreement with Ramond, Ellis and Kaspra each took a two-hour shift, with the guards covering the rest. Thankfully, the night passed without incident.

Ramond joined Inga as soon as everyone was stirring.

"One of my men has found fresh paw prints not far from where the horses were tethered. I examined the prints myself. I've never seen an animal with paws that size. My men are on high alert." He appeared no more troubled than usual, in spite of the news.

"Thank you, Ramond. I'll warn Kaspra and Ellis to be especially wary."

He fixed her with a measuring gaze. "I don't doubt you have good reason for keeping your own counsel. If you want me and my men to be effective though, it would help to have some indication of what we might be facing."

Inga waved Emmela to her side. "Could you please get Alexis, Kaspra, and Ellis?"

Emmela turned away with a nod.

While she was gone, Inga turned back to Ramond. "The chief master told me I could trust you. It's time I took you into my confidence. You can share whatever seems appropriate with your men. Emmela is aware of everything I'm about to tell you, and she will give you direction should anything happen to me."

As soon as Emmela returned with the three mages, Inga gave all of them a brief outline of the background to the mission and its purpose. She omitted any reference to the book, but otherwise gave a complete account.

The mercenary gazed calmly back at her. "My men and I answer to the chief master and therefore to you. Nevertheless, all of us call Periton home. We're not looking for a confrontation with a member of the royal family."

Inga didn't waver. "The king gave his explicit approval for this mission—in writing. He assured the chief master there will be consequences for anyone who interferes with it, including the prince."

A slight flicker of Ramond's eyebrows was his only reaction to this news. Nodding his head respectfully, he returned to his men.

"Not much seems to fluster that one," offered Emmela.

"No. And before long we might have good reason to appreciate it," Inga replied.

VOLUME 3—RENEGADE

CHAPTER 23

For the best part of two days, Kylen and the twins had been walking as fast as they were able, trying to keep up with the long strides of the mage. Breaks were infrequent and never long enough.

Putting on a burst of speed, Kylen caught up with their leader. "We'll never catch Lars and Petria at this rate," he said breathlessly.

"Don't imagine I'm unaware of that," the mage replied. "They were out of range of your farsense faster than I expected. That must mean they're traveling on horseback, and they're pushing their animals to the limit."

He steepled his brows in frustration. "There's a reason for their sudden haste, and I can't figure out what it is." His face cleared. "At least we know roughly where they're going."

"To the mountains?" asked Kylen.

"To the mountains," agreed his mentor.

"Would you like us to arrange for some horses?" asked Jonno.

"I would not," Dalthinir replied tartly. "We won't be needing horses."

Bella rolled her eyes, Jonno snorting in response.

"I should warn you," the mage continued, "The two of you will need to remain behind when we get closer to the mountains. Just for a while, and purely for your own safety."

"It won't affect us, because by the time you get there we'll have grown old and died," said Bella. Neither her face nor her tone displayed the faintest hint of irony.

"But we'll send our grandchildren," continued Jonno seriously. "You can leave them behind instead."

Both of them burst into laughter.

The mage ignored them. He'd told them clearly he didn't want them around when it became dangerous, and perhaps he thought that would be the end of the subject. If so, he didn't know the twins as well as he thought.

Kylen wasn't going to utter a word though, not when Dalthinir was finally including him in the action.

He decided to change the subject. "If we don't need horses, how will we get to the mountains?"

"I've been giving that a lot of thought," was all he got in return.

With little to distract them as they walked, Kylen decided to raise a subject that had been niggling away at him. *Ode to the Fallen One* had captured his imagination, and he was eager to know more about it. Since the mage had been unusually guarded on the topic, he decided to approach the matter indirectly.

Sidling up to him, he asked, "This book that Lars and Petria want— why is it so dangerous?"

"Every book written in the dragon tongue is dangerous. Even opening such a book can have devastating effects. To read one aloud is much worse. But few have the destructive potential of *Ode to the Fallen One*. Every mage learns about its history. The book is known to have played a role in the Great Desolation."

"What's that?"

His mentor eyed him for a long minute. "How much did Olatiren teach you about the origins of the kingdom where we live, the Kingdom of Periton?"

"He told me that it was once a province of a much larger kingdom."

Dalthinir nodded. "At one time the kingdom of Methesia was prosperous and thriving, spanning the entire continent. The capital was Ettaran. It is said that it was fair to behold and a center of culture and commerce. By night its lights outshone the stars. It was regarded as a wonder of the world. The kingdom's mages were numerous and powerful, and their many achievements enriched the kingdom. The ruler had two sons, and he sent them to rule over outlying provinces so they could gain experience. The crown prince oversaw Tantel, the larger of the two provinces, from its capital Antilin. The younger brother was installed in Periton in our own capital of Cambrick.

"At the height of the kingdom's glory, a terrible calamity came upon it, leaving much of it devastated. It is referred to as the Great Desolation. The capital was destroyed, the king and its citizens along with it. The provinces ruled by the king's two sons largely escaped the ruin, protected by mountain ranges that separated them from the rest of Methesia. The provinces became independent kingdoms."

"Why didn't the crown prince become king of everything that remained?"

"Because the two brothers had a falling out. They were estranged and fought a bitter war for many years."

"Why?"

The mage sighed. "It was over a woman. It's a story for another time. What's important is that dragons were responsible for the destruction of Methesia."

"But I thought you said dragons are extinct! They were driven away by the mages."

"That happened as a direct result of the destruction of Methesia. After the dragons turned on the kingdom, the mages united to fight them. Working together they were ultimately victorious. Few of them survived though. So much knowledge was lost. It was a dark time. Ettaran and everything surrounding it was ruined. It remains an uninhabitable wasteland to this day—no one goes there. Tantel and Periton limped on, gradually rebuilding their strength. Both kingdoms are relatively prosperous today. Nevertheless, the Compact based in Cambrick is a pale shadow of the mage council that gathered in Ettaran during Methesia's heyday."

Lost in his thoughts, Kylen had nothing to say.

"Dragon magic is perilous," Dalthinir concluded grimly. "Almost as perilous as dragons themselves. But unfortunately, historians agree that human mages today have access to a small fraction of the power wielded by dragons. And the greedy have always lusted for more. Allowing Lars and Petria to succeed will only lead to further devastation."

Kylen was left with a great deal to ponder. He only realized later that he'd come away from the interaction with more questions than answers about *Ode to the Fallen One*.

He shook his head in frustration. There had to be a way to satisfy his curiosity. He would keep looking until he found it.

THE SUN WAS NEARING the horizon when Dalthinir approached him, a thoughtful look in his eye.

"I've allowed myself to become much too preoccupied," he said. "It's time we continued your education."

Kylen nodded in anticipation. The more he knew the better.

"The mage senses we've covered so far are mage smell and mage touch. Today we'll talk about the ability to create illusions. We refer to it as mage taste. The mage becomes a kind of chef, manipulating the taste buds of the imagination with illusionary magic."

He grinned when he saw the look on Kylen's face.

"I can see you think it's odd to draw a link between illusionary magic and taste. I did too when I first learned about it. But it does make sense. The idea was popularized many years ago by Master Ella, who pointed to the way spices and other flavorings are used either to mask or to enhance the taste of food. She suggested that illusion is similar, because it masks or enhances the appearance of reality."

"Are you able to create illusions?"

Dalthinir shook his head. "Not many mages are capable of it. Emmela is one of them." He stroked his beard distractedly. "I'm sorry to say that some mages dismiss mage taste as being somehow lesser than other magical senses."

"Why?"

"Because they're snobs." He frowned. "Magical snobbery is no less ugly than any other kind of snobbery."

His face cleared again. "I haven't told you what mage taste is capable of. There are different forms of illusionary magic, but the most basic expression of it is to make something appear different from how it actually is. A more unusual expression of it is to make something disappear."

"You mean it actually disappears?"

"Not at all. The object isn't gone—it just appears to be. Illusionary magic doesn't actually change anything, and no matter what form it takes, the effect is only temporary."

Kylen wasn't sure whether to be relieved or disappointed. "Does it affect anything apart from what you can see?"

"That's a good question, Kylen. I like it when you're paying close attention! Someone with strong ability can create illusions that affect other physical senses as well. For example, if a dog is made to look like a skunk, the animal might smell like a skunk as well. Equally, if a real skunk is made to disappear, any lingering trace of its smell might disappear too."

It sounded impressive. "Does Master Emmela have strong ability with mage taste?"

"She does, although I've had very little opportunity to see her in action."

It seemed like a good time to raise another issue he had been curious about.

"Can mages use up all of their power?"

"Not permanently. Power isn't like a cup that's empty once you've drained it. It's more like a pool renewed by a spring. You can take water from the pool, but the spring will replace it. If you take too much water too quickly, though, you might empty the pool. The spring will fill it up again, but it will take time."

"What happens when you use too much power too quickly?"

"You get weary. Physically weary. It takes time to recover."

"Is it worse for someone who's old? Or someone who isn't physically strong?"

"No, being old doesn't seem to affect the amount of power you have, or your recovery time. The condition your body's in doesn't seem to matter either."

"Do all mages get tired after using the same amount of energy?"

"No. The most powerful mages get tired more slowly, and they also recover more quickly. And it isn't just about the amount of power. One mage might be able to deliver a powerful burst of power for a short period, while another might be capable of delivering a weaker burst of power over a much longer period. Just like some people are good at running fast over short distances, and some are better at running more slowly over long distances. The most powerful mages are capable of doing both."

"Did dragons run out of power?"

Dalthinir smiled. "You have a lot of questions! I believe the answer was no. As well as possessing greater magical strength, dragons are thought to have possessed unending power, which means they could keep using power for as long as they wanted."

The lesson came to an abrupt end as the light faded. Kylen was left with plenty to think about.

It took a while to find somewhere suitable to camp for the night, but eventually they settled down to sleep after sharing a simple meal.

Kylen fell immediately into a deep slumber. As he slept, he dreamed.

He found himself standing once more in the dark near the ruptured ash tree. This time the old woman came right up to him. She was wearing a hood, and he could see nothing of her face in the dark, but she swayed in his direction. "Destiny! Destiny!" she croaked.

Her bony finger jabbed in his direction. "The child of prophecy is you! YOU are the one!"

He stumbled backward, trying to distance himself from her.

"Power!" she shrieked. "Power will rise in your hands!"

A mighty wind rose abruptly, snatching him into the air. The woman quickly dwindled in size below him, but her final words reached him still. "Doom! Doom upon us all!"

Waking with a start, he found he was sweating profusely. Trembling and still haunted by the dream, he got up and wandered about in an attempt to recover his composure.

"Are you all right?"

Startled, he looked up to find that Bella had joined him. She peered up at him, concern in her eyes.

"I'm fine," he told her, lowering his head to hide his face. "Just a little uncomfortable in the night." He was determined that no one would ever learn of his dream.

Working hard to appear normal, he rejoined the others.

The little party cleared their campsite, setting off again as dawn was lighting the sky.

Some time had passed since Kylen last detected another mage apart from Dalthinir. At the location where they built the bridge, the glimmer of mages in Cambrick had been on the limit of Kylen's range. When he headed north in pursuit of Lars and Petria, the Cambrick auras were soon beyond the reach of his farsense. He was therefore taken by surprise later in the day when he again detected auras from the direction of the capital.

"A group of five mages has left the capital, Dalthinir," he announced.

"Who are they?"

"Inga and Emmela. I don't know the other three."

The mage's eyebrows had gone up in surprise. "Where are they headed?"

"In this direction. And they're moving quickly."

"When are they likely to reach us?"

"Maybe late today or tomorrow morning."

After musing for a few moments, Dalthinir told them, "We'll stay well away from roads and open country. I'll hide our glimmer. Let me know once they're about to reach us, Kylen."

Kylen had thought they were already walking quickly. He and the twins were soon in for a surprise. They were almost forced to run to keep up.

He brought them to a halt within sight of a broad river. They were in the open, but it didn't seem to bother him.

"There are no fords across this river," he told them. "It's too deep and too wide. There are no bridges for the same reason. There's a ferry further to the east, though. They'll head for that. We will wait here until they're gone."

The mages did indeed head toward the east. It seemed to take forever, but they eventually crossed the river and continued north.

Dalthinir had not been idle. After spending a considerable period hunting along the riverbank, he called out triumphantly.

All of them hurried to his side. He was standing beside what remained of a small boat. Structurally it appeared sound, but it had holes in the sides as well as in the bottom.

"What use is that?" asked Jonno. "It's going to sink the minute you put it into the water. And the river is flowing west, anyway. A boat won't take us in the right direction."

"Let me worry about that," the mage replied calmly.

"Do you think Inga and her party are well clear of the river?" he asked Kylen.

"They must be, because they're moving quickly again."

"Time for a test, then," said the mage with a smile. "Who would like the first ride?"

"Me," replied Bella without hesitation.

"Wonderful. Everyone can give me a hand getting it into the water."

Between them they carried the boat to the water's edge, placing it gingerly into the water.

When the others stepped back, Jonno continued holding onto it. "It will disappear downriver in a moment if I let it go!" he told them.

"I thought you said it would sink," said the mage with a grin.

All of them looked at it more closely. The holes were there, but no water at all was coming into the boat.

"How are you doing that?" asked Kylen. He sensed an expenditure of power, but it wasn't significant.

His mentor smiled happily. "Most of the credit goes to you, Kylen. It was your idea to use a sack. All I did was establish a waterproof sack around the boat. Jump in, Bella."

Climbing nimbly into the boat, she settled herself in the stern. "Don't worry, I'm a good swimmer," she said.

Jonno let go reluctantly. The boat floated free, with the invisible waterproof sack keeping the inside dry. It was quickly swept downriver.

Then, impossibly, it began to move against the current, returning to the riverbank where it was launched. To Kylen's amazement, he barely detected any use of power.

The mage was perspiring. "That took a lot of effort," he said, helping Bella onto the riverbank before physically hauling the boat out of the water.

All of them must have appeared equally puzzled, because after flopping down exhausted onto the ground he at once began to explain. "As long as the boat is floating, the right amount of pushing magic will move it in any direction we need."

"But even that tiny amount of effort exhausted you!" said Jonno.

"It wasn't just the pushing that wore you out, it was shielding it from the mages nearby," Kylen ventured.

"Yes! Well done, Kylen! I can't use my magic freely, because the mages would be able to detect it. But I could use my power to conceal all traces of magic while you do it."

"Is that going to work?" asked Kylen. "Will we be able to move the boat against the current once all four of us are onboard?"

"No one's around. Let's find out."

"I can't swim!" Kylen reminded him.

"If it comes to that, I'll keep you afloat the same way I'm keeping the boat afloat. You could do it yourself if you needed to."

"When we needed to escape the mages after we first met, you swam, and you pushed me into the water with a branch!" Kylen reminded him. "Why didn't we do something like this?"

The mage raised his hands helplessly. "Apart from the fact that there was no boat for me to use, an idea like this didn't occur to me at the time. I would never have imagined it would be this easy to keep something afloat."

He waved at them. "Enough talk! In you all go!"

The others climbed into the boat. Kylen followed somewhat nervously.

Once aboard he tried giving the boat a magical push. It lurched forward so violently they barely managed to stay aboard. Considerably sobered, he tried again, this time with much less power.

It took some experimentation to get the speed and direction working as he wanted, but before many minutes passed the boat was skimming over the water heading upriver.

"Pull into the bank again, Kylen!"

Kylen obediently redirected the boat toward the shore. They had almost reached the riverbank when the boat hit a submerged root, pitching all four of them into the water. Reaching out desperately, Kylen managed to grab hold of the side of the boat. Dalthinir must have been as good as his word, because he sensed that even if he let go he wasn't going to sink. He clung on tightly anyway.

The mage was the first to reach dry land, and he moved quickly to help Kylen from the water. After slapping his shivering apprentice cheerfully on the back, he helped the twins ashore.

Having reached dry land, Kylen glanced back at the boat. Astonishingly, it didn't appear more damaged than it was already.

"That water's cold," grumbled Bella.

"Never mind," chuckled Dalthinir. "I'll get a fire going. We'll soon have you all warm."

All of them were soon warming themselves before a roaring blaze. They continued to soak up the warmth until their clothes began to show signs of drying.

"You seem able to access your power reliably now, Kylen," ventured the mage.

"It's thanks to you! It was your suggestion about using my gut instead of my head that made all the difference."

The mage smiled. "It wasn't my idea. An older mage suggested it to me when I was first learning. I should have thought of it sooner."

Kylen shrugged. He was just glad he finally knew what to do.

"Did pushing the boat wear you out?" asked the mage.

He shook his head. "I don't feel at all weary. I enjoyed it!"

"It was incredible!" Jonno enthused. "Apart from the dunking, that is! Why aren't we making use of what's left of the daylight?"

"Think about it," said the mage patiently. "What will people say when they notice a boat gliding upriver by itself with four people in it? Especially if they look closely and see that the boat is full of holes."

"I suppose when you put it like that..." conceded Jonno.

"We'll travel at night as much as possible. It should be safe enough if we keep to the middle of the river."

Bella had finally stopped shivering. "Will this river get us all the way to the mountains?"

The mage shook his head. "If I remember my geography correctly, we can follow this river northeast. It will merge with a river that flows in a southerly direction from the Drakkenridge Mountains. If we follow that river north, it should get us roughly to where we need to go. I've walked in the region before, and I know both the river and the terrain. We're fortunate that it's late summer. The river from the mountains can become quite wild during the spring thaw."

He glanced up at the sky. "It will be dusk soon. I suggest we all rest for a couple of hours. Then we can make a proper beginning."

CHAPTER 24

After a few nights on the river, Kylen had become adept at moving the boat through the water. The mage was responsible for keeping it afloat and masking their magic.

"My power seems to be increasing," he told the mage. "I was expecting I'd be worn out by now. Is it like climbing onto roofs—the more you do it, the better you get at it?"

"I can't say," Dalthinir replied. "To begin with, I don't yet know the limit of your power. I can only say you show unusual potential. As for me, I'm managing to do my share, but only barely."

The following night tested them to the limit. They had reached the junction of the two rivers at last, and it was apparent even in the darkness that the passage would be unusually hazardous.

"Take us in to the bank, Kylen. We can't attempt this in the dark. We'll have to risk doing it during daylight hours."

Kylen took them to the northern bank of the river they had been traveling on. The river flowing from the mountains in the north now joined their river a little ahead of them to their left.

Once they had pulled the boat from the water, they gratefully took the opportunity to sleep through what remained of the night.

When he got up the next morning, he found the mage peering out at the river, a frown creasing his face.

He pointed at white water boiling endlessly over a series of rocks. "We'd never have made it if we tried to get across that in the dark."

"Can we do it the daylight?"

Dalthinir glanced along the bank. "We'll carry the boat as far upriver as we can. That might get us past the worst of it. Beyond that?" He shrugged. "It's impossible to say."

Jonno had joined them. "Won't the boat be too heavy?"

"You'll make it lighter for us, won't you?" asked Bella, stepping up beside them.

"We will indeed, Bella," said the mage. "We'll start as soon as we've broken our fast."

The ground along the western bank of the new river proved to be rocky and uneven. Even with the boat lightened magically, it was large enough and awkward enough that carrying it became extremely challenging, even for a short distance. All of them were suffering from stubbed toes and sore feet before they'd been at it for an hour. Another hour later, the ground had become impassable.

"This is as far as we go," said the mage, slumping to the ground in exhaustion.

The boiling water that marked the joining of two rivers lay well below them now, but a series of rapids still stretched off into the distance upriver.

"I've been here during the spring thaw," Dalthinir told them. "Ironically, this section of the river isn't nearly so difficult then, because the water level is high enough to cover those rocks completely."

"It's a pity we're not on the other bank," said Jonno.

Whenever Kylen had glanced across the river previously, the opposite bank had been largely obscured by rocks and trees. Now he saw a broad meadow stretching along the eastern bank of the river. Directly opposite them, and for as far as he could see upstream, the meadow reached right to the edge of the water. It almost seemed to be mocking them.

"Why don't we go to the other side?" suggested Bella.

"How are we going to do that?" asked Kylen, unable to prevent himself from sounding grumpy.

"We can retrace our steps," she said calmly. "Once we're back where we landed, it might be possible to sail safely to the other side."

Kylen stared at her incredulously. "But that will take us the rest of the day!"

"It's a good suggestion," said Dalthinir. "She's using her head. It will cost us a lot of time, but I can't see an alternative."

With no better ideas on offer, Kylen gave in to the inevitable.

Carrying the boat back down the riverbank proved no less frustrating than carrying it up, but they made it back to the place where they had started without incident.

Launching into the first river again, they crossed to the far side where the water was less turbulent. Then they traveled upriver past the junction and crossed to the northern bank once more. Before long they were able to go ashore across from their original landing place. Now on the eastern side of the new river, they began hauling the boat once more along the riverbank in the direction of the mountains.

As Kylen had predicted, it took them the rest of the day to reach the meadow. They arrived as the light was fading.

Throwing themselves down in exhaustion, all of them fell at once into a deep sleep. Kylen didn't stir before the sun rose.

THE MORNING HAD ALMOST GONE by the time they were beyond the rapids and ready to launch the boat again. The relatively even ground on the eastern bank of the river had continued for some distance, but eventually it too gave way to rocky ground. Although their path had never become impassable, it cost considerable time and effort before the most dangerous stretch of the river lay behind them.

As with the previous day, Kylen had used his mage touch ability to lighten the boat while Dalthinir masked his use of magic. Continuous physical exertion and uninterrupted magical toil had wearied them all. Tempers were showing signs of becoming frayed, and even the normally long-suffering Dalthinir had spoken irritably to Jonno a couple of times.

Nevertheless, the mage was unwilling to lose two entire days to the troublesome set of rapids. Having sighted no one for several days, the risk of being observed seemed small. With clear water ahead of them, they climbed aboard once more and resumed their journey.

So began the most perilous part of their river journey.

For three hours they made good progress. The river was narrower and the flow faster than the previous river, but Kylen had no difficulty steering around the rocks they encountered. However as the shadows were lengthening they found a new set of rapids waiting for them.

Dalthinir scanned both banks of the river. "From the look of the terrain, the western bank appears more promising," he called, his voice barely carrying over the roar of the water.

Responding with a brief nod, Kylen guided the boat to the riverbank and leaped ashore, holding the boat while the others alighted. All of them worked together to pull it from the water.

"We'll need to carry it past the rapids again," the mage announced, to a chorus of groans.

With no good reason to delay, they set off immediately. After struggling upstream for more than an hour, they were relieved to find they had left the rapids behind.

Eyeing the sun critically, Dalthinir shook his head. "It's too late to risk the river. We've earned a break—we'll rest now and continue in the morning."

Kylen slumped to the ground exhausted. His power wasn't close to being depleted, but the concentration required to constantly scan the river for hazards had worn him out.

All of them woke refreshed at dawn.

"How much further do we need to go?" Kylen asked.

"Perhaps two or three days, providing we don't encounter too many more obstacles. Can you detect any mages?"

Kylen shook his head.

"That suggests we're ahead of them. It's one thing we can be grateful for."

The morning passed quickly as they followed the river into the mountains. They had barely entered the foothills, but Kylen glanced upward to see snow-capped peaks towering above them in the distance.

He glanced up to find the mage watching him.

"Do you feel it too?" Dalthinir asked. He jerked his head toward the mountains.

Kylen nodded reluctantly. "It feels...dangerous."

He hadn't wanted to admit it to himself, but a sense of menace had slowly been growing as they drew ever closer to the peaks of the Drakkenridge Mountains.

The mage nodded. "The danger is real. We'll need to leave Jonno and Bella behind soon."

Thankfully the twins weren't within earshot. They wouldn't be at all impressed, but Kylen was beginning to understand why the mage felt so strongly about it. They had plenty of raw courage, but courage wouldn't be enough to deal with whatever was waiting up there.

"Time to go!" called Dalthinir.

Once more they climbed aboard the little vessel. Once more Dalthinir kept it afloat while Kylen drove it forward.

The afternoon was drawing on and the mountains towering ever higher when Jonno called a sudden warning as they rounded a bend in the river. "White water!"

The rapids were upon them before Kylen could adjust the power driving them forward. There was no chance to search for a suitable landing place. Plunged into turbulence with barely an instant to decide, Kylen saw only two choices: press on, or remove the power entirely and allow the current to sweep them back the way they had come. He chose to press on.

Water churned forcefully around submerged or barely visible rocks, and Kylen's heart raced as he wrestled with the boat, driving it through the maelstrom. Tossed about wildly, narrowly missing one obstacle only to scrape noisily over the next, they lurched from one direction to another.

Then suddenly they were through, and moving steadily through calm water. Kylen heaved a massive sigh of relief.

The noise of the water had been increasing. Rounding the latest bend in the river, they quickly discovered the reason. A new and even more uncertain set of rapids lay a short distance ahead.

With the river rushing through a channel bounded by jagged rocks on both sides, landing the boat was out of the question.

"We have to go back!" yelled the mage.

Kylen responded immediately. As the flow of power ended, the current gripped the boat, sweeping it downriver faster than he could have imagined. The previous rapids were looming rapidly, and he hastily applied power to slow the boat down.

It was neither the time nor the place for a first attempt at an extremely tricky maneuver. Underestimating the power required, he failed to slow the boat sufficiently. Swept inexorably forward by the roiling waters, it smashed down hard onto a partially submerged rock and broke apart.

Kylen was pitched into the water. He needed to at least try to protect himself, but everything was happening too quickly. Tossed about mercilessly, his head sustained a heavy blow from a passing rock.

Everything went black.

Kylen wandered alone in the dark. He had no idea where he was or how he came to be there. All he knew was he needed to keep moving forward.

The stillness of the air and the faint echoes of his footfalls suggested he was in a huge enclosed space. Reaching down, he felt the ground beneath his feet. As hard as it was smooth and even, it could only be solid rock.

He shuffled forward cautiously, unable to guess when his groping feet might suddenly meet nothingness, plunging him into a fissure. Then as he proceeded, a dim light began to grow. It had no obvious source. It revealed he was in a vast cavern, featureless and dull.

The light ahead began to grow, thanks to reflections from a large body of water.

Moving forward more quickly, he reached the edge of an underground lake. No ripple disturbed its mirror surface, and no waves lapped gently on the shore at his feet.

A small boat glided steadily toward him. No visible boatman steered it, and it moved without obvious means of propulsion. It came to a halt immediately before him.

Without fully understanding why, he stepped into the boat and sat facing forward on a thwart across the middle of the little craft.

The moment he was settled, the boat sped away from the shore, heading into the heart of the lake. He was not alarmed. He felt strangely detached.

It seemed impossible to keep track of time in this place, but eventually he saw an island rising from the lake. The boat came to rest on a small beach, and he stepped out onto fine white sand.

He knew what to do. Setting off at once, he headed inland.

At first the ground sloped gently upward, but after a while he found himself climbing steadily. The ascent seemed effortless, and he was not breathing heavily when he reached the top.

Peering around in the dim light he saw that the water surrounding the island stretched into the distance on every side. Then he noticed a wooden staff lying on the ground. Taller than him, it was undecorated at its base. The upper section had been ornately carved in the shape of a dragon at rest.

A deep voice sounded, its tone dispassionate. "Take it."

He stared uncertainly at the staff, making no move to obey.

"Take it!" boomed the voice.

His arm reached downward, almost of its own accord. Asserting his will, he brought it to a halt barely a hand's breadth from the object.

A violent wind rose up, buffeting him as it swirled about. The roar of the storm gave voice to a fierce rage, and he crouched low in fear.

On impulse he glanced up to see a dark mass plunging down through the storm, spreading out to engulf him.

Everything went suddenly white.

CHAPTER 25

Even as he was being propelled into the water, Dalthinir acted on his promise to protect Kylen. A waterproof sack enveloped the helpless apprentice, quickly reinforced with a layer of protection. The mage could only hope he'd been in time both to prevent him from drowning and to protect him from injury.

There was little more he could do for Kylen. Enveloping himself in a sack of his own, he tried to catch sight of the twins. As he cleared the rapids he caught a brief glimpse of Bella's head. Thankfully she had made it through as well. She was trying to reach the only stretch of the riverbank accessible from the water. In no time he had wrapped her in a sack and given her a firm push in the right direction.

Jonno was dragging himself out of the water by the time Dalthinir spotted him. Thanks to the mage's assistance, Bella wasn't far behind him. He joined them on the riverbank.

"We need to find Kylen!" he said.

"He can't swim!" Bella exclaimed, her face creased with distress.

"I put some protection around him," Dalthinir assured her. "But there's no telling how far downriver he might be when he makes it to shore."

They set out the moment they were capable of doing so. Thankfully the ground beside the riverbank was reasonably even, and they hurried along it, peering into the water and along both banks for any sign of their friend.

An hour passed with no hint of the missing youth. Even Dalthinir's farsense failed to detect the faintest sniff of power. Determined not to yield to his darkest imaginings, he was nevertheless becoming increasingly concerned. After two hours, they were back in the foothills. With the light beginning to fail, the need to find Kylen quickly was becoming pressing.

"Look!" Bella called suddenly.

A flock of swallows was sweeping in and out above two rocks near the far side of the river.

"Do you see where those birds are flying?" she asked. "Is there something in the river between the rocks?"

Peering across the water in the fading light, Dalthinir thought he could dimly see something between them.

"I'm going to investigate!" he called.

Buoyed up by a waterproof sack, he struck out for the rocks. The current tried to drag him away, but he fought it with pushing magic. Even before he reached the rocks he knew it was Kylen. The protective sack was still in place, but his apprentice was not moving.

"Kylen!" he called.

There was no reply.

Positioning himself upstream of the rocks, he began tugging at Kylen's limp body. He was wedged in tight. Becoming desperate, the mage drew upon his magic and wrenched him free. Then he pushed them both to the bank as rapidly as he could. As he reached dry land, he realized that in his distraction none of his magic had been masked. He didn't care.

Jonno and Bella helped drag Kylen ashore. Swiftly examining him, the mage saw to his immense relief he was still breathing. A dark bruise on the side of his head hinted at the reason for his state of unconsciousness.

"Can you heal him?" asked Bella.

He shook his head. "I'm sorry to say a situation like this is beyond my skill."

"When will he wake up?" asked Jonno.

The mage shrugged helplessly. "All we can do is wait and hope for the best. In the meantime, we won't be moving him. We'll camp here tonight."

The mage spent an anxious and restless night at Kylen's side. Even though he knew there was little point, he constantly checked to satisfy himself the youth was still breathing. In the early hours of the morning he drifted off to sleep.

He woke to find Kylen conscious again. His relief knew no bounds.

"How are you feeling?" he asked gently.

"My head hurts," Kylen replied. "I'm not sure I'll be able to do much with the boat for a while."

"Forget the boat! Can you see clearly?"

A slow and thorough check of his apprentice's condition convinced the mage he had a good chance of recovering fully.

"You need to rest," he told Kylen sternly. "Promise me you won't get up and won't use any magic—not unless I give you permission."

Kylen nodded his agreement.

Moving away from him, Dalthinir stared absently off into the distance. After ten years of hiding, he had finally been drawn into the open. At first it had been to rescue a newly awakened and highly vulnerable young mage. Now he saw himself hurtling toward the greatest crisis Periton had faced in generations.

It was hard to believe the two situations were unrelated. Kylen had appeared at an unusually critical time. It was tempting to wonder if there was a higher purpose behind it.

He sighed. Who could comprehend the mysterious designs of Providence?

He called the twins aside. "We can't afford to wait here for Kylen to heal," he told them. "I could leave him behind with the two of you, but it's impossible to know what's going to happen. Something tells me he will be needed there. It'll be a few days before he can get around normally though. That means we'll need to build a stretcher."

Jonno nodded immediately. "I'm familiar with stretchers. They used one at the farm a few years ago."

"Can you scout around for some suitable materials?"

"Definitely!"

They were gone in a moment. He wasn't surprised—people usually needed something to do at times of crisis.

By noon they had built a crude stretcher.

The moment he saw it, Kylen protested. "I don't need that! I can walk on my own!"

"I've seen cases like yours before," the mage replied. "People who don't give themselves time to recover after a head injury suffer for it later. You won't be doing anything except resting for a few days."

The only response was a grunt.

At that moment Dalthinir noticed Kylen was leaking power again. With the distraction of all that had been happening he'd somehow failed to notice it. The power wasn't significant, but any mage in the vicinity would be able to detect it. He masked the leakage at once.

He wouldn't have considered asking Kylen to do it. In his condition it wouldn't have seemed right. There was one question his apprentice might be able to answer though.

"Can you detect any glimmer?"

After closing his eyes for a moment, Kylen replied, "Only yours."

It was encouraging that he could still detect magical auras. It remained to be seen if his range had been affected.

ALL OF THEM rested for a full day before resuming their journey. This time Kylen was lying dutifully on the stretcher.

Although the others had agreed to rotate the role of bearer between the three of them, Dalthinir intended to do much more than an even share of the work. Thankfully he was able to call upon his abilities to lighten the load.

Even so, the bearers set off acutely aware that a long and arduous journey lay ahead of them.

WHEN CONSCIOUSNESS RETURNED, it left Kylen groggy and with a pounding headache. He remembered nothing after allowing the boat to run with the current.

Nothing apart from his strange dream. Overwhelming as the experience had been, it seemed distant and unreal as he peered about, disoriented in the daylight. The impact of it faded quickly, to the point where he soon struggled to remember any of the details.

The pain in his head gradually eased as the hours passed, and he felt increasingly alert. Being required to rest for an entire day was a big challenge, and he became even more uneasy the following morning when Dalthinir confined him once more to a stretcher.

By the time the day ended, the bearers could only collapse to the ground in exhaustion. When a new day dawned and Dalthinir still insisted on using the stretcher, Kylen began to feel distressed.

The effort it cost the bearers was increasingly obvious. Seeing the noonday sun beat down mercilessly as Jonno and the mage struggled to carry him over difficult terrain, Kylen could remain silent no longer.

"Let me at least help lighten the load! It wouldn't be any effort."

Dalthinir would have none of it. "You need to rest!" he insisted. "That means a rest from magic as well."

Kylen groaned in exasperation. He was feeling remarkably well. In fact he was brimming with energy. In spite of his recent head injury, he could scarcely remember a time when he'd been thinking so clearly.

He was also bursting with power. A great deal had changed since his power was first awakened. It was welling up inside him now, begging to be used.

Lying on his back he could see clouds wrapped around the upper reaches of the mountains, as if cloaking deep mysteries hidden there. His instinct told him that extraordinary dangers awaited him in those mountains. Yet he was not afraid.

An eagle glided into view, and at once he saw the world through the eagle's eyes. The experience was no product of his imagination— this time he was certain. Below he saw three figures clustered around the stretcher, progressing slowly through a rough and broken land-scape. He discerned at once the route they needed to take, and he saw that carrying a stretcher across the terrain ahead would soon become impossible.

Tilting its wings, the monarch of the skies rode the thermals southeast. Before Kylen lost contact with it, he glimpsed through its eyes a group of people heading toward the mountains on horseback.

The sight prompted him to reach out with his farsense. He immediately sensed that Lars and Petria were in the group. Reaching out further, he saw a group of five mages behind them. Only two of them were known to him: Inga and Emmela.

His bearers stumbled, dragging his attention back to the present. Bella had taken Jonno's place with Dalthinir, but a quick glance was enough to reveal that all three of them were in a state of exhaustion.

"What's wrong?" he asked, baffled.

Putting down the stretcher, they slumped to the ground.

Dalthinir contemplated him wearily before answering. Finally he shrugged. "You've been leaking power. At first it was easy to hide it for you, but the power has been growing in strength. It's pouring out of you now, and masking it isn't easy. At first I was able to lighten the load, but I had to stop. We've been forced to rely on physical strength to carry the stretcher."

Appalled, Kylen shut off the leakage immediately. He needed no instruction. It was the work of a moment, and it cost him almost nothing.

"I'm so sorry!" he said in dismay. "Why didn't you tell me?"

"I wanted you to rest."

"I truly appreciate your concern, but it's time for me to walk on my own two feet," said Kylen decisively, leaping up from his makeshift bed.

Seeing the alarm on the mage's face, he added, "I'm not just being foolish. I don't understand why, but I'm stronger than I've ever been. My power is fully accessible to me. Fully! And I know how to use it."

Dalthinir opened his mouth, but Kylen didn't give him time to speak. "I know where Lars and Petria are right now," he continued, "and I know where they're headed. There are others with them as well. Inga and Emmela are following with three other mages. They must be almost a day behind."

Before the mage could respond, he added breathlessly, "If we're going to have any hope of catching them, I need to lead. The terrain is impassable ahead. We'll have to divert a little to the south."

All of them were staring at him.

Dalthinir's mouth was hanging open. "You've stopped the leakage," he said. He seemed unable to decide between being relieved and astonished. "How do you know there are other people with Lars and Petria?"

"I saw them. Through the eyes of an eagle."

"Mage sight," breathed Dalthinir in wonder. "I haven't even told you about it!"

He must have seen his apprentice's quizzical look. "It's very rare, but mage sight gives the ability to borrow the senses of non-human creatures—seeing through their eyes, and sometimes hearing through their ears. Even borrowing the other senses of the animal." He shook his head. "I don't know of anyone who can do it apart from you."

He stared at the youth, his face unreadable.

"Very well," he said finally. "I'm willing to let you walk on your own. And if you know where they're going, you should lead. Where are they headed?"

"I don't know how to describe it. They don't seem to be heading for a location. It's more of a place and time."

"What does that mean?"

Kylen shrugged. "I can't say. I don't understand it myself. There's a powerful magical emanation of some kind. Not power being used, and not a magical aura. That's all I can say."

"I sense it too," the mage confirmed, "and I can't account for it either. Whatever it means, we need to reach Lars and Petria before they can do any damage. Will we reach them in time?"

"We might. If we hurry."

Dalthinir turned to the twins. "Thank you for helping us. I never intended for you to come this far, but I freely acknowledge that we needed you. If you return to the river now you should be safe. You can wait for us there."

"We're not going," said Jonno stubbornly.

"If you leave us behind, we'll follow you anyway," added Bella.

The mage covered his face with his hands.

"I don't think it's our place to push them away," said Kylen. "I had no idea what I was getting them into when I encouraged them to leave the city, but I do know we wouldn't be here without them. This is their journey too. They have as much right to be here as we do."

"Perhaps so," said Dalthinir reluctantly. "I'm not confident I'll be able to protect them, but maybe you can."

Kylen winced. "I can't make any promises—I don't know what we'll be facing. I'm not saying they need to come with us. I'm only saying we shouldn't try to prevent them if that's what they want to do."

The mage gazed at each of them in turn. "Very well. I won't try to stop you."

Both of them grinned in triumph.

"Don't think I'm doing you some kind of favor," he told them grimly. "This could end very badly for all of us." He sighed. "But if you insist on joining us, we'll face it together."

"Then it's time to go!" said Kylen.

From that moment the apprentice became the leader. With the eagle's view of the landscape fixed in his mind, he guided them forward.

CHAPTER 26

Petria was the first to emerge from Lady Mardell's final way house at the foot of the Drakkenridge Mountains. The first glow of dawn had begun to lighten the sky.

Prince Evran followed her out, his captain at his side.

The captain peered at the barn beside the main building where the horses had been left. "Where are the guards?" he growled. "If they've fallen asleep on their shift they'll regret it."

He strode purposefully toward the barn. With no guards at the entrance, he disappeared inside. No more than a minute passed before he raced from the barn, his face pale.

"Your Highness, please remain here!" he called urgently.

Without waiting for the prince to respond, he thrust his head through the entrance and bellowed, "Get up! All of you! Report to me at once!"

Lars emerged, frowning at the captain. "What's all the yelling about?" he demanded indignantly.

Ignoring him, the captain turned to the prince. "Both of the guards are dead, Your Highness. They've been torn apart! And the horses are gone."

The prince rounded on Lars. "You're the only one here capable of setting wards and providing shields. Did you do so?"

"Of course I did," Lars replied frostily. "I set wards on the main building. No one told me your men were incapable of looking after themselves!"

Petria moved quickly to redirect the conversation. "How are we going to manage without horses?"

Turning his back pointedly on Lars, the prince addressed himself to Petria. "Horses are useless in the mountains," he told her. "Before long we would have sent them back here with a couple of the men anyway. We only need them for the return journey."

As he spoke, men were scrambling out of the building.

The captain lined them up. "We had visitors in the night," he told them grimly. "Big cats most likely. They're common in these mountains. We're two men down now." He stabbed a finger. "You two dig a trench and get what's left of them into it." Seeing their faces he growled, "Be grateful it didn't happen on your shift!"

He faced the remaining two. "Take a good look around the area. And be careful! I've had enough surprises for one day!"

The men moved away to do his bidding, their reluctance painfully obvious.

The morning was spent by the time they set out. On foot and reduced in number, every member of the party was more cautious than ever. The captain deployed the remaining guards two at the front and two at the rear of the group, and Petria could see that none of them were pleased with the assignment.

After the messy deaths of their comrades, all of them subtly tried to position themselves as close as possible to Lars. It was hardly surprising. They undoubtedly saw the mage as their only certain guarantee of protection. She couldn't help wondering how much interest he had in their well-being.

By the time the sun set, the party had reached the foothills of the mountains. After lighting a fire, they sat down to eat. Without packhorses to carry supplies, the food was simple and the portions meager. They could expect no better until they returned to Lady Mardell's way house.

After the meal the prince confronted Lars. "Well?" he demanded bluntly. "Are you planning to protect the entire party tonight?"

"I will be setting wards around our whole camp tonight, Your Highness," he replied coolly. "I didn't do so last night because you assured us you were bringing the best of your guards. I had no desire to embarrass you by doing their job for them."

Petria winced. She was stuck with Lars through no choice of her own. Banadin had at least given her seniority over him, and she intended to keep it that way.

Lars hadn't finished. "Don't imagine your men will get a night off duty though. My wards will only give us warning. They won't protect us. I can only maintain a shield when I'm awake, and I need sleep just like anyone else."

After building up the fire, they settled down for the night.

Few of them got any sleep. The silence never felt comfortable, even when it wasn't punctuated by loud growling on every side. The predators responsible for the noises must have been dangerously close to the camp.

Lars in particular was tired and irritable when the sun finally rose. "If one of those beasts comes close enough, I'll put a shield around its head and choke it!" he growled.

After what he'd done to Adrastas's dog, she didn't doubt it.

They resumed their journey in the morning with every member of the party on edge. Their path, initially over even ground, turned rough and broken, resulting in the line gradually becoming strung out as they clambered over rocky outcrops and slipped and slithered across expanses covered with loose rocks and shale.

By the time the sun was making its way toward the western horizon, they were climbing steadily. Positioned near the front of the group, Petria was startled by a sudden cry of terror. She looked up in time to see a wildcat of enormous size pouncing on the guard leading the party. Before the animal could spring away with its victim, she sent a fireball slamming into its haunches. The cat dropped the guard with a piercing scream before scampering away to vanish among the rocks.

Petria hurried to the guard. Sprawled awkwardly on the ground, he lay bleeding freely from jagged wounds. His arm appeared to be broken. Retrieving bandages from the pack on her back, she leaned down to dress his wounds.

The group gathered around, some of them glancing nervously about them.

"Where did that fire come from?" asked the captain.

"You'll find that our Master Petria has quite a liking for fire," said Lars dryly.

"Can you heal him?" the prince asked.

"Neither of us have healing ability," Petria replied. "He won't be able to go anywhere. We'll have to leave a couple of men behind with him."

Lars looked at her as if she were mad. "You can't be serious! They'd end up as meat themselves. And look at him! He won't survive another night."

The guard was in shock and he'd lost a lot of blood. His situation certainly didn't look promising.

"Our priority is to protect the prince," said the captain firmly. "Leaving guards behind is not an option. Especially now we're down to half strength. We won't be staying unless the prince stays."

The prince was clearly torn. "It's an impossible situation," he said, shaking his head.

"We can't afford delays," said Lars forcefully. "Time is against us."

Ignoring him, Petria moved away from the group and began gathering sticks.

"What are you doing?" demanded Lars.

"I'm going to build a fire. It will keep him warm, and it might offer him at least some protection."

Lars glared at her.

She stared back at him with narrowed eyes. "Leave if you want to. I'll catch you up later."

He could rage and storm for all she cared. The truth was he couldn't afford to lose her, and he knew it as well as she did.

The prince joined her, and the remaining guards quickly did the same. Lars didn't say a word, but it was obvious he wasn't happy. She ignored him.

Once enough wood had been gathered, she built a fire, igniting it with her magic. She made sure that plenty of wood lay within reach of his good arm.

"I'm sorry I can't do more," she murmured. If he heard her, he gave no indication of it.

"I'm ready to leave," she informed Lars.

"An idiotic waste of time," he growled. He turned immediately and headed back up the slope.

"From now on we stay close together," called the prince.

The two men at the front immediately closed in on Lars.

"Back off!" growled the mage.

Letting him pass, they congregated around Petria instead. She rolled her eyes but didn't send them away.

After a few minutes she looked back. The injured guard was already lost to sight.

Would he still be alive at dawn? Would another predator finish him off?

She quickly decided that it didn't matter. His death would be regrettable, but there was nothing she could do to save him. And she needed to harden herself. Two men had died already, and many more would die in the upheavals anticipated by Banadin. Great things were rarely achieved without sacrifice.

She didn't allow herself to be distracted for long. There were more important things to think about. She returned her attention to the task before her.

Progress was now slower than ever. Their way led ever upward, and frequent rest breaks became necessary. As the sun inched closer to the western horizon, they came upon a small plateau.

"We'll stop here for the night," the prince announced.

He approached the two mages. "Are you sure we're heading in the right direction?" he asked quietly.

"We can't point you to an exact location, Your Highness," Petria told him. "But we're definitely heading in the right direction."

He nodded in satisfaction before turning away.

Petria was staring fixedly at the mountains towering above them. "It's as the parchment said," she murmured. "The book is drawing us to it."

❄

INGA SOUGHT out Emmela as the party was setting up camp for the night.

"I detected a surge of power," she told Emmela quietly. "Not long before dark."

"Do you know who was responsible?"

"I didn't recognize the scent."

Emmela's eyes went wide. "Dalthinir?"

"I suspect so."

"Where was it?"

"In the direction of the mountains. To the west."

"Are we going to divert toward it?"

Inga stared thoughtfully into the distance. "I don't think so. Something tells me we're going the right way."

"Do you think Lars and Petria would have noticed?"

"It's impossible to say." Inga smiled wryly. "Either way, I have the feeling things will get interesting."

WHEN A NEW MORNING dawned they set off again. Sensing that time was becoming short, Inga had called for the pace to be increased.

Late in the day they paused to give the horses a break. Inga was sitting with Emmela. "Did you sense that?" she asked sharply.

Emmela shook her head. "What was it?"

"A brief surge of power."

"Could you smell who did it?"

"It was Petria."

"Where?"

Inga pointed. "Straight ahead of us. We're going in the right direction."

Their conversation came to an end as Ramond approached them. "We need to decide about the horses," he told them.

They looked at him quizzically.

He pointed toward the mountains. "We've almost reached the foothills. If we're planning to climb those peaks, horses will be a hindrance. Starting from tomorrow we'll need to walk. We can't leave the horses here though, even under guard. They'll be too vulnerable to predators. The best option is probably for a couple of the men to escort them somewhere safe. I spotted a suitable place on the way here and pointed it out to the men. It means more walking on the return journey, but at least we'll know horses are waiting for us."

Inga nodded. "That sounds sensible. Do whatever is needed in the morning."

She was appreciating even more the wisdom of including Ramond and his men in the party. Without them the horses would have become a significant problem.

"We're grateful to you, Ramond. You'll need help again to keep our camp protected tonight. I'll speak with Kaspra and Ellis."

As with the previous night, Kaspra and Ellis each agreed to take a two-hour shift. The guards would cover the rest on the understanding they could call upon the mages if the need arose.

Kaspra took the first shift. Perhaps predators sensed the magical shield around the campsite, because everything was peaceful during her two-hour stint. The situation changed dramatically after she lay down to sleep, leaving only wards in place.

An hour after a pair of guards had taken their turn to watch, the screaming of horses roused the entire camp. Inga sprung up and prepared to defend herself.

Alexis must have been the first on the scene because a fireball suddenly banished the darkness. Inga saw dark shapes prowling near the horses.

The voice of Ellis rang out. "We're protected again! I have a shield in place!"

Men came running with torches, revealing a huge cat inside the shield. As the cat readied itself to pounce on the men, it suddenly slumped to the ground, snarling helplessly.

"Don't worry!" exclaimed Kaspra. "I've wrapped it in a protective shield. It won't be going anywhere."

Ramond stood at alert with sword drawn. "What are we going to do with it?" he asked.

"Can you move it over there?" asked Kaspra, pointing away from the camp. "It can't harm you."

Three of the men tried to manhandle it into the indicated position. The animal was so heavy Ellis eventually provided some magical assistance.

"I'm going to move the protective bubble around the cat," he explained. "Once it's outside the barrier, Kaspra can release it from her shield."

The men watched in fascination as the mages carried out the two actions with what appeared to be effortless ease. Finding itself suddenly free, the cat slunk away into the night.

Ramond's attention had already shifted. "Do we still have all the horses?"

One of the men on guard answered immediately. "The horses were terrified, but I think we got there in time."

"I'm not asking what you think. I'm asking you to check," growled Ramond.

Everything went quiet as the men moved among the horses.

"They're all here, and none of them appear injured!"

"Well done, men," said Ramond, sheathing his sword. "You've handled yourselves well under difficult circumstances."

Inga joined her fellow mages. "Thank you for your help," she told them. "I'm sorry to have to say it, but it's become obvious that the campsite won't be safe without magical help. And unfortunately, there isn't a lot Emmela or I can do to contribute."

"We'll have to manage without much sleep for a while," said Ellis.

The others nodded. "We'll make it work."

Inga settled for the night with a keen awareness that their challenges were probably only beginning.

CHAPTER 27

The morning sun showed bleary eyes everywhere. No one in Inga's party had slept well. Mounting up, they rode until the terrain slowed the horses to a walk. Then they dismounted for the final time.

As soon as provisions from the packhorse were distributed among the others, Ramond selected two of the men to take the horses to safety. The men left within the hour, and those who remained headed deeper into the foothills the moment they were gone.

Kaspra positioned herself near the front of the group while Ellis covered the rear. Between them they intended to ensure the group was protected throughout daylight hours.

Ramond and a couple of his men were skilled trackers, and they soon discovered signs that others had passed that way.

"Should we follow them?" Ramond asked.

Inga nodded. "Don't let us get too close though. We're not here for a confrontation. Our role is to monitor what they're doing."

Barely an hour later an urgent cry from the leading tracker halted the column. Ramond hurried forward, with Inga close behind.

A man lay beside the embers of a fire. Blood soaked a crude bandage, and his face was pale. He appeared to be on the brink of death. One arm was unnaturally bent, and his other hand was tightly grasping a smoldering piece of wood.

"Kaspra! Quickly!" called Inga.

Hurrying to join her, the younger mage bent over him. "He's almost spent," she said.

"Can you help him?"

She turned to Inga. "He's lost a lot of blood. I probably can't do much more than ease him." The look on her face said a great deal more than her words.

Inga watched as she worked, sensing the power that flickered over the helpless man. He released a deep sigh.

"What happened?" asked Kaspra gently.

"Giant cat," he managed. "Master Petria sent...a fireball."

That explained the power surge Inga detected the previous day. Petria had driven the cat away, but she'd been too late to protect the guard.

"They...left me."

"The prince?" asked Inga.

His eyelids closed once in a rough approximation of a nod.

"Are Master Lars and Master Petria with him?" she asked.

He stared back at her, almost as if he didn't understand, before slowly blinking again. The effort of speaking had been too much. His eyes closed.

"Can we move him?" asked Inga.

Kaspra shook her head. "He isn't strong enough. I can stay with him and protect us both though." She lowered her voice to a whisper. "It doesn't look hopeful."

"I'll discuss the situation with Ramond and Emmela."

Turning away, she called, "It's a good time to stop for a break. We all need a rest."

She waved Ramond and Emmela over.

"What are you planning to do?" asked Ramond.

"We can't just leave him here alone," said Emmela.

"Apparently the previous party did," observed Ramond.

"And I intend to make sure Lars and Petria are held accountable for that decision," Inga told him darkly. "Mages take a vow to care for those under their protection. Unless there are exceptional circumstances. It will be for the Compact to decide whether the circumstances were exceptional in this case."

"They did at least build a fire and leave plenty of wood behind," Ramond pointed out. "He wouldn't have lasted long otherwise."

"That would have been Petria," said Emmela. "She's always loved fire. And she isn't quite as heartless as Lars."

At that moment Kaspra joined them, a despondent look on her face. "I'm sorry to say he's gone. He'd been trying to tell me something. The effort was too much."

"What did he say?" asked Inga.

"I think he was trying to warn us about whatever attacked him. If I understood him correctly, two other guards have been killed as well. One of the creatures tried to take him last night, but he was able to protect himself with a burning branch."

"How many men were in their party?" asked Ramond.

"He didn't say," she replied.

Digging a grave was out of the question in that location, so they quickly made a cairn, piling rocks over his body. Then they resumed their journey.

Their path led ever upward, and frequent rest breaks became essential. Emmela joined Inga on one of the breaks. "There's something strange about these mountains," she murmured, staring up at the peaks.

"'Ominous' is the word that comes to mind," Inga replied.

A sense of urgency had been building within her, and with it a fear they would arrive too late. With no idea what they might be in danger of missing, she was determined to get there in time.

Farsense allowed Kylen to locate the mages at any time, but birds of prey offered a wealth of other information. Thanks to the keen eyes of an unsuspecting hawk, Kylen had counted the exact number of people in both of the other parties. He detected Petria's surge of power with farsense. But an eagle allowed him to see Inga's companions tending to the dying man the following day. Strangest of all, he felt the raptor's displeasure when the body disappeared under a mound of stones.

Wildcats tracked each party, and raptors tracked them in their turn, hoping to share the scraps after a kill. Kylen was not concerned about the predators. His power had swollen to the point where he was confident of protecting his entire party even while asleep.

Control over his mage sight was increasing too, along with a familiarity that came only with experience. Even after a bird had disappeared from view he was now able to maintain a connection.

Much could be gleaned from the penetrating gaze of a bird. He knew the prince's party was well in front of the others, but he also knew that the path before them would not take them where they wanted to go. A backtrack was unavoidable—he had discerned it long before they did. He also noted that Inga's party was steadily gaining on them.

Above all, he knew his own party needed to move faster to arrive in time. The destination was clear in his mind, as it surely must be by now to each of the mages winding their way ever higher into the mountains.

What waited for them there was less than certain. The encounter would be perilous, but beyond that he could be confident of nothing.

"Is there a way past the overhang?" called the prince, frustration adding a harsh edge to his tone.

"No. We'll never make it," the guard called back.

Petria watched dispassionately as the guard cautiously retraced his steps. While the man was undoubtedly telling the truth, it was evident to her he had no inclination to push himself to the limit. Why would he? None of the guards could afford to become injured—not when they knew the prince and his party would abandon them to their fate and walk away.

As the man rejoined them, she caught a glimpse of a wildcat lurking among the rocks above. If he had found a suitable path, he might not have lived to report it.

"We must go back and find another way forward, Your Highness," the captain was saying. "You cannot afford to risk your life unnecessarily."

The prince contented himself with a disgruntled glare.

Lars was more predictable. "What a delightful day to be strolling about aimlessly in the mountains," he said.

"You're supposed to be leading the way," growled the prince. "If you've suddenly decided you don't know where you're going, it's well past time you told us."

"I know where I'm going. I never claimed I knew the best way to get there!" Lars retorted. "You were supposed to supply a guide! Do I need to remind you that this entire effort will be for nothing if we don't get there in time?"

Petria turned her back on them. "Lead on, captain," she called.

For a fleeting moment she wondered what had become of the guard they left injured on the mountain. He surely couldn't have made it through the night.

A more pressing question pushed him from her mind.

"You said Master Inga was putting together a party to follow us, Your Highness," she said to the prince. "When would you expect them to reach the mountains?"

"Why would they be heading for the mountains?" asked Lars. "They can't possibly know where we're going."

When she didn't respond, he added, "If she's fool enough to show up here, it might give the wildcats something more tasty than us to feast on."

Apparently savoring the thought, he returned his attention to the path before him.

Petria glared after him. It was becoming apparent that stressful situations brought out the worst in Lars. Not for the first time she wondered what possible role Banadin had envisaged for him in his new order.

She scowled. Try as she might, she could not banish Banadin from her thoughts. He was a subtle and manipulative man, and it wasn't until well after his passing that Petria began to glimpse the true depths of his cunning.

Ten years after his death the conspirators who survived him had gathered to hear his final instructions. Not long after that fateful meeting, she had been sought out once more by the same member of the Notaries Guild.

He had bowed respectfully. "The will of Master Banadin contained a further addendum. It instructed us to deliver this letter to you two weeks after you met with the larger group." After handing her a sealed document bearing her name, he bowed once more and left.

Finding a place where she would not be disturbed, she had opened the letter. Then, with her heart pounding, she had read it.

Master Petria,

I left instructions with my legal representative to destroy this communication either if you failed to attend the meeting I arranged or if you left within the first few minutes. If you remained in the meeting, he was instructed to deliver it two weeks later.

You are receiving this because you have chosen to embrace a key role in my new order. Well done!

I am sure you have been curious about the reasons why I selected you. Some of those reasons I freely communicated to you. The first and most obvious reason is that you have many admirable qualities. Further to that, you were not satisfied with the existing order or with your current lot in life. Your limitations frustrated you, and you longed for much more. Having from your earliest days been routinely denied opportunities to improve yourself, you were predisposed to embrace change. Enough so that the idea of overthrowing existing institutions did not greatly trouble you. These were necessary qualities in every person I chose.

I want you to be aware there is another compelling reason for you to pursue change—a reason that has everything to do with your own self-interest.

I made careful inquiries into your background and character before choosing you. I therefore know you had good cause to be angry after what was done to you in your early years. In particular, the way your father and your aunt treated you was unforgivable. When I learned of their supposedly accidental deaths, I felt the circumstances seemed remarkably fitting—a house fire in the case of your aunt, and the more gruesome situation in which your father met his end.

By now you are beginning to realize that I have uncovered the truth. I fully understand why you turned on them after your magical awakening. In my eyes you simply enacted justice. Unfortunately, those in authority cannot be expected to be equally understanding should they find out what you did.

I have never exposed you, and the need to do so will not arise while you remain faithful to me and my wishes. Remaining safe from me does not mean you can ever afford to relax though. I learned the truth through nothing more than careful inquiry. Whether they are enemies or friends, others might one day do the same.

You urgently need my new order. More than most. You will never be truly safe until you take your rightful place at the helm.

More accurately it is your new order, of course. I merely initiated it, inspired by my magical patron as you are aware.

Trusting that this finds you well and actively preparing for the great task that lies before you.

Master Banadin

PETRIA HAD BROKEN into a cold sweat as she read the letter. At last she knew the truth—he had chosen her in large measure because he knew he had a hold over her. Having unearthed her darkest secrets, he could have—and would have—used them against her whenever it suited him.

His message had swept away any lingering delusion that anything about her cause was noble. Apart from that, it changed nothing. Having committed herself, she intended to see it through to the end.

Nevertheless, it was infuriating to know that Banadin had been in the grave for ten years and still she wasn't free of him. Receiving this letter had been conditional on her remaining in the meeting. It was easy to guess what might have happened if she walked away. And she hadn't missed the subtle threat at the end of the message. Banadin had undoubtedly left other instructions with his legal representatives that were conditional on her actions in the future. Whatever happened during the eclipse, there would probably be a message to the Compact to expose her. It would serve as a vigorous prod to ensure her break with that body, whether or not she had acquired unlimited power.

She didn't doubt that each of her fellow conspirators had received similar letters. Perhaps Banadin was setting out to curb any hesitancy among them. Perhaps he was simply gloating from the grave.

Embittered by her recollection of the letter, her thoughts returned to Lars, at that moment walking ahead of her up the mountain. Banadin was undoubtedly manipulating him too, but she didn't care. She was thoroughly sick of him. He was deluding himself if he expected her to give him the second talisman.

The next time they paused for a break, she sought out a quiet spot behind a large boulder and retrieved from her backpack Banadin's two identically fashioned clenched fists. She wrapped a hand protectively around one of the golden talismans. The other she placed on the ground before her.

It would be a simple matter to draw upon her magic to destroy the exposed talisman with fire. Lars would sense her use of power and want to know what she was doing, but she could tell him she had been chasing off a wildcat.

Then she remembered his words. *You need to be aware that I will do nothing to help unless you give me one of the talismans.*

She scowled. When the time came to open the book she would need both of the little objects.

All at once she knew what she needed to do. First she transferred the talisman in her hand to a secure pocket in her backpack for safekeeping. Then, picking up the other and willing it to trap her magic, she sent off a fireball.

To her immense satisfaction, nothing happened. Holding the little golden fist aloft, she willed it to release the captured magic. A fireball immediately streaked off into the distance, chasing an imaginary wild-cat. The talisman had done its job. With a gratified nod she placed it in a second pocket.

The strategy had worked. The second talisman's capacity to store magic was now greatly diminished. She would give it to Lars when he was ready to open the book.

He would discover the truth, of course, but not until after the magic had erupted. By then it would be too late.

EVERYTHING HAD CHANGED SO QUICKLY for Dalthinir. After being entirely alone for years, he'd suddenly acquired an apprentice and two dependents. Momentous as those changes had been, it was only the beginning.

He couldn't reasonably describe the twins as dependents, of course. Not once he'd seen them in action.

Finding a way to describe them accurately hadn't been straightforward. A fisherman once told him that pearls were formed when an irritant slipped inside the shell of an oyster, and on reflection he decided that the description expressed perfectly the impact of Jonno and Bella on his life. Intensely irritating as they were at times, they had demonstrated their worth over and over again.

They had undeniably slipped past his guard. He had come to care about them as if they were family.

Consequential as the arrival of the twins had been, it was nothing compared to the upheavals that had followed the earlier arrival of Kylen. Taking on an apprentice had forced him out of his isolation and into danger. But brief as the apprenticeship had been thus far, Dalthinir could no longer think of him as merely an apprentice. Not since the blow to his head. Or was it since arriving in the Drakkenridge Mountains?

Whatever the trigger had been, Kylen was unquestionably developing into a force to be reckoned with. If his abilities offered any indication, he might one day be numbered with the legendary mages of old.

Having come to these mountains to challenge Lars and Petria, Dalthinir now freely acknowledged he was playing a secondary role to his apprentice. Nevertheless, he knew his own role was far from over.

Kylen might command greater power, but without support his lack of experience might one day prove costly. And like anyone else, he would be at great risk if power ever became an end in itself for him. Dalthinir had seen first hand the consequences of the unbridled pursuit of power.

Learning to wield magical power was only one aspect of traditional mage training, of course. Studies needed to include at least a smattering of science, geometry, algebra, history, geography, sociology, languages, human studies, non-human studies, systematic thinking, and problem solving. And it didn't end there. Responsibility lay heaviest on those who commanded great power. It had long been recognized that every mage needed a firm foundation in law and ethics.

It was true that Olatiren had provided Kylen with a solid start in a number of these areas, but the training had predated his magical awakening. Everything he knew had since taken on new meaning, and the possible applications of his knowledge had expanded dramatically. In acquiring him as an apprentice, Dalthinir had accepted responsibility for helping him navigate this strange new landscape.

The form of his training was also important. Dalthinir favored apprenticeship because apprentices learned by observing the way their mentors exercised power as they went through life. And they benefited from having a mentor at their side as they began to use power themselves.

Valuable as any kind of training might be, it wasn't enough. Lars and Petria had been thoroughly trained by the Compact, as had Banadin before them. Each of them in their own ways had demonstrated that knowledge, intelligence, and power could be frightening when held by a person without integrity. Dalthinir regarded the development of character as an essential life journey—one that anyone wielding power needed to embrace.

Yes, there was more than enough for him still to do to assist Kylen's development.

Someone needed to look out for the twins too. When it came time for a confrontation, Kylen would have plenty else to think about.

At that very moment, his apprentice came alongside him. "There seem to be a lot of birds in these mountains."

Dalthinir peered at a large flock flitting nearby, many of them darting surprisingly close to the two mages. "If you mean the swallows," he replied, "I've been here before, and I've never seen anything like it."

Kylen gazed up at them thoughtfully for a while. Then he returned his attention to Dalthinir. "Are the other mages within range of your farsense yet?" he asked hopefully.

"If you mean Lars and Petria, then yes. I've been able to sense them for a while now."

For some reason Kylen seemed to take comfort from the news.

"What about Inga?"

The mage shook his head. "They're still out of range, for me at least."

A haunted look had come into Kylen's eyes. "What are we supposed to do? I mean when we catch up with Lars and the others."

The mage didn't try to spare him. "We can reasonably expect Lars to attack us. I'm less certain about Petria and the prince."

"But you said there are laws about mages using magical power against other people," Kylen said in alarm.

Dalthinir's face was grim. "The law isn't going to stop someone like Lars. Not if we're in the way when the book is within his grasp."

"We can protect ourselves with a shield. But how are we supposed to stop him? And what if we don't succeed?"

The mage gazed back at him calmly. "I cannot give you a settled answer. But I can say one thing with confidence—inevitable as the advance of evil might seem, as long as people dare to oppose it, its triumph can never be certain. We will remember that, and we will do the best we can."

CHAPTER 28

Inga's column came to an abrupt halt. Before she could move forward to find out why, she spotted Ramond heading back toward her.

"Is there a problem?" she asked.

He pointed forward. "It's the path the other group has been taking. I've discussed it with our best tracker, and both of us agree it makes no sense."

"Why not?"

He gazed upward at the peaks soaring above them. "It's hard to explain. Call it experience if you like. They're heading for a dead end. We're sure of it."

"What will that mean?"

"They'll be forced to retrace their steps. If we're still following them when they do that, at some point the two groups are going to meet face to face."

She peered upward. When they first left Cambrick in pursuit of Lars and Petria, she had no clear idea where they were going. Now it was as clear as a mountain stream.

"They're going in exactly the right direction," she told him. "Can you get us up there without hitting dead ends and without us bumping into them?"

"As long as you know where you want to go, we'll find a way to get you there."

In the short time she had known Ramond, she had learned to value him highly. "We'll follow your lead," she promised. "I'm confident you'll guide us onto the best path."

He accepted it calmly. "I'll confer with my tracker."

They resumed their journey a few minutes later, heading directly across the slope on an easterly bearing. It wasn't the right direction, but she was willing to trust Ramond.

Thirty minutes later they came to a fissure leading upward. The tracker guided the party into it without hesitation.

The hour that followed taxed Inga's strength to the limit. Just as she was beginning to seriously question her ability to continue, they emerged onto a gentle slope. Looking down she saw they had gained altitude significantly. The place where they had turned aside from tracking the prince's party was now hidden from view. That was something to be grateful for. She had no desire for her party to be seen when the others returned to their starting point.

Ramond appeared at her side. "Can you show me the final destination?" he asked.

She immediately pointed upward and to the left.

He nodded. "I'll check in with you from time to time to make sure we're still on track. And we'll aim to approach it from an angle so the two groups are less likely to meet."

"Thank you, Ramond! We're fortunate to have you with us."

The next few hours included some hard climbing, but it didn't compare with the extraordinary exertion required to scale the fissure. With the daylight beginning to fade, Ramond and his tracker found a vaguely flat area where they could camp in relative safety.

"We've seen no sign of wildcats for many hours," Ramond told Inga.

"Perhaps they don't venture this high," she replied.

"Perhaps." He didn't sound convinced. "Whether they do or not, your mages need to sleep. I suggest we build fire pits around our camp. My men and I will remain on guard for the next four hours. After that your people can take shifts through the night."

Inga readily agreed to the proposal, and for a time the site buzzed with quiet activity as they prepared for an uncertain night in an unforgiving environment.

Uncomfortable as the conditions were, Inga fell asleep almost immediately. She was deeply immersed in a strange and unsettling dream when she was startled awake. Sitting up, she tried to make sense of the clamor of shouts mingled with ferocious snarling. The firelight flickered on a wildcat of frightening size crouching a short distance away, confronted by determined men with sharp spears.

Her movement caught the animal's attention. Springing suddenly forward, it pounced. Moving too slowly to escape, she was knocked to the ground. Slavering over her, the terrible mouth plunged down to fasten around her neck.

Yet the teeth failed to penetrate her skin.

Snarling in fury, the cat snapped with greater force. To no avail.

Unable to penetrate the protective bubble that had surrounded her, the animal drew back in frustrated rage as men came at it with loud cries.

"Thank you, Ellis," she breathed, staring wide-eyed at the young mage who had hurried to her side.

The cat bounded away, leaving the whole camp awake and on high alert.

Kaspra appeared. "I've established a shield around the site," she reported.

"Thank you!" Glancing quickly around, Inga was relieved to see that no one appeared to have been injured.

The pounding of her heart had barely stilled when a savage growl close at hand almost startled her out of her wits. With an effort she calmed herself, reminding herself that Kaspra's shield would keep the beasts at bay.

Having begun badly, the night did not improve. When dawn finally banished the darkness, Inga felt as if an eternity lay behind her. No one had slept at all. The persistent growling of predators had kept them restless and unsettled throughout the night. With their destination close at hand, they more than ever needed to be alert. A sleepless night was not going to help.

She sought out Ramond. "I see no value in delaying our departure," she told him. "We might as well get underway."

Unruffled as ever, he responded with a firm nod. A few minutes later they were climbing upward again.

She saw no trace of wildcats. Were they nocturnal, or were they serving some other purpose? With no way to answer such questions, she decided to put them from her mind. The details of their environment were a distraction she couldn't afford.

As they drew ever closer to their destination, a tingling sensation traveled slowly up her back, settling on her head. She felt sure her hair must be standing on end. It was as if the atmosphere had become so saturated with magic it was coating anyone who came into contact with it.

She felt simultaneously bolder and more somber. Yet at the same time she was conscious of tension slowly building, pressing in on her. It felt like the whole mountain was somehow holding its breath.

Emmela was climbing beside her.

"Do you feel it too?" asked Inga.

"I feel as if I could shout out loud," her friend replied. "Except it would intrude upon the solemnity of the place."

The other mages were gazing around with wonder. Inga guessed they were similarly affected.

Ramond's men were another matter entirely. The group had come to a halt at the base of a rock slope, and many of the men had sat down where they were.

Approaching their leader, she asked, "Are your men well? They look uneasy."

Ramond stared back at her. "I'm not sure I can ask them to go any further." An unreadable expression flashed across his normally tranquil face. "There's something...not right about this place. Up there especially." He jerked his head up the mountain. "It feels...it feels as if we don't belong."

She cast her eye about. "This is as good a place as any to stop. Why don't you all get some rest? I'm sure you could use it."

Nodding tightly, he left to speak with his men.

Inga drew together Ellis, Kaspra, and Alexis. "Ramond and his group are not coping too well up here. Could you please stay with them?"

"There's certainly something very strange about this place," Ellis replied with a nod.

Kaspra had a strange look in her eye. "I'm not sure whether to feel exhilarated or alarmed," she said slowly.

Alexis was more matter-of-fact. "We'll make sure no harm comes to them."

"Thank you," Inga said gratefully.

She gazed up the mountain. "I know what you mean—I've never experienced anything like this place. Emmela and I will climb higher. I want to know what's up there."

Emmela looked uncertain, but she didn't argue, and when Inga separated from the little group she soon joined her.

Thankfully they had no need to scale a cliff face to continue their upward journey. Nevertheless, the slope before them became ever steeper, forcing Inga to concentrate entirely on where to place the next foot.

Fewer than thirty minutes passed before the slope flattened out. Ahead of them their path was blocked by a stone wall. The air was throbbing with power. They had reached the place. Yet there was no obvious way to proceed.

Examining the wall more closely, she saw the faint outline of what appeared to be a door. No handle or keyhole interrupted its smooth surface. There was no obvious way to open it.

After both mages had poked and prodded it in growing frustration for several minutes, Inga gave up. "This door needs to be opened magically—I'm certain of it. I'm going back to get some help."

"I'm not staying here alone," Emmela told her emphatically.

After a quick shrug, Inga began retracing her steps. Climbing down was no less challenging, but it was at least a little quicker.

The other mages quickly gathered around the moment they arrived. "We believe we've found the right place," Inga told them. "But we're going to need help to get in."

"I'll join you," replied Ellis eagerly.

"Me too," said Kaspra.

Inga frowned. "Only one of you. And only until we find a way in. I'm not comfortable leaving Ramond and his men without strong protection."

"You go," Kaspra told Ellis.

The climb seemed somehow longer and more difficult the second time, but the three of them finally reached the door. Panting with exhaustion, Inga bent low with her hands on her knees.

When she finally straightened, she saw that Ellis had already moved to the door to examine it.

"What do you think?" she asked him.

"I suspect this door is designed to keep anyone out who doesn't have magic—mage touch ability in particular. I'm going to try to open it."

No change of any kind was visible, even though she could sense him using energy. The magic around them was so overpowering she could barely catch the scent of his magic.

He continued to try for so long she began to despair of him ever succeeding.

Then abruptly a grinding sound shattered the stillness, and the door began to move. In a matter of moments it stood ajar.

"Well done, Ellis!" she exclaimed.

"I have no idea what I did to make it open," he told her frankly. "It was nothing more than dumb luck. I'm not confident I could do it again."

She smiled at him. "Call it whatever you like. The important thing is you succeeded."

Leading the others inside, Inga found herself in a small open space enclosed by rock on all sides.

The mages spun slowly around, trying to absorb what they were seeing. Three sides were enclosed by rock walls that stretched upward to perhaps twice Inga's height. Beyond that, Inga could see open sky. There was no roof. To the left of the entrance towered a jumbled pile of rocks, closing off the space.

The lower section of the rock walls was smooth and featureless.

Above head height, the wall appeared crumbled and broken. She was no mountaineer, but she guessed that attempting to escape from the room by climbing upward would be extremely dangerous. The entrance they had used offered the only way in and out.

At the opposite end of the pile of rocks a roughly fashioned stone block stood before the wall of rock. The stone resembled a plinth with nothing apart from a large rock perched on top of it. Beyond that, the room was empty.

There might be little to see, but the magic that surrounded them was almost overpowering.

"I should get back to the others," said Ellis reluctantly. "Do you think you'll be safe if I leave the door open?"

"Probably not," Inga replied. "If the door shuts, you might not be able to get it open again! We'll come with you."

The three of them filed out, with Ellis the last to leave. The moment he cleared the door, it closed shut with a grinding snap.

"You managed to close it without any difficulties," Inga observed.

"That wasn't me!" he replied. "The door shut by itself."

Inga's eyebrows went up in surprise. "Now I'm doubly grateful that Emmela and I didn't remain inside."

Emmela was looking pale. "I wouldn't have wanted to be trapped in there."

"Rejoin the others, Ellis," said Inga. "We'll look around for a while, then we'll join you."

With a quick nod, he disappeared back down the slope.

It didn't take long for Inga to decide there was little worth seeing outside the room.

"The magic in the air is almost overwhelming," said Emmela. She spoke softly, as if anxious to remain inconspicuous.

Inga nodded. It was difficult to keep her senses sharp.

Distracted by the impact of the environment, she failed to notice until too late that someone was approaching.

A woman's voice rose exultantly. "The book is near! I can sense it!"

A harsh voice cut her off. "Get out of my way! You're blocking the path!"

She instantly recognized the voices. Somehow in the mad frenzy of this place she had failed to sense their glimmer until they were upon her.

So it was true that Lars and Petria were seeking the book. Jonno had reported accurately what he overheard while eavesdropping.

A shiver of fear shook her to the core. She could only guess what these two might be capable of. They had already taken fearful risks in pursuit of forbidden power.

Inga had always known what she might be up against. The unpredictability of their behavior was the reason she had brought three mages who matched their abilities. Now she needed them, not one of them was within reach.

How could she have been foolish enough to send Ellis away? Neither she nor Emmela had any hope of defending themselves if the two mages became aggressive.

Lars reached the open ground before the door, immediately followed by Petria.

Both Inga and Emmela stood frozen, in full view, on the far side of the door. There was nowhere for either of them to hide.

CHAPTER 29

The unwelcome necessity of backtracking had tested Petria's patience to the limit. As for Lars, he was ready to explode.

Irritated though she was by his behavior, she shared his frustration. The total solar eclipse would not wait for them. It would take place the following day whether they arrived on time or not.

The prince hadn't come entirely unprepared. He had included in his retinue a guard capable of guiding them through mountainous terrain. Unfortunately, he was the same person they had left battered and bleeding among the rocks, with nothing but a fire to protect him from predators and the cold.

The prince approached Petria, pointedly ignoring Lars.

"You seem sure you know where to go," he said, "but you're unable to provide details of how to get there. Experience has demonstrated we can't use a direct approach. That means we'll be forced to try an indirect approach."

Leaving Lars as a bystander to the conversation wasn't going to improve his temper. Nevertheless, Petria was just as ready as the prince to ignore him. A person unable or unwilling to control his tongue didn't deserve to be consulted.

"I've directed one of my guards to lead us. He isn't a mountaineer, but he does at least have some experience trekking in the wilderness."

There was nothing better on offer. The party followed as their new guide led them in a different direction. The light began to fail before they had traveled far, but their progress offered promise for the following day.

"Set up camp here," ordered the prince. His three remaining guards hastened to do his bidding.

"Can we rely on you to provide protection?" he asked the two mages.

"I'm willing to take a shift," Petria replied.

Lars barely managed a grunt.

They began at once preparing to sleep.

"Get away from me!" snarled Lars, glaring at two of the guards who had dared to settle beside him.

"What else do you expect?" asked the prince sourly. "It's hardly surprising that people crowd you when it's obvious you're interested only in protecting yourself."

Petria decided it was safest not to comment, not least because the prince had positioned himself so that he was almost touching her. She didn't need to be told it had nothing to do with her feminine charms.

From this unpromising start, the experience quickly degenerated into a waking nightmare.

Snarling and growls surrounded them almost from the moment the light faded completely. Petria sent fireballs streaking into the night, but they didn't silence the noises for long.

Although Petria had volunteered to take a shift, she had no ability to place a protective shield around the camp. It therefore fell to Lars to protect them all.

In spite of his irritability she never doubted he would do his part. It had nothing to do with selflessness. Arriving at their destination seemed barely within reach at that moment. They had no hope of arriving in time unless they all worked together, and Lars had enough sense to realize that.

He didn't disappoint her.

When the sun rose, she glanced around anxiously. To her relief, every one of them had made it through the night alive and uninjured.

Alive they might be, but none of them had slept, and tempers were short by the time they set off. Lars was becoming more agitated with every hour that passed. Petria might not have been showing it, but she too was increasingly alarmed as the time for the eclipse drew closer.

Fortunately for them all, the new guide was demonstrating an uncanny knack for choosing the right path. They were once more moving directly toward the destination. After an hour of steady climbing, they paused for a break.

"We're very close now. Can you feel it?" she whispered to Lars excitedly.

"Of course I can feel it!" he snapped. "You're not the only mage here!" He shook his head in disbelief.

Not willing to dignify his words with any kind of response, she turned her back on him and moved away.

Seeing the prince close at hand, she went straight to him.

"There's something very strange about this place," he said. "It feels...unsafe."

"There is dragon magic at work here. All of us can feel it," she told him. "It's time for us to find the book, Your Highness. It's vital we're in place before the eclipse begins." She paused. "I'm sure I don't need to tell you it will be very dangerous when that happens. Make sure you stay well clear until we call you."

His eyes narrowed, but after a moment he nodded. "I'm sure I don't need to remind you of our common purpose," he said pointedly.

"I haven't forgotten," she assured him.

He jerked his head toward Lars. "And what about the genius in the group? Will he remember this is not solely for his benefit?"

The sarcasm might be well deserved, but none of them could afford to get distracted. "He'll play his part," she promised firmly.

At that moment, one of the guards hurried to the prince. "Another group is nearby!" he exclaimed. "I've just caught sight of them."

"Where?" asked Petria.

He pointed. "There's a place we can safely observe them."

She nodded, and the three of them crept forward to the vantage point he had referred to. Looking down, she saw five men she didn't recognize. They had the look of fighters about them. With them were three mages, Alexis, Kaspra, and Ellis. Alexis had abilities that closely matched her own. Kaspra and Ellis had similar abilities to Lars.

There was only one possible conclusion. They were looking at the group sent out by Adrastas. Supposedly it was under the leadership of Inga, although she was nowhere to be seen.

She shook her head in frustration. Why did these people have to arrive at the critical moment?

The prince had been eyeing the group and their surrounds. He signaled Petria and the guard to join him.

As soon as they returned to the others, the prince said urgently, "There's a slope full of loose rocks above the other group. We could climb beyond it and start raining rocks on them. If it doesn't bury them, it should keep them busy for a very long time."

After a moment's consideration, Petria nodded. "That might give us time to do what we need to do. Just make sure they're completely distracted until the eclipse begins. Once that happens it will be too late for them to intervene."

He nodded.

"Don't put yourself at risk, Your Highness," she added.

He shrugged it off. "Few prizes worth having come without risks."

Calling together his remaining guards, he set off.

WITH THE ATMOSPHERE BUZZING, Kaspra had been unable to relax. Then a large rock landed beside her, barely missing her head. Looking up in alarm, she saw small figures moving on a ridge above. As she watched, two of them released other rocks.

Shouting a warning, she hastily activated a shield.

The slope above them was steep, and the rocks hurled from above were dislodging other rocks as they plummeted down. New missiles were quickly launched, in turn dislodging more rocks. Some of the boulders rolling down the hill were frighteningly large in size. None of the party would have long survived the initial onslaught without her magical shield.

The shield held firm when the rocks struck it. However many of them were now resting on it directly, increasing the pressure on the shield.

It occurred to Kaspra that Inga and Emmela might need support. The attackers above them must surely be members of the prince's party. If they were, Inga and Emmela were likely to come under attack as well, and at a time when the three mages capable of protecting them were fully occupied defending themselves and their companions.

There was nothing she could do about it though. Her own situation was about to get much worse.

Spurred on by their success, the attackers had redoubled their efforts. They were dodging fireballs now, but Alexis had joined the defense too late. The entire slope above them was on the move.

"Ellis!" she screamed, pointing upward.

He didn't answer. Already feeling the strain, she could only hope his attention was focused entirely on a shield of his own to strengthen their defenses. They were going to need it to survive the avalanche roaring toward them.

Petria couldn't begin to guess how Adrastas's pursuers had found them. It made no difference though—they had arrived in time.

It would be up to the prince and his men to keep the other group busy. It wouldn't need to be for long. The total solar eclipse was almost upon them.

She was climbing steadily, panting hard from the exertion. Lars was no less eager, but he couldn't keep up with her. Both of them knew the way to go. They were being drawn.

They must be so close now. The atmosphere felt thick—it was as if she was wading through a bog.

Then the slope leveled out. A wall of rock loomed ahead of her.

Lars joined her, breathing heavily.

"The book is near! I can sense it!" she said excitedly.

"Get out of my way!" he snapped. "You're blocking the path!"

Ignoring his rudeness, she stepped forward to examine the rock face. "The door is exactly as the parchment described!" Stepping back she traced its outline with a finger. Knowing it was there had certainly made it easier to find it.

He moved into position in front of the door.

She couldn't help herself. "Two presses at the top, two at the bottom, and three on each side of the door. Then hard in the middle!"

"I know what the parchment said," he sneered. "I don't need you to teach me."

"Well get on with it, then," she snapped back.

He completed the sequence, and a rumble of protest sounded. Then the door slowly ground its way open.

Pushing through, Lars stepped into the enclosed space. Unwilling to let him out of her sight even for a minute, she hurried in after him.

The doorway led into a room with a smooth, level base. High walls of rock rose on three sides, the lower section smooth and the upper section crumbling. Equally tall, the fourth side consisted of rocks heaped chaotically.

The lower part of the walls of rock seemed too smooth to be natural. Someone—or something—had carved out this place. No roof covered the enclosed space; sunlight was streaming into it.

Glancing around, she immediately spotted a thick pedestal fashioned from rock, with a large, crudely shaped boulder sitting on it. Apart from that, the space was completely empty.

"Well, go on!" said Lars impatiently, pointing to the boulder. "This is your moment."

"The eclipse hasn't started yet."

"What difference does that make? The parchment wasn't clear about what the eclipse applied to. We didn't need it to open the door. Maybe the book can be released from the boulder beforehand as well. There won't be time to get it wrong during the eclipse. You might as well try using fire now."

Turning from him with a shrug, she faced the boulder. "Very well. I'd suggest you stand well clear if you value your precious hide."

Calling upon her power, she directed heat at the boulder, gradually increasing it until every inch of visible surface was glowing red. Nothing happened. Intensifying the heat, she continued until she had nothing left to give. The boulder remained intact.

With an exhausted grunt, she abandoned her exertion.

"You're not trying hard enough," he growled.

She scowled back at him. "I've done this plenty of times! Rocks always crack under that much heat. This whole place is infused with dragon magic. It must be protecting the rock."

Weary from her effort, she sat down. "I'm going to rest," she told him coolly. "I need to reserve my energy for the eclipse. Don't bother talking to me. You won't get a reply."

"Do you sense that?" Kylen pointed off along the mountainside.

Dalthinir nodded. "Power, and from two mages!" He paused. "Now a third! I don't recognize the scent of any of them."

"Inga's people?"

The mage nodded. "Almost certainly. We'll see if they need help."

They hurried forward, Kylen taking the lead. He felt his own power swelling. It had never been more accessible, his mind never clearer.

The other mages could not have been far away, but it was taking too long. When a hawk swung into view, he borrowed its eyes.

"I can see where we need to go," he reported. "We need to hurry. Three mages and a group of men are under attack. A few others are positioned above them, and they're pushing down rocks. There's a shield around the lower group, but a huge mound of rocks and soil has piled around it. There must be enormous pressure on the shield. One of the mages is sending fireballs against the men above, but it isn't slowing them down."

All of them were already exhausted, but they put on an extra spurt.

"We're nearly there!" Kylen told them. They were roughly level with the upper group, and he pointed toward them. Then he pointed down to the beleaguered mages.

"It looks like we need to do something about the higher group," said Dalthinir, breathing heavily.

"We can handle that," said Jonno. "You two are the only ones capable of helping the lower group."

The mage looked unconvinced.

"Go!" urged Bella, brandishing her slingshot. "You already know we can look after ourselves."

He nodded reluctantly. "Be careful!" he implored them. "It will be the prince and his men. They're trained to fight!"

The twins hurried away.

"Come with me, Kylen!"

As soon as they found a location that overlooked the lower group, Dalthinir stopped.

"We need to stay out of sight," he said. "I'll strengthen their shield."

Kylen eyed the scene critically. He didn't doubt the twins could end the downward flow of rocks, and sensing the power Dalthinir was lending to the shield he was confident the people below would be well protected. None of it dealt with the debris piled against the shield though. Looking at the sheer volume of rubble, the men above must have triggered a landslide.

Overflowing with power, he decided to lend a hand. Not far from the shielded area he spotted a ridge with a sheer drop on one side of it. Scooping up the rubble, he sent it flying over the edge.

The people within the shield stood watching as the mound gradually diminished in size. Shouts from above hinted that the twins were beginning to attract the attention of the prince's men.

A hawk offered Kylen a closer look at the scene above.

"A couple of the guards are heading for the twins," he told Dalthinir. As he watched, the twins began to target them. "One of the guards has gone down!" he said. "The twins are incredibly accurate with those slingshots."

Then he became alarmed. "The twins need help! Another guard has been climbing above them, and they don't seem aware of him."

"Finish clearing the rocks and dirt away from the shield," said Dalthinir. "I'll protect them."

The mage immediately headed in their direction.

Redoubling his efforts, Kylen cleared the last of the debris. It didn't exhaust him at all. Then he set off after Dalthinir.

Now wrapped in shields, the twins had resumed their barrage. But they still seemed unaware of the soldier above them. Then he began to throw rocks.

Kylen snorted in contempt. The missiles were sailing beyond the twins. Even without protection, they would be at no risk of being hit. Then one of the rocks smashed into the ground beside the mage. He suddenly realized the twins weren't the target. The missiles were aimed at the man protecting them.

Just in case Dalthinir wasn't protecting himself, Kylen wrapped a hasty shield around him. He was too late. Taking a glancing blow to the head, the mage had fallen to the ground.

Hurrying to him in a panic, Kylen examined him. Another rock landed so close beside them that chips of rock hit Kylen in the face. Like his mentor, he had been solely focused on protecting others. He belatedly protected himself.

Then with a shock of horror he realized that with Dalthinir down, the twins would no longer be protected. Looking up, he saw guards almost upon them.

Furious at the men who had injured Dalthinir—perhaps even killed him—he abandoned defense, instead wrapping every guard he could see within a restrictive sack.

"Down here! Hurry!" he called to the twins, waving frantically. Seeing them picking their way toward him, he redirected his attention to the mage.

To his relief, he saw that he was breathing. He was unconscious, but alive. A gash on his head oozed blood freely.

Jonno reached his side first. "Men from Inga's group are going after the guards."

Dalthinir opened his eyes. "What happened?" he asked weakly. He looked pale.

"You were hit on the head. You need to rest," Kylen told him.

"Lars and Petria?" the mage managed. When there was no response, he added weakly, "You'll have to stop them."

"Me?" Kylen had never imagined confronting them without Dalthinir at his side.

The mage had closed his eyes. He didn't bother to answer.

His apprentice got up. "Don't let anything happen to him!" he told the twins.

Turning toward the source of the magic, he began to climb. Seeing men from Inga's group reach their attackers, he released them from their containment. Suddenly freed, they slumped to the ground. He ignored them. Inga's people could deal with them.

The auras of Inga, Emmela, Lars, and Petria lay ahead of him, clustered together at a single location. Even without their glimmer, he would have known exactly where to go.

CHAPTER 30

Inga stood rigid as Lars and Petria reached the door and glanced around. To her astonishment, both of them looked right through her.

It took a moment to grasp the obvious truth—to the eye of any onlooker they weren't there. Emmela had used her ability to create an illusion. She had succeeded in hiding them both.

The most surprising aspect of the illusion was that Inga could still see Emmela. Somehow neither of them were affected.

Emmela nudged her. Raising her eyebrows inquiringly, she pointed back down the slope.

Shaking her head, Inga pointed firmly to the ground they were standing on. She wasn't going anywhere.

Emmela's only response was a calm nod.

Inga listened as Petria revealed the method of opening the door. Once it stood ajar, Inga boldly followed the two mages inside. Emmela followed close behind. Positioning themselves against the nearest side wall, Inga and Emmela stood watching silently.

To Inga, two things seemed apparent. First, Emmela had used gestures rather than speech when asking her earlier question. That suggested the illusion was visual only. It therefore seemed reasonable to suppose that any careless sound might give them away. Second, when Inga had indicated she wanted to stay, Emmela showed no concern about her ability to maintain the illusion.

There was one thing Inga did not understand. Why hadn't Lars and Petria detected Emmela's use of power? Was Emmela somehow able to mask it? Or was masking it a side effect of the illusion itself? She realized she had forgotten much of what she learned about mage taste. It probably wasn't surprising given that she had never seriously needed it before. Clearly she had some catching up to do.

There was another possibility. The magical energy of this place might be so great it was blotting out the magical scent, much as the noise of people shouting made it impossible to hear a whisper.

More importantly, there was a great deal she didn't understand about what Lars and Petria were doing. She listened intently as the two mages argued, then watched with bemusement as Petria heated the boulder. Petria spoke of a parchment and a total solar eclipse. Where had this information come from?

The only thing she could say with certainty was she had no intention of missing whatever was about to happen.

Preventing the two of them from doing something foolish would be problematic. Kaspra and Ellis might have the power to restrain them, but they were waiting below with Ramond and his men.

At the very least, Inga and Emmela could act as witnesses. It was going to be impossible for Lars and Petria to keep their actions secret.

Then she noticed that the daylight was steadily fading. The sun was nowhere near due to set, and she didn't immediately grasp the significance of the failing light.

Then it hit her. A total solar eclipse was beginning.

As the light faded, Petria's heart began to pound.

"Quickly!" shouted Lars. "This is the moment!"

Once more she turned toward the boulder on the stone pedestal. Once more she poured heat onto it, aggressively increasing the intensity.

The light grew dimmer, but it wasn't yet completely dark. The outside of the boulder was glowing red. Then a moment came when the daylight failed completely. With a mighty effort she cast every remaining glimmer of heat onto the boulder.

With a deafening crack, the boulder split in two.

Silence fell.

The effort had exhausted Petria, and for a moment neither of them moved. Then Lars rushed to the pedestal.

"It's here! The book is real, and it's actually here!" His voice was quivering with excitement.

She hurried to his side. Both of them peered down at it in awe, straining to see in the darkness.

Dim light was gradually growing in strength.

"The eclipse must be ending," she said urgently. "Take it while you still can!"

Raising it with mage touch, Lars carefully lifted the book from the pedestal and turned it over slowly.

Sturdy covers protected pages of treated animal skin—either parchment or vellum. The book was thick, perhaps fifty pages in all. The covers appeared to have been made from thin wooden boards covered by leather.

The only embellishment on the front cover was a series of spidery characters burned into the leather. The script was not known to her.

"I can't read it," she said.

"The language is ancient—undoubtedly draconic," he replied. "But it shouldn't matter. The power is released by opening it."

He turned to her. "Give me one of the talismans."

After seeming to hesitate, she retrieved the one she had previously limited from her backpack and held it out. He snatched it from her hand. She ignored his rudeness, quietly retrieving the other talisman for herself.

"Are both talismans untouched?" he demanded.

She nodded, hoping her face would not betray her.

"Then you won't mind exchanging them," he said shrewdly. He held out his right hand with the talisman in his open palm.

She scowled at him for a moment. Then she snatched the talisman from his hand. Almost dropping it, she bent low, thrusting out both hands to retrieve it. Straightening, she held out her other hand and deposited a talisman on his palm.

After glancing suspiciously at it for a moment, he returned his attention to the book.

Petria couldn't resist a smirk. Having anticipated a challenge of the kind from Lars, she had resorted to sleight of hand, a trick she perfected in her youth after seeing a wandering tinker perform it. It had allowed her to return the same talisman to Lars. And he was clearly none the wiser.

Lifting the book nervously with mage touch, he prepared to open it by the same means.

She held her breath, her whole body trembling with the tension.

His mage touch pulled gently at the cover, but nothing happened. He tried again, more firmly this time, but it still refused to budge.

Petria was the first to recognize the cause. "It's magic! Someone is preventing you from opening it!"

"Who would dare to hinder me?" he growled, his face growing red.

"I don't know," she replied in bemusement. "I don't recognize the scent."

Spinning around together, they saw an unfamiliar figure framed in the entrance. It was a spindly youth, one she had never seen before.

"Who are you?" demanded Lars.

Intuition offered her a surprising answer. "You're Kylen, aren't you?" she asked.

He didn't reply. But he didn't deny it.

She nodded slowly. "That will mean Dalthinir is somewhere nearby."

"Dalthinir?" Lars's face twisted with rage. "He dares to show his face?"

A grim smile came to Petria's lips. "It seems our renegade mage has taken it upon himself to prevent us from releasing the magic."

As THE LIGHT FADED, it became almost impossible for Inga to see what Lars and Petria were doing. But she could hear clearly enough. When Lars called on Petria to act, the boulder began to glow red once more.

The parchment they had mentioned earlier must have provided the inspiration for whatever they were trying to do. It apparently had something to do with the moment of eclipse. Why Petria needed to bake the rock was far from obvious, but she guessed it was a necessary step in finding the book.

Then the boulder shattered.

She scarcely dared to breathe.

At first when Lars raised the book she could see nothing. Then the light grew, and she found she could dimly make it out.

Hearing him say that opening the book would release the magic, she glanced at Emmela with horror. The interaction about a talisman alarmed her even more. Was it possible they thought they had found a way to protect themselves from the effects of opening the book?

Someone had to stop them. There was no one else who could even try.

Knowing that any attempt at intervention would prove as futile as it was dangerous, she nevertheless prepared to throw herself at them.

She was too slow. Before she could move, he tried to open the book. And failed.

Astonished by Petria's assertion that Lars was being prevented from opening the book, Inga failed at first to notice Emmela pointing frantically toward the entrance.

"You're Kylen, aren't you? That will mean Dalthinir is somewhere nearby," Petria was saying.

A thrill traveled slowly up her spine at the mention of Dalthinir's name. He might yet save them all.

"Where is your master?" demanded Petria.

Inga stared wide-eyed, the same question burning in her own mind.

She glanced at Kylen. What was he doing there? Did he have even the slightest awareness of his danger?

And where was Dalthinir?

"If the renegade is so determined to interfere with us, it's time we returned the favor," said Lars.

Pieces of rock began breaking free from the walls and flying at the youth. Most of the rocks missed, but one hit him on the arm, drawing blood. While he was distracted, the entire upper section of the wall beside him broke free. Inga watched in horror as a massive pile of rubble plummeted toward him.

The sound of the rock breaking loose alerted him, and he looked up as it was about to reach him. He ducked instinctively, but he had no need. Bouncing harmlessly off an invisible shield, the rocks piled up around him on the ground.

"Dalthinir's protecting him!" cried Petria.

Even before the rubble came to rest, she began lobbing fireballs. They didn't reach the shield, instead changing direction to sail around the open space. None threatened Inga or Emmela, but Petria and Lars were reduced to dodging and ducking frantically. Lars must have quickly established a shield of his own, because they were soon standing upright again.

A new fireball roared toward Kylen, closely followed by two more. This time all three fell harmlessly to the ground, stopped by his shield.

Lars was beside himself. "Why won't he show himself?"

Then he cried out in astonished fury. Pulling free from his control, the book sailed slowly through the air, directly toward Kylen.

Petria was shaking her head in frustrated amazement. "Dalthinir isn't doing this," she growled. "It's him!" Her stabbing finger singled out Kylen.

"Use your talisman to capture his magic!" demanded Lars.

"Never!" she retorted angrily. "Use your own!"

Lars ignored her. A nasty look appeared on his face. Eyes narrowed, he stood perfectly still, focusing his attention on the youth in the entranceway.

After what Lars had done to Adrastas's dog, Inga knew better than anyone what he might be trying to do. But there was nothing she could do to help Kylen. His shield had proven effective against physical objects, but would it protect him from an assault of this kind? She waited fearfully for the telltale signs of an imminent collapse.

Kylen's eyes opened wide. Abruptly forgotten, the book fell to the ground.

Beads of sweat appeared on the face of Lars, yet Inga could see nothing obvious in return for his effort.

Pale but determined, the youth remained standing. Somehow he had managed to blunt this attack as well.

In growing astonishment, Inga recognized that Petria was right. She stared at Kylen in wonder. Who was this youth? How could he be a mage? The Compact certainly hadn't awakened his power. Was it possible that Dalthinir had somehow done it?

More importantly, did Kylen have designs of his own on the book? He commanded great power—that much was obvious. Might he emerge as a bigger threat than Lars and Petria?

Having failed in his attempt to disable Kylen by attacking his body, Lars furiously sent a new stream of rocks in his direction. While the youth was once more distracted, Lars retrieved the fallen book, using his magic to return it to its previous position. Then he gaped in astonishment, staring directly at Inga and Emmela.

Glancing at Emmela, Inga saw that she had slumped to the ground, stunned. A bruise on her head suggested a stray rock had struck her a glancing blow. Her illusion had faded, exposing their presence.

Inga saw no hint of surprise on Kylen's face at their sudden unmasking. Before she could make sense of that, Lars was upon her. Hooking an arm around her throat, he pinned her firmly from behind.

"Perhaps you don't know who this is," he snarled, addressing Kylen. "It's Dalthinir's dear, dear friend, Inga. I can stop her heart in an instant. And I'll do it too, unless you immediately drop the shield around this book. Oh, and don't imagine you can shield her from me. You're too late! I've already put a shield around us both."

Inga's heart pounded as she braced herself for the inevitable. The youth had no reason to protect her, even if he could.

Then she caught a glimpse of the haunted look in his eyes. To her horror, she saw he was ready to comply with Lars's demand.

An anguished cry burst from her lips. "No! You mustn't do it, Kylen!"

Emmela had recovered herself enough to call out, "Listen to her, Kylen! He'll only destroy everything!"

Inga stared in dismay as the young mage hesitated. Faced with impossible choices, he was clearly struggling to decide how to respond. How could anyone so young and inexperienced be expected to handle a situation like this?

Dalthinir would have known what to do. Where was he?

Then Lars began to gag. Releasing Inga, he bent double, retching violently.

Inga looked on in bewilderment. Kylen must surely be responsible. The youth had repelled a similar attack on his own body. Either Lars didn't possess the same ability or Kylen had penetrated his defenses.

Rushing to the support of Lars, Petria came to a sudden halt. Her face pale, she began gagging herself.

Then a voice spoke calmly. "I can take it from here, Kylen."

Ten long years had passed since that voice last reached her ears. Upon hearing it, a chaotic confusion of joy and grief overwhelmed her.

Looking up, she saw him. Apart from a gash on his head, he had barely changed. She registered instinctively that he was too thin, and that his robe desperately needed replacing. She saw too that the worry lines in his face were deeper, and flecks of gray highlighted the unkempt mass of his hair. But the inner serenity that radiated from him hadn't changed a bit.

She steadfastly refused herself any outward display of emotion. Nevertheless the truth would be denied no longer. She had loved him from the moment they'd met. It was a doomed devotion, destined to remain forever unrequited. But she loved him still, and she always would.

Belatedly she noticed that Lars and Petria had slumped to the ground. They lay breathing peacefully, their gagging at an end.

Kylen was speaking. "I'm sorry, Dalthinir. I was trying to do something like that, but I didn't know how."

Dalthinir smiled. "There's nothing to be ashamed about, Kylen. You stopped them! You've done well, and under extremely challenging circumstances."

Both Petria and Lars appeared to have dropped small objects when they fell to the ground. Noticing them, Dalthinir came closer and picked them up. Holding them up, he examined them closely.

"I've seen something very similar to these before, when I was a child. An old mage had one. He used it for parlor tricks. It trapped small bursts of magic, and he was able to release the magic later. They're very limited though. He told me that the amount of magic they can store is determined by the magic used to create them. That means they're limited by the power of the mage who created them."

He glanced down at the prone mages. "Opening the book would have released an overwhelming torrent of magic. Did these two imagine their little trinkets were capable of trapping it all? They were fools if they believed they could use them to acquire unlimited power while sparing the kingdom from destruction." He shook his head in bemusement. "Who could have put such ideas into their heads?"

Putting the golden fists carefully on the ground, he trained elemental fire magic upon them. Soon nothing remained except two small golden puddles.

While he was distracted, Emmela had regained her feet. She made no attempt to hide her discomfort. Indebted to Dalthinir or not, she clearly hadn't forgotten he was a renegade. "I'll get Ellis and the other two," she mumbled, heading outside.

Inga ignored her. "That gash on your head looks serious," she told Dalthinir sternly. "Did you lose consciousness?"

"Yes," Kylen told her. "He did briefly."

"It needs to be attended to."

Swinging a small pack from her back, she rummaged inside and extracted some dressings. "Come with me," she ordered in a no-nonsense tone.

Dalthinir hesitated, glancing at the two sleeping mages.

Following his gaze, Inga bent low and briefly examined them. "From the look of them they won't be going anywhere for a while. How long do you expect them to be out?"

He shrugged. "It's difficult to say. I've only ever done this kind of thing with sick animals. Maybe a couple of hours?"

"Emmela will be back with the others before then. In the meantime you're coming with me."

"I'll get you into trouble, Inga," he said, a worried frown on his face.

"If you think I care about that, Dalthinir, you don't know me very well." Taking his arm, she steered him firmly through the entrance.

The mage made no attempt to resist. She caught a hint of a smile twisting his lips as he met Kylen's gaze, then he allowed himself to be swept along beside her.

CHAPTER 31

Kylen stood alone inside the rock-enclosed room, relieved that the confrontation was over and astonished that it had ended as smoothly as it did.

He'd been ready to do almost anything to save Inga. He couldn't help himself. He heard Bella's voice in his memory. *Kylen has always been drawn to the helpless.*

He had a great deal to thank Dalthinir for. There was no telling how it might have ended without him.

With his mentor at last enjoying time with Inga, he had no desire to interrupt them. They deserved whatever moments they could snatch together.

On impulse he glanced around the strange little room. He had arrived to chaos and conflict, offering him no opportunity to examine it. His eye was caught by the empty pedestal. Without knowing how, he sensed that the book belonged on it.

Glancing down, he noticed it lying on the ground. Bending low, he tried to pick it up. He couldn't do it. Then it occurred to him to lift it with mage touch magic. Raising it by that means, he brought it to the pedestal.

He stared down at it. One small book had led to so much confusion, so much trouble. He shook his head in wonder.

Words were scratched on the leather cover: *'Ode to the Fallen One.'*

Dalthinir's refusal to tell him anything of substance about the book had succeeded only in stirring his curiosity. Now it lay before him. A sudden desire came over him to read it.

Yet he hesitated. He'd been told that just to open it would lead to the kingdom being destroyed.

What if that wasn't true though? It seemed so extreme. Could anyone really be certain about what would happen? It made sense that any kind of power would be dangerous in the hands of people like Lars and Petria, but he wasn't looking for more power. He was merely curious.

Still he hesitated, another part of him refusing to be so easily convinced. Hadn't he and Dalthinir been racing against time solely to prevent the book from being opened? How could he risk even the possibility of kingdom-wide destruction just to satisfy his curiosity?

But the inner wrestler refused to quit. He told himself he was being ridiculous. There was plenty of hearsay floating about, but what evidence was there to support such an alarmist position? Surely there could be no harm in a tiny peek.

An obvious solution presented itself. He would open it slowly and carefully. If anything bad started to happen, he would immediately slam it shut again.

With him almost in the act of opening it, a voice broke across his thoughts.

"Are you sure you want to do that?"

He started guiltily, the book slipping from his control to fall directly onto the pedestal. The instant it landed, a boulder materialized, encasing it entirely. He stared down at it in astonishment.

Set free from the book, he belatedly recognized its seductive allure. Even encased in rock he could feel its pull.

But who had challenged him? He spun slowly around to identify the owner of the voice.

At first he saw nothing but a jumble of rocks at the opposite end of the room. Then he stared in stupefaction as the illusion was stripped away and the truth laid bare. How could he have believed himself to be looking at rocks?

His heart skipped a beat, his eyes almost popping out of his head.

A huge dragon crouched before him. Mottled green in color with purple streaks on its folded wings, it seemed at once relaxed and poised for action. The feet at the end of its great legs sported long and menacing claws. He didn't doubt that a single slash from one of those claws would end his life in a moment.

The dragon's voice sounded once more, a discordant blend of growl and purr.

"So we meet again, little human."

His jaw went slack. What could the creature mean? No one could possibly forget an encounter with a dragon. Not unless they had lost their wits.

How could he respond to such a greeting?

A more pressing question confronted him. How could he face such a being and live? If he had doubted that dragon power was unmatched, he could doubt no longer. The magic all around him did not flow from the location—he sensed that it streamed unceasingly from the creature before him. The intensity of it was beyond anything he could have imagined.

He could not hope to survive. Not when every report depicted dragons as destructive and evil.

Defiance rose up within him, puny though he might be.

"Why do you hate us so much?"

The two huge orbed eyes stared dispassionately back at him from the scaled head. A hint of smoke wafted from the creature's nostrils. It offered no response.

He stood with heart pounding, horrified at his own audacity.

The creature before him had no need of magic to deal with someone like him. It had only to open its mighty jaws and roast him with fire, or sink its fearsome teeth deep into his fragile flesh. He could not convince himself that his magic would protect him.

He had once seen a cat playing with a mouse. For the first time he understood how the mouse must have felt.

"Are you going to sport with me?" he asked nervously.

Still there was no answer.

Dalthinir had told him that mages once united against the dragons, and that they had been victorious. Clearly they had failed to finish the job.

"Dragons destroyed Methesia, and they would have destroyed humankind completely if they hadn't been driven away. Why? What made you do it?"

With his questions ignored, he became bolder. "Are dragons born evil?"

The intimidating mouth opened strangely. Was it smiling? "No creature is born evil, little mouse," the dragon replied calmly. "Evil is a choice. It has been so from the beginning."

Little mouse? A deep flush crept up Kylen's face. Surely the creature couldn't read his mind. Could it?

"So why did dragons choose evil?" he persisted stubbornly.

Any trace of purr had vanished from the voice. "You lay claim to great knowledge, young Kalmithien."

He frowned in puzzlement. Who or what was Kalmithien?

The huge orbs pinned him with their unblinking gaze. "Answer me this if you know so much. Were you there when my grandsire gamboled at the feet of the Merciful One as He walked in the Garden in the cool of the evening?"

Kylen had nothing to say.

The voice became a rumbling growl, and smoke billowed from the great nostrils. "Were you there when the mages of Methesia chose madness? Did you watch, confounded, as Master Arbilis invoked the dark magic?"

Discomposed by the impact of the dragon's authority, he struggled to comprehend its words. What was the creature implying? Was it suggesting that renegade mages had been responsible for the destruction of Methesia?

He shook his head numbly. Whatever the cause of the devastation, the dragon was right about one thing. Kylen had witnessed none of these things.

Then doubt asserted itself. Why should he believe a creature like this? Dragon magic led only to folly and madness. It was forbidden for a reason. Lars and Petria had lusted after it to their own ruin. He had almost failed the test himself.

"I refuse to believe you," he declared obstinately. "I reject dragon magic, and everything associated with it!"

"It is too late for that, Kalmithien."

He stared at the dragon blankly.

"I saw you perched atop the roof in Cambrick, peering into a room where oath breakers huddled in the candlelight, charting a course for a new desecration. I dropped from the sky, and my wings overshadowed you."

The great head tilted provocatively. "It was I who awakened your magic."

Kylen's heart skipped a beat. Surely it couldn't be. It was unthinkable.

But it must be true. Why else had his power swelled as he approached the mountain? He had been approaching the very source of his magic.

Dalthinir had told him that dragons once awakened magical power in mages. The mages that emerged could only have been renegades. They must have been evil, because dragon magic was tainted. That was not a matter of debate. He bowed his head in horror and dismay.

How much time passed as he stood rooted to the ground he could not say. But when he looked up again he discovered that the dragon was gone. Not hidden by illusion as before. Gone.

The atmosphere no longer tingled with power. An inexplicable feeling of exultation had swelled within him as he ascended the mountain. That was gone as well.

The conclusion was inescapable—all of it had flowed from the dragon. He had sensed an unusual magical emanation well before they arrived at this place. For some reason the dragon chose not to mask it.

The dragon might be gone, along with every trace of its presence. But his own power remained, stronger than ever. He could sense it.

The words of the old woman on the hillside flooded into his mind. *The child of prophecy has awakened! He will rise up in power, and the mountains will shake. Our doom rests upon his shoulders.*

She had visited him again in a nightmare. *Doom! Doom upon us all!* she had cried.

Too distressed to think clearly, he covered his face with his hands.

At some point he became aware he was not alone. Spinning around, he found one of the mages from Inga's group staring at him. He'd never met the mage, but he recognized his aura.

"What was all that about?" the mage asked, a confused frown on his face.

Blood rushed to his face. "You witnessed it?"

"I saw you standing in front of a pile of rocks and speaking gibberish. If that's what you mean, then yes, I witnessed it."

Kylen almost burst into mad laughter. He didn't know whether to be relieved or humiliated. Somehow managing a tight smile, he nodded to the mage and headed into the open.

The mage had neither seen nor heard the dragon. Stranger still, he hadn't understood a word Kylen was saying.

Had the dragon been speaking a different language? If so, how had a conversation been possible? Kylen knew no languages apart from his own.

For one glorious moment his spirits soared as he dared to believe he had imagined the whole incident. If the interaction was only in his mind, he had no reason to believe he'd been awakened by a dragon.

Then reality imposed itself. The dragon's presence couldn't be dismissed so easily, however much he wanted to do it. The magic in the atmosphere had been palpable—Dalthinir had felt it too. And it had disappeared with the creature.

No, the dragon had been real. And it had undoubtedly awakened him as it claimed.

The more he considered it, the more he could find no other explanation for why the creature had spared him. Dalthinir had made it clear that dragons hated humankind.

His shoulders slumped in dismay. His access to magical power had been difficult to accept at first, but over time he had slowly become comfortable with it. Everything now took on an entirely different meaning in light of the revelation about his awakening. Dalthinir had never understood how awakening was even possible without involvement from the Compact. What would he say if he ever discovered that a dragon had done it?

He had thought it grossly unfair to be cast as a renegade just because the Compact had not trained him and overseen his awakening. He could protest no longer. What could he be if not a renegade? No other label fit.

The only thing he desired was solitude. Head down, he let his feet take him where they would. Anywhere, so long as it was far from other people.

CHAPTER 32

Inga stood beside Emmela, Ellis, Kaspra, and Alexis facing a panel of their peers. The panel had been assembled by Chief Master Adrastas.

"This inquiry is in session!" called Adrastas importantly. "As all of us are aware, a team was sent in pursuit of Lars and Petria. That team was led by Master Inga. Our purpose today is to review the outcome of the mission along with the conduct and actions of the team."

Waving toward a row of empty chairs positioned at one side, he encouraged the team members to be seated.

He began by calling forward Ellis, Kaspra, and Alexis. The morning light faded as the three mages, interrupted by many questions, described the journey, the constant danger from predators, and the invaluable contribution of Ramond and his men. Panel members exchanged dark looks when they heard of the wounded man left behind by the prince's party. The dark looks turned to anger when the mages described the attack on their campsite at the top of the mountain.

"What did you do when the prince and his men attacked you?"

"We protected the campsite with shields," Ellis told them. "But I thought we were finished when they precipitated a landslide."

"How did you escape?"

"A boy and a girl had arrived with Dalthinir, and they drew off the guards with slingshots. No more rocks came down after that. And almost at the moment I thought our shield was about to collapse, it was strengthened unexpectedly."

"Who strengthened it?"

Ellis exchanged glances with the others. "Dalthinir," he replied reluctantly. "By the time he arrived, half of the hillside was pressing down on our shield. We were trapped below it. We couldn't go up or down, and there was no safe space on either side. And both of us were beginning to tire."

"How did you escape the debris?"

"It was cleared away."

"How?"

"By magic."

"You and Kaspra removed it?"

Ellis shook his head. "We were hard pressed just keeping the shield in place."

"Are you saying that Dalthinir did it?"

Ellis hesitated. "Possibly." Once more he exchanged glances with the other team members. "We think it was more likely to have been the other person traveling with him. A youth, apparently called Kylen."

This remark was met with general skepticism. "Are you suggesting another mage was present? An unknown mage with no connection to the Compact?"

The team members could only shrug.

"Why didn't any of you apprehend Dalthinir or this unknown youth?"

Ellis looked bemused. "You mean apart from the fact that they'd just saved us?" With no response forthcoming, he shrugged, "Actions of that nature would seem to be the team leader's responsibility. But it was obvious that all of us combined weren't powerful enough to do any such thing."

Adrastas steered the inquiry back to safer ground. "So Ramond apprehended the men who attacked you?"

"Yes," replied Alexis. "The three men and their captain were kept under constant guard during our return journey to Cambrick. Ramond turned them over to the royal guards as soon as we arrived."

Adrastas nodded. "I expect them soon to be tried. Some of you will be called upon to give evidence."

"What happened to Prince Evran?" asked Master Kothlar.

"Ramond sent a couple of men to capture him, but he evaded them," Alexis told him. "We have no idea where he is now. It's possible he didn't make it out of the mountains alive. Wildcats are especially dangerous during the hours of darkness."

"And what of Lars and Petria?"

"They were eventually disabled at the top of the mountain," said Kaspra.

"By whom?" asked Adrastas.

"Master Inga and Master Emmela can provide details," Kaspra replied. "But we understand that Dalthinir was responsible."

Her answer provoked energetic conversation among the panel. They spoke too quietly for Inga to hear what they were saying.

"Then why didn't Lars and Petria return with the team?" asked Kothlar.

"We had them under magical restraint and also under guard when we left," Kaspra replied. "But while we were still in the mountains, wildcats attacked our party again. Ellis and I were called upon to shield the campsite."

"Who asked you to do that?"

"Master Inga," she replied. "Unfortunately, we weren't able to maintain the magical restraints as well as shielding the campsite. During the confusion they managed to escape into the night."

"What became of them?"

"We don't know. We saw no further sign of them."

This evidence provoked more loud muttering among the panel.

Emmela was called next. She described the confrontation in the rock-enclosed room.

"You're saying that an unknown mage—a youth called Kylen— succeeded in defending himself against both Lars and Petria? And that he prevented Lars from opening the book?"

"That's what appeared to be happening."

"And you'd never seen this person before?"

Emmela shook her head. "I didn't recognize him. Or the scent of his magic."

"But Dalthinir knows him?"

"He clearly did from the way he spoke to him."

Kothlar's brows had drawn together. "An unknown mage can only have come from Tantel."

Adrastas interjected. "There has been no request from the mage council in Antilin to allow one of their number to travel to Periton. That suggests this Kylen is a Tantellan renegade who has fled the kingdom and somehow made his way here."

Inga stole a glance at the chief master. He would undoubtedly be considering the possibility that Kylen was not a renegade. If that were the case, it could only mean the Tantellans sent him to Periton on a covert mission. She didn't believe it for a minute.

How had Kylen's magic been awakened? Dalthinir would undoubtedly be able to answer the question.

She frowned. She couldn't afford to think about Dalthinir. The inquiry demanded her full attention.

Kothlar had resumed his questioning of Emmela. "What did the renegade do when he arrived?"

"Kylen had been trying to physically disable Lars and Petria, but he was distracting them and not much more. When Dalthinir arrived, he immediately put them to sleep."

"So this Kylen attacked two Compact mages, intending to magically disable them?"

"Yes. Lars had an arm around Master Inga's neck at the time. He threatened to stop her heart if Kylen didn't release the book."

"Why wouldn't Kylen release the book?"

"I can't say. I presume he didn't want Lars to open it."

"And Dalthinir attacked them as soon as he arrived."

"He rendered both of them unconscious."

"So he and Kylen both attacked two Compact mages."

Emmela frowned. "Yes. But they also prevented them from harming Master Inga."

"And the way Dalthinir spoke to Kylen suggested he knew him

well?"

She nodded.

"Did he do anything else?"

"Lars and Petria dropped two small objects when they went to sleep. They were shaped like fists and appeared to be made of gold. Dalthinir said he'd seen something similar. It was used to trap small amounts of magic and store it for later use. It was used for parlor tricks."

"I've never heard of such a thing," said Kothlar skeptically.

"I have!" called Master Gunnith. He must have been the oldest mage in the Compact. "It was used exactly as you described."

"Dalthinir wondered if they believed they could trap the magic released when the book was open," Emmela continued.

"Thereby preserving the kingdom while leaving them with vast amounts of stored power," snorted Gunnith. "They were fools if they believed any such notion!"

"Dalthinir said almost exactly the same thing," she told him.

"What became of these objects?" asked Kothlar.

"Dalthinir melted them. With fire magic."

"Did you speak with Dalthinir while he was in the room with you?" Kothlar continued.

"Of course not! He's a renegade!"

"What about Master Inga? Did she speak with him?"

Emmela avoided eye contact with Inga when answering the question. She related Inga's interaction with the renegade, and her decision to treat his wounds.

"So Master Inga conversed with a known renegade, and then tended to his injuries?"

She nodded uncomfortably.

"How did Dalthinir sustain these injuries?" asked Master Kothlar.

Emmela turned to the other team members.

"The prince's guards attacked him," Kaspra replied. "While he was strengthening our shield."

"So you're telling us that a renegade acted in your defense?" The questioner didn't hide his skepticism.

Kaspra could only shrug. "We've already told you that."

Finally Adrastas called Inga. "Do you concur with the evidence presented thus far, Master Inga?" he asked.

"I do," she said without hesitation.

"Including Master Emmela's testimony about Lars and Petria, and in particular what they did with the book?"

"Yes," she replied. "All of her statements were accurate."

"Master Inga," said Kothlar. "The book, *Ode to the Fallen One*, seems to have been the cause of the conflict and confusion. We've heard from Master Emmela that Lars found a way to get access to it, although she was miserly with the specifics of how that was achieved." He glanced briefly at Adrastas before continuing. "The matter is extremely sensitive, of course, so I will not probe for further information. But I am anxious to know what became of the book. Can you please enlighten us?"

"I think Master Alexis can best answer that," she replied, turning to him.

Alexis rose to his feet. "Once the debris was gone and Ramond began pursuing our attackers, I wasn't needed at the campsite. So I headed up the mountain to see if I could help Master Inga and Master Emmela. I met Master Emmela on her way down. She briefly told me what had happened. I continued to the top and peeked into the room. Kylen was there on his own, holding the book by magical means."

"Did he open it?"

"No. He dropped it onto the pedestal. The moment it landed, a boulder encased it."

His testimony was greeted with stunned silence.

"Did he do that?"

"I don't know, but I suspect not. I had the impression he was as surprised as I was."

"So he never opened the book?"

Inga rolled her eyes. "If he had, you wouldn't need to ask the question."

Kothlar ignored her comment. "Did he see you, Master Alexis?"

"No. I kept out of sight."

"What did this Kylen do next?"

Alexis frowned. "It was strange. He stood in front of the pile of rocks at the other end of the little room and babbled."

"Babbled?"

"Yes. I couldn't understand a word he was saying. Eventually he noticed me."

"What did he say?"

"He asked me if I'd witnessed it. I told him I'd seen him speaking gibberish in front of a pile of rocks."

"It sounds as if he was embarrassed," suggested Adrastas.

"He certainly seemed to be," Alexis confirmed.

"Either that or the youth is unhinged," offered Kothlar. "If so, it's an alarming development. A second renegade with significant power is bad enough without him being deranged as well."

Alexis sat down.

One of the panel members regarded Inga grimly. When he spoke, his voice was stern. "In view of the unusual gravity of your mission, Master Inga, could you please explain to us how it was that you left the mountain on friendly terms with Dalthinir, not to mention an entirely new renegade who is most likely from Tantel? And how you presumed to return to Cambrick without Lars and Petria?"

This last question was the final indignity for Inga. Having lost all patience with the questioning, she turned to Adrastas. "Is this a trial, Chief Master?"

He frowned. "Of course not. Why would you think that?"

"The grim looks on your faces and the stiff formality of the proceedings might have something to do with it. And the impertinence of the panel in questioning my role. Maybe it also has something to do with the guards ready at the door in case I try to run away."

"There's no need for sarcasm, Inga. While this isn't a trial, some might argue that a trial would be appropriate under the circumstances. You failed to retrieve Lars and Petria, and if we have been informed reliably, you consorted openly with the renegade Dalthinir."

Inga stared at him with eyes narrowed. "May I remind you, Chief Master, that the reason you sent me after Lars and Petria was—and I quote—'to keep an eye on them?' There was never any suggestion of apprehending them, much less retrieving them."

He nodded uncomfortably. "You are correct."

"Further, you speak now of retrieving them because they not only recovered the forbidden book, *Ode to the Fallen One*, they very nearly succeeded in opening it. Yet I seem to recall you were completely dismissive of any possible threat related to the book. If I remember correctly, your exact words were, 'I simply can't take it seriously. You're worrying for no reason, Inga.'"

Adrastas winced. "I freely admit I was wrong about the book."

"You speak of consorting with Dalthinir. You've already heard that it was Dalthinir and his associate Kylen who rescued the party attacked by the prince and his men. More importantly, they then prevented Lars from opening the book. Without their intervention, a disaster of catastrophic proportions would have been visited upon our kingdom."

The chief master had gone silent.

"It was only thanks to the efforts of Dalthinir that we were able to take Lars and Petria into custody in the first place. If he had been free to travel with us to Cambrick, they would still have been with us when we arrived. Without his support, their escape on the return journey was little more than a foregone conclusion."

She glared at Adrastas and his panel. "Have all of you conveniently forgotten that they stood in this very room and insisted that destroying Dalthinir should be the primary focus of every mage in Periton? Their motivation should now be perfectly obvious to every one of us. They painted Dalthinir as a dangerous monster for one reason only: they correctly deduced that he was the one person capable of preventing them from finding and opening the book. Far from being dangerous, Dalthinir acted with great courage, taking considerable risks in the process. Our entire kingdom owes more than we could ever repay to this 'monster.'"

Her passion spent, she allowed her shoulders to slump in weariness. "Finish your inquiry, Adrastas. I will be the first to acknowledge that we have a great deal to learn from what has happened. But when you bring your findings, don't denigrate any of those who risked their lives repeatedly in pursuit of Lars and Petria." She directed a respectful nod to her colleagues on the team.

Then she looked directly at Emmela. "And don't *any* of you dare to demonize the man who risked his life and freedom to save us from our own blindness. We cast him aside as a renegade—a man worthy only of death. Yet he chose to rescue us rather than despise us."

Emmela had gone bright red. She bowed her head, unable to meet Inga's eyes.

Master Kothlar rose to his feet. "All of us would do well to heed Master Inga's words. Some among us challenged the wild claims about Dalthinir made by Lars and Petria. We did so with far more justification than any of us realized at the time. We must learn from our mistakes, but we can and should also celebrate a fortuitous escape from a terrible disaster." Then he sat down abruptly.

After bowing to Inga, Adrastas addressed the panel. "Do any of you have further questions?"

All of them shook their heads.

"In that case we will retire to discuss our findings. Please take the opportunity to refresh yourselves," he told Inga and her team. "We will call you back when we have concluded our discussions."

Summoned once more by the chief master, Inga returned with the others to hear the panel's rulings.

Adrastas wasted no time. "On behalf of my colleagues, I would like to express appreciation for the extraordinary efforts of the whole team. Your mission was undertaken in an environment of danger and uncertainty, and the Compact is grateful for what you have done. You were tested beyond anything we anticipated, and we are grateful to you for carrying out your duties above and beyond what might reasonably have been expected of you."

He locked eyes with Inga. "As leader of the group, Master Inga, you faced a number of extraordinary challenges, including a threat on your life. Although the panel expressed considerable discomfort at your interaction with Dalthinir, we also acknowledge the exceptional circumstances of the mission, and appreciate your steadfastness in the face of great danger. In view of the complexities of the situation, we decided against imposing sanctions. Nevertheless, we wish to make it clear that engagement of any kind with a renegade has always been, and remains, strictly forbidden, by duty as well as by law."

He turned away without offering her an opportunity to respond.

"I regret to say that as a result of the actions of Lars and Petria, they are, as of this moment, formally stripped of their Compact membership along with all their titles and privileges. As of now they are declared renegade. This action has not been taken lightly, but it is a necessary step in view of the damning testimony against them by two reliable witnesses."

He sighed. "It also seems that a young mage who wields enormous power has somehow appeared in the kingdom. It is impossible to guess at the consequences. But it is sobering to consider that the mission began with a single renegade, and ended with four. None of us can ignore the danger the kingdom faces as a result. I need hardly remind you that the Compact bears legal responsibility for dealing with renegades. All of us will be called upon in the days to come to play our part in responding to what can only be regarded as an escalating threat."

He nodded to them all. "Thank you for your participation. I hereby declare this inquiry at an end."

Later that day Inga was tracked down by Adrastas. He found her sitting alone in a secluded corner of the Compact grounds, enjoying the afternoon sunshine.

He was shaking his head. "We have recently received two missives from the long-dead Banadin, if you can believe it. Through his legal representatives. The letters separately accuse Lars and Petria of a range of crimes, including murder! We have yet to investigate the claims, but it's difficult to imagine this case becoming more bizarre than it already is."

Seeing she wasn't going to be drawn, he squatted down in front of her, frowning in bemusement. "Was it really necessary for you to be so blatant about treating Dalthinir's wounds? The man is under sentence of death! I barely persuaded the panel not to sanction you. You know how serious that would have been."

Inga snorted. "It isn't difficult to guess why they allowed them-selves to be persuaded. You needed 'two reliable witnesses' to declare Lars and Petria renegade. If I'd been punished, or even formally repri-manded, you would've only had one."

He gave her a wry smile. "You don't miss much, do you, Inga?"

She pressed on. "As for the law, I'm well aware that Dalthinir is under sentence of death. But don't expect me to treat him like a monster. I'm not a cactus, and I never will be."

"A cactus? What does that mean?"

"A cactus uses its sharp points to impale anything that comes close enough."

He laughed. "That's an apt description for a number of people I work with."

She was in no mood for laughter. "Sometimes, Adrastas, you show about as much human feeling as the paper your precious laws are written on. The law is supposedly there to serve people!"

"I don't disagree. But one important way the law serves people is to deal with those who refuse to come under it."

"I'm not going to argue semantics with you. You want to define Dalthinir as a monster purely because he's a renegade. Fine. But don't expect me to do it. I almost died up there! Lars used *my life* as leverage. He would have stopped my heart without blinking if it suited his purposes. There's your monster, if you're looking for one! Lars and Petria abandoned an injured man to die alone on the mountain—that's the kind of thing monsters do."

She threw up her hands in exasperation. "Monsters don't save the lives of every person on my team. You're even willing to overlook the fact that Dalthinir and Kylen saved the entire kingdom!"

She glowered at him. "Think of them as monsters if it makes you happy. But when someone shows compassion at great risk to them-selves, I won't hesitate to show them compassion in return. Even if the entire Compact is looking on!"

He shook his head helplessly. "You're a very decent person, Inga. No one disputes it. But like it or not, anyone outside the law has to be dealt with. And when it's a mage, dealing with them is our respon-sibility."

And with that he left.

His arrival had driven away her tranquility. Sadly, it didn't reappear with his departure.

Looking up, she discovered that clouds had moved across the sun. It felt like a depiction of her life in recent days.

Clambering to her feet with a sigh, she headed back to her quarters alone.

CHAPTER 33

Trudging along behind the others with his head down, Kylen tried to make sense of everything that had happened on the mountain. He couldn't dismiss from his mind the memory of the dragon, staring at him with its orbed eyes. The creature was physically imposing—terrifyingly so. He didn't doubt that its scales would blunt a thrust from the sharpest spear.

The air had throbbed with its power. From the little he'd seen of human mages and their magic, he wondered how all of them together could drive away a solitary dragon.

Dalthinir came alongside him. "You seem a little flat, Kylen. I'm sure what happened back there was very taxing, but I hope you know you should be very proud of the way you conducted yourself. You showed great compassion and unusual mastery."

Kylen managed a half-hearted nod.

The mage gazed at him thoughtfully. "You mentioned earlier that the book isn't accessible now. What happened to it?"

"I dropped it onto the pedestal. A boulder immediately appeared and enclosed it."

Dalthinir's eyebrows went up in surprise. "Some kind of magical protection by the sound of it," he mused.

Kylen offered no comment.

"Perhaps a distraction might be useful," Dalthinir offered brightly. "I still haven't told you about the remaining mage sense, which is mage hearing. It's quite rare. I'm not aware of any mage who has it. It's the ability to understand any language without needing to learn it. The mage becomes a linguist or polyglot by magical means. The ability even encompasses non-human languages. It isn't just about understanding languages either. It allows a mage to communicate in any language. You might notice I didn't say speak in any language. Communication might not always involve the use of vocal cords, especially with non-human languages."

Kylen became suddenly attentive. "Does this ability allow a mage to speak with dragons?"

"It does. Records suggest that dragons spoke solely in their own language. They must surely have been capable of communicating through human languages, because they would have possessed some equivalent of mage hearing. But for some reason they never did. Perhaps they were unwilling to stoop so low. Consequently, only those with mage hearing ability were ever able to communicate directly with them."

So Kylen himself had mage hearing ability. And dragon language was the gibberish he was overheard speaking on the mountain. Any lingering hope that he'd imagined the interaction was finally dashed.

"Curiously," Dalthinir was saying, "a literate mage with mage hearing ability is also able to read and write foreign languages. Literacy trains a mage to perceive meaning in the scrawl of written words, and once that has been achieved, mage hearing unlocks magical comprehension of all written language. Mages with the ability are said to learn to read and write more quickly than others."

He glanced at Kylen. "As it happens, you learned remarkably quickly yourself."

"Is dragon language written as well as spoken?"

"Yes, draconic speech was transcribed as a written language. At the time of the dragons' betrayal of humankind, draconic texts of any kind were declared extremely dangerous and strictly forbidden. By law, any scrolls or parchments in draconic language must be destroyed by burning immediately upon discovery. Every mage who joins the Compact takes an oath to uphold that law."

Kylen remembered the words of the dragon. *I saw you perched atop the roof in Cambrick, peering into a room where oath breakers huddled in the candlelight.*

"What about *Ode to the Fallen One*? Was that written in dragon language?"

"Most certainly. Which means Lars would never have been able to read it," the mage noted with a snort.

"Why did he want it so badly then?"

"Great power is released just by opening such a book. He must have hoped he could get access to some or all of that power."

"How could that be possible?"

The mage shrugged. "I suspect he'd somehow become convinced that the talisman he was holding would capture and store the power for his later use."

Kylen wondered if Methesia had been destroyed in a similar way. Suspecting that Dalthinir might stop talking if he asked about it directly, he steered in a different direction.

"Why was Lars opening it? Why him and not Petria?"

"Only a person with mage touch ability can open such a book. For that reason it fell to Lars. They both had talismans, so perhaps they both expected to benefit from the release of power. I imagine they agreed to work together once they had acquired all this power. How that would have worked in practice is an interesting question."

Kylen remembered clearly the title on the cover of the book on the mountain. The fact that he had been able to decipher it provided further confirmation of his mage hearing ability. What uncontrolled power might he have released if he had opened the book? The thought was terrifying.

"Dragon magic is tainted, isn't it?"

"Yes, but such considerations wouldn't trouble a person like Lars."

The words of the dragon came to mind. *Did you watch, confounded, as Master Arbilis invoked the dark magic?*

"Did Master Arbilis have mage hearing ability?"

Dalthinir looked at him sharply. "Where did you hear that name?"

Flustered, Kylen struggled to come up with an answer. "Somewhere," he stammered. "You told me about a powerful mage who became a renegade and did a lot of damage. Was that him?"

The mage was looking at him strangely. "No. Arbilis was a powerful mage, certainly, but not a renegade. He lived during the time of Methesia's destruction."

Kylen's heart skipped a beat. So the dragon had named a real mage. And if the creature was to be believed, it was that mage who had brought about the destruction. The dragon had described itself merely as an observer.

Then he frowned, berating himself for his own folly. How could he believe anything said by a dragon?

"Did one of Inga's people mention Arbilis?" persisted Dalthinir.

He shrugged helplessly. "I don't remember much of what they said. There was a lot going on."

To Kylen's relief, the mage let it drop. He told himself he needed to be much more careful speaking about anything that involved the dragon.

Jonno and Bella had been walking a short distance behind, and Jonno now jogged forward to catch up with them.

"Where are we going?" he asked.

"We're heading east, but we'll stay within the borders of these mountains," Dalthinir told him. "I expect it will be safest to avoid populated regions for a while."

"What about avoiding wildcats?"

"Both Kylen and I can protect us against predators of the non-human variety."

Once the light began to fail, they made camp. Bella soon had a small fire crackling welcomingly.

"Could you please put a shield around the campsite, Kylen?" asked the mage. "And can you mask it?"

He nodded.

"Will you be able to maintain it while you're sleeping?"

He nodded again.

Dalthinir considered him for a moment before adding, "While

you're at it, do you think you can block out wildcat noises? I'd be grateful for some uninterrupted sleep for a change."

"I think so."

The mage raised his eyebrows admiringly. Then he headed for Bella's fire where Jonno was dressing a couple of rabbits he had snared. Heaving a huge sigh of appreciation, he sat down.

Dalthinir's requests said more plainly than words how highly he rated Kylen's abilities. He was willing to entrust the safety of them all to a largely untried youth.

Kylen knew he should be flattered, but he couldn't help wondering what the mage would think if he knew that the protection was provided courtesy of dragon magic. Tainted magic.

When they settled for the night he lay down eager for the release of sleep. But sleep eluded him. He heard again in his memory the dragon's voice. *Evil is a choice. It has been so from the beginning.*

He had no conscious desire to be evil, but he was tainted, and he knew of no way to break free of it. He himself had almost done the very thing all of them had worked so hard to prevent Lars and Petria from doing.

He tried to imagine what it would be like to go back, to return to his life as it had been before the night on the rooftop. Living on the streets had been hard, but he'd been contented enough. Then he remembered his missing finger. If it weren't for his magical power he would be missing an entire hand. That loss would have changed his life significantly.

Restless and uncomfortable, he twisted and turned beneath his blankets.

When sleep finally took him, he dreamed.

Once more he found himself on the hillside with the divided tree. This time the old woman looked directly at him. "Tainted!" she cried. "He has chosen evil!"

"No!" he protested. "It isn't true!"

But the woman either didn't hear him or ignored his denial. "DOOM!" she cried, louder than ever. "DOOM upon us all!"

Kylen woke trembling to find Dalthinir at his side.

"It isn't true, Dalthinir!" he insisted, still struggling to separate the dream from reality.

"I'm sure you're right, Kylen," the mage said comfortingly. "Whatever it was, you can put it from your mind. It was nothing but a bad dream."

Sitting up, he tried to stop his body from shaking. By the time he finally conquered the tremors the others were sound asleep again.

Lying down, he abandoned any attempt at sleep.

Evil is a choice. It has been so from the beginning.

If the dragon had been right about nothing else, maybe it had been right about that one thing. He had no desire to choose evil—he rejected it with his whole being.

Maybe he truly was doomed, no matter what he chose. If so, he was powerless to change that. But if he couldn't choose his destiny, he could at least choose the way he behaved. He could choose to reject any inner voice that urged him to justify folly and evil.

To whatever extent it was up to him, he would strive with all his might to turn the tainted magic against itself and use it for good.

And he wasn't alone. Dalthinir had promised to guide him, and he knew the twins wanted the best for him. Even the dragon had played a part, interrupting him when he was on the brink of yielding to a terrible temptation.

By the time the sun rose he had come to a decision. Even if he couldn't save himself, he would continue to save as many strays as he could. He would never turn aside from the helpless. And for as long as his magic obeyed him, he would bend it to the same purpose.

Looking up, he saw a large flock of swallows darting about in the dawn light. They seemed to be pursuing insects, but to his surprise a constant stream of them were peeling off from the main flock and swooping close to him.

"You seem to attract them, Kylen," said Jonno, pointing to the swallows. "When we were searching for you in the river there were swallows flying around you. That's how we found out where you were."

"He's right," agreed Dalthinir. "And there was another large flock when we were heading up the mountain. They seemed attracted to you as well."

"Swallows are a symbol of hope and good fortune," said Bella. "I think it's a sign."

Kylen peered up at the birds. Maybe it was a sign.

The timing couldn't have been better if it was. Because if there was one thing he needed at that moment, it was hope.

The End

The saga continues in *The Riven Land,*
Book 2 of Allan N. Packer's series
The Ruptured Kingdom

LIST OF CHARACTERS

- *Adrastas* - Chief Master (head mage) of the Compact in Periton
- *Alexis* - Peritonian mage with the ability to manipulate all of the elements (earth, air, fire, and water)
- *Arbilis* - Methesian mage in earlier times
- *Banadin* - Peritonian mage who died some years previously
- *Bella* - twin of Jonno; daughter of farmers; close friend of Kylen
- *Clarree* - Peritonian mage (male, deceased)
- *Dalthinir* - renegade Peritonian mage
- *Durvaryn* - king of Periton; married to Queen Karolin with 2 children: Firan, a son aged 8, and Layla, a daughter aged 6
- *Emmela* - Peritonian mage with strong illusionary magic ability
- *Ellis* - Peritonian mage with moderately strong ability to control, manipulate, and move objects by magical means
- *Elspeth* - a girl Kylen met and befriended on the streets of Cambrick
- *Evran* - prince of Periton, younger brother of King Durvaryn
- *Firan* - prince of Periton; son of Durvaryn and Karolin

- *Garmer* - Peritonian mage (male, deceased)
- *Grudem* - a friend of Dalthinir's living in Camberton, the town outside the walls of Cambrick
- *Gunnith* - elderly Peritonian mage
- *Inga* - Peritonian mage with strong farsense ability
- *Jonno* - twin of Bella; son of farmers; close friend of Kylen
- *Karolin* - queen of Periton; married to King Durvaryn with 2 children: Firan, a son aged 8, and Layla, a daughter aged 6
- *Kaspra* - Peritonian mage with moderately strong ability to control, manipulate, and move objects by magical means.
- *Keemun* - son of Grudem and Marta
- *Kothlar* - Peritonian mage with strong ability to move objects magically
- *Kylen* - orphan initially living on the streets of Cambrick
- *Lars* - Peritonian mage
- *Layla* - princess of Periton; daughter of Durvaryn and Karolin
- *Mardell, Lord* - Peritonian nobleman; Royal Chancellor; married to Lady Mardell
- *Mardell, Lady* - powerful Peritonian noblewoman married to Lord Mardell
- *Marklo* - Peritonian nobleman
- *Marta* - wife of Grudem, living in Camberton, the town outside the walls of Cambrick
- *Olatiren* - Kylen's tutor in his early years on the streets.
- *Petria* - mage with moderate elemental magic capability controlling fire
- *Ramond* - mercenary leader; childhood friend of Adrastas
- *Rostem* - Peritonian nobleman
- *Roza* - Peritonian mage (female, deceased)

NOTE FROM THE AUTHOR

Thank you for reading *The Hard Edge of Magic*—I hope you enjoyed it. Please consider leaving a review. Reviews make a huge difference to me as well as benefiting other readers.

I also very much appreciate feedback from my readers. I'd love to hear from you—please feel free to send me an email.

The saga of the Ruptured Kingdom continues in *The Riven Land (The Ruptured Kingdom Book 2)*. See below for an outline of the book.

To be kept up to date on new releases, sign up to my newsletter mailing list at *www.allanpacker.com*. New subscribers will receive an exclusive bonus novelette—a prequel to *The Hard Edge of Magic*. The novelette, *The Renegade,* reveals the process that led to Dalthinir becoming a renegade, while providing important background to the wider story. The novelette is described below.

A second exclusive bonus novelette is also available to subscribers —a prequel to *The Cost of Knowing* from my first epic fantasy series, *The Stone Cycle*. The novelette, *The Rending,* is a complete story that can be read independently from other books in the series.

Is anything worth being hunted and despised?

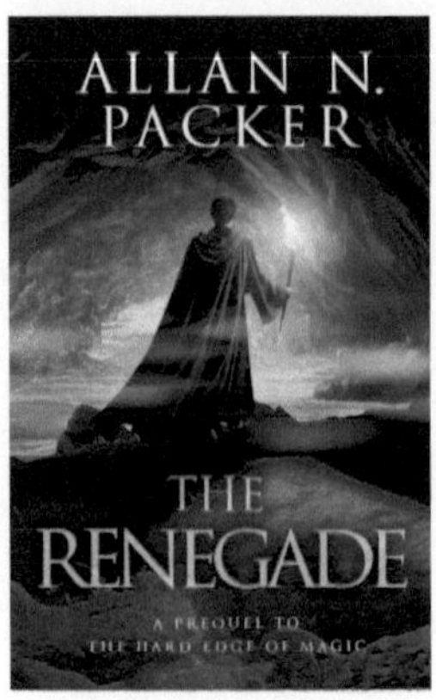

Dalthinir's life quickly unravels when he acts on suspicions about a fellow mage. After desperately using magic to escape an attempt on his life, he finds himself on trial for murder.

But more is at stake than his reputation. In their greed for power, reckless mages are willing to risk a release of magic so powerful it will destroy the kingdom. He alone recognizes the peril.

Prohibited from taking action, Dalthinir must decide what he is prepared to lose for the sake of the kingdom. Can he sacrifice everything he cares about to become a scorned and hunted renegade?

The Renegade is also available in print and audiobook editions at online bookstores.

Mortals are flickers of candlelight before a power that shatters kingdoms.

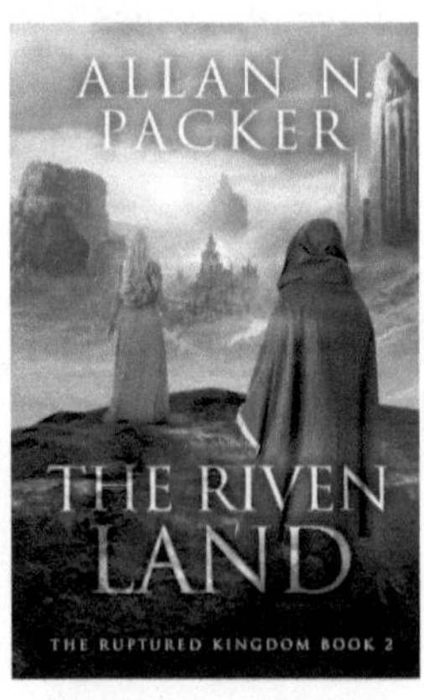

Fleeing certain death, a young woman shrouded in mystery arrives in Periton. Rescued by the renegade mages Kylen and Dalthinir, she sets out with them for the ruined kingdom of Methesia.

Hunted relentlessly by unseen enemies, the fugitives risk everything in crossing the border and heading for the former capital of Ettaran.

Dangers multiply as the doomed city

draws closer. The truth about its sinister reputation must soon be exposed.

What they find in Ettaran could destroy them all. Mortals are flickers of candlelight before a power that shatters kingdoms.

The Riven Land is available in ebook, print, and audiobook editions at online bookstores.

RESEARCH NOTES

Spoiler Alert!

The reader is advised to avoid this section before finishing *The Hard Edge of Magic.*

Shrew-Ashes and other Superstitions

Every one of the superstitions described in *The Hard Edge of Magic,* from horseshoes to toads on the path, have been embraced in different parts of the world over long periods.

The incident where a baby was passed through a cleft in an ash tree might seem bizarre, but it isn't without precedent in human history. The scholar Cecil Torr, reminiscing about life on Dartmoor, described how a baby with an abdominal rupture was passed through a cleft in an ash tree in a similar fashion. Preserving a long-standing tradition, the father had split the ash tree and wedged it open with blocks of oak. After passing the baby through three times he removed the blocks of oak and bandaged the ash trunk, expecting the baby to heal along with the tree. The baby in question was born as recently as 1902.

The superstition involving stroking cows with branches cut from a shrew-ash was described by Gilbert White, writing in Hampshire in 1776.

The following sources offer more information about shrew-ashes:

https://www.countrylife.co.uk/nature/ashes-to-ashes-is-this-the-great-trees-last-stand-211209

https://www.layersoflondon.org/map/records/a-shrew-ash-tree-with-healing-powers

Total Solar Eclipse

First noticed in 2134 BCE by Chinese Astronomers, Total Solar Eclipses occur when the New Moon passes between the Sun and the Earth, casting a dark shadow onto the Earth. The Moon only partially blocks the Sun in annular and partial solar eclipses. During a Total Solar Eclipse, the Earth is plunged into complete darkness for a few minutes.

While Solar Eclipses can be observed several times each year, Total Solar Eclipses are rare. A Total Solar Eclipse takes place somewhere on the Earth every 18 months, but much more rarely at any specific location. In the U.S., one was observed in 2017 and astronomers expect another in 2045.

Refer to https://rarest.org/nature/astronomical-events for more information.

Other Sources of Inspiration

I found inspiration from a couple of sources that give insights into historical periods now lost in time:

• Gilbert White's fascinating *The Natural History of Selborne*, written in the late 1700s, was a useful reference for both natural phenomena and human behavior in a period untouched by the far-reaching changes accompanying the modern era.

• *Meditations* by Roman Emperor Marcus Aurelius Antoninus proved to be another interesting reference. Marcus Aurelius was a devoted follower of the Stoic philosophy. Dalthinir would have had a lot in common with him.

ACKNOWLEDGMENTS

My warmest appreciation goes to my wife Merilyn, who patiently reads and rereads drafts, never failing to provide invaluable feedback along the way.

Special thanks to my beta readers, Adrian Herber, Roly Edwardes, Samuel Pryor, Deborah, Stephen, and Alison George. Their feedback makes a huge difference. My grateful thanks too to my beta listener, Arpenny Hart, who provides great feedback on the audiobook draft.

My developmental editor, Mary Novak, has made a major contribution to this story, pointing out gaps that needed filling and areas that needed strengthening.

James has stepped in as my new proofreader and done a very thorough job! I am grateful to him.

My grateful thanks go to Brian Plush for the awesome map. He's done it again!

Thanks to 100 Covers for the great cover design.

Finally, my gratitude goes to God, the source of creativity and the generous provider of purpose, grace, forgiveness, and so much more.

ABOUT THE AUTHOR

Allan Packer writes epic fantasy. *The Ruptured Kingdom* is his second series, following *The Stone of Knowing* and subsequent stories in *The Stone Cycle* series.

Allan grew up surrounded by books and became an avid reader during his childhood. In his university years fantasy displaced science fiction as his favorite genre, thanks primarily to J. R. R. Tolkien. He later shared this love with his four children by reading *The Lord of the Rings* to them aloud—a three-month marathon he completed twice during their formative years.

Born in Australia, Allan has lived and worked on three continents, and spent one quarter of his working years abroad. Having worked as an IT professional throughout his career, he was first published as a technical author.

Today he lives with his wife in Adelaide, South Australia, at the heart of a growing and geographically distributed extended family.

Allan is currently working on the latest installment in his series *The Ruptured Kingdom*.